Maefair

IA Mullin

Maefair

Redsands Book 2

By
IA Mullin

Avio Publishing

Maefair—Redsands Book 2—by I.A. Mullin

Published by Avio Publishing, LLC
PO Box 293, Eaton CO 80615

Edited by Mark Graham and Ann Tinkham of Mark Graham Communications, Denver, Colorado.
Proofread and cover design by Deanna Estes of Lotus Design, Fort Collins, Colorado.
Cover illustration by Kathy Bornhoft.

ISBN-13 978-1-946023-04-9 paperback
ISBN-13 978-1-946023-05-6 ebook
ISBN-13 978-1-946023-06-3 hardback

Check out Magewood.com or on facebook @authorIAMullin for new releases and additional content from IA Mullin.

Check out AvioPublishing.com for more about Avio Publishing, LLC.

Maefair is dedicated to my family who love me no matter what I do, to my father who taught me to work hard, and my mother who let me learn about my own characteristics in my own time.

Thank you, I love you.

Contents

Redsands

CASHAINS
TANZAMELL
PRICINLIA
Castant Estates
Clain Estates
King Carloth's Castle
COANDOR
LENTIER
Draukshar
Abdshar
Reine's Crossing
Eastridge
Lotal Estates
Camp
Kenhol Estates
Mira's Plateau
Maefair
Pandensy
Glancenar
The Beach
Quway Estates
Versith
Ruberic Estates
Incland Estates
Roana Estates
Herinsford
Pavlatach
Map of Redsands
Kingdom Border
Province Border
Doquib Estates
Bram's Fen
Main Road
Secondary Road
Path
Flaznek Estates
Grudent
West Cove
Arndt Estates
Mystillion
Ranat Estates
Western Sea
Southern Tip
Turmult Gulf
N
0
100
miles
Bandit Camp
GREAT MOUNTAINS

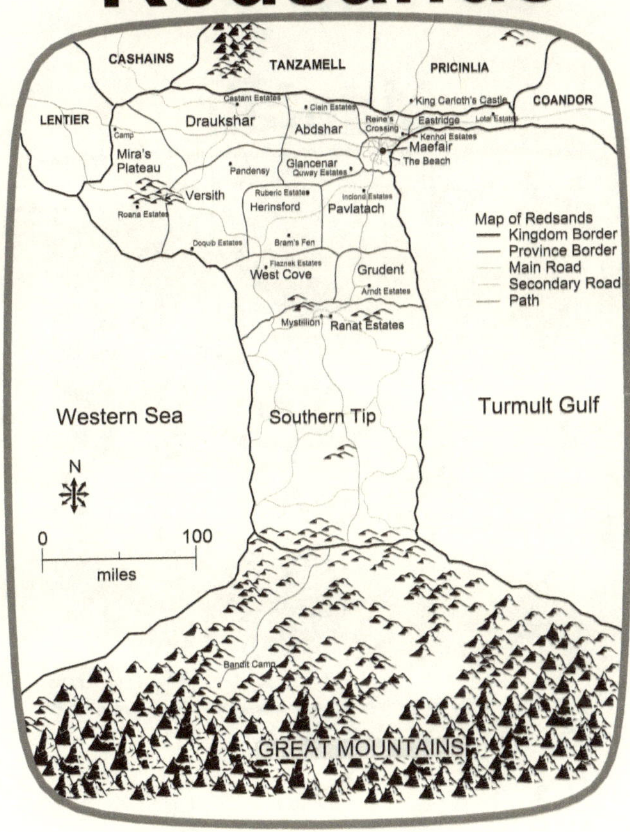

Maefair

↑ Titlf Forest
Tournament Grounds
North Road
Market
Palace
Horse Market
Market
Market
Castant Manor
Maefair Courthouse
Roana Manor
Threine Estates
N
0
1
mile

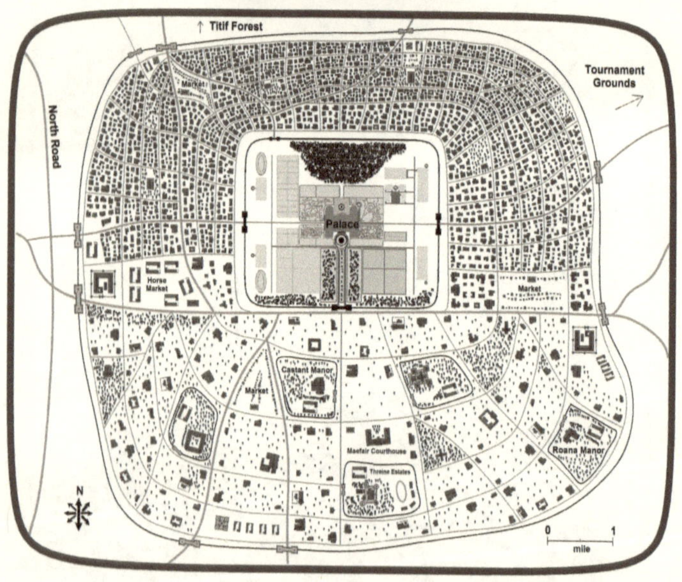

Maefair Royal Palace

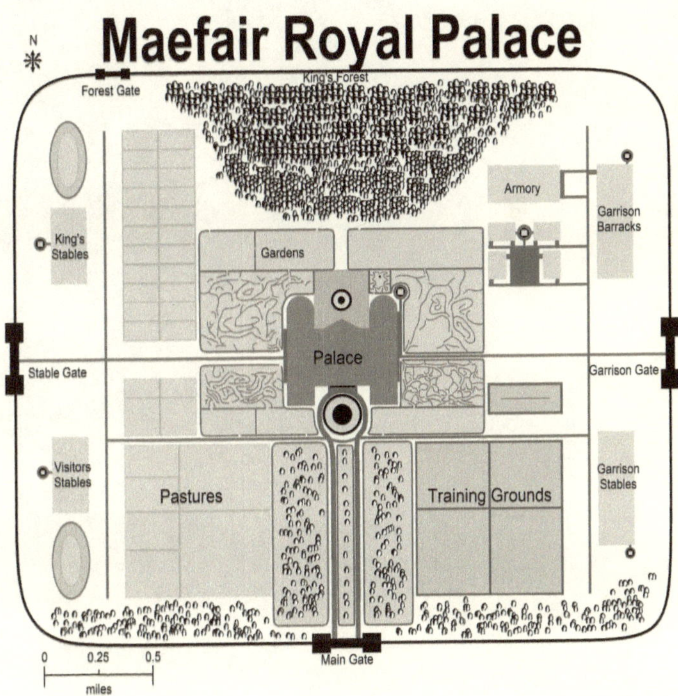

1

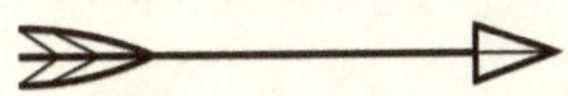

It was a cold late autumn day, and the market of Mystillion was half empty. The young lioness named Marilana paid for a basket of apples, hung her satchel over her shoulder, and pulled the hood of her cloak over her head. She turned for home.

She hadn't gone more than a block before she heard someone calling her name.

"Marilana! Marilana, wait!" It was Klay, her longtime classmate. The burly black bear hurried up to her, breathing hard and clearly distraught. A dozen paces behind and even more out of breath was Caton, a slender silver fox and another of Marilana's school mates.

"Klay! Caton! What's the matter?" Marilana asked, seeing the look on their faces.

"Earek is in trouble. Brittia is putting her foot down," the bear growled. "Adrek just fetched one of the magistrates from the courthouse."

"That's right," Caton said. "And I just saw Vavinta walking this way with Brittia, Merchant Sleater, and Headmistress Ceta. Earek has been putting Brittia off for months now. She doesn't like being ignored, and she does not like anyone challenging her authority, especially the way Earek has been lately."

"Brittia doesn't have the authority to tell people how to live," Marilana said coldly.

"No, but she can make life difficult for anyone who stands in her way," the silver fox said quietly.

"We cannot get involved," Klay said. "But Earek has been our friend for a long time. He has deflected Brittia's anger from the rest of us for years. Help him, Marilana. Please. Anything you can do."

"Don't worry. Earek may suffer some, but he will survive the day," Marilana said firmly. "I can't offer much assistance, but I will do what I can. Thank you for letting me know what's going on."

Marilana turned in the direction of Merchant Yulan's shop. As she approached, she noticed a restless crowd beginning to form in the square. She made her way to the front of the crowd just as two of Merchant Sleater's merchant guards were escorting the black leopard from his father's shop. Earek seemed surprisingly calm as he looked around the crowd. His eyes came to rest on Brittia. The alluring lynx was flanked on one side by her father Merchant Sleater, her mother Corlda, and her aunt Headmistress Ceta. On the other stood Earek's father Merchant Yulan and Earek's mother Xyta. Earek's older brother Adrek, his wife Vavinta, and one of the magistrates stood just behind them. Brittia caught sight of Marilana and her smug look turned to a cold smile.

"Marilana, step forward. I'm glad you are here to witness this. You are the cause of this unpleasantness after all," Brittia said haughtily.

Marilana didn't move and gave nothing away with her expression. She thought she knew what Brittia was up to, and, if she was correct, Earek would be faced with a number of life-changing decisions. Brittia looked around at the crowd, nodded to Merchant Yulan, and then fixed Earek with a self-satisfied look.

"Earek, you are my second son," Merchant Yulan said with resignation. "It has been brought to my attention that you have been fraternizing in a manner unbefitting of your station.

We must have a resolution to this situation. Miss Brittia has been trying to help you see your proper path."

"Earek, I can understand that you needed time after your best friend left last summer," Brittia said levelly.

She was referring to the sudden departure of Marquiese, a young lion son of a high-class Merchant who ranked equal to herself. After three years in Mystillion he had suddenly left without warning. Most of the populace of Mystillion assumed he and his Merchant family had moved to some other provincial town where trade would better benefit the family. Marilana and Earek both knew that he had not really been a member of that family, and that Marquiese had in fact returned to the royal city, Maefair, under dire circumstances. Neither of them had heard from the young lion despite his promise to write.

"It was hard for all of us to accept that Marquiese left without a word to anyone. However, it has been nearly five months. It is time for you to leave the past behind you and start looking toward the future."

"Brittia, just get to the point," the black leopard said in a bored voice. "Just tell everyone that you're mad because I am friends with Marilana. Tell everyone that you expect me to wait on your every want and need. Just say it out loud; you're mad because your favorite backup suitor doesn't want to court you."

"Earek, this is your last chance," the lynx said coldly. "Renounce your friendship with Marilana or face the consequences."

"You do not control my life, Brittia," Earek said firmly. "I will not renounce my friendship with anyone simply because you demand it, nor will I spend any more time as your fall back."

"Very well," Brittia hissed. "Merchant Yulan you know what we discussed."

"Earek, please reconsider," Merchant Yulan pleaded.

"No, Father. I will not end my friendship with Marilana," Earek proclaimed. "Nor will I be at Brittia's beck and call just because it is expected of me."

"Very well," Merchant Yulan sighed. "You leave me with no choice. If you refuse to act as a proper merchant son, I am forced to disown you. From this moment on, you are no longer part of my family."

Earek looked momentarily shocked; he had known such a turn of events was possible, but hearing the words clearly stung. He then smoothed his face to a calm mask. Marilana gritted her teeth in anger, but knew she could not do anything to stop the proceedings; this was the way of things in the Kingdom of Redsands. Brittia knew it as well and smiled smugly.

"Magistrate, did you record all of this exchange?" Brittia asked imperiously.

"Yes, I did," the magistrate said, shaking his head. "Sad business that it is."

"Magistrate, while you are recording, you can record my next edicts as well so that no one forgets my words," said a strong voice rising up from the crowd.

The voice belonged to no less than Lady Annabella Ranat, Great-Lady of the Southern Tip, the most noble of lions, and Marilana's longtime ward. The crowd parted, all bowing and curtseying respectfully, and Lady Annabella and her entourage stepped forward.

Lady Annabella walked serenely to the open area, allowing a wave of whispers and murmurs to spread through the crowd. The noble lioness stopped between Marilana and Earek and waited for the tremors to dissipate.

Brittia straightened from a deep curtsey and smiled broadly.

"Lady Annabella what a lovely surprise," the lynx said brightly. "You grace us with your presence."

Lady Annabella chose not to acknowledge Brittia's overture. Instead, she turned her attention to the lithe old lynx who ran Mystillion's schoolhouse. She said, "Headmistress Ceta. The newly orphaned Earek, once of Merchant Yulan's family, will continue to attend Mistress Rose's class and will finish his last year of Finishing School as if he were still a merchant son."

"I am sorry to ask, My Lady, but are you then taking responsibility for him?" intoned the magistrate hopefully.

"I am the Lady of the Province of the Southern Tip and the county of Mystillion. It is my responsibility to make sure all individuals, without regard to caste or privilege, are properly cared for, and that includes orphans and the homeless," Lady Annabella replied dryly. "As such, I have taken an interest in today's proceedings."

"As you say, My Lady."

"Furthermore, Headmistress Ceta, you will make sure that Orphan Earek is properly taught, and you will send me monthly reports on his progress. You will not discipline him, however, nor will you discipline Marilana any longer," Lady Annabella announced.

"My Lady, how can I keep order if I'm not allowed to discipline the students in my school?" Headmistress Ceta protested, wringing her paws agitatedly.

"I will deal with any and all disciplinary action needed for these two," Lady Annabella said calmly. "You will, of course, still discipline any of your other students as needed."

Marilana swallowed both her surprise and jubilation and forced an expressionless face once again. Lady Annabella turned and motioned to two of her guardsmen.

"You two will escort young Earek to Merchant Yulan's house and make sure that he is allowed to gather up his possessions. Then you will escort him safely to his destination," Lady Annabella told the men and then looked at Marilana. "Marilana, no more hiding. Attend me now."

Marilana made a quick curtsey and moved to follow Lady Annabella from the market.

"Lady Annabella!" Brittia called, quickly stopping Lady Annabella as she turned away. "Excuse me, My Lady. You have not yet replied to my messages. When, may I ask, will you start my training?"

Lady Annabella turned a cold look on the lynx.

"Know this. I choose who to train and when," the Great-Lady said coldly. "Merchant daughters would do well to remember their place. Merchant Sleater, you would do well to teach your daughter courtesy and manners."

Brittia looked like she had been slapped. Marilana almost felt sorry for her, almost. Lady Annabella and her entourage set out and Marilana hurried to follow. She glanced back and saw Brittia staring furiously after Earek as the black leopard was escorted away by Lady Annabella's guardsmen.

*

"Marilana? Are you there? It's Earek."

When Marilana heard Earek calling to her, she quickly disarmed the many traps that protected her forest cottage and ushered Earek inside.

Before going in, she waved at the two guardsmen who had accompanied Earek's passage, and they turned their horses and set out east toward Lady Annabella's estates. Marilana rearmed the dozen traps as she worked her way toward the entrance and closed the door behind her.

Earek sat slumped in the chair facing the fireplace and stared into the dancing flames. Marilana smiled down at him and then sat on the floor next to him.

"So here we are again," Earek said sadly. "Three years ago it was Jarek who they disowned. Now it is me."

Earek's younger brother Jarek had joined Lady Annabella's provincial army against his family's wishes and was now a respected soldier gaining his own honor, and making his own place in the county. Earek had been nearly devastated by the separation from his brother, but Marilana had made sure they had been allowed to visit each other, earning her the gratitude of both brothers and increased respect from her friend Marquiese.

"Earek, it is not as bad as it seems," Marilana said gently.

"Really?" Earek sighed and looked at her. "Where am I going to live? What am I going to do? I have no rank. I no longer have any family ties to offer to a future bride. At least Jarek wanted to become a soldier and that supported him. What do I have? Nothing."

"Excuse me? Nothing?" Marilana said, slightly hurt. "You gave up everything for my friendship. I don't consider that nothing, not today anyway. I don't have any rank. I can't get you a future bride. However, my friendship can give you what you need."

"I doubted you when Jarek was disowned, and look what you did for him," Earek said, shaking his head. "Alright, Marilana, my dear friend, what do you have up your sleeve this time?"

"First, Lady Annabella is leaving tomorrow to go to Maefair for the annual tournament. She will return in a little over a month after the Winter Council and the start of the new year. When she returns, she has invited you to start attending my etiquette lessons with her. She is going to teach you higher etiquette and proper courtesy. Second, when she returns, she wants you to start sparring practice with me every morning so that I can teach you how to use a bow and sword, as well as other weapons and horsemanship. Under Captain-General Zariff's supervision, of course," Marilana said happily. "Third, Lady Annabella is giving you a choice as to where to live. You can live in the barracks as a new recruit and learn to be a soldier. Or you can live in the officers' apartments in Mystillion."

Earek sat blinking at her for a long moment.

"Why?" he asked finally. "Why would she do this for me? The extra training, providing some place for me to live, and I assume some sort of arrangement for food. She doesn't have to do this for me."

"No, and she is not doing it just for you," the lioness said, smiling. "She knew I would want to help you, so she decided that if you chose my friendship over a future with Brittia that she would grant my requests. You have to finish school with me, and you have to accept her discipline if necessary. However, you have room and board. You do not have to find work until next year when you come of age unless you find something that you like before then. You have a chance to make your own life."

"Why do I get the choice of the officer's apartments?" he asked suspiciously.

"I'm not the only one who wanted to help you," Marilana said slyly.

"Jarek of course," the black leopard said in wonder. "But he lives in the barracks. That's everyone, isn't it? Just you two?"

"You'll find out soon enough. Come on. He's waiting for us," Marilana said, jumping to her feet and gathering up her bow and quiver.

Earek got to his feet and grabbed the pack containing all his worldly possessions. They hurried through the woods until they came to the southern part of the town of Mystillion. They entered town via the main road, and Marilana led Earek to a stone house up the street from the courthouse. Earek knocked, and a panel slid open in the door. A pair of inquiring eyes peered out. They heard a grunt of recognition, a lock clicking, and then the door swung open. The guard was a scruffy old badger. The leopard standing next to him was a younger version of Earek, although with the normal black-spotted yellow coloration.

"Ah, you made!" Jarek cried with a wide smile. "Come in. Come in."

Jarek wrapped an arm around his brother's shoulders and led him and Marilana into a small sitting room. "Sit. Sit," he said, offering them chairs.

"You look well," Earek said. "But I still can't figure out what you are doing here?"

"I couldn't wait to tell you. I got a promotion to Lieutenant last fifnight," Jarek said with a proud grin. "These are my new quarters."

"That's fantastic," Earek said, equally as proud. "Congratulations!"

"Yes, thank you. Plus, I heard what was going on with you—sad business, my brother—and I asked Lady Annabella for permission to let you stay with me."

"Really? Thank you, but . . . ," Earek looked around at the cramped quarters.

"Don't worry this is just the common room. This house has multiple suites set up for Lady Annabella's officers, and their wives for those who are married. It is a good place for someone to start a family, if they so choose, and then move into a larger house when they have saved up enough to purchase one.

"Lady Annabella said she has no problem with you living here with me until we decide on some other arrangements. The deal is that you have to uphold the code of honor just like the rest of us soldiers. You will have to do some basic training with the new recruits to learn the laws of rank, and, of course, you will have to finish school as Lady Annabella decreed. But if you live here with me, I will make sure you are fed and clothed. What do you say?"

"I never thought I would be dependent on my baby brother for my room and board, but I like it. I accept your offer," the black leopard said, smiling. "Thank you, Jarek."

"Not at all," Jarek said with a shrug. "It's my turn to look out for you for a while, that's all."

"I'm glad for you, Earek. It's a good arrangement," Marilana said with a smile. "I'll let you get settled in and take word of your acceptance to Lady Annabella. She wanted to know your decision before she leaves tomorrow."

"Marilana." Earek reached out and touched her lightly on the shoulder. "Thanks, for everything."

"It is my pleasure, my friend," Marilana gave him a playful wink and walked to the door. "I'll see you tomorrow at school. Don't be late."

*

Marilana was uncommonly nervous as she escorted the children to school the next morning. Brittia had stopped walking to and from school since Marquiese had left, and many of her classmates had followed her example. Marilana didn't mind. She had never cared much for escorting Brittia, and she certainly didn't miss the daily insults.

Marilana took a deep breath and walked into Headmistress Ceta's office. The Headmistress glanced at her and then waved at the vault. Marilana stowed her weapons and left the office without a word. She met Earek at the door to Mistress Rose's classroom. He smiled at her.

"Lady Annabella said no more hiding, remember?" he said quietly. "Are you ready?"

"I can only do as I must," Marilana said, sighing.

The bell rang, and they went inside. Mistress Rose nodded to them, and they took their seats. Brittia, not surprisingly, ignored them completely.

When everyone had settled down, Mistress Rose said, "Good morning, class. Let us get started. We have one month to review the rules of etiquette and law before your final exam. We will also review every dance we have learned to this point. After the New Year, we will focus all of our time on the Dance of the Seasons so that we are ready to perform on your last day of school. We have a lot of work to do, so please stay focused." Her gaze settled on Marilana. "Marilana, you will act as hostess today. Earek, you will serve please."

Brittia's smirk last only until Marilana took over the class. Brittia had always enjoyed Marilana's apparent lack of etiquette, but Marilana had always hidden her true skills. Today she acted as Lady Annabella had trained her. She directed everyone as to her preferred seating arrangement and introduced each and every one as if for the first time. She acted the perfect host for a formal dinner, and Earek served the five-course meal to Marilana's exact specifications. By the time the meal was over and Marilana had dismissed the class for a break, Brittia was fuming. Mistress Rose said nothing to Marilana as she left the classroom, but kept Earek so that he could eat lunch and discuss his performance.

Marilana went out to the schoolyard and joined the younger students she tutored during the lunch break. Marilana had half expected Brittia to call a halt to her tutoring after Lida had moved away, but she had let it continue. Lida was the young daughter of the merchant family who had housed Marquiese during his years of hiding in Mystillion. Lida had braved convention when she first asked Marilana to help her during school. It was a dangerous act—after all Marilana was a peasant, and peasants were not normally allowed to interact in that way with the merchant class.

Britta, the highest ranking child of the merchant caste here in Mystillion, had at first protested, but due to Marilana's quick wit, changed her mind to an attitude of nonintervention. She had simply said that tutoring was work befitting a servant. Marilana tried to ignore Brittia's hateful stare during their break and sighed when the bell rang, sending them back to the classroom. The lioness knew that dance practice would just make Brittia even madder, but there was nothing to be done about that.

Marilana walked inside and joined Earek at the side of the classroom.

"Today I would like to review the Courtship Dance," Mistress Rose said calmly. "You have all been doing well with it, but for the moment I want only three dancers to join me for demonstration purposes. The rest of you will watch carefully to see the differences between what we have been learning, the dance form called low style, and the grander form of the dance called high style. Brittia and Earek, please take your positions to perform the courtship dance as we have been learning it. Marilana, please take your position to perform high style. I will act the part of the male opposite you."

Murmurs swept the room when the rest of the students heard this, many of whom were clearly appalled—Marilana had to this point been the worst dance in the class. Marilana paid them no mind. She stepped smoothly forward and took the simple parchment fan Mistress Rose held out to her. She took up the appropriate starting position and focused on the dance.

"Girls, you will compare Marilana's form to Brittia's form," Mistress Rose continued, ignoring the whispers. "Boys, you will compare the form I use to Earek's form."

Marilana cued off Mistress Rose as she talked the class through each step. When they had gone through all the steps slowly, Mistress Rose increased the pace with each of the next three rounds.

"Alright, I do not expect you to necessarily learn high style, but I do want you to be able to recognize it," Mistress Rose said patiently. "Now I want you all to break into pairs."

Brittia took her place next to Earek, but Mistress Rose stepped between them and directed the lynx toward Diof, a lanky zebra. Then she said, "If you need guidance on the steps, you can watch Marilana and Earek here at the front of the room."

Brittia faltered and her face flushed with anger. Marilana ignored her and took up the beginning position of low style across from Earek. She held the fan in front of her face as was traditional, blocking his view. They danced the rest of the afternoon; Mistress Rose used Marilana and Earek to illustrate the various points of the dance and ignored Brittia's fury. Marilana was relieved when the final bell eventually rang. She hurried to Headmistress Ceta's office and retrieved her weapons. She was not surprised when the Headmistress followed her out to the schoolyard.

Brittia was waiting for them, her paws on her hips and a scowl painted on her face.

"So this is what Lady Annabella meant when she told you no more hiding," Brittia spat angrily. "You have been pretending not to know etiquette and dance for two and a half years. I have never been so insulted. A peasant should not have the knowledge that you do, let alone outperform members of a higher caste. You should be severely punished for this. We are going to the magistrates immediately."

"No, we're not," Marilana retorted firmly. "You can go to the magistrates and complain if you wish, but I have a duty to escort these students home. That is what I intend to do. Lady Annabella allowed me to hide my skills because I did not wish to insult you. She has ordered me to stop hiding those skills, so I will do as she wishes. She is my warden. She is also my disciplinarian. She is the only one who has the right to give me orders. I am a Noble Ward. I will no longer try to cater to your feeling of superiority. We both know better."

Marilana turned her back on Brittia and started away.

"It was you, wasn't it," Headmistress Ceta called to her coldly. "You were the girl in the golden costume at the Winter Masquerade."

Marilana turned and looked back up at her thinking back to almost one year ago. She remembered clearly the gathering of all the students in finishing schools from across the province, and the noble guests Lady Annabella had arranged. She had enjoyed that night, the dancing freely, the magnificent golden costume Lady Annabella had made for her, and the stolen dance with Marquiese. She had run away from that celebration without revealing her identity.

"Yes, that was me. And I am no longer hiding," Marilana replied levelly. She turned again and walked out of the schoolyard.

2

“Brittia, have you received a letter from Marquiese?” Marilana asked carefully during their lunch break. It had been six months since Earek had been disowned by his family. Marilana and Earek spent most of their time together, and their friendship had strengthened remarkably. Earek lounged against the fence not far away watching her try to talk to Brittia.

“What do you care if I have heard from Marquiese? It’s not as if he liked you. He used you for his homework and nothing more,” the lynx retorted.

“He said that he would write to me, and he hasn’t yet,” Marilana explained levelly. “I just wondered if anyone else had heard from him.”

“Well, he never told me he would write, and I know he would have had he intended to. Besides, I care not. He is no longer here and no longer of importance in my life. He left nearly eleven months ago. If he hasn’t written by now, he never will.” Brittia turned on her heels and strode away.

“Don’t listen to her. She doesn’t care about anyone but herself,” Earek said, stepping up beside Marilana. “He said that he would write, and we can’t give up hope. Not yet.”

“Brittia’s problem is that she has no pride. She hurts others as a way of making herself feel better,” the lioness commented.

The black leopard shook his head and said in a most sarcastic tone, “Come on. We have another fun afternoon of preparations for the Dance of the Seasons ahead of us. What could be better?"

They went inside and found Headmistress Ceta waiting impatiently for the class to find their places. When the last chair was filled, she called everyone to order.

"As you know, there are two fifnights, only ten days, left before you perform the Dance of the Seasons," the diminutive lynx announced imperiously. "It is time for me to give you all your final positions for the dance. Your class is larger than the past few classes, and so you will all be expected to focus on your individual parts. And I expect perfection."

She unrolled a length of parchment and read out the names and what part each student would perform. Marilana was not surprised that Brittia was named Lady Season or that neither she nor Earek were named for any part.

A murmur of excitement rose from all who supported Brittia's starring role, but it was interrupted by a knock on the open door.

"Please excuse the interruption," Lady Annabella said stepping into the classroom. The girls all curtseyed and the boys all bowed from their seats, and the Great-Lady of the Province added. "Actually there will have to be some changes to that arrangement, Headmistress Ceta."

"Lady Annabella, what a pleasant surprise," Headmistress Ceta said in a tight voice. "What changes, if I may ask?"

"Master Arndt has requested the pleasure of dancing with this class for the Dance of the Seasons," Lady Annabella announced calmly. The murmurs once again swelled, and she allowed them to dissipated before saying, "He will of course be dancing the part of Lord Time. He has requested that Marilana dance the part of Lady Season, as she has proven herself to be the best dancer in the class and a logical choice. The best remaining dancers will lead the chorus, so those positions go to Brittia and Earek. Are there any objections?"

"No, My Lady," Headmistress Ceta replied coldly. "The arrangements will be made."

"Very well, my seamstress will make Marilana's and Earek's costumes, and the others will be managed by Merchant Yulan," Lady Annabella said firmly. She looked around the classroom at a cluster of stricken expressions. "We do not want to be embarrassed in front of Master Arndt and his family, so I expect all of you to learn your parts well and do your best."

Marilana's heart sank. She had been more than relieved when she had been left off the dance roster. Now she would be partnered with Master Arndt, a jaguar whose motives she did not trust, and would surely be facing the wrath of Brittia and her sycophants for taking her place in a dance Marilana had no interest in.

Marilana took a deep breath. Despite her reservations, she was determined to perform to the best of her abilities, especially given Lady Annabella's faith in her.

*

The last day of school came much quicker than Marilana wished. She and Earek had been practicing together for the big dance and helping each other with their respective parts. Marilana could dance her part in her sleep, but she was still anxious. She could also tell Lady Annabella was nervous about the performance. The great-noble had told the lioness and black leopard to spend all of their time practicing, even at the expense of their chores and other studies. This was unprecedented.

The exception was their morning sparring sessions. These they were not allowed to miss. Earek had made good strides. He was getting quite good at sword fighting, and he was a fast learner. His footwork was excellent, probably because he was also such a good dancer. The rest of their time they spent dancing.

The practice should have been more enjoyable, Earek smiled every time as he lead her through the steps, but Marilana kept remembering the last time she had danced with Marquiese. They had danced purely for the joy of it, almost exactly a year ago, in the meadow by the lake with only the sound of the waterfall in the background. She had the distinct feeling that the Dance of the Seasons would hardly be as enjoyable, especially partnered with Master Arndt.

Despite Marilana's dread, the day arrived, shining bright.

Marilana took a deep breath to calm her nerves as Lady Annabella's carriage stopped in front of her house. She went outside and Captain-General Zariff, her mentor and long-time friend, was waiting for her. Marilana lifted the pale green skirts of her spring dress with one paw and accepted the elder lion's proffered paw.

"You look lovely," he said.

"Thank you," the lioness said with a small smile.

Zariff helped her into the carriage and she settle on the bench opposite Lady Annabella. Marilana had gotten dressed at her house instead of at Lady Annabella's castle in order to avoid Master Arndt. The Arndt family, great-nobles of the neighboring province Grudent, had arrived at the castle the day before, and Jarek had informed her that Master Arndt and Master Warhaim had scoured the entire estates surreptitiously looking for her and asking questions of the staff about her. She was not sure what was going to happen after the dance; if the two jaguars attempted to corner her, she would have a decision to make: to relent or to fight.

"Marilana, Master Arndt has asked to dance the Courtship Dance with you," Lady Annabella said evenly. "I told him that you would agree to the dance, but only if it was strictly an exhibition dance. He agreed to the condition. Dancing this dance will not result in you entering a courtship with him. I do not want you to out dance him, however. He is already slightly insulted that I waited this long before revealing your identity to him; I do not want him to be further insulted. Is that understood?"

"Yes, My Lady." Marilana sighed with resignation.

Master Arndt had been enthralled by her ever since the Winter Masquerade when she had danced so well with him, before running off without revealing who she was. She was less worried that he and his brother were mad at her, and more concerned that they wanted a closer acquaintance. They arrived shortly at the market square. Earek met them at the carriage and bowed to Lady Annabella.

"Headmistress Ceta and the Arndt family await you on the platform, My Lady," the black leopard said formally.

"Thank you, Earek," Lady Annabella replied with a smile. "Please escort Marilana to the dancers' area."

Earek bowed again and then waited for Marilana. He looked very handsome in his brown and blue costume representing the earth and sky. Marilana descended the step to the ground and checked that the circlet of flowers and colorful ribbons was still well secured on her head. She straightened the long ribbons tied around her wrists as they started to walk through the crowd to where the dancers were waiting.

"You'll do fine," Earek said quietly to her. "And you could hardly look more fabulous."

"Earek, I may have to disappear after the dance," she told him.

"Whatever happens, Marilana, I'm your friend. If you need help, I will do anything I can to help you," he replied seriously.

"Thank you, my friend," Marilana smiled at him.

"Ah, so this is the lovely lioness that I have been waiting to meet," Master Arndt said as they emerged from the crowd into the dancers' area.

Earek bowed to Master Arndt and then went to join the rest of their classmates. Brittia gave Marilana a withering glare and then turned her back to them. Marilana curtseyed deeply and tried not to blush with embarrassment as Master Arndt examined her off-the-shoulder strapped dress. She kept her eyes lowered.

"Thank you for dancing with my class today," Marilana said to break the silence between them. "I am sure that your performance will make this dance today the best Mystillion has ever seen."

"Well now, that depends on you," Master Arndt said coolly. "Are you going to run away before the end again?"

"I apologize for that, Master Arndt," she said quietly. "I was not ready to let my skills be known at the Winter Masquerade, and so I hid my identity. I am not hiding my skills any more. So I will not be running away today."

"Well, that is something," Master Arndt said levelly. "Come, it is time for us to give the crowd a dazzling performance."

They took their places with the rest of the dancers, and Mistress Rose cued the musicians. The music began, and the Dance of the Seasons was officially underway. Marilana focused on the dance, knowing every step as if she had choreographed it herself, and performed it without overshadowing Master Arndt. The jaguar was not the best dancer in Marilana's opinion; his skills, in fact, had not gained much grace since the Winter Masquerade, but he was still the best dancer Mystillion had seen perform as Lord Time.

The audience loved the show. They erupted into cheers and applause as Lord Time finally caught the elusive Lady Season to end the dance, and she swooned in his arms, arching her back. Marilana felt very exposed, supported only by Master Arndt's arm and every eye in the square rapt upon her.

Eventually, the music of this final scene faded gently away. The other dancers moved in unison back to the dancers' area, but Master Arndt and Marilana remained frozen. The music began to build again, and Master Arndt lifted her back to her feet and spun her around to face him at arm's length. He released her paw and bowed as the first notes of the Courtship Dance sounded. Marilana unfurled the fan that had been hidden among the ribbons at her wrist and curtseyed to him in the first position of low style. They danced slowly at first and then faster and faster as the music built. Marilana listened carefully to his breathing as the dance progressed and it became increasingly more ragged. Finally, she spun to a stop, gracefully dropped to one knee, and placed the fan artfully on the ground between them. She was breathing hard, but not nearly as hard as he was.

The crowds cheered and applauded even louder.

Once again, Master Arndt offered his paw, and she let him help her to her feet. Together they bowed and curtseyed to Lady Annabella and the Arndt family. The rest of the dancers joined them, and they bowed as a troupe. Three times they again bowed and waved. The applause continued for several minutes longer until the dancers all made their way back out of the dance area. Mistress Rose caught Marilana's eye and gave her a proud, yet tearful smile. The crowd swarmed the dancers area, accosting the dancers, and congratulating one and all on such a fine performance. Master Arndt gently twisted Marilana's paw around so that it rested on his arm, but he kept his other paw over hers and made sure that she could not slip away from him. Marilana forced a polite smile as members of the community approached them and commented on how amazing the dance was. Marilana couldn't help thinking that tomorrow all of these same creatures would gladly chase her out of town with sticks for having the audacity to act so above her station.

Marilana curtseyed deeply to Lord and Lady Arndt. The elder jaguars complimented her on her skill as a performer. Marilana cringed inwardly at the suspicious and calculating look in Lady Arndt's eyes as they moved on. The youngest jaguar, Master Arndt's sister, Mistress Graita, was simply dismissive and moved past without so much as a glance. Marilana stole only a furtive peek at Master Warhaim's face when he complemented her and was not surprised to see a hungry look in his eyes. The younger jaguar remained nearby for the rest of the afternoon. He spoke and flirted with some of the other girls, including Brittia, but Marilana knew he would stop her from getting far if she somehow slipped away from his brother.

Marilana felt like a trap was slowly closing around her as they talked to the creatures of Mystillion and occasionally danced. Her one hope was that Lady Annabella had some plan in mind. Earek, thankfully, also seemed to be nearby throughout the course of the afternoon. He danced with a number of girls and laughed with his former peers as if equals, but he also somehow remained only a little way away from her. She was glad for his presence. He never met her eyes, but even so she gained a sense of calm every time she spotted him.

It was late in the evening when Brittia approached Marilana and Master Arndt.

"Master Arndt," she said breathlessly, and gave him a deep curtsey. "I have never seen a finer dancer. You gave the performance such a strong, commanding aura; I almost felt that you were truly controlling time. I know my heart beat faster."

Brittia gave him a look of pure adoration and twisted her scarlet and white dress in such a way to give Master Arndt the fullest picture of her curves. Marilana could feel Master Arndt pulling away from her and knew he was tempted by Brittia's flirtations. If only it were true, Marilana thought hopefully. However, Master Arndt's grip tightened on her paw a moment later, and he moved closer.

"I have to say, Marilana," Brittia said when she saw Master Arndt pull away. "You did well enough; at least you did not embarrass the whole town by the limitation of your skills."

The lynx turned on her heel and stalked away. Master Arndt led Marilana through the crowd in the opposite direction. Eventually they reached the area where two carriages waited. Lord and Lady Arndt were climbing into the first carriage. Master Arndt pulled her closer and turned to face her. Marilana looked up into his eyes for the first time all day. She was not surprised to see the lust in his eyes. She shoved down her panic and gave him a polite smile.

"You will return to Lady Annabella's estates with me?" he asked quietly, although Marilana felt it was more of a command.

"Actually, Marilana will ride with me," Lady Annabella said, the elder lioness and her entourage stepping up behind the pair. "She will not be at my castle tonight, although she will see you and your family off in the morning."

"As you wish, Lady Annabella," Master Arndt said with a cool smile. "Until tomorrow then."

He released Marilana at last and she curtseyed as he climbed into the carriage followed by Master Warhaim and Mistress Graita. Marilana turned as the carriage pulled away and followed Lady Annabella into her carriage. The young lioness collapsed onto the bench and sighed. Lady Annabella smiled proudly at her.

"You have done very well, Marilana," Lady Annabella said warmly. "I can tell you do not like Master Arndt very much, and I have to say I do not much like his family either. They are, however, powerful in their own way. I like to keep them happy. No reason for them to see me as an enemy. I do not trust those boys, however. I'm going to let you out close to Brittia's house. I trust you can make it home without being followed from there."

"Yes. Thank you, My Lady," Marilana said with relief, taking the gray cloak Lady Annabella held out to her.

"I expect you at the castle bright and early tomorrow morning. I will have a change of clothes in your room for you to wear while we send the Arndt family on their way," Lady Annabella said evenly.

"I will be there," Marilana replied with a smile.

The carriage stopped, and Marilana climbed out. She waited for the carriage to pull forward before walking lightly into the forest. She moved deeper into the woods and paused only briefly among the low grass of a thicket. Then she swung the cloak around her, pulled up the hood, and leapt through the trees without a sound.

She didn't go far before circling around back to the road. She was not surprised to see two horsemen wearing the crest of the house of Arndt examining her tracks where she had entered the forest.

The pair, both badgers and clearly excited at the prospect of tracking a lone lioness, moved steadily into the trees. Marilana followed them at a distance, as silent as her bandit-garnered title of The Ghost suggested. They were fifty feet from the road when they stopped suddenly at the edge of the thicket.

"Where is the trail?" the old badger asked, surprised.

"I don't see it. It was clear as day to here, and now it's just gone," the younger one said angrily.

Marilana smiled and slipped away, leaving them completely befuddled. She made her way carefully through the trees to her house. She scouted carefully in the gloom until she was sure there was no one watching the house. Quickly, she descended to her garden wall, stepped through her traps to the back door, and slipped inside.

*

The next morning, Marilana rose early, as was her way. She conducted her usual patrol for bandits. Finding no signs, she hurried to Lady Annabella's castle as she had been instructed. She was surprised when she entered the stableyard to see an extra carriage being hidden behind the carriage house. She wondered what that might be about, but only briefly; she had far bigger concerns on her mind.

She hurried to her room in the servant quarters and found a simple lavender dress waiting for her. She changed quickly and made her way up to Lady Annabella's rooms. She waited for several hours, wondering at the delay. She tried to read a book, but was far too distracted.

Finally a servant came to the door and announced that the Arndt family was ready to depart. Marilana followed Lady Annabella down to the main steps of the castle. The carriage displaying the Arndt family crest stood ready in the yard, and the escort of Lord Arndt's guardsmen waited on their horses. Marilana spotted the two men who had tried to track her the night before. She suppressed her smile and stood patiently behind her lady.

Lord and Lady Arndt led the family down the steps of the castle. Marilana forced a polite smile and curtseyed.

"Lady Annabella, I thank you for entertaining us." Lord Arndt smiled easily and bowed to Lady Annabella.

"Thank you for attending such humble events, Lord Arndt," Lady Annabella replied. "May The Goddess grant you a safe journey home."

"Lady Annabella, you simply must get me those dress patterns. Graita would look lovely in such delicate finery," Lady Arndt said.

She smiled, but Marilana noticed that the smile did not touch her eyes and knew the words were simple pleasantries. Master Arndt stepped up to Marilana, and she looked up into his cold, lustful eyes. He smiled at her, showing his sharp white teeth.

"Lady Annabella has assured me that we will meet again sometime in the near future," he said quietly catching her paw and pressing it to his chest. "I will think of you every day until we are together again."

"May The Goddess grant you peace until that day, Master Arndt," Marilana said with a polite smile and a curtsey.

He kissed the back of her paw and then followed his family to the carriage. Master Warhaim smiled hungrily at her as he waited for his brother to climb in. Marilana returned his smile politely and wondered with disgust if they had agreed to share her between them. *Well, we'll see how to avoid that,* she thought darkly.

Marilana stood by Lady Annabella as the carriage rolled out the gates and down the road. Surreptitiously she rubbed the back of her paw on her skirt to remove the lingering feel of Master Arndt's lips. Lady Annabella heaved a sigh of relief and turned to her ward.

"Come along, I know you are eager to change." Lady Annabella smiled. "You did very well this morning. You were polite yet did not give any indication as to what might happen at your next meeting with Master Arndt. That was very diplomatic of you."

Lady Annabella walked with Marilana down to the servant quarters.

"Did you have any trouble last night with Master Arndt's men?" Lady Annabella asked as they entered Marilana's room.

"No," Marilana laughed. "It was a simple matter. Thank you for intervening for me."

Marilana's eyes widened when she saw a rolled and sealed parchment lying on the pillow at the head of her bed. She crossed the room with cautious steps and picked it up. "What is this?"

"Why don't you open it?" the noble lioness suggested kindly.

The parchment was sealed with plain red wax. Her name was written across the front in neat, crisp writing. Hesitantly, she broke open the seal and unrolled the letter. The paper was the finest she had ever seen, and the elegance of the script matched it perfectly.

It read:

Dear Marilana,

I am sorry that I have not written to you sooner. My father is very stern. He had to be absolutely sure that you were trustworthy before allowing any communication. I have convinced him at last and would now like to ask if you might consider coming to visit my home for a few months. A friend of my father's is visiting Lady Annabella currently, and he has agreed to offer you passage on his return to Maefair, if you would be willing.

I have missed you, our long conversations, and your laughter.

If this invitation finds you willing, I will have someone waiting for you when you arrive in Maefair.

Hoping to see you soon.

Your friend,

Marquiese

Marilana sat down on her bed and read the letter through several times. Her surprise was so genuine that she could hardly believe it. She had been waiting for months for some word from Marquiese. Now suddenly the young lion writes to her just as she finishes school and the only thing in the letter is an invitation to visit. No indications about how he has been or if he is safe; just that he has made arrangements, assuming, as he put, she was willing.

"What is it, Marilana?" Lady Annabella asked concerned. "I can't tell if the news is good or bad. Speak up, child."

Marilana blinked. She came to her feet and passed the letter to Lady Annabella. The noble lioness read the words with a calm expression and then nodded. She looked at Marilana expectantly.

"Well?" Lady Annabella prompted warmly. "Do you want to go? If you do you should really ask your warden if she will allow it."

"Go to Maefair?" Marilana sounded slightly stunned. "Well, yes, I do, but . . . ."

Her voice trailed off.

Lady Annabella smiled kindly and said, "Marilana, you have finished school. You have done everything I have asked of you and with nary a complaint. You deserve some personal time. Go. Visit your friend. See the royal city. I give you my permission."

"What of my duties?"

"I'll have your chores suspended until further notice. And Hosten can take care of your horses," her warden said gently. "Now I expect you will need to write a letter for Child explaining your situation and pay a visit on Earek. Pack a light traveling bag. Your ride plans on leaving tomorrow at dawn. I know it is short notice. He is a fine and trustworthy gentleman, and I'll make arrangements for him to accommodate you if, like Marquiese says, you are willing. If so, you will join him here first thing tomorrow. If you need anything, Marquiese knows how to reach me."

"At dawn tomorrow. Yes, it is short notice, but not that short. And yes, of course I will write to Child and pay a visit on Earek," Marilana mused thoughtfully.

Lady Annabella turned to leave, then stopped at the threshold.

"Marilana, there is one more thing." She met Marilana's eyes. "Do not take any weapons with you. Not your bow or dagger. Not even your throwing knives. Understand?"

"No weapons?" Marilana said, surprised.

"I think it would be best." Lady Annabella nodded firmly. "Remember, you do not need weapons to make you deadly. Your intelligence is your best defense. I'll see you off in the morning."

Marilana sat on her bed for a while, still in shock, and stunned at the speed at which things were moving. She looked down at the letter in her paws. A slow smile spread across her face. A pleasant heat coursed through her body. She remembered the discussion she had overheard between Lady Annabella and Marquiese the day he left, almost twelve months ago, one month shy of a full year. Whatever conditions they had wanted met, seemingly had been. Marquiese had requested her presence in Maefair, and Lady Annabella had apparently decided that she was ready for such an encounter.

Marilana jumped up and quickly changed her clothes. She grabbed a few things from her little room and hurried out of the castle and through the gates. She ran to her house and packed her travel satchel and herb bag. She did not bother with a bedroll, but packed a few travel rations just to be safe. With her packing done, she hurried back out of the house and ran through the forest to Mystillion. She hurried up the steps of the officers' apartments and knocked quickly on the door. The view window on the door slid open, and the guard inside peered out at her.

"I need to speak with Earek" Marilana said quickly. "Is he here please?"

"He is. One moment." The guard slid the view window closed. She heard the lock disengage. The door opened. The guard led her into the sitting room and went to fetch Earek. Marilana paced the length of the room ten times before she heard footsteps.

"Marilana! What's the matter? What's happened?" the black leopard said, hurrying into the room. "Is everything okay?"

"A letter arrived today! Marquiese wants me to visit him! The carriage he arranged for me leaves tomorrow!" The words spilled out of her mouth, and she held the letter out to him. "Look."

"Wow, that's great!" Earek read the note, and the words brought a smile to his face. "Look at this paper. It's so white. And Marquiese's writing. It's like a master scribe's."

Earek passed the letter back. He reached out and hugged her warmly. "I'm so excited for you. Is there anything I can do for you while you're gone?

"Thank you, everything's been taken care of." Marilana shook her head. "But what you can do is keep up your sparring practice."

"Don't worry. I'll go to Lady Annabella's estates with Jarek tomorrow and report to Captain-General Zariff as usual."

"Earek, what if you get invited too?" the lioness said. "Wouldn't that be wonderful."

"Don't worry about me. I'll manage without you." Earek laughed. "You just go and have a great time, alright? Tell Marquiese hello for me. And make sure to tell him I stood by you even when it cost me my family. I want him to know that."

"I'll tell him." Marilana smiled. "I'll see you soon, my friend."

Earek walked her out, and Marilana waved goodbye. She hurried back to her house and wrote a letter to Child, the orphaned deer Marilana had trained as a bandit hunter, explaining where she had gone and asking her to take care of the house and garden. Then she went to bed and spent several hours staring at the ceiling wondering what tomorrow would bring.

3

Marilana arrived at Lady Annabella's estates before dawn. She went into the working horse stables and stopped at Storm's stall. She rubbed the magnificent stallion's nose and ears fondly and whispered to him like she always did. She didn't like leaving the horse, even for a day, but she knew Lady Annabella would take good care of him. She said one last good bye to him and then went out to the stable yard.

Captain-General Zariff was waiting for her and motioned her toward the castle steps and the carriage waiting for her there. Marilana made her way around the carriage and waited on the steps. She had only been there a few moments when the doors opened behind her. Lady Annabella and an older, regally dressed leopard descended the steps toward her.

"Marilana, good." Lady Annabella smiled. She gestured toward the leopard and said, "This is Sir Withers Castant of Draukshar province. He will see you safely to Maefair."

Sir Castant took Marilana's paw briefly and said, "We will have a grand old time, young lady. Never fear."

"Thank you." Marilana curtseyed.

"Remember your manners and etiquette," Lady Annabella said to her. "I will see you again soon enough, but the dawn is breaking and it is time to go. Farewell my dear, safe journey."

"Farewell, My Lady." Marilana smiled warmly.

The old leopard was already climbing into his carriage. Marilana took a deep breath, gave her satchel to the footman, and then she climbed in after him. She settled on the red velvet bench opposite the leopard. He smiled kindly at her again and then knocked for the driver to start. Marilana leaned over and watched Lady Annabella and her estates disappear behind the trees. They took the North Road, and Marilana watched the forest she knew so well and the life she had always depended on quickly pass out of sight.

"Have you had anything to eat yet this morning?" the old man asked lightly, indicating the covered basket on the bench next to him.

"I'm fine, thank you, Sir Castant," Marilana replied quietly. She tried to think of something to say. "Have you known Lady Annabella for long?"

"Lady Annabella and I have been friends for many long years," he said brightly. "You have no need to fear me. Young Marquiese spoke highly of you and asked if I would be so kind as to make sure you arrived at Maefair safely. He said you are a highly skilled war horse trainer. I am a Knight of the Realm and competed in many tournaments in my youth. Tell me, do you train your war horses to ride first or acclimate them to the sounds of battle first?"

His question was surely meant to relax Marilana, and it indeed served its purpose. She returned his smile and they discussed horse training techniques for most of the morning. She found that Sir Castant was very knowledgeable and easy to talk with. At lunch, the old leopard uncovered the basket, and Marilana was pleased to learn that Lady Annabella had provided them with a picnic lunch they could share without stopping.

Sir Castant said he hoped she would make it to Marquiese's home in time for dinner, and so he had ordered a fast pace. They spent most of the afternoon discussing jousting techniques and other sports of horsemanship, and the city of Maefair grew ever larger on the horizon.

It was late afternoon when Sir Castant looked out the window and smiled.

"Well, we have come to Maefair at last, and I see your next ride waiting for you," he said warmly. "If you ever find yourself in Draukshar and in need, I would be honored to help in any way I can. Take care of yourself. I have a feeling we will meet again sometime."

"Thank you for the ride, Sir Castant," Marilana smiled. "I am in your debt."

"Nonsense. I was just glad I could be of service. You made the journey much more enjoyable with your pleasant company," he replied. "Farewell, Marilana."

Marilana climbed down from the carriage, took her satchel from the footman, and waved as the carriage drove on. She turned and took a look around. The city was more beautiful than she had ever imagined and none of the many stories she had heard did it justice.

There were big expensive buildings, stone laid streets, and perfectly tended gardens. There were creatures of all types in splendid garb, fancy carriages, and shops as far as the eye could see.

As she stood in awe of her surroundings, a pleasant looking young doe came up to her and said, "You must be Marilana. This way please."

The servant took Marilana's satchel and gestured toward the waiting buggy.

Marilana took in every amazing detail as she climbed in and took her seat. The buggy was white with one red velvet seat. It was covered with a white cloth roof that came down into a short fringe of red tassels suspended with delicate gold strings. The young doe climbed to the driver's perch and took up the reins. She was dressed in a long, white dress with a long-tailed red overcoat and golden buttons that matched the buggy. She also wore small white boots and a tall red top hat. Her large ears were pulled back in a gold net under the rim of her hat. The working horses were a perfect match, both bright white with red blinkers and red harnesses lined with small gold bells that tinkled softly as the horses moved.

Marilana watched as much as she could as they drove through the west part of the city to a large, golden gate. Two uniformed guards allowed them in, one on either side of the gate. The guards wore blue slacks and blue coats with a red sash from right shoulder to left waist, and golden buttons down the middle of the front. There were guards in the same uniforms in the guard towers on either side of the gate. The sides of the drive were lined with trees and flowers. In the distance Marilana could hear the neighing of horses. They drove around a large marble fountain, water cascading over the statue of a crowned lioness—Marilana recognized the visage of the ancient Queen Maebala from her history textbook. The buggy came to a halt in front of long marble steps leading up to tall, wooden doors carved with exotic trees, ancient heroes, and strange writing. She climbed down from the buggy and the doe returned her satchel.

Marilana swallowed nervously as she looked around at the surrounding wings and front steps of a massive white stone building that could only be described as a palace. A male gazelle in white, red, and blue livery and two guards carrying halberds stood waiting for her at the top of the steps. "Do you carry any weapons?" the gazelle asked officially.

"No," Marilana replied.

"Very well. Know that the peace of the Royal Palace is not to be broken on pain of punishment determined by the severity of the offence, and no weapons are allowed to be carried in the presence of royalty without permission," he recited. He opened the palace door. "Follow me."

She barely had a chance to take in the grandeur of the vast palace entry hall before being led into a large side room.

"Wait here while your presence is announced," the servant said and closed the door.

Marilana allowed her feet to carry her around the room and her eyes to marvel at its size and majesty. Beautifully painted scenes of forests and flowers adorned every wall. She wondered briefly to whom she was being announced. The servant had not even asked her name. Marilana only hoped she was in the right place; it would be very embarrassing if there had been a mistake and she had been brought here instead of some noble who had been left sitting on the side of the road. The thought put a smile on her face despite the gravity of the situation.

Soon she heard footsteps. A moment later, the door opened, and a young lion walked in with a pair of guards and a servant. Marilana curtseyed quickly and then cautiously let her eyes drift upward. He was dressed in blue pants and a blue coat with a creamy undershirt and a red sash crossing his chest from left shoulder to right waist. His luscious mane was growing in well. On his head sat the golden circlet of the Crown Prince, which she had seen only once in a portrait Lady Annabella had shown her as a child. Her thoughts froze. She didn't believe that she, an orphaned peasant from the Southern Tip, was here in the Royal Palace in the presence of a prince. It had to be a mistake. Then she focused on his face and looked into his warm, sparkling green eyes.

"Welcome, Marilana, to my home," he said, with a regal smile.

"Marquiese?" she gasped. "But . . . ?"

"Yes, I am the Crown Prince of Redsands. And yes, my true father is King Rylan," he said proudly.

Marilana curtseyed again, feeling suddenly very uncomfortable and even a little frightened.

It must have shown, because Marquiese reached out and touched her shoulder lightly. "Do not worry. I asked you here to repay you for your friendship. Here you will be treated like a lady," he said reassuringly. "I am so glad that you are here."

"And I am honored to be here," she replied quietly.

"Your room is waiting. You will find clothes more appropriate to the surroundings. If there is anything you need or any way we can make you more comfortable, do let me know."

Marquiese gestured to a slender red fox and said, "She will show you to your room so you can change and freshen up. Dinner will be served shortly. I will see you there."

Marquiese shared a warm smile, gave her a reassuring nod, and turned away. Marilana watched as the Crown Prince of the Kingdom of Redsands departed and felt her half-starved lungs fill with air.

She felt very shy and quite embarrassed as the serving girl led the way to her room. Once she was alone, she took a few moments to compose herself and then cautiously explored her new surroundings. Her room was large—to say the least, her whole cottage could have fit in it with space to spare—and very well appointed. She had her own bathing room, and it was filled with all sorts of perfumed ointments, soaps, and lotions. Her large four-poster bed was surrounded with lacy white curtains and sat on a slight dais in its own portion of the room. The rest of the room's furniture was set in groups according to use.

A wardrobe sat next to a dressing table with a large open area where a lady would presumably be dressed by her personal servants. There was a writing desk and an oil lamp. There was a table with six chairs for private dining. Grouped around the window were a couch and two chairs for entertaining visitors. There was even a pair of glass doors that opened onto a balcony. The balcony was likewise furnished with a couch, two chairs, and a sheltered table. It over looked the gardens and the road leading to the stables. From that spot she could see over the garden trees to acres of paddocks and the stallions, mares, and foals stabled there.

The opulence was all slightly overwhelming, but Marilana didn't have time to think about it. She needed to get ready for dinner with royalty. She went back inside and crossed to the wardrobe, taking a deep breath before opening the doors. Her wardrobe was filled, as she had suspected it would be, with beautiful evening gowns, everyday walking dresses, riding clothes, and more shoes, hats, scarves, and accessories than Marilana thought she could wear in a year. The cut of the clothing still marked her as a noble ward, but the material was much finer than she would have ever chosen to wear.

Marquiese was indeed going to treat her as a lady and clearly expected her to look the part. Marilana chose a light blue evening gown with short white sleeves, a white belt, and a light blue lace veil that lay gently down the back of her head and around her ears. Marilana marveled at how beautiful everything was. And even though Lady Annabella had taught her the art of wearing such finery and the proper etiquette for a gathering of nobles, she felt completely out of place.

Marilana was still staring at herself in the mirror when someone rapped sharply on her door. She opened the door and found a plump tigress glaring back at her. The woman wore a black evening gown with a blue slash diagonally crossing her chest. Marilana knew that the slash marked her as part of the royal family, but she could not place her. The tigress' claws had been trimmed and polished. Every inch of her fur had been carefully placed and oiled. Meeting the scowling dark eyes, Marilana felt sure she was about to be scolded for pretending to be of a higher caste. She curtseyed carefully, and waited for the woman to speak.

"I am Prinka. My son would like to talk to you," she said flatly.

Prinka. Of course, the King's wife, Marilana thought. She could tell from the tone of the woman's voice that she was not pleased about having been asked to fetch a guest, if indeed that was the case.

Marilana closed the door behind her and followed Prinka down a flight of stairs and along a hallway to the main floor and the wing that housed the palace's guestrooms. She wondered why Marquiese would choose a room in such a lonesome area. She also wondered why Prinka had referred to him as "my son," instead of "The Prince" or "Marquiese." They stopped in front of a door with no markings, and Prinka held it open.

"In here," she said.

A single candle lit the room. The air smelled of mold, fish, and seawater. Prinka closed the door with an ominous click as soon as Marilana had cleared the threshold. Marilana blinked to adjust her eyes to the sudden darkness and could barely make out a shadowy figure leaning against what appeared to be a table.

"My name is Frishka. I'm Marquiese's stepbrother. Step over by the candle," said a harsh, cold voice from the dark.

Marilana held her breath and stepped cautiously toward the candle. A thousand questions raced through her mind. She hated the dark room and the stench and the uncertainty. She wanted to be as far away from this place as possible, but she also knew better than to speak or resist without cause.

"Good. Now turn around slowly," he said.

As Marilana turned, she caught the glint of the figure's eyes, but little else. She did not linger. As a member of the royal family he was surely a powerful individual, and she did not want to anger him. Nonetheless, she would have given anything for a sword in her paw just then, and the feeling of danger grew ever stronger the longer she stood in the darkness.

"Thank you. That's all for now. I may have a use for you in the future. Go now. Marquiese is waiting for you," he sneered.

The light from the hallway blinded Marilana as a servant opened the door, but Marilana neither flinched nor gave in to the urge to run out of the room. She walked carefully out the door and followed the servingman back down the hallway. Marilana wondered why Frishka had mocked Marquiese as he had done; she also wondered what he had meant about having a use for her. *Not likely*, she thought.

They arrived at the dining hall, and she pushed the encounter with Frishka as far from her mind as possible.

The dining hall was a long room with two rows of carved and gilded tables and chairs facing a head table on a slight dais. The King's large gold throne sat at the middle of this raised table with a slightly smaller throne to the King's left for the Crown Prince. Two ornate chairs sat to the King's right, which Marilana assumed were meant for Prinka and Frishka, and one less ornate chair to the Prince's left.

Already many guests had arrived, and the atmosphere grew increasingly festive. Marilana spied Marquiese talking with a group of young men—a tiger, two leopards, and a tall and powerful looking elk—and he saw her not a moment later. He excused himself from the group and hurried over.

"Good evening," he said formally. He offered his arm and escorted her onto the dais where the King and his party were to be seated. Marquiese indicated the chair to the left of his own, and Marilana took her seat, feeling very exposed and very out of place.

"You look very nice this evening," Marquiese whispered to her as they watched the rest of the guests find seats.

"Thank you, kind Prince," she whispered shyly. "As do you."

Marilana looked into Marquiese's familiar green eyes and relaxed slightly. When she looked aside, she saw Prinka entering the hall followed by a royally dressed tiger Marilana assumed to be Frishka. He, too, was primped and polished like his mother. But while she was rather plump, he was bony and wraith-like. He face had a sunken, mean look. Like Prinka, he was wearing solid black with a single broad blue stripe extending from the left shoulder to the right waist opposite that of the guards' red slash. He gave Marilana an evil smile as he walked past, and she shifted uneasily in her seat.

"You have already been taken to his chamber, I presume," Marquiese said, suddenly frowning.

"Is that a bad thing?" she asked warily.

"Was it lit only by a single candle?" he asked quickly.

"Yes . . . ."

"Then it is alright for now. He just wanted to frighten you," he replied with relief.

"Well, he managed distrust and unease," Marilana whispered, wondering how that was a relief. Before she could say any more, however, the room filled with the sound of great trumpets, and a door opened behind the dais. Everyone arose. Through the door strode the most royal lion Marilana had ever seen. On his head sat a wide circlet crown of gold with a middle band of diamond-studded silver. Golden highlights flowed through his thick, rich brown mane. He wore a gold embroidered blue suit. A red velvet cape rimmed with blue fur draped down his back. His eyes were kind and welcoming, but just as proud as Marquiese's. King Rylan sat between his son and Prinka and then spread his arms wide, gesturing for the guests to be seated and for the dinner to begin.

Marilana had never enjoyed such a dinner, though "enjoyed" may not have been the right word. More than once it occurred to her that she should be counted amongst the servants instead of sitting with the royal family. She tried to relax and enjoy the company of the young lion she had come so far to visit as he guided her through the menu. She sampled several wines and ate far more than she normally would. Finally, after laughingly refusing any more desserts, she sat sipping water and watching the gathered nobility say their farewells to King Rylan. Frishka and Prinka had left during the dessert course and Marilana hadn't been sorry to see them go.

She studied the nobles and felt grateful at least that Lady Annabella had insisted she practice her etiquette as much as she had. She was happy to have shared such a meal with Marquiese, but there was so much she wanted to talk to him about, so much she *needed* to talk to him about. Unfortunately, she couldn't help feeling slightly uneasy with him.

After all their guests had left, Marquiese and The King turned to her.

"Marilana, I must bid you goodnight," Marquiese said formally, accenting his words with a slight bow. "I shall see you tomorrow. Rest well."

Marilana was surprised by his abrupt departure and disappointed that she did not have a chance to speak with him alone. After all, she had come so far just to see him.

Marquiese nodded to his father, and then, with a brief smile, turned and walked away. Now here she was standing a matter of feet from the King of all Redsands, and the royal lion held her with penetrating green eyes very like his son's. Then he held out his paw, indicating the door behind the dais.

"I have heard so much about you, Marilana, and now I am finally graced with your presence. Come," King Rylan said in a deep, rich voice.

Marilana followed The King into a well-appointed, if simple sitting room. It was comfortably furnished with armchairs and end tables and was well-lit with oil lamps. She had the feeling that it would be a good place for company or quiet reading. She settled nervously into the armchair her host had indicated, and he sat facing her with great interest.

"Marilana, thank you for accepting the invitation to visit Marquiese. He has spoken very highly of you and your trustworthiness. As you know, I am King Rylan. I am Marquiese's blood father. I think you are disappointed that you have not gotten to speak with Marquiese in private yet, but I asked him to wait until I could have a few moments with you," King Rylan said shrewdly. There was a silver serving set on one of the end tables, and the King poured tea for them both as was his duty as host. "I want to get to know you better, most certainly. But I also want to share certain information that will help you make the most of your visit."

"Thank you," the young lioness said politely.

"Marquiese has told me much of your history, including your unfortunate capture by bandits as a small child, but I want to hear it from you. Please, tell me as much about your life as you feel comfortable discussing."

"If you wish," Marilana said, shifting nervously. She began with her parents leaving her in Lady Annabella's care and allowed the story to carry through with few exceptions to the present day. After a time, she found herself relaxing in the cozy room.

King Rylan was a good listener. He was patient and had a calming air that Marilana found comforting. He reminded her of Marquiese, as well as Lady Annabella. His questions prompted her to expound on certain events she hadn't expected to reveal, including her skills as a bandit hunter.

"Yes, I know much about your prowess. You are known as The Ghost," he said. "I have also been told about your skills in horse training."

Marilana acknowledged this with a courteous nod, and the comment led to a brief discussion about jousting techniques.

It was nearing midnight when Marilana finished telling King Rylan about the three years Marquiese had spent in Mystillion. She fell into a thoughtful silence as King Rylan refilled their teacups.

"Sire," Marilana asked hesitantly, "why did Marquiese attend my school and make friends for three years posing as a merchant's son?"

"I wondered if you would ask that," he said, sighing heavily. "It all started seven years ago when I was mediating between two countries, both my enemies. The two had been at war with each other for many years and were hoping for peace. That was when I first met Prinka. She was the daughter of one of my enemies, a princess of Ankenhun, but we spent some time together, and I fell in love with her. She was a beautiful tigress then, and so happy and full of life; hard to believe when you look at her now. My wife and Queen had died a few days after Marquiese turned five, and I had not met anyone who could make me feel the way Prinka did. Well, the two countries agreed on the peace settlement that I proposed, so I came back home to a motherless nine-year-old boy who I spoiled at every turn and allowed to do whatever he wanted.

"A couple days later, Prinka showed up on my doorstep. She had run away. Doing so, I told her, would bring war to my kingdom. For that, she was sorry. But I loved her and so let her stay."

"And did war erupt?" Marilana asked, leaning forward in her chair.

"Luckily not, though her father was extremely angry with both of us. I sent her to him, and she explained everything. He came to the wedding, and we signed a peace alliance between our kingdoms. It was a full year later when Frishka showed up; he was thirteen at the time. I sent a letter to Prinka's father inquiring about her son. His reply was not kind. Her father informed me that the boy had no father that he knew of. Also, that the boy had made choices against the Crown and so had been disowned by the family. Prinka had not seen her son since he had been disowned two years previous. She said she could see changes in his character, and she believed that a strong father figure would help him find the right path. She begged me to give the boy a chance.

"She is my Lady-wife, but not my queen, so I was reasonable and accepted him as a second son and named him a Lord. Of course, the second son has limited inherence rights as long as the first son is alive. I should have listened to Prinka's father and kept the boy at a greater distance.

"Frishka challenged my decision. He said he was older and therefore deserved to be my heir. When I refused, he challenged Marquiese to a duel declaring the victor should be named champion and my rightful heir. Luckily, Marquiese was a much better swordsman even though three years younger. When Marquiese won the duel, Frishka swore he would be second to none. He tried several times to kill Marquiese and had several of Marquiese's companions attacked."

"Oh, my goodness," Marilana whispered.

"During his time away from his mother, Frishka had befriended a strange, secretive young lion who we only knew as Confidant, and together they committed a number of very cruel acts. This Confidant was eventually banished from the kingdom, but even then Frishka was relentless. I knew Marquiese was in increasing danger. I threatened to disown Frishka, but Prinka would not allow her son to be put out again. The time came when Marquiese needed to spend a year of study elsewhere in accordance with the inheritance law. I did not want to let him go. We both agreed that Frishka would surely attack him without sufficient protection, but the time of study had to be completed for Marquiese to be truly recognized as my heir."

"I was unaware of such a law," Marilana admitted.

"Yes. For merchants and peasants it does not apply, for nobles the time is only a month, but for royals it is a full year. It is meant to help the heir find his or her own heart and path. So, for Marquiese's own safety, he joined a merchant family and moved to Mystillion. Given the situation, I was not told where my son had gone or if he was well. All I could do was hope for the best. We had agreed that after the year was up, he would send me a message and return.

"Prinka pleaded constantly with me to name Frishka my heir, but I refused to change my stance. When I did not receive word from Marquiese at the end of the year, she claimed he had forfeited his inheritance. What Prinka and Frishka did not know was that Marquiese had sent a letter to his childhood friend, Enton Castant, who had recently taken his father's place as one of my advisors. Marquiese's situation called for him to remain in hiding longer. He said he would send word when he was ready to return. After almost three years I received a letter from Merchant Colbran saying they had to move again and asked permission to send Marquiese home. I read between the lines of the letter and understood that Marquiese needed to return at once.

"When Marquiese arrived home I ordered two guards to watch him at all times. I was pleased and slightly saddened by the changes that had occurred in his character. He is much more mature and much wiser. He has also been very untrusting. I am glad for these things, but I also could tell that he had seen death up close. When he told me of his near capture by bandits, and the men he killed, I was saddened by the loss of his innocence so far from home. It was a lesson he needed to learn, but also a terrible one."

"And what of Frishka?" the young lioness asked.

"So far he seems to have accepted his role and Marquiese's new found confidence. I am also sure he will not remain so peaceable. Marquiese secured his position firmly before he came and talked to me about you. He has convinced me of your character. Of that I have no question. That I am as strict as I am has nothing to do with you, rest assured. It is because Frishka may want to use you in his plot to get rid of Marquiese."

"Sire, if you please, I am concerned as well that Frishka may do just that," Marilana said, fearful for Marquiese's safety. "He has already tried to frighten me and said that he may have a use for me in the future. Is there is a guard you would trust to stand by my door?"

"You are brave to make such a selfish statement in front of a king. You would request a personal guard to protect yourself when the Crown Prince is the one in danger?" he said watching her closely.

She looked shamefully at the floor, the color rising quickly to show through the thin fur on her cheeks.

"Forgive my presumption, Majesty. I was thinking only of protecting Marquiese. Lady Prinka took me to visit Lord Frishka's rooms earlier this evening. A single candle lit his rooms and he said he just wanted to get a look at me. At the time, I did not know who he was or any of the dangers that he represents, but the experience made me uncomfortable and wary. That was when Frishka said that he might have a use for me. I did not know what he meant, but now I fear that he will try to use me against Marquiese as you fear. Perhaps it might be better if I return to the Southern Tip."

"You are a kind and caring person Marilana. Marquiese is lucky to have you for a friend," King Rylan said, his words and smile both gentle. "I had already planned on assigning a guard to watch over you, but your request proves that you have grasped the serious nature of the situation. I am not surprised that Frishka has already started to make his impression on you. He uses a single candle when he wants to test someone's fear and how easy they are to manipulate. He prefers to be feared and tends to disregard female intelligence. I tell you this to put you on your guard, but I do not think you need to leave us quite so soon."

"Thank you for the warning, Sire," she said gravely. "I will remain vigilant, but I will sleep better knowing that there is a guard watching my door."

King Rylan sighed. "I fear that even guards will not help. Marquiese has assured me that you are loyal and will be able to protect yourself. Allow me to request that you be on your guard at all times while you are here. And please help protect Marquiese as well."

"Of course, Sire. I will do my best."

The guard arrived shortly thereafter. His name was Karndel. He was a young cheetah, strong, courteous, and above all loyal to Rylan and Marquiese. When he entered the room, he bowed to the King and tipped his blue guard's hat to Marilana. He accepted his orders to keep Marilana out of harm's way and provide escort around the palace, and then stood silently by the door.

"It is getting late. I should be retiring to my room," Marilana said, hiding a yawn behind her paw.

"Might we continue our talk tomorrow after dinner then? I would like to speak in more detail about your horse training," King Rylan said, sounding glad to broach a more joyful topic.

"I look forward to it, Sire," she answered gladly.

*

By the time Marilana reached her room, she felt as if she had known King Rylan much longer than a single evening. She was, however, extremely worried about all that she had learned during their conversation. It troubled her that there was so much distrust among the royal household.

Karndel took up his guard at the door and assured her of his diligence. When Marilana went inside, a young caracal maidservant was waiting for her. The servant curtseyed.

"Mistress Marilana," she said humbly, "I'm Altia, if it pleases you. Prince Marquiese chose me specifically to act as your personal assistant while you stay at the Royal Palace."

"Thank you, Altia," Marilana smiled at the young caracal. Small and slight of stature, she had beautiful tawny fur and black tufted ears. "I think it would be nice to have someone that I can rely on to help me find my way around. Please, just call me Marilana; I stand as low as anyone can. I am the orphaned child of peasant scholars."

"Very well, Marilana," Altia replied with a small smile. "But if I might say, you stand higher than most guests at the palace because you hold the regard of the Prince. He also said you were the noble ward of Lady Annabella, and that places you in high standing. He gave orders to treat you as nobility, and so that's what we will do."

"I understand his orders," Marilana said, sighing. "But please in private don't treat me as anyone higher than a fellow servant. I'm uncomfortable enough acting as he wishes in public."

The caracal came to assist Marilana out of her fine dinner gown and into a simple sleeping gown. Marilana noticed the girl frowning in thought.

"What are you thinking?" she asked.

"Oh, forgive me, Marilana," said Altia with a start. "I should be more attentive to my duties."

"No need for an apology, Altia," Marilana said gently, "I just wondered what you found so worthy of such deep thought."

Altia smiled shyly. "I was wondering why you said you were uncomfortable in public? When I saw you at dinner, you seemed to be very much the lady the Crown Prince said to treat you as."

"Really?" asked Marilana surprised, "I was so nervous and fidgety that I felt sure anyone could tell I should have been serving dinner instead of eating it at the head table."

Altia giggled, "I probably would feel the same. I will try to help you feel at home. You really did a fine job at dinner, though. I have seen many of the high born ladies do much worse."

Marilana relaxed a little and thought about what Altia had said as she climbed into the large soft bed. Maybe she could act the part of a lady; after all, she had been trained extensively in etiquette by a wonderful and noble teacher.

*

The next morning, Marilana stood at the window of her rooms looking out at the beautiful morning. She had slept well enough, given her long journey the day before and her first dinner at the Royal Palace. However, she had woken this morning lost in thought. She had dressed in a simple walking dress of pale green and had eaten the breakfast of porridge and fruit that Altia had brought for her. Then, not knowing what else to do, she had tried to distract her thoughts by thoroughly searching and analyzing her rooms. Even when she found what appeared to be a hidden door in the bathing room, she could not stop thinking about Marquiese.

Now she stood staring out the window thinking back over the years she had spent with him in the Southern Tip and saw it all in a new light. His secret had never seemed overly important back then; he was a great friend and someone she was certainly attracted to—despite her attempts to smother such attraction for sake of her position—but she had never dwelled on his past. Now she knew who he really was and why he had kept his identity so secret. Many of the things he had said and done were much more than they had seemed. She understood him better now that she could see the truth. It pained her deeply, but she decided it would be best if she broke off their friendship. She was a risk to his safety, and they had no future together. It would not be easy to accomplish. She knew Marquiese would object.

A knock on the door interrupted her contemplations, and she turned expectantly toward the door. Marquiese strode in, smiling broadly. Behind him, she saw two guards and the cheetah named Karndel taking up positions in the hall.

Marquiese closed the door and walked briskly toward her. As he drew near, Marilana gave him a low formal curtsey.

"Your Highness," she said simply.

Marquiese stopped his approach two paces from her and crossed his arms, frowning deeply.

"Marilana," he said quietly, "I am still Marquiese. When we are in private, please dispense with the formality."

"We are who we are, Highness," she replied levelly not meeting his eyes. "I am the lowest of your subjects, while you are the Crown Prince, to whom I am sworn through Lady Annabella to serve."

"So this is the way it is to go." He sighed. "I have imagined this meeting thousands of times and this was the logic that I had hoped not to have come from you. I had thought that our friendship would mean more, and that to you the Crown would not be an impediment. However, I should have known this is what you would say. After all, it is what you say about Lady Annabella too."

"I am speaking the truth," Marilana replied firmly.

"You are putting up walls," he countered. "The truth of the matter is that you are here at my request because you are my friend. A very special friend. If you did not still want to be my friend, you would not have accepted my invitation."

"That was before I knew your secret. Now I feel like I barely know you at all," Marilana said quietly.

Marquiese smiled and replied softly, "Yes, Marilana, I am the Crown Prince, but the truth is that without those years spent in the Southern Tip, I would not be the person I am today. You know me, and you know how I changed. You were the one who showed me the people I am supposed to rule someday. You were my tutor, but you taught me more than school ever could. You taught me to look beyond the social status and to listen to the peasants because they are the ones who support all of the upper castes. You showed me the problems that the common people face every day and how the nobles' points of view can affect those problems. You helped me learn how to be a better king. For that I will be forever grateful. Beyond that, you also saved my life on multiple occasions and are the reason that I am safely where I am today. I asked you here so that I could reveal my secret in person because I respect you and consider you to be a true friend."

Marilana looked down at her paws. "That is part of the problem, Marquiese. I keep thinking back on all those time that I put your life at risk. If I had known who you were, I would never have taken you into such dangerous situations. It is true that I saved your life more than once, but I also put you at risk. For that I am ashamed."

"No, Marilana," the regal lion said, stepping close to her and placing a paw on her shoulder, "I took those risks. I put my life in your paws. Those were my decisions, and you cannot take the blame just because you did not know my true identity."

Marilana did not look up. "Lady Annabella did."

"At first she just suspected. After she cornered me at your house, she knew fully the extent of the situation. She promised to keep my secret and said that you were probably the best person to stay close to. She knew I had to play the part of a merchant and take risks. She said that you would keep me safe and you did." Marquiese chuckled, shaking his head. "Do you remember the Winter Masquerade? My father nearly fainted when I told him about switching with Earek for a dance."

Marilana looked up with wide-eyed horror. "You took a terrible risk that night. If Master Arndt or his brother had recognized you! I can hardly bear to think what could have happened if your enemies had found you there. And when the knights came to see my horses, any of them would have recognized you on sight." She shook her head, filling her lungs and calming herself. "The bandits were searching for you. Someone knew you were there."

"Someone *suspected* I was in the Southern Tip. I have not found out how or who. Frishka has not given me any indication that he suspected I was in the Southern Tip. He is my greatest threat and the reason I was in hiding. However, do not dwell on what ifs, Marilana, please. As my father says, what is done is done, and the only thing left to think on is how to move forward from here. Besides, the Masquerade was worth it. That one dance was worth it."

"How could one silly dance be worth risking your life? You are the Crown Prince, and your life is infinitely more valuable than a dance at a county school," she scolded.

"County school or palace feast," he said lightly, "I would risk my life again to see you in that dress and dance with you once more."

Marilana felt the heat rise in her cheeks and her stomach suddenly seemed to be full of butterflies. She realized at that moment that she could never break off their friendship. She cared for him too much.

Marquiese raised his eyebrows in surprise, "Of all the reactions I was prepared to witness, seeing you blush was not one of them."

Marilana turned abruptly toward the window breathing fast and pressed her paws to her heated cheeks.

"Forgive me, Highness," the lioness said breathily, "I do not know what has come over me."

"Marilana, my friend," Marquiese said gently, "I should be the one apologizing. I did not mean to embarrass you. I know why you keep those wardrobes at your cottage secret, although I hope you can enjoy wearing some fancy dresses for a time. I want to thank you for sharing your knowledge, life, and home with me in my time of need, and now I want to return the gesture and share my home with you. There is danger here; you will have to be careful. I have enemies, lots of responsibilities, and very few friends. I trust you to be here. I am asking you to take a big risk and remain here for a while; I want you to know me as I truly am."

He took a step close, reached out, and touched her shoulders lightly. "Will you still be my friend, Marilana?"

Marilana turned back, breaking the physical contact, and studied his sincere green eyes.

"Why did you stay after the first year?" she asked seriously.

"So Father spoke of that," he said studying her eyes. "I stayed because you showed me the injustices of the higher castes. I needed to learn the truth of the matter. Also you told me about the bandits, and I knew they were hunting me. I needed to stay hidden a while longer."

"Were those the only reasons?" she asked, her eyes still holding him.

"At the end of the first year, yes," he nodded seriously. "There was a time when I almost rushed back here. You remember when Lady Annabella delivered bad news to me at your house? She came to me and told me that my father had fallen ill. I was torn between returning to defend my father or remain in the Southern Tip. I chose to remain because I had not fully solved the mysteries that I had found there. I was troubled for fifnights after, wondering if I had made the right decision. Once my father recovered, I felt justified in my choice as well as relieved that he was better. Later, I almost considered not returning. That life was a good one. I was free of my duty, had very little responsibility, and had two of the best friends I could ever have dreamed to find.

"Lady Annabella saw the decision I was challenged with and helped me determine a better course of action. Still I lingered longer than I should have. In the end, the bandits made my decision for me. Once they discovered my whereabouts, they would have been relentless in hunting me. I had to leave. Even then I feared the loss of your friendship; I feared that I had left you with too many questions and not enough answers. Now I have given you the answers and may still lose you. It is your choice."

It was his turn to hold her eyes. "Friends?"

She studied him a moment more before nodding and saying, "Friends." Then she smiled. "I have missed you, Marquiese. I am glad you convinced me that I should not run from being your friend."

"I have missed you too, Marilana," he said warmly. "Come sit with me. I want to hear everything that has happened this last year, especially at the end of the year ball. Lady Annabella told me she invited Master Arndt to dance with you again. What happened? Was Brittia furious?"

Laughing, they sat together on the couch and spoke of many things. But Marilana chose not mention the exhibition courtship dance with Master Arndt. Somehow it just didn't seem the right time to mention that detail. The lioness relaxed as they talked, realizing the handsome lion sitting next to her was, after all, the same person despite his lofty rank.

4

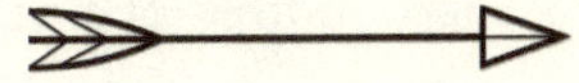

Marilana was busy in the days that followed. She spent much of her time with Marquiese when he was not otherwise occupied with the many duties of the Crown Prince. She walked with him in the gardens, went driving with him through the countryside, or rode with him through the forests. She herself enjoyed all the new sights and the beauty of Maefair and the surrounding lands, but what she cherished the most were all the things Marquiese had wanted to share with her but had not been able to during his time in Mystillion.

He returned her tutelage by teaching her the nuances of court life and how to read the currents of the nobility. He built upon Lady Annabella's teachings and soon she began to recognize how to further use the skills that she had learned. Her confidence in public grew day by day, and she felt less out of place at his side.

Altia also helped Marilana feel more at home in the palace. The young caracal was very knowledgeable about the nobles and the undercurrents of palace life. She had started as a kitchen helper and had since become a member of the cleaning staff for the Royal Family Apartments. The slender cat chatted almost constantly as she worked, and Marilana found she liked the girl more all the time. Altia talked most about her life in the palace and in the city. Her great-aunt Gwina had raised her after her parents' deaths, and Marilana was pleased to learn that the elderly caracal was an Herb Mother and had some knowledge of the old ways. Altia was thrilled to learn that Marilana was knowledgeable in herb lore and the old ways as well and asked permission to tell Aunt Gwina about her. Marilana was happy to agree to the request and hoped to meet the Herb Mother in person some time soon.

*

A fifnight after Marilana's arrival, Marquiese came to her room just after breakfast and said he had a surprise for her. She laughed as he led her down several corridors and a flight of stairs, and then stopped in front of a pair of age-darkened wooden doors.

"Why will you not tell me where we are going?" the lioness asked him for the fifth time.

"I told you it is a surprise! Why are you not satisfied with that answer?" he responded with a laugh.

"I am excited, and I want to know!"

"Well you can stop asking because we are here. But of course I have to blindfold you."

"Blindfold! You never said anything about a blindfold!" she exclaimed as Marquiese pulled a blue satin sash out of his coat pocket.

"Now just stand still," he said as he walked behind her. He carefully reached around and pulled the sash over her eyes, then tied it off. Butterflies fluttered in Marilana's stomach as his claws gently brushed her fur.

"How am I supposed to walk—" she started to protest when he laid his paw over her mouth.

"Hush, you talk too much. Trust me," he said quietly.

He took her paws in his and gently led her forward. She could hear the creaking of heavy hinges as one of the doors opened in front of them. She felt light suddenly touch her face. Beneath her feet she could feel a plush carpet.

"Are you ready?" he asked releasing her paws.

"Yes!" she whispered. He took the blindfold away from her eyes and she found herself looking at a wonderful sight.

There in front of her was an L-shaped room two stories tall with floor-to-ceiling windows on one side looking out over the palace entrance and shelves filled with books covering every other available space. At the end of each arm were spiral staircases covered in gold that led to an elevated walkway. The main doors were at the "top" of the L and the other arm extended along the windows, cleverly hiding the far staircase from the door. The floor was furnished with plump armchairs, rocking chairs, writing tables, and all manner of lamps. The carpeting was indeed plush red, speckled with blue.

"Oh, Marquiese! It is wonderful!" Marilana gasped.

"My Lady, please keep your wits about you and respond to Prince Marquiese as His Royal Highness!" said an elderly snow leopard seated behind a desk.

"No, it is all right, Sir Libor. This is my personal friend Marilana. She has the privilege of addressing me informally," Marquiese said to the man. Then he glanced at the lioness at his side. "Marilana, this is the Royal Library, and this is Sir Libor, the Royal Librarian and my longtime tutor."

"Pleased to meet you, Sir," Marilana said quietly, curtseying.

"My dear child, no need for that. I can see that you are quite respectful of the library already. If you ever need my help, you are free to ask," Sir Libor stated gently, clearly flattered by the courtesy. "Please enjoy."

"Marquiese, how did you know I would love this?" Marilana asked softly.

"I remember that if no one could find you at school, home, or at Lady Annabella's stables, you were in a library somewhere with your nose in a book." Marquiese laughed. "Seriously, though, I wanted to bring you here before I left. I have business outside the city which requires my attention."

"When do you leave?" she asked, frowning slightly.

He took her paw in his and squeezed it gently. "I leave immediately. My escort is already waiting for me. Enjoy the library; I know Lady Annabella would be pleased if you continued your studies here. I will be gone for almost two days. I should be back in time for dinner tomorrow."

Without another word, he turned and strode out of the library. Marilana moved over to the windows from which she could see the front steps of the palace and the fountain of Queen Maebala. She watched as Marquiese exited the palace, mounted his horse, and rode off with his escort of guards and servants. She suddenly felt very alone.

"What can I help you find, Mistress?" asked Sir Libor from behind her. "Anything at all?"

She turned and found him smiling kindly. He held out the satin blindfold. She took it gently and tucked it into her belt pouch.

"I find that time always seems to pass quicker if I devote my mind to some study or another," he said lightly.

Smiling she followed him back toward his desk and thought about what studies she should pursue first.

*

Marilana was quiet and nervous while Marquiese was away. She spent much of her time in the library studying one of the history books Sir Libor had pulled down for her. King Rylan even allowed her to eat dinner in her rooms that night. Marilana didn't miss Frishka's inevitable sneers, but she did miss the company. Every evening since her arrival at the Royal Palace, Marilana had joined King Rylan in his sitting room after dinner. Several times he had introduced her to minor lords and ladies of Maefair, and she had enjoyed her evenings immensely.

Not this evening, however. Despite the fact that she had lived alone for seven years, the lioness felt lost and lonely sitting in her rooms watching the sun set over the gardens. She spent most of the next day awaiting Marquiese's return and the prospect of dinner in the dining hall.

When dinner finally arrived, Marilana returned Marquiese's warm greeting with her own bright smile and after eating, he surprised her by joining her in his father's sitting room. Marilana did not have to wonder why for long.

"How did your business in Bram's Fen go?" King Rylan asked sitting in his customary armchair.

"Lord Ruberic was more than willing to assist me," Marquiese said levelly.

Marilana frowned. She recognized Bram's Fen as the home of Brittia's cousin Demdrake. The merchant son had caused her nothing but trouble the few times he had been in the Southern Tip, and the last time he had visited, Marquiese had spoken against him in front of Lady Annabella. The handsome Prince remained standing and did not look at her.

"You managed the situation in an unbiased fashion?" King Rylan prodded.

"I did my best, although my feelings supported the lawful resolution," Marquiese replied.

"May I ask what happened?" Marilana asked suspiciously.

"An ... acquaintance ... of ours was in some legal trouble. I went to Bram's Fen to make sure justice was fulfilled," Marquiese said cautiously and met her eyes.

"You went to settle your score with Demdrake," Marilana said disapprovingly.

"No, that was just an added benefit," Marquiese said seriously. "Demdrake was apprenticing with a young Knight of the Realm who will go nameless for now. Over the past six months, fourteen young girls of both low-class merchant and peasant castes have been seriously abused. In the last month three have died. It was well known that the Knight was responsible, and that Demdrake was involved. It was also in their right to do as they wished with girls of lower castes. However, the Knights of the Realm are supposed to adhere to the code of chivalry, and the Council of the Brotherhood decided that they could not look the other way any longer.

"They spoke to the local magistrates, but the Bram's Fen Merchant Council—led by Merchant Branish, Demdrake's father—opposed any action. There was a stalemate. It looked as if the Knight and Demdrake were going to get away without punishment again. The magistrates and the Council of the Brotherhood needed help; they needed someone with higher authority to intercede. One of the Knights on the Council told my father about the predicament. My father recognized Demdrake's name from my account of the incident in the Southern Tip and sent me to Lord Ruberic, Great-Lord of Herinsford, the province in which Bram's Fen is located.

"Lord Ruberic accompanied me to the courthouse in Bram's Fen. He suggested that I remain outside the courtroom since I had a prior disagreement with Demdrake. Lord Ruberic listened to the case and decided that the Council of the Brotherhood was in the right. The Knight was stripped of his title and family name and was sentenced to a fifnight in the stocks. Demdrake was to be sentenced likewise. But his father led a vehement opposition to the sentence."

"I am sure Lord Ruberic was less than pleased," King Rylan commented seriously.

"He was furious to have a merchant oppose him to such a degree," Marquiese said darkly. "He sentenced Demdrake as he intended, and then stripped the entire family of their caste. The rest of the Merchant Council ceded to Lord Ruberic, and the magistrate recorded the decree. I have never seen Lord Ruberic so angry.

"When the accused were led out of the courtroom, Demdrake saw me and started to threaten me. He was furious to find that I was behind his family's demise. When the former knight recognized me, he gave Demdrake a good kick and told him to shut up. Lord Ruberic rounded on Demdrake and told him that if he continued to threaten the Crown Prince in such a manner, he would be sure to have him executed immediately.

"Demdrake gaped like a fish out of water. He looked up at the circlet on my head and the insignia on the uniforms of my guardsmen, and the truth hit him. He fainted right there and had to be carried out by the town garrison."

"You did well to remain outside the proceedings. Lord Ruberic coped with the situation with his customary decisiveness." King Rylan nodded his approval. "It is unfortunate that so many had to suffer before others put a stop to it."

"No one would have stopped it at all if the man had not been a Knight of the Realm," Marilana said sadly. "The upper castes have no reason to stop such abuse. It is their supposed right."

"There are many flaws in the caste laws, Marilana," King Rylan said gently. "That is one of the reasons we have bandit hunters. You protected many girls from Demdrake while he was in the Southern Tip and limited the degree of abuse. I wish the people of Bram's Fen had a bandit hunter like you. Unfortunately their last bandit hunter was killed in a skirmish a year ago, and the town had no one who could stand against the abuse."

"That is unfortunate," the lioness said with a pronounced sigh. "Bandit hunters are hard to find. I hope one will choose to protect Bram's Fen in the near future."

"On a good note, Demdrake got what he deserved," Marquiese said firmly.

"He will have to watch out for the peasant fathers now." Marilana smiled. "He no longer has the right to abuse their daughters, and they can take their own revenge. One consequence of your action however is that Brittia will be finding out your secret soon and will spread it to the rest of the Southern Tip."

The Crown Prince nodded. "That is true, and it brings me to the second thing I want to discuss. There is someone in Mystillion who I would rather tell my secret to in person, rather than let him find out from someone else. I owe him that much, Father."

"Your friend Earek, I assume," the regal lion said to his son.

"Yes. May I please invite him for a visit," Marquiese asked. "Marilana knows him well and we both trust him."

"What will he do if he has to choose between friendship and mortal danger?" King Rylan asked seriously.

"He is the second son of a wealthy merchant, yet does not seek wealth for his own. He will not harm me of his own free will," Marquiese said honestly.

"Actually, that is no longer the truth," Marilana said, grimacing. She looked into Marquiese eyes. "I did not tell you before because it did not feel like the right time. But you should know before inviting him."

"Know what, Marilana?"

"Earek's family disowned him."

"What? When?" Marquiese exclaimed in outrage.

"Last fall, just before Lady Annabella left the Southern Tip for the Annual Tournament."

"Why would they do that? Earek was the perfect merchant son; he would never have disgraced his family."

"You are forgetting that they disowned Earek's younger brother just because he was determined to become a soldier."

Marilana shook her head sadly. "Brittia forced it on them because Earek refused to break off his friendship with me."

"Brittia," Marquiese muttered, "I should have known. That was when Lady Annabella told you to stop hiding your skills, too, wasn't it?"

"Yes, it was. And after watching what Brittia did to Earek, I was not sorry to prove she was not the best in the class in either dancing and etiquette or the laws of the land," Marilana said firmly. "I was proud of Earek for choosing his own course and not letting Brittia dictate his life."

"Is he all right?" Marquiese asked.

"Lady Annabella set him up with a place to live and made sure he could finish school. Just a few days before the end of school, he swore oaths of service to Lady Annabella in return for all her assistance. He was supposed to study with her chamberlain this summer."

"He seems to have a good heart and to be a loyal friend. Marilana, will you vouch for this Earek?" King Rylan asked her seriously.

"Yes, Sire, I will," Marilana responded calmly. "I have never seen him take action against anyone unless forced too. He has been training with me and is becoming skillful with sword and bow, but he has been skillful in diplomacy for many years. He holds his honor to the highest degree."

"Very well, it seems that both of you are very fond of this young leopard and I will have to trust your judgment. However, if I don't approve of him, he will be sent away and will not return. Do we understand each other?"

"Yes, Sire!" Marilana and Marquiese replied, their smiles filled with excitement.

5

Another fifnight passed in pleasantries, studies, and idleness for Marilana. She was not used to having so much free time without chores and patrols. Marquiese was frequently busy with his duties, and she spent her time getting acquainted with her surroundings. The staff and palace guards were beginning to know her better. She made frequent visits to the kitchens, gardens, and stables, and had quickly learned the warren of hallways throughout the palace. Altia, the energetic and diminutive caracal, had become a fast friend, frequently stopping by for a quick chat, passing on servant gossip or suggestions on what to wear for the various occasions both in the palace and the city.

One night, Marilana returned to her rooms after her regular after-dinner talk with King Rylan to find Altia pacing by the dim light of a single candle. Marilana frowned; she had sent word to the serving girl that she would be late and that Altia could go to bed without waiting for her. Finding the girl agitated in the dark worried Marilana, but she waited to see if Altia would speak first. Altia quickly and silently helped Marilana out of her evening gown and readied her bed.

Marilana finally broke the silence, saying, "Altia, what is the matter? You are nervous as a sparrow in the dark. Why did you not light the lamp?"

Altia twisted her paws together as she stood by the bed.

"Marilana." Altia started hesitantly. "Can I . . . I need . . . may I ask you for some advice?"

"Of course you can," Marilana replied with a smile.

She patted the bed, and Altia sat eagerly on the edge. She smiled nervously and twisted her apron in her paws.

"Well, there's this man. He's a fine and handsome cheetah," Altia said quickly. "And I don't know what I should do. Should I act bold and try to catch his attention, or act timid and hope he notices me? Or maybe I should just stay away from him? I just don't know. I just don't know . . . ."

"Hold on, Altia. Why are you asking me? My experience with males is, well, not much to brag about. Maybe you should ask Aunt Gwina. I'm sure she could help you much more than I can."

Altia paused and looked puzzled, "Well, I just thought you would know the best way to get a male's attention. After all, you have the attention of the Prince. Most of the females in the palace, both noble and peasant, would give anything to be in your place."

Marilana laughed. "I did not know he was the Prince when I first met him. I thought he was the spoiled first son of a snobby merchant."

"No! Really?" exclaimed Altia, completely shocked. "But you and he are friends and the way you act together . . . . Well, I just assumed you somehow flirted your way into his good graces."

Marilana blushed. In a most gentle voice, she said, "That is not the way it should work, Altia. Those women who flirt and flatter their way into a male's life are not always being honest. They may want a man's favor because of his power or position or wealth. Also a male that favors a woman because of the way she flirts or the promises she makes may not want anything more than to get a pretty body into bed with him."

"I'm sure this man is not that way," stated Altia, but then she hesitated. "How can I be sure? I only know him in little ways. Like when we pass in the hallway or chance meetings in the kitchens. We have only talked a few times. I don't know if he really has noticed me or if I'm just another servant in his place of work."

"How often do you have these chance meetings?" Marilana asked with a smile. "Are you arranging them? What does he do when he sees you?"

Altia thought for a moment, "Well, we seem to meet once or twice a day, but I am not doing it on purpose. Usually I'm busy with some kind of work and he will smile and nod to me as he goes about his own work."

"Is this how he acts toward the other servants? Has he addressed you by name or you him?"

"Well, he is always courteous to the creatures around him, always polite," she mused. "He did surprise me one day by addressing me by name. I remember because it was the first time I had really paid him any mind. He stopped me in the hallway outside the kitchen just as I was taking in a clean load of towels. 'Miss Altia, you dropped this!' he said and placed a towel on top of my load. He seemed a bit awkward, but opened the door for me. He returned my smile when I thanked him."

"Who is this fine and handsome cheetah?" Marilana asked with a smile. "He sounds like he has been watching you for some time without doing more than being polite."

"He is an officer in the palace guards." Altia smiled shyly. "Do you think he likes me?"

"I think you both want to find out. I think you are both worried about being too forward, and I also think it would be good for you to talk when you are not working."

"I don't know, Marilana." Altia shook her head warily. "What if he just wants to get me alone, like you said?"

"I'm not suggesting you let him," Marilana replied. "Is there another servant you are friends with, maybe one of the older kitchen staff? You two could take a walk on the barracks path just after his shift change, see if he comes by."

"What then? What if he comes, what do I do? What if he doesn't come?" Altia fidgeted nervously.

Marilana reached out and placed her paw over Altia's paws, holding them still.

"Lady Annabella once told me that if you want someone to think about you, you need to be seen. Even if he doesn't stop to talk to you, at least you had been seen. Make it part of your routine and go for a walk every day at the same time. Be patient, and you will find out if he wants to talk to you. Smile at him when you pass in the halls, and say hello. No matter what you do, it should not make you feel uncomfortable. If you do not act like yourself, he will not know the true you."

Altia relaxed and smiled. "Thank you, Marilana. I may not have been right about how you and Prince Marquiese became friends, but I was right about asking you for advice. You know how to read people better than you let on."

"Perhaps I do, but I will not trust that skill too much," Marilana warned. "There are too many people who can and will act to deceive."

"Like Lord Frishka," Altia said with disgust.

"The servants don't seem to like him much. Nor do they talk about him much," Marilana noted.

"You never know when one of his serving men or one of his mother's women is listening around a corner. Some of the other men report to him as well, for pay of course. He deals harsh punishment for disrespecting him or his mother."

"None of the other women report to him directly?" asked Marilana curiously.

"He makes us uncomfortable, and we avoid him at all costs. He looks at us like we are bugs that need to be smashed or pies to be eaten." Altia shivered. "You need to be careful as well. I have seen him watching you with that hungry expression, too."

"Does he assert himself on the women servants?" Marilana asked with disgust of her own.

"Not on the servants. Others are not so safe. The ladies and the noble daughters have turned away his advances easily enough, but the peasants and merchants of the city are not so lucky. He prefers the peasants, I think, because they have no ties to the nobility and no one bothers to find out what happened if one disappears."

"I thought as much." Marilana grimaced. "That kind of man is dangerous. He works in the shadows and doesn't mind spilling blood to get what he wants."

"I think he enjoys spilling blood," Altia added with another shiver.

They sat in silence for a moment, each lost in her own dark thoughts. Finally, Altia stood. "I should be going," she said.

"Altia," Marilana called to her. "Why did you not light the lamp?"

Altia sat sheepishly back down on the bed.

"I dismissed you for the night, yet you were here waiting to talk to me," Marilana stated gently. "The Head Maid doesn't know you are here, does she."

Altia swallowed nervously. "No one knows I am here. I needed advice. So I returned to your rooms after I was dismissed. I was worried that Mistress Refrona would disapprove of our friendship, and I thought it might be better if we didn't make it public knowledge. I don't want to appear to be overstepping my station."

"I understand the friendships that can occur between a servant and the one they serve. I agree that those friendships and any conversations are private," Marilana replied seriously. "I am also aware that you are not my servant. You serve me only at the request of Prince Marquiese. I am grateful that you have graced me with your friendship. I will do what I can to prevent any harm coming to you through me. I promise never to mislead you with my intentions."

Altia relaxed a little and smiled.

"So," Marilana continued. "How did you sneak into my rooms and how are you planning to sneak out again?"

Altia fidgeted. She looked away, frowning. "I can't tell you."

"You accepted the possibility of telling me when you chose to come here in secret. You chose to trust me, at least in part."

"I am sworn to secrecy, Marilana. I cannot tell you," Altia said seriously.

"Very well," Marilana replied sternly. "You will not tell me that there is a secret door in my bathing room, but will you tell me how many people know about it?"

Altia looked appalled. "Who told you about it? Only the most trusted know about it."

Marilana smiled slyly. "No one told me about it. I found the outline of what I suspected was a well-hidden door the first morning I was here. You just confirmed that I was right."

"No one has ever found it before. No one."

"Yes, well, I am a bandit hunter. I am a very skilled tracker, and I am trained to discover much that is secret. The door is very well hidden, and it took me a good while to discover the outline. Unfortunately, I could not discover the mechanisms to open the door. I am concerned that someone may use it with ill intentions. Use it to harm Prince Marquiese. I need to know who knows about it."

"You are a bandit hunter?" Altia said, shocked. "Does Prince Marquiese know? Is that why he brought you here?"

"Yes, he knows." Marilana smiled gently. "He brought me here because I am his friend. He trusts me with his life. And I trust him in return. I was kidnapped by bandits when I was a little girl and made it my life's work to hunt those that terrorize children and families. I am not here to hunt; however, if Prince Marquiese or King Rylan made such a request, I would hunt anyone for them."

"I do trust you," Altia said after a long moment. "I did not tell you about the door, and I will not show you how it works at this time. Perhaps in the future, I may tell you the secret, but not tonight. I will tell you something of it because you are His Highness's friend and you are right that someone could use you against him. It is said to have been built a very long time ago by a king who was paranoid about his safety. He held against a revolt and a siege in this palace and made many renovations to make the Royal Palace more secure for his family. He had a mistress who stayed in this room. He had the secret door made so that he could visit her, or to hide if need be. That is why this room is called the Mistress's suite by the staff, though none know about the secret door. Only the most trusted of the Royal Family's Personal Servants know of the secret door, three others and I. The Head Maid does not know of it. It is a closely guarded secret, kept by us to be revealed to the king only at great need."

"So Marquiese and Rylan do not know of it?" Marilana asked surprised.

"No." Altia shook her head. "It is said that the old king took many of his secrets to his grave. The secret of the doors he entrusted to one servant, and so it has been kept ever since. I was told only after proving my loyalty to be unbreakable. Please, Marilana, don't tell anyone."

"I too am a loyal servant of the royal family and so I swear to keep this secret as the servants before me. To be revealed to the king only at great need," Marilana promised solemnly. "Now it is late, and we both need sleep."

Altia hesitated, then threw her arms around Marilana. Marilana returned the embrace warmly.

"Thank you, Marilana. My friend," whispered Altia.

"Good night, my friend," replied Marilana.

Altia quickly and quietly took the candle and disappeared around the corner and into the bathing room. Marilana listened for any sound, but the light disappeared with only the soft patter of Altia's slippers. Clearly, the secret door was very well crafted.

*

The next day Marilana and Marquiese waited excitedly for Earek's arrival. They tried to stay busy. They spent the morning in the stable yard assisting the stable master. Marilana loved working with the palace horses, and the stable master was thrilled when he heard she had trained so many of Lady Annabella's horses.

After lunch, Marilana took a long bath and dressed carefully. She selected an elegant, dark blue walking dress and then went to the library to wait. Sir Libor was away on some errand, and the library was empty. The lioness found a book on the history of Maefair and settled into a high backed chair with her back to the door, facing the windows. This was by intent; the more difficult it was for someone to see her, the better.

Earek was arriving from Mystillion by carriage, much as Marilana had. A buggy would carry him to the Royal Palace, and the lioness kept a close eye out. Not long after she had opened her book and well before she could immerse herself in the text, a light buggy appeared driving smoothly down the long drive from the distant gate. Marilana sat up, a smile tugging at the corners of her mouth. The buggy stopped in front of the steps. A single bag was unloaded. A passenger stepped down and took the bag. It was not Earek. Marilana studied the young yellow leopard for a moment, wondering who he was. Then she spotted a second passenger exiting the other side of the buggy, and this was indeed the black leopard she had long called friend.

Earek had no baggage and looked as if the driver had let him off at the wrong place. Marilana's grin broadened. She set the book down on the table and waited silently. Soon the library door opened, and she heard a servant say, "Wait in here, young sir, while I announce your presence."

The door closed and Marilana heard footsteps whispering in the plush carpet.

"How was your ride, young sir?" Marilana asked suddenly, still hidden from view.

The footsteps stopped. The lioness watched the distorted reflection in the base of a silver lamp.

"Long, but pleasant," Earek said, his narrowed eyes panning the room. "I have traveled all the way from Mystillion in the Southern Tip, if you must know. If I may ask, where are you? And who am I speaking to?"

"How is everyone in Mystillion? I have not been there for a while," she asked cunningly, knowing that her voice would echo slightly off the windows and obscure her location.

"Everyone is doing fine for this time of the year," he replied, quietly moving toward a group of chairs and now clearly enjoying the charade.

"And the school yard? Are the marigolds in bloom yet, Earek?" she asked, hardly containing her smile. At this, the black leopard stopped. He peered toward the windows. Laughing, Marilana sprang to her feet and faced her friend.

"Marilana! It is you!" he cried, excitement overflowing in his voice. "What are you doing here? For that matter, what am I doing here? And where did you get such a fine dress?"

They embraced, both of them laughing. "So many questions. Come and sit," Marilana said, offering him a chair and taking one herself that this time gave her a clear view of the doors.

"Tell me everything," she said.

"Tell me first what I am doing in the library in the King's Palace, for goodness sake," he demanded.

"That is someone else's secret to tell," she said evasively. "Now fill me with stories long and short and spare no details."

And so he did. Stories of Jarek and Brittia, of Lady Annabella and her estates, of his training and his new life as an apprentice chamberlain. Through it all, they laughed just like old times, and it was, for that hour, exactly like old times.

Eventually, they heard footsteps approaching the room. Marilana stood and Earek followed her lead. However, instead of a servant opening the door and announcing the arrival of the Prince, his cruel and devious stepbrother, the emaciated tiger Frishka, slipped in. At the sight of him, Marilana stood straighter and took a half step closer to Earek. Except for their nightly dinners, she had seen neither Frishka nor his mother since her first night in the palace. She wondered what he was up to.

"So. This is your friend?" Frishka said in a mocking tone, making his way toward the arm of the library that was hidden from the doors, his cruel eyes raking over Earek. "And that of my foolish stepbrother? Earek. Do I have the name right? A black leopard. Not the smartest creature, but one easily manipulated."

"You apparently know nothing of black leopards," Marilana said coldly. "And I will, if need be, call the guard."

"Oh, he won't come. Conveniently, he's running an urgent errand for Mother," the tiger smirked. He pinned Earek with his eyes. "We will talk again sometime."

"I don't think so," Marilana answered for her friend.

They heard another set of footsteps in the hallway. "Well, well. Here comes the Prince now." He sneered in Earek's direction.

As the door opened, Frishka disappeared around the corner and a voice called out in a loud voice. "His Royal Highness, Prince Marquiese."

Marilana curtseyed low. Earek began to bow, but paused mid-bow and looked up, his eyes wide.

"You always were a little slow to catch a name." Marquiese laughed. Earek, mouth gapping wide open, looked from Marquiese to Marilana and back again. Both were laughing at his half-bowed, gapping figure.

"Ma-a-Marquiese?" Earek finally stuttered in surprise. "You? A prince?"

"Yes, my friend. King Rylan is my father. He has allowed me to invite you here in return for the friendship you so willingly gave me during my time in Mystillion," Marquiese answered. He gave Earek's arm a squeeze. "So good to have you here, my old friend. We shall talk later. I want to hear everything. In the meantime, guests are already arriving for dinner. I shall see you both there."

He turned and departed the library in the escort of two guards.

"Wow," Earek said when Marquiese was gone. "I hadn't expected that."

"That was quite obvious," Marilana teased.

A servant entered the room a moment later and her eyes fell on Earek. She said, "May I show you your room, Master Earek?"

"Oh, yes. Thank you." Earek and Marilana followed the servant down several hallways to stop at the door next to Marilana's own room. His room was as large as hers except for the balcony. In its place were two door-like windows that opened inwards with a railing on the outside. His bed was adorned with feather pillows, but unlike hers, it was carved dark wood enclosed with a dark red silk curtain, not lace. His wardrobe was full of clothes cut in high-class merchant style, but made of very fine cloth.

"So?" Marilana said with a smile. "Will this do?"

"I think this will do quite nicely, yes."

"See you at dinner then," she said. "I must get changed."

Earek watched Marilana walk to her rooms and then went back to his wardrobe. He chose a dark red suit that made his black fur look even richer. When he was ready, he walked down the hall to Marilana's room, where a guard at the door eyed him suspiciously.

"Yes, hello. I'm Earek, and . . . ."

Just then, the door opened, and Marilana stepped out in a full sweeping, dark blue evening gown.

Earek stared. "My goodness. Aren't you stunning."

"Thank you, good sir. And you look quite presentable yourself," Marilana said with a grin.

Earek stepped forward and offered her his arm. "Might I escort you to dinner, fair Lady?"

The guard took a threatening step forward, but Marilana quickly interceded. "It is all right, Karndel. Earek is the friend who arrived today from the Southern Tip," she told the guard with a smile. Then she turned to Earek. "Do you not mean to ask if I will escort you to dinner, considering that you do not know where dinner is served?"

Laughing, she took the black leopard's arm. They set out toward the dining hall with the guard close behind. Earek was as happy as he could be to have Marilana with him. He had missed her friendship the past two fifnights. When they arrived, Marquiese was talking with the young leopard who had ridden to the Royal Palace in the buggy with Earek earlier in the day.

When he caught sight of Marilana and Earek, the lion Prince excused himself and hurried over. He offered his arm to Marilana and led the pair to the head table. He directed Earek to the chair that had been added next to Marilana. Then he grinned. "You are both here. I can hardly believe it. I am so glad you are. Now make yourself at home."

Earek was nervous to be sitting at the head table with all the nobles staring at him. He was uncomfortable wearing high-class merchant clothing again as well, he had resigned himself to peasant cut clothing since his family had disowned him. He turned to speak his thoughts to Marilana, and noticed her warily eyeing the pair of tigers that were seated at the other end of the head table. They watched him unabashedly and occasionally looked at the young leopard he had arrived with. Their whispering made Earek uncomfortable and he remembered Marilana's reaction to the male tiger in the library. If Marilana found tiger worthy of her suspicion, then he would try to be equally as wary.

Soon the trumpets blew, and everyone stood to welcome King Rylan. Earek was so awed at the sight of the King that he barely remembered to bow. And then the food began to arrive, plate after plate. By the time dessert came, Earek could hardly eat another bite.

After all the guests had said good night, King Rylan took Earek into the sitting room to talk. The two of them talked late into the night, and when Earek's new personal guard finally escorted him back to his room, he was exceedingly relieved to finally reach his bed.

While King Rylan and Earek chatted, Marilana and Marquiese went out to the gardens. The three guards trailed them at a fair distance, affording them privacy. This was the first time they had truly spent their evening time alone, just the two of them. True, they had spent considerable time alone while Marquiese resided in the Southern Tip, but this night felt different. Tonight, it was just the two of them without Marquiese's secret hanging over their heads. The moon was big and bright and dusted the gardens with a silvery illumination. The flowers appeared silver and grey as they walked silently down a garden path. They stopped at one of the many small water gardens and watched a school of small fish shimmering brightly in the moonlight. Marquiese carefully picked a silver lily and held it out to Marilana. Her paw brushed his as she accepted it.

"Thank you. So beautiful." Suddenly she felt unusually shy. Nervous butterflies fluttered in her stomach. She smelled the flower and turned away without meeting his gaze. They walked further down the path until they reached a gazebo with a high roof that blocked the moon and allowed them to see the millions of stars sparkling overhead. It was a warm night with only a slight breeze and perfect in every respect.

They sat on the gazebo's stone bench, and Marquiese laid his paw over hers as comfortably as if he had done so a hundred times. The butterflies fluttered once more in Marilana's stomach, but she did not pull away this time.

"What a beautiful night!" she said as a way of directing her thoughts away from his paw.

"We should do this more often, for it amuses me to see you acting this way," Marquiese said.

"If it would amuse Your Highness, I could sing and dance as well," she said, sitting straighter.

He laughed and held tighter to her paw. "I suppose you would, but . . . ,"

"Oh! You cruel prince!" she cried before he could finish.

She jumped up and tried to pull her paw away. Suddenly he stood and spun her around, so that she was suddenly face-to-face with him, their faces mere inches apart. He held her paw and caught her waist with his other paw. Marilana froze, staring up into his green eyes. He had grown taller during the year they were apart, she had to look up into his eyes.

"No singing. But please dance with me," he said softly.

Humming, the elegant lion started moving in the steps of a simple waltz. Marilana let her steps flow, easily following the dance he had chosen. She watched his eyes the whole time and felt her nervousness melt away. When the dance was over, they stood for a very long moment, lost in each other's gaze. Then Marquiese led her back to the bench. He wrapped his arm around her shoulders, and she leaned against him. Together, they looked up at the stars.

"You are very beautiful tonight. Your fur, shimmering like silver silk, and your eyes sparkling like the stars," he said quietly. Then his voice faltered slightly and he cleared his throat. "What I said before . . . well, it came out all wrong. I meant only that I have never seen you in such a state of peace. You are usually so tense watching for threats, so aware of your surroundings yet not able to enjoy the beauty of life. I meant only that I was enjoying your company so very much."

Marilana felt the nervousness returning. She twisted the lily in her paw and fixed her gaze on the stars.

"The way you look tonight, you belong among the most beautiful flowers and deserve the best treatment I could ever muster," he whispered, his eyes watching her.

"Look. The constellation of the Hunter. It's rising," she said, changing the subject so he would not see her blushing.

"Yes, and over there is the Dragon," he said and leaned toward her to point it out.

Marilana blushed furiously. She tried to focus her thoughts on the stars and away from his closeness. Marquiese spoke quietly, telling her of how he used to sneak out of the palace at night to play in the gardens. Marilana could not quite banish the nervous flutters of her stomach, but regained her outward control enough to enjoy listening to his stories and talk easily with him.

They talked until the moon began to emerge along the west eave of the gazebo, their conversation easy and intimate––and perfectly natural. Eventually, Marquiese stood and offered her his paw. He helped her to her feet. Paw and paw, they walked slowly back to the palace doors and up to her room.

"Good night, my fair maiden," he said softly. He bowed and kissed her paw. "Such a special night."

"Good night, My gracious Prince," she replied with a curtsey so deep she was almost kneeling. He smiled warmly at her before turning and walking away down the hallway. She watched him walk out of sight, then turned and went into her room.

As she closed the door behind her, she leaned her back against it and pressed her paws against her cheeks as the color rushed into them again in yet another blush.

Why can't I stop blushing? She thought frantically. This can't happen. I have to stop this. I can remain his friend without it going further, can I not? Yes, if only he were not so charming. But don't forget. I am but a peasant and he, well . . . . And yet he asked me to come, so I can't refuse to go on walks with him. That would be just too rude. Not to mention the fact that I want that time more than anything. No! What am I thinking! He is The Prince! I cannot let him forget his duty and future. I cannot offer him what a noble lady can. He must marry well. I am just a peasant. Even if I'm fond of him . . . no, I cannot. He cannot. He must stay honorable for the good of the kingdom.

The argument continued in her head as she got into bed, until she finally decided that if things continued the way they had tonight she would have to go along with it and just not be surprised when it eventually ended as she knew it would have to. He had his duty to marry well, and she would just be a memory. She smiled softly at the lily resting on her bedside table. She started to drift off to sleep, and her last thought was that she would enjoy every moment as long as it lasted.

6

Three days after Earek's arrival, Altia woke Marilana at first light relaying King Rylan's request for an early breakfast. As Marilana dressed, she noticed a wagon and ten riders leaving the palace on the stable lane. She could only just make them out in the dim light, but she was sure one of the riders was Marquiese.

"Please, sit, Marilana," King Rylan said when she entered the breakfast room. "Thank you for joining me on such short notice."

"It is my pleasure, Your Majesty," she said with a deep curtsey. She took her seat, and the question that had been on her mind burst out of her mouth. "May I ask where Marquiese is off to this morning?"

"There is a tournament in Precinlia, one of our neighbors to the north. One of our closest allies. The event is a celebration of the coming of age of Princess Clara. She has asked that all of the princes of age come and battle for her paw in marriage," he replied excitedly.

"I see. Very exciting. And what if she does not like the prince who wins?" Marilana asked.

"A very good question. However, I don't think that Clara has to worry about that. The best two princes in the allied kingdoms are Marquiese and Prince Dansho of Lentier, our neighbor to the west. Clara has grown up with them both. I think she favors Marquiese a little bit more, although she has not seen him for many years, and may have become closer to Dansho in his absence. In any case, that is the purpose of this tournament."

"And does the tournament have anything to do with your breakfast invitation, Sire?" the lioness asked politely.

"Yes, Marilana, it does. You see, to enliven the tournament, Clara has asked that an eligible princess or great-lady of each kingdom attend as well so that each prince will have a lady's color to ride for. Since our kingdom has no princess, Marquiese asked if you would come and offer the red and blue of Redsands. Would you consider it?"

"Oh! Yes, I would love to! Such a privilege," she exclaimed. "However, I am not a great-lady or even a noble. Will it not insult other royalty and nobles at the tournament that I have been granted such an honor?"

"If they are wise, they will not question my word," he replied, lightly dismissing the matter.

"Of course, Your Majesty, your word is my law." She smiled.

"One other thing. Your friend Earek went with Marquiese to see what a tournament looks like from the floor. He will join us in our box for the Jousting of the Champions."

"Wonderful!"

After breakfast, Altia helped Marilana change into the very special dress that Marquiese had ordered for the occasion. It was cut in noble style. The full floor length skirt of fine blue cloth had red satin ruffles tapering down the front and the tight, over-the-shoulder strapped bodice was of the same tantalizing blue cloth. The straps and neckline were accented with a ruffle of the red satin. The dress was completed with ties at the waist, also red satin, to be fashioned in a bow in the back with long tails that fell gently with the skirt. Last but not least was a red lace veil and blue circlet for her head. Marilana was nervous about wearing the dress, but she allowed Altia to dress her anyway.

It fit beautifully.

When the fitting was complete, Altia insisted on applying a light layer of powder to Marilana's face. It was just enough to highlight Marilana's features. She blushed with pleasure at the thought of Marquiese seeing her dressed so nobly. She tried not to think about all the other people who would also see her.

"My word! Marquiese will be quite pleased seeing you looking so much like a great-lady. I am sure of it!" King Rylan exclaimed as they gathered beside his royal carriage.

"Do you think so?" she asked timidly.

"Of course! Do not worry. Marquiese said you would be treated as a lady here in Maefair, and this is one of the many tastes of nobility," he said helping her into the carriage.

"There are so many people at these types of tournaments! Do you really think I will do, offering the colors of the kingdom?" she asked as the carriage started forward.

"I do. And so does Marquiese," the King said seriously. Then he shared a comforting smile. "You are very nervous. Know that we have a separate box from all the other royalty. And while you will be visible to all, no one will know how nervous you are simply because you carry yourself with such grace. And remember, all of the other ladies will be nervous, too." He smiled once again. "Now you will try to have an enjoyable time, will you not?"

"Yes, no matter what happens, I will enjoy the day."

They spent the rest of the journey discussing horses and jousting. The ride seemed long, but it was only mid-morning when they reached the city hosting the tournament. Marilana was still nervous, but she knew she could act proud and strong with King Rylan by her side. The thought that bothered her the most, however, was not standing with royalty and nobility. It was that she might well be witnessing the end of her time with Marquiese. She knew Marquiese did not intend to hurt her, but she wondered why he would have her come and watch a tournament where the prize was marriage to a princess, especially if he did not see her as anything more than a friend. Marilana was sure he was more than able to win the tournament. For one, he was an excellent combatant. And for another, she had, after all, trained him.

When they neared the tournament grounds, the shutters were closed over the windows so that they would be protected from the growing crowd of spectators. It was not unusual to see a show of opposition for certain royalty or nobles at these events. It normally had nothing to do with politics, but rather who was betting on whose champion. "As with so many things, it comes down to money," the King told her.

Marilana could hear the occasional thud of a rotten vegetable hitting against the side of the carriage, and King Rylan winked at her and said, "Someone out there is obviously betting against Marquiese and wants us to know it."

The carriage pulled up to the unloading platform; the receiving area next to the platform was crowded with royalty from the many other attending countries.

Two servants unloaded the baskets containing their lunch and took it into a small building that stood at the edge of the tournament field. There were many other such buildings, each marked by a different flag, they were obviously the boxes in which the royalty of the various kingdoms sat. The commoners sat in stands between the royals' boxes.

Opposite King Rylan's box rose a longer, slightly taller box. This was the host kingdom's box, and Princess Clara and her family would sit there.

As the carriage pulled away, King Rylan offered Marilana his arm. They mounted the steps to the receiving area and began moving from one noble or royal to another. The King introduced her as the Lady Marilana of the Southern Tip. This disturbed Marilana at first. She knew that it was against the law to impersonate someone above his or her caste, but King Rylan seemed not to think anything of it.

The kings, princes, and lords were mostly friendly and polite. Some were a little too friendly as they smiled at her and kissed her paw.

The queens, princesses, and ladies, on the other paw, gave her tight-lipped smiles while eyeing her suspiciously. Soon King Rylan led them to the box displaying the flag of Redsands, a rearing red lion on a blue field. Once inside, the servants offered them an early lunch, and Marilana breathed a sigh of relief. Lunch was light fare, mostly fruit and nuts, but Marilana was too nervous to eat and King Rylan declined much of the food as well.

"You did very well to smile with such grace at the various ladies in attendance," the King told her. "They know that the Southern Tip is the border province, which apparently means 'less civilized' in their eyes. By their expressions, I would say they almost expected you to walk on four legs. Sometimes I wonder how they ever got to be called 'ladies.' I was glad to see you act even more refined than they were. I am very proud to have you here, Marilana."

"Thank you, Sire," she replied quietly.

"I also noticed that quite a few of the competing knights were watching you rather closely. I believe that you are going to create quite a stir today. Clara might have more competition from you than she had thought. She was one of the princesses that you did not get to meet, but I saw her talking with some of the other ladies. When they pointed you out, she waved dismissively. She will be quite surprised to see how many competitors ask to ride under your colors." The King laughed.

Marilana gave him a small smile, but she only cared about the intentions of one prince. Marquiese had not been among the competitors greeting the royal and noble spectators. Marilana assumed he was in the competitors' tents preparing for the tournament.

"There are thirty-two knights competing today," King Rylan explained while they waited, both sipping cucumber tea.

"But only fourteen are princes and only the colors of competing princes are represented by a lady from his kingdom. The other competitors are knights from the allied kingdoms testing their skills against each other and the princes. All tournaments are open to knights. However, if any knight is foolish enough to win this tournament, he should probably plan on ending up in the stocks for affronting Princess Clara. Better to make it to the last round of the Jousting before bowing out. That way they gain honor by standing down to a Prince of the Realm. Quite a lot of honor."

"Is Marquiese is the only knight representing Redsands today?" Marilana asked.

"Yes. For various reasons, none of our other knights chose to compete in this tournament." The King did not elaborate.

Just then, a crescendo of trumpeting horns gained the attention of the watching crowd. With the sounding of the horns, King Carloth and Princess Clara, lions as regal as any Marilana had seen, stood up in the Hosts' box and waved to the cheering crowd. When the crowd quieted at last, King Carloth lifted a red rose out before him and took a step forward.

"Thank you all for attending this grand event," he called in a strong voice. "The prince who wins this tournament today will have the pleasure of entering a courtship with my beloved daughter, Clara, Crown Princess of Precinlia."

Again, a roar filled the arena, and again King Carloth waited for the roar to dissipate. When it did, his voice rose and he called, "Let the tournament begin!" and dropped the rose.

The spectators cheered wildly as the rose hit the floor of the arena. Marilana watched with interest as a team of squires hurried into the arena and hoisted a large construct onto four support polls. Fourteen rows of thirty-two rings in the colors of each of the princes' kingdoms hung below the wooden cross beams. Each knight would collect one ring of each color by riding under the construct and hooking the rings on his lance. This first round was not an elimination round. It was a demonstration of the knights' skills and a show of honor to the kingdoms in attendance.

Marilana watched critically as the knights rode single file around the arena. She spotted Marquiese and studied his posture as he guided his mount. He met her eyes as he rode past with his visor raised. His eyes sparkled, and he smiled mischievously at her. She liked the way his armor fit him. It seemed natural on him, and he moved easily with his mount. He was clearly relaxed and focused, just as she had trained him to be before a challenge of arms. After all the knights had circled the arena, they began to pass under the construct and collect their rings. Marilana smiled broadly when Marquiese collected all fourteen rings in one pass. Not many of the other knights did as well, and most had to make multiple passes to collect all fourteen.

Once the rings had been collected, the knights circled the arena one at a time and stopped to bow to the Hosts' box. Once the knights had all acknowledged the hosts, the squires hurried in to remove the rings construct and set the arena for the first round of eliminations.

"I know you are well acquainted with the skills and feats of a tournament, but am I correct that this is your first time watching one?" Rylan asked as the squires arranged jumps and obstacles.

"You are correct, Majesty. I have never had the chance to attend a tournament before," Marilana replied.

"Well then, I will tell you some of what to expect in the next several rounds," he said. "The next three rounds will be elimination rounds based on points. Each round commences when the knights first enter the arena. They will ask a lady from the crowd for the honor of riding under her colors. Then perform the feats required for that round. After all the knights have completed the round, the eight with the lowest scores will be eliminated. The knights remaining will continue on to the next round. The last round is the Jousting of Champions. Eight knights will compete in that round, and the winner is proclaimed Champion of the tournament."

"It would appear that this round is a challenge of horsemanship," Marilana said, indicating the obstacles being quickly assembled on the floor.

"Indeed it is. The next round is a challenge of archery. Then comes a challenge of skill with the lance," King Rylan said. He then pointed toward a small basket resting next to her chair. It was filled with oversized red and blue kerchiefs. "When a knight approaches and asks for your colors, take one of these kerchiefs and give it to him with a smile. The knights will ask for favors in each round, so you may give the same knight your colors more than once, but only one knight may ride under your colors in each grouping."

As the squires left the arena, Marilana drew a kerchief from the basket in the event that a knight actually approached her. She had her doubts.

The first group of eight knights raced into the arena and angled toward the spectators. Two of the knights raced toward Princess Clara, and the first to arrive was rewarded with her colors. Marilana was surprised when one of the others drew rein in front of her.

"I would be honored, My Lady, to receive the red and blue from your lovely paw," he said with a slight smile.

"It is my pleasure, Sir Knight," Marilana said, rising smoothly and extending the kerchief to him.

The knight accepted the colors, bowed, and then rode off to take his place with the others.

"That was graciously done." King Rylan smiled approvingly.

"I like the lines of his mount. He should do well," Marilana noted.

"He is a Knight of Precinlia, though I must confess I do not know his lineage. Or that of his mount."

Marilana smiled as King Rylan chuckled, then took a calming breath. The round began to the sounds of cheering and clapping. First one knight and then the next attempted the jumps and obstacles, some with more success than others, and the audience responded accordingly.

Marilana was pleased that the knight bearing the colors of Redsands scored well, though she wasn't surprised. What did surprise her was that a knight from the next group also asked for her colors. And when it happened again with the third group, she realized that King Rylan had been right: the competitors had taken notice of her. Both knights accepted her colors graciously, and both performed well over the jumps.

Finally, Marquiese and his mount appeared, racing into the arena with the fourth group. Marilana watched as he and another knight angled toward the box occupied by Princess Clara. Marquiese arrived first, so the second knight changed course immediately and crossed the arena to the Redsands' box. Marilana could now see that he was a lion like Marquiese and Princess Clara. Marilana answered his request by extending the red and blue kerchief to him and marking the exchange with a smile. He raised the red and blue kerchief in front of his visor, then made a flourish and bowed to her. He smiled, but his gray eyes remained cold.

Marilana watched him closely as he cantered off and then shared a brief glance with the King.

"That was Prince Dansho of Lentier," he informed her. "Dansho and Marquiese trained together at times growing up and they were well matched last time they competed."

Marilana watched Dansho and Marquiese as each navigated the jumps and obstacles with exceptional skill to the delight of the audience. Dansho did very well, but Marilana smiled proudly when Marquiese achieved the highest score. After the fourth group left the arena, eight knights entered on foot and lined up before the Hosts' box. They bowed in unison and then climbed into a roped off section of seating, a polite round of applause marking their departure from the event.

"Those were the eliminated knights," King Rylan told her. "They have paid their respects, and will now watch the rest of the tournament as spectators."

"I see," the lioness said as the squires once again swarmed the arena and removed the jumps and obstacles. At one end of the arena, an arrow wall was erected to protect the spectators, and five targets were arranged in front of it. Marilana was impressed with the difficulty of the shots, though they would have posed very little difficulty to someone of her skill level.

As soon as the squires finished, the first group of eight knights charged in and claimed colors. Marilana smiled as another knight drew rein in front of her, another lion. She extended the red and blue to him. He met her eyes curiously as he bowed, then moved off to prepare his short bow.

"Clara is not very pleased with your popularity," King Rylan chuckled, eyeing the Hosts' box. "That was Prince Zandor of Coandor, our neighbor furthest to the east. He and Marquiese have never really agreed on much, but they seem to agree today."

Marilana blushed slightly and looked across the arena at the young lioness sitting in the Hosts' box. Clara glared at her with her arms crossed, and Marilana bowed her head, hiding a small grin.

"I do not mean to make her angry," she said softly.

"Do not worry about it," King Rylan said, smiling gently. "Clara has a temper, but it is her own fault for inviting other ladies to come to the tournament. It is not something for you to be ashamed of. If anything, you should be pleased by how many of the young men are showing interest in you."

Marilana watched Prince Zandor shoot his flight of arrows from horseback. The round allowed one arrow per target, and scores were awarded by how close to the center each arrow struck. Prince Zandor scored the best in his group.

"He shoots well," Marilana noted.

"Zandor will certainly move on, but how far remains a question."

The second group entered as the first group left, and Marilana gave her colors to yet another knight. He did not do so well. His horse frisked and danced so that his arrows went wide and one completely missed the intended target. Marilana shook her head.

"Knights competing at this level should have better control of their mounts," she commented as the crowd voiced their disproval.

"On that we agree," King Rylan said as the third group of knights raced into the arena. Marquiese and Dansho were again competing in the last group of the round, and again they both raced to claim Clara's colors. Marquiese reached Clara first, so Dansho once again reined his mount around and claimed Marilana's colors. Marilana smiled at him, and he again gave her a sweeping, if emotionless bow.

The crowd roared with each shot, cheering hits and jeering misses. Marilana was proud to see Marquiese hit the center of every target. It seemed he had continued to practice all that she had taught him. She wondered if he had asked her to come so that she could see that her efforts toward his training had paid off. Marquiese received the top score for the round with Dansho second and Zandor third. The eight lowest scoring knights once again paid their respects to the hosts and joined the other eliminated knights.

The tournament was now down to sixteen participants, and the noise in the arena echoed the tightening of the competition.

A pair of servants entered their box between the change-over and offered them cider. On the tournament floor, the squires dismantled the archery targets and erected four polls for the fourth round, a test of speed and efficiency. Eight rings were hung from each of four polls. The eight knights who could collect the two rings of his color by the use of his lance and deposit them without knocking off anyone else's rings would advance to the Jousting of the Champions.

Marilana gave her glass back to one of the servants as eight knights entered the arena. She sighed as yet another knight asked for the honor of riding for her colors; it wasn't that she lacked an appreciation for the honor they were bestowing on her, but there was really only one prince she truly wanted to give her colors to and he had not yet approached her. Putting a smile on her face, Marilana gave the knight the red and blue kerchief and was rewarded with a return smile. Then competition began.

Marilana watched intently as two knights at a time attempted to retrieve their rings. Hooking a ring with a lance took careful aim. Hooking a specific ring quickly without knocking any other rings off took timing and control of both the lance and the mount. Some were more successful than others, and the audience was not shy about expressing their appreciation.

Marquiese and Dansho entered with the second group. Their race for Clara's colors again favored the Prince of Redsands, and again the Prince of Lentier claimed the red and blue from Marilana. Both performed well and tied for the top score. Marilana tried to stifle her disappointment that Marquiese was showing so much favor to Clara. She wondered if it was time for Marquiese to turn his attentions to a woman of his own caste; yet, she could not stifle the slight hope that he was up to something. She kept remembering his mischievous smile at the beginning of the tournament.

When the round ended, eight more knights paid their respects to the hosts and joined the eliminated knights, spectators now for the Jousting of Champions.

A moment later, Marilana and King Rylan heard footsteps, a knock on the box door, and a voice that the lioness recognized well.

"Earek," King Rylan said, greeting him with genuine gusto.

"Your Majesty." He bowed and then gave Marilana a wink. "My Lady."

"Young Sir," she said with a smile.

The King waved him in. "Come sit with us and tell us what news you have from the tents. How is Marquiese faring?"

"His Highness is in good spirits, Your Majesty," Earek said taking the seat next to the King. "He is happy with his scores so far and anxious for the joust."

"Good. He should be happy." The King laughed. "He has gotten a nearly perfect score."

The squires finished setting up the list, and the first two competitors entered the arena. Marilana breathed a sigh of relief as Dansho claimed Clara's colors for the first time. Clara was obviously pleased to finally present him with her colors, and he made a show of accepting her favor.

"This should be a good match," King Rylan told them. "Prince Dansho verses Prince Akadine of Rucdign. Rucdign is an ally, but is situated to the north of Precinlia. Dansho and Akadine have had a fierce rivalry for years. Akadine is Dansho's equal on horse, although Dansho has previously been the better swordsman. We shall see."

Marilana watched with interest as the two princes charged each other. With a loud crash, both lances splintered and flew apart. A roar of approval swept over the crowd as the horses reached their respective ends and turned.

The princes grabbed fresh lances and charged again. Again their lances splintered on impact, but this time Prince

Akadine was thrown violently from his mount. Cheers echoed throughout as Dansho dismounted and drew his sword. Prince Akadine rose from the ground and gripped his weapon. The ringing of steel on steel rang loud and fast as the two attacked. Back and forth they fought, turning, twisting, and lunging. The afternoon sun glinted off their swords and armor, and dust rose from the floor. Finally with a twist and thrust of his sword, Dansho disarmed Prince Akadine and the match ended. The arena exploded. Prince Akadine retrieved his sword and both princes bowed to the Hosts' box. Marilana raised her eyebrows in surprise as Prince Akadine joined the eliminated knights.

"He is eliminated?"

"For today's tournament, the Jousting of Champions is an instant elimination round," King Rylan explained. "Each match will eliminate one of the competitors while the winner will move on to the next set of matches. With eight knights, we will see four matches in the first set with the four winners moving on. There will be two matches in the second set, and the two winners will face off in the last match to determine the tournament champion."

"But would it not be better for all the competitors to face each other to determine who the best truly is?"

"If the goal were to determine the best, yes," King Rylan agreed. "But Princess Clara already knows who she wants to reach the last match. She chose to have the first rounds be tests of skill so that the competitors could determine the best eight. Now the competitors have to consider if they want to win her courtship. If not, they will allow their opponent to get the advantage."

"Just as Prince Akadine did," Marilana said thoughtfully. "He did not fight as hard against Dansho as he could have, though most in the audience may not have seen it."

"Yes, indeed. He let Dansho get the advantage. I am pleased that you were able to see that." King Rylan smiled.

Marilana watched the next pair of competitors charge along the list. Neither of them had asked for her colors or for Princess Clara's. Both were knights, not princes, and Marilana expected the winner would make sure to lose the next match. They fought fiercely against each other, however. Both broke three lances before one was unhorsed, but the one who had been unhorsed was significantly better with the sword. Tall and broad, he attacked quickly and pressed his opponent hard. Marilana was impressed with his speed for such a big man. He disarmed the other and then sportingly shook his paw.

"That one will be a competitor to watch in the future," King Rylan mussed. "He is one of Prince Dansho's guard officers, and I have a feeling he has been training with Dansho. Their styles are very similar."

Marilana watched both men bow to the Hosts' box, and the loser took his seat with the other knights. Marilana smiled politely as the next pair of competitors entered the arena, and Prince Zandor approached her for the Redsands' colors. He accepted the red and blue with a short bow, his armor glistening.

Marilana glanced in Clara's direction as Zandor rode to his end of the list. The Princess was glaring at her again. The other knight had not asked to ride for Clara's honor, which meant this was the first time she had not given her colors when Marilana had.

"Not to worry. Prince Zandor and Clara have never gotten along," King Rylan explained, seeing her dismay. "He is competing just to prove he can and that she is not in a position to manipulate him."

"I do not approve of him using me to spite her," Marilana said, her frown telling.

"You are her biggest competition at this tournament." King Rylan chuckled. "He probably would have been happier to have chosen a color other than the red and blue, but he is clearly playing you against Clara and enjoying every minute."

Marilana tried unsuccessfully to suppress the flush of color in her cheeks as she watched Prince Zandor charge his opponent. She winced as Zandor's lance struck the other knight solidly and unhorsed him without breaking. Zandor dismounted and quickly disarmed his opponent. It was not a good showing, and the audience showed their disapproval of the knight with a round of spirited boos. All in good fun, according to King Rylan.

Marquiese entered the arena as Zandor exited and rode directly to Clara's box. Marilana watched her smile broadly at him. Marquiese's opponent approached Marilana, and she gave him the red and blue and her most polite smile. She thought it amusing that Marquiese was facing an opponent riding under the colors of Redsands; after all, he was the future King of Redsands.

The riders took their places. Marilana leaned forward as they charged down the list, lances cradled. She griped the arm of her chair tightly as both lances struck and splintered. Marquiese managed to remain in his saddle, but his opponent crashed to the ground. Marquiese dismounted quickly and drew his sword. His blade flashed and darted as he pressed his opponent. The knight was good, but not as good as Marquiese, and he lost his sword to a swift back-arm parry.

Marilana breathed a sigh of relief and sat back in her chair as Marquiese shook his opponent's paw. And then, as had the combatants before them, they bowed to the Hosts' box.

Dansho rode past Marquiese on his way to claim Clara's colors for the fifth match. Marilana was surprised when his opponent, the man King Rylan had identified as one of Dansho's men, approached her. She could now see he was a brown bear. She extended her kerchief and smiled politely at him. The knight studied her face far longer than he might have before taking the red and blue and bowing. Without giving too much thought to the knight's reaction, Marilana turned her attention to the match and watched with interest. Dansho unhorsed the bear on their first pass with a well-placed lance. On foot, they strove against each other, and Marilana could see that they were well matched and knew each other's style. After several fierce blows, however, Dansho succeeded in knocking the sword from the bear's paw, and it was clear to her that the knight had no intention of trying to best his commander. They bowed respectfully to each other and then bowed to the Hosts' box.

The tension in the arena rose as Marquiese and Prince Zandor entered the arena for the last match before the final joust. Not surprisingly, Marquiese rode to claim Clara's colors, and Prince Zandor asked Marilana for hers once again. She extended the red and blue to him for what she hoped was the last time. As the two lions faced off, Marilana reminded herself to control her breathing. Their mounts rumbled down the list, dust flying, lances poised. Marilana gasped as the lances crashed on the first pass, their splintered remains flying in every direction. Both riders tumbled to the ground, their armor clattering loudly. Marilana knew that Prince Zandor had no interest in courting Clara, but he apparently was not going to give in to Marquiese without a fight.

They drew their swords and attacked. Marilana watched closely as they danced and circled. This, she observed, was not the fast and pressing attacks she had seen in the other matches. This was a more cautious and calculated fight. Lunge, parry, retreat. Attack, parry, press, retreat again; Marilana watched the quick exchanges and leaned forward with anticipation as they each strove for an advantage. Then Marilana saw an opening and smiled when Marquiese took it. He spun inside Zandor's attack and pinned his opponent's sword arm under his own. With an outward thrust, Marquiese sent Zandor's sword spinning away. It was over. The crowd cheered enthusiastically, and Marilana sat back in her chair, relieved. Marquiese and Zandor shook paws and offered tribute to the Hosts' box, bowing deeply.

Then Marquiese turned and quickly went to retrieve his charger for the final joust. As he was mounting, Prince Dansho took advantage of the moment and raced across the floor to claim Princess Clara's colors for the last match. Clara clapped her paws enthusiastically at his request, graciously extended her kerchief, and smiled broadly.

When Marilana saw this, she worried that Marquiese would be disappointed having to ask for someone else's colors, but he seemed relaxed as he guided his mount around the arena.

Marilana's breath caught as her friend halted in front of her.

"Might I have the honor of accepting the red and blue from your most graceful and beautiful paw?" he asked seriously.

"It is my pleasure and honor to grant your request and bestow the red and blue upon you, My Prince," Marilana replied just as seriously.

Marquiese gave her a deep bow and then smiled broadly before spurring his mount away. Marilana sat on the edge of her seat and clutched one of the kerchiefs in her paws. This was an anxious moment. Both Marquiese and Dansho had fought extremely well, so predicting a winner was near impossible. Both had their followers, and a wall of cheering and applause swept through the arena.

The flag was raised and the two attacked fiercely. Marilana watched every move. They each broke three lances before Dansho was unhorsed. Marquiese dismounted and drew his sword. Dansho did the same. They faced off. Dansho seemed to gain a quick advantage. Marquiese seemed … tired. Marilana could see that he was a step slow, and she frowned as the lion took several quick steps in the wrong direction. It was a critical error. With a fast and graceful turn, Dansho stepped in and disarmed him. It was over. The arena exploded.

Marquiese shook Dansho's paw and then both bowed respectfully to the Hosts' box. The winner raised his paws in victory. Marquiese turned and strode calmly toward the exit without a second glance. Dansho waved to the cheering crowds and eloquently went to claim his bride. Clara was obviously overjoyed at the turn of events. Marilana could see King Carloth announcing Prince Dansho as the tournament champion, but she could not hear his words over the raucous cheers of the crowd.

Marilana sat back in her seat, shocked by the outcome. She watched as Marquiese left the field and noticed his head held high. She noticed something else as well. It seemed to her that as he neared the gates his step became the brisk step of someone who had been hiding his energy and was now claiming some victory that no other could fathom.

He lost the match on purpose, she thought as King Rylan and Earek came to their feet. Marilana held the thought firmly in her mind and stood as well.

She heard Earek saying, "Thank you for letting me join you for the Jousting of Champions, Majesty." His bow was deep and respectful.

"It was my pleasure." King Rylan smiled.

"Is there anything I can do for you before I rejoin Prince Marquiese, Sire?"

"Please pass my congratulations on to Marquiese for a champion performance."

Earek bowed to King Rylan, smiled at Marilana, and then turned and left the box. King Rylan offered Marilana his arm. He patted her paw gently and led her out of the box and onto to the loading platform. His carriage and entourage were already waiting, and so he helped her into the carriage and climbed in behind her. As the carriage moved slowly away, Marilana watched as the swarming masses milled about the tournament fields; the celebration, she realized, was just starting. Her eyes moved beyond the crowd and settled on the competitors' tents. Marquiese had declined to marry Clara, and Marilana was left to wonder why.

Once they were away from the crowds and out of the host city, Marilana turned away from the window and found King Rylan watching her. He gave her a knowing smile.

"Sire?" she asked, bemused by his expression.

"Marilana, I knew Marquiese was going to come in second. He told me before he left this morning that he did not wish to marry Clara."

"But, Sire, why not?"

"Because Clara holds no attraction for him. He achieved what he wanted to achieve today."

"He lost on purpose, Sire."

"Of course you would see that. Most would not." The King shared a satisfied nod. "Marquiese proved to Dansho that he could have won if he had truly wanted to, but chose not to."

Marilana sat back and returned her eyes to the window in thoughtful silence all the way back to Maefair.

Marquiese was quite pleased with his performance. He had fought well and come in second, exactly as planned. He had one last task to perform before returning home. He turned to the Noble-Commander of the Palace Garrison and said, "Master Castant, get the horses ready and have everything packed up, if you would. Earek and I are going to go congratulate Dansho. We will be back shortly."

"I will have the squires do the packing. I am coming along with Your Highness," replied the young leopard.

"Why is that?" the Prince wondered.

"I am sorry, Your Highness, but I heard that Dansho is in a right fury at you. That is all I know, but that is all I need to know. If there is trouble, I intend to be there."

"Very well, come along." They set out, and Marquiese turned his attention to Earek. He said, "So how did you like the tournament?"

"It was very exciting," the black leopard replied. "I am glad that Your Highness brought me along."

"How did Marilana fare during the jousting?"

"She sat on the edge of her seat the whole time. I thought the kerchief she was holding was going to be torn to shreds every time you received a blow," laughed Earek.

"Well, apparently the excitement is not over yet," Marquiese said with a mischievous grin.

The three young men walked through the lanes of tents toward the one dedicated to Prince Dansho and his weaponry. They turned a corner and ran headlong into Dansho and two companions—one a rather large horse and the other a rough-skinned water buffalo.

"We were just on our way to find you!" called Dansho in an overly friendly manner.

"Really? Is it not customary for the loser to come congratulate the victor?" retorted Marquiese.

"Of course it is. Under normal circumstances."

"And is there something abnormal about the results of the tournament?"

"Only that you lost on purpose," Dansho said in an accusatory voice. "Do not deny it, Marquiese. You went into the entire tournament determined to come in second place."

"You fought very well today, Dansho. I was tired from my match with Zandor, and that dismount advantage you had on me today was over-powering," Marquiese replied calmly.

"You will not dissuade me so easily," Dansho growled. "Your skills have improved dramatically since being away, and I admit that you would have beaten me had your efforts been true."

"You are questioning my efforts, are you?" Marquiese said, his voice still calm.

"You dishonored Clara by giving in to me. She is crushed to think that you would choose that Southern beast over her."

"Highnesses, I think you should both calm down and discuss this as reasonable individuals," Master Castant interjected quietly.

"Stay out of it, Castant," Dansho growled without looking away from Marquiese.

"That so stated Southern beast is the most honorable female I know and will be a great-lady. I will not allow you to dishonor her," Marquiese said, the anger suddenly coloring on his face and stiffening his posture.

Dansho was surprised at Marquiese's sudden change in demeanor. They'd had their occasional disagreements, but Marquiese was usually calm and sly, hardly ever showing his true emotions. Now the outrage was plain on both his face and in his stance.

"So you did choose that beast over Clara," growled Dansho darkly. "I am horrified to think that you would do such a thing! You have known Clara all your life. We trained together for this day, striving against each other to win her favor. In these last years while you were away, I courted her favor alone and yet you were always her favorite. Now you disgrace her. I cannot believe that you had that peasant lioness stand as a noble in the presence of royalty. I will fight for Clara's honor here today and forever more!"

Dansho snatched his dagger from its sheath and lunged at Marquiese with all his might. Marquiese dodged the attack easily and caught Dansho across the back of his shoulders. Dansho landed face first on the ground. Dansho's two companions lunged at Marquiese, but Earek and Master Castant were ready for them. Earek ducked low like Marilana had taught him and easily tripped the charging horse to the ground. Master Castant was struggling with the buffalo when King Carloth rounded the corner and froze at the sight of the unfolding encounter.

"You there! What is the meaning of all of this?" King Carloth called. The six of them withdrew, all eyes falling on the King. "Marquiese! I am ashamed of you! I never thought that you, of all people, could be such a sore loser as to break the peace of the tournament!"

"Your Majesty, I am sorry. I meant no disrespect. We—"

"We just had a little disagreement," Dansho said, finishing the thought. He stood up and brushed himself off. "It is settled now. Prince Marquiese was just leaving."

"You two have always had your disagreements, but never before have you stooped so low. You have both grown into your own during these last years. Which led me to believe that you had grown beyond the physical brawling of boys," King Carloth chided.

"Yes, Your Majesty. We should know better. I am sorry I let my temper direct my actions. My apologies, Dansho." Marquiese offered his paw to the lion.

"My apologies as well, Marquiese," said Dansho coolly grasping Marquiese's paw. "You really have changed. I do not think I know you very well anymore."

"I have been taught to see better," replied Marquiese. "Perhaps I will get the chance to share some of what I learned with you and Clara if the occasion arises. I must apologize too, that I will not be able to attend the tournament ball tomorrow. I have other matters that require my attention. I regret that I will be leaving Clara without a partner for the occasional dance. However, since Marilana is also unable to attend, leaving you without a partner for those same dances, I would ask that you take my place with Clara. I expect you to make sure the Princess enjoys herself.

"As for now, I need to take my leave; I still have a long ride home before dark. Again, congratulations to you, Dansho, and please pass my congratulations along to Clara. I hope she is happy." He turned to the King and shared a small bow. "Farewell, Your Majesty. Good evening to you all."

He, Earek, and Castant turned and walked away without another word. They were just outside their tent when Marquiese caught sight of Prince Zandor watching them from the shadows.

"Wait for me a moment," he said to Castant and Earek. "I have to speak with someone privately."

"Prince Zandor," he said, approaching the lean lion.

Zandor shook his head and lowered his voice. "That could have been managed better, don't you think?"

"If you mean Dansho and Clara, I suppose you are right."

"Of course I mean Dansho and Clara. They are furious with you. You know as well as I that both are quick to anger and hold grudges until those grudges are satisfied."

"So they have not changed much," Marquiese suggested.

"Not in the slightest. But you have changed." The two lions studied one another. Zandor was a few years older than Marquiese and had yet to choose a bride. In Coandor, Zandor's homeland, they did not force a prince to marry when he came of age, but allowed him several years to make an educated choice. The people of Coandor placed high value on scholars and knowledge. Zandor was no exception. He was a good combatant, but he was also both intelligent and cunning.

Zandor shook his head and grinned. "I want to congratulate you, Marquiese. You managed to cause considerable upheaval among the royals and nobles here today."

"For someone who also did not desire Clara's paw in marriage, I would have expected you to respect my choice."

"I was not talking about your choice to come in second," Zandor said, smirking. "I am talking about Lady Annabella's new heir. Bringing the lioness here before Lady Annabella made her choice public was a huge risk. I can see why you did it, and I congratulate you on catching that one. I can see her intelligence as well as her beauty. I am disappointed that I will not have a chance to dance with her tomorrow. I think I would have enjoyed that. Judging from her lack of confidence, however, I am willing to bet she does not know Lady Annabella's intentions."

"How do you know so much about Marilana and Lady Annabella?" Marquiese asked darkly.

"I am neither blind nor deaf," Zandor said easily. "It did not take long for the rumors to reach my ears."

"What rumors are those?"

"That the girl was your peasant friend from the Southern Tip. I know you and your father would not have presented her as a lady without sound reason. The only way she can become a great-lady, as you suggested to Dansho, is if Lady Annabella has chosen her as her heir."

"So you heard what I said. That was careless of me."

"You and he caused quite the ruckus." They stared at one another. Prince Zandor smiled. He said, "So when will Marilana find out?"

"She is in the middle of her month of study as required of noble heirs," Marquiese replied cautiously. "Information that you will keep between the two of us, I am sure."

"You are not the brash young lion you once were," Zandor said watching Marquiese closely. "Perhaps we shall have the chance to talk again in the future. Perhaps we might come to better understand each other."

"Yes. Perhaps so," Marquiese said.

"And I hope that I get the chance to speak with Marilana as well at some point. I imagine she has some fascinating insight on any number of scholarly subjects."

"Her parents were scholars, and she inherited much of their insight." Marquiese smiled slightly. "I think you would enjoy speaking with her. She has taught me much. Congratulations on your performance today, I enjoyed our contest of arms."

"I wish you had lost to me, I would have loved to have prevented you and Dansho from facing each other and to have ruined Clara's tournament by tossing down my lance to one of you in the final match. However, I think I prefer it this way. You managed to ruin much more of Clara's grand plan by bringing Marilana. And congratulations to you. You really have matured well. I wish the same were true of Dansho and Clara. Which leads me to caution you. Do not underestimate their anger. Farewell, Marquiese," Zandor said turning away.

"Farewell, Zandor," Marquiese replied sincerely.

Marilana stood at one of the estate's yearling pastures scratching the ear of a bay filly and thinking about the events of the day past. Karndel leaned on the fence nearby.

She and King Rylan had arrived at the palace in the middle of dinner, and he had escorted her from the carriage straight to the head table. It had been lonesome sitting at dinner with an empty seat on either side of her. She felt exposed. Every time King Rylan addressed her, she found Frishka leering at her. Feeling too impatient to return to her room, she decided not to change her dress after dinner and instead to come out to the pastures to wait for her friends' return.

The night had started out warm enough, but a cool breeze had picked up. Marilana was on the verge of going back to the palace when she saw the caravan enter through the stable gate. She waited nervously for Marquiese. Eventually she saw six people making their way toward her, including Marquiese, Earek, three guards, and the young leopard who had arrived at the palace the same day as Earek. Marilana was interested to meet the leopard who seemed to spend much of his time with Marquiese.

"Marilana! My Lady, why are you waiting out here? This breeze is too cold for you to be out here without a cloak. You will catch a chill," Marquiese said when he saw her.

He pulled his cloak off and wrapped it around her shoulders. She blushed when she saw that his coat hung open and the laces of his shirt were casually undone at the neck. He had an air of relaxed informality that accented his handsome features.

"Your Highness, now you will catch cold. I am much more used to the cool summer nights than you are," Marilana argued, trying to remove his cloak.

"Do not worry about me. I can take care of myself," he said softly. He placed his paw on her lower back and gently directed her to face the yellow leopard. "Marilana, this is

Master Enton Castant. He is one of my father's top advisors and my close friend, as well as Noble-Commander of the Palace Garrison."

"Hello," the lioness said, her surprise genuine. "Your father would be Sir Castant?"

"Yes, Lord Withers Castant, Great-Lord of Draukshar. He speaks well of you and wishes for you to visit him sometime," Master Castant said with a slight bow.

"Tell Lord Castant that I would very much enjoy visiting him sometime soon," replied Marilana warmly, hiding her surprise at finding the old leopard was really a great-noble. "I must confess I have not heard of a Noble-Commander. What does the position entail?"

"It is not a position of the guards," Master Castant explained as they began to walk leisurely toward the palace. "The garrison officers report to me for the everyday duties. That prevents the King and Prince from becoming bogged down by menial tasks such as checking duty rosters, supply requests, and managing every little problem that comes our way. Of course, if the problem requires it, I have sufficient rank to approach the King or Prince at any time. If I am unavailable or absent from the Royal Palace, the reports are given to the Commander of the Royal Family Guards, and he can then consult with the King."

"It sounds like a position of high trust, and high honor," Marilana commented.

"It is," Marquiese said. "Master Castant not only watches my back, but he helps me and my father run the palace smoothly."

"They keep me running, that's for sure," Master Castant said ruefully.

Marquiese laughed easily. He shifted his arm around Marilana's waist as they walked toward the palace, and she felt her cheeks flush again.

"So, Marilana, how did you like the tournament?" the Prince asked, their eyes meeting.

"It was very exciting," the lioness said brightly. "I was pleased to see your scores. And, I must say, your skill with the sword has not diminished."

"Always the trainer," Marquiese said, looking from Earek to Master Castant and chuckling.

"I was surprised when you let Prince Dansho win, however. Clearly it was an intentional act. King Rylan told me you did not wish to court Princess Clara," Marilana said levelly.

"That is true," Marquiese said easily. "I used to think I would marry her one day. The marriage would have united the two kingdoms under one family. She will inherit from King Carloth, and I will inherit Redsands. Together we could have wielded far greater power than we do now. But after spending time in the Southern Tip, I no longer seek that power. Redsands is one of the most powerful kingdoms as it is. It controls the largest amount of land, even if some of the other kingdoms are more populous. Joining Redsands with Precinlia would create a powerful union outside the influence of the other allied kingdoms. It would likely have produced a large amount of fear from our allies, and possibly even war from our enemies. I chose not to pursue that future.

"Dansho is second in line for the throne of Lentier, and so his marriage to her will not end in a power struggle. I had not seen Clara or Dansho since before my time in the Southern Tip, and I have to admit they are far more arrogant than I remember."

"What about Prince Zandor?" Earek asked. "You and he seemed to have a good conversation before we left."

"Prince Zandor is not as arrogant as I thought. He is intelligent, and I am afraid I never gave him the credit he deserves."

"I was very impressed with your duel with him," Marilana said.

"That was the most difficult of any of my matches," Marquiese replied. "Had I not trained with you, I doubt seriously I would have won. He is more cunning than the other knights, and he was certainly motivated to beat me."

"But why?" Marilana asked curiously. "To spite Clara?"

"Indeed." Marquiese laughed. "When a competitor throws down his lance to his opponent, he indicates that the prize is not worth his efforts. That is what Zandor wanted. To throw down his lance in his match with Dansho and to prevent me and Dansho from facing each other so that Clara would not have seen which of us was the better suitor. It would have defeated her whole reason for holding the tournament and added insult to injury."

"But would that not have caused a lot of harm in the relationships between their kingdoms?" asked Marilana.

"Not really. Clara insulted him first. She proclaimed that the tournament was for all eligible princes, but did not invite Zandor. He was within his rights to compete, and his insult to her would have been expected if he made it to the last match. Dansho's anger at the dishonor would have been a bigger problem, but I am sure Zandor would have managed Dansho skillfully."

"Unlike Your Highness," Master Castant muttered darkly. "And as mad as Dansho and Clara seemed to be, I would not be surprised if they are already planning something drastic."

"What did you do that made Princess Clara and Prince Dansho so angry?" Marilana wanted to know.

"Nothing that you—or anyone else—need to worry about," Marquiese said as they entered the palace. "So tell me, how was dinner? I am starving."

The talking continued as the men ate a late dinner, but did not return to the subject of Dansho and Clara, even if Marilana had hoped it might. Instead, she listened to the tales the three men told about the tournament, and when the meal was over, Marquiese walked with Earek and Marilana to their rooms.

"Goodnight, Marilana. Goodnight, Highness, and thank you again for taking me among the tents today. I enjoyed the experience," Earek said with a slight bow before entering his rooms.

"I hope you are not too bruised from today's competitions," Marilana said when she and Marquiese paused outside her door. "I could make a tonic for you. It would sooth the pain and help you sleep."

"Thank you. But no. I will be fine. A bit sore, but back to full health in a few days." He took her paw in his. "I wanted to apologize to you for missing the tournament ball tomorrow. Lady Annabella gave her permission for you to attend the tournament, but she said you should not attend the ball."

"Lady Annabella is right. I am only her ward, and I should not be attending balls with royalty," Marilana said firmly.

"Nevertheless, I would have liked to complete the experience for you. I was glad to see you wear that dress today." Marquiese smiled at her. "And from all the rumors and complements I heard among the tents, the other competitors were glad you wore that dress too."

"Thank you for inviting me," Marilana replied, lowering her eyes and blushing furiously.

"It was my pleasure, Marilana," he said, gently kissing her paw. "Good night."

As Marquiese walked away, Marilana pressed her paws to her stomach trying unsuccessfully to control her flutters.

7

The next two fifnights passed in a blur for Marilana. She and Earek spent time each day studying in the Royal Library. Some days Marquiese would join them. Some days he took them on rides.

Master Castant frequently joined them as well, and he often took Earek with him to run errands, conveniently leaving Marquiese and Marilana with time alone.

Marilana liked the mysterious leopard and thought he would make a good friend, but he seemed leery of getting too close, as if something was holding him back, perhaps some danger she could not see.

Marilana and Marquiese continued to take walks after dinner. Marquiese seemed slightly different after the tournament, seemingly more relaxed and yet more nervous from moment to moment. It was almost as if he had made a decision, but was unsure how to move forward. Marilana did not prod. If he needed her help or counsel, she only hoped he would ask.

Day by day, the young lioness was feeling more and more at home in the palace. She had been visiting for nearly a month and could not help but wonder how much more time she would have with Marquiese.

On the last day of the fifth fifnight of her stay, Marquiese took Marilana on a ride through the Titif Forest north of the royal city. They were escorted by three guards, including Karndel, Marilana's personal guard. She noticed that the guards managed to keep a respectful distance while scanning the forest from every angle. They watched every movement and listened to every sound.

Marquiese wore his sword as usual, but Marilana was unarmed. She understood now why Lady Annabella had insisted that she leave her weapons in Mystillion; it was, after all, frowned upon to be armed in the presence of royalty. But Marilana had never gone single day much less five fifnights without her bow or her dagger, and she would have felt better with some kind of weapon on her person now. She was, after all, a bandit hunter, and a bandit hunter without her tools of the trade was both a contradiction in terms and a less than intimidating sight.

Still, it was a beautiful summer morning. The sky blazed a brilliant blue and the air was more spring-like than summer. The birds sang happily in the tall trees. The Titif Forest's offering of oaks, aspens, and birch could not help but lift the spirits. Marilana noted the heavy growth of underbrush along the road, and the lack of it back under the thick canopy, always alert to her surroundings.

The two rode peacefully, talking quietly, and taking in the beauty of the day. This road was close enough to the city and well patrolled, so they had little fear of attack. They stopped in a clearing for lunch and then decided on a different route back to Maefair.

This road curved deeper into the forest and was heavily shaded. A gentle breeze had the leaves in the trees dancing, and birds sang lively choruses.

They were rounding a bend in the deepest part of the forest when suddenly Marilana's horse reared up and knocked her out of the saddle.

"Marilana! Are you alright?" cried Marquiese. He jumped down beside her and offered his paw.

"I am fine," she said, coming to her feet. "But something spooked my horse and whatever it was must be close."

Karndel had also dismounted and was holding the reins of Marilana's snorting and dancing horse when both his mount and Marquiese's whinnied in alarm and bolted down the road. An instant later, a tiger and a cheetah, both heavily armed, swung out of the trees and knocked the two remaining guards from their horses. A third attacker—this a powerful brown bear in leather and mail—swung onto Marilana's horse at the same moment.

"Quick! Run, Your Highness!" Karndel pulled Marquiese toward the side of the road. Marilana was close behind.

"Look out!" she shouted as their attackers turned the horses on them. Marilana leapt forward, pushing Marquiese into the underbrush and out of harm's way. Her cry ended in a yelp, however, as the bear swept her up with one arm, pulled her up on to the saddle, carrying her off.

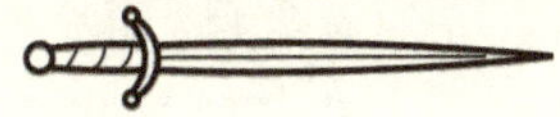

Marquiese righted himself and looked down the road, watching in disbelief as the three men and their mounts raced away with Marilana.

"Marilana!" he yelled, knowing it was futile. He jumped to his feet and turned to his guards. "Karndel, run with all speed back to the Royal Palace. Get a legion of horsemen and return as swiftly as possible."

"Yes, Highness." The cheetah turned and sprinted away.

"You two," Marquiese said to the remaining guards. "We're going after them. Follow me."

"Your Highness, wait! This is too dangerous. We cannot risk your life," the senior of the two guards interjected. "This could lead to a trap."

"Your concern is noted, Urdan, but we have to get Marilana back. If we wait, we could lose the trail. We must press on. Now! That is an order!"

"Yes, sir!" both replied, saluting with fists to chests.

The three set off down the road, easily following the tracks of the running horses. The trail was clear until they came to a place where the trees grew close overhead and the brush was thinner on the roadsides.

"Sir, the horses left the road through here," Urdan said, indicating a break in the underbrush.

"Use your kerchief to mark this place for the legion," Marquiese said quietly.

"Yes, Your Highness." The caribou tied his blue kerchief to a low hanging branch, and they plunged into the trees.

Marilana twisted in the saddle and felt the bear's arm tighten around her waist. Her arms were momentarily free so she grabbed at the reins of the horse with one paw and grabbed for his dagger with the other. She pulled the blade from its sheath. The rider, however, was well trained. He was stronger and had longer arms. He directed the horse with his legs and managed to knock the dagger from her paw.

Without a weapon, Marilana resorted to an unarmed attack. She struck her captor with several solid punches to his face. The bear raised one arm to block her, so she changed tactics and elbowed him in the stomach. He grunted even with his armor taking most of the blow, but did not loosen his hold on her. Eventually, he grabbed one of her wrists. Twisting in the other direction, Marilana reached forward, grabbed the reins with her free paw, and jerked the horse sideways. As the horse turned, she rammed her shoulder into the bear's side. The force of it threw him off the horse. He still had a hold of her, however, and pulled her to the ground with him. The horse whinnied loudly and darted away into the trees.

The other two took immediate action. The cheetah went after the horse. The tiger jumped off his horse and tackled

Marilana as she rolled to her feet. Together, the bear and tiger pinned Marilana to the ground on her stomach. She could tell by their movements that they were trained soldiers.

"What do you want with me? Where are you taking me? You are not bandits, so why are you kidnapping me?" Marilana yelled, her voice challenging and fearless.

The cheetah returned with two horses, hers and the one belonging to Karndel.

"I found a second stray. We can tie her to her own horse and save ourselves the trouble of carrying her."

"Good thinking. Get the rope," replied the leader.

Marilana slammed her boot heel into his ribs. He grunted and then twisted her around onto her back and sat on her legs. The tiger reached across to hold her shoulders down and she bit at his paw. He jerked back with a growl, but did not let go of her arms. The cheetah sprang forward with a long rope in tow and began to tie Marilana's paws together.

She knew her strength was no match for these three. If she had been armed, she would never have been caught in the first place. She chided herself for becoming complacent and letting her guard down. These three were well trained and strong; at least they were not bandits. They were too mannerly; they did not strike her, and they used only enough force to subdue her. She would not try to kill them if the chance availed itself; she wanted to know who they worked for. Still, she did not want them to reach their destination because that could spell her doom. She also knew that Marquiese would be doing everything in his power to follow their trail, so giving him more time was a definite priority.

She stopped struggling and focused on her breathing as they lifted her into the saddle and tied her paws to the saddle horn of her horse. The bear took the reins and mounted his own horse. The moment before he was fully in the saddle, Marilana spurred her horse, and the chestnut mare reared up.

The bear was pulled from his saddle, but he refused to let go of her reins. The tiger and cheetah dismounted again.

"We're wasting time," the cheetah hissed. He jumped toward the frantic horse, causing it to buck and twist. Marilana lost her hold and was knocked out of the saddle. Her arms twisted as the horse spun. She could not pull herself back up into the saddle, so she let herself move with the horse, cooing, "Whoa, Sweet, whoa now! Hush now. Calm down. That a girl."

Hearing her voice, the horse slowly pulled up, its racing heart calming with each word. The lioness continued to speak until the mare dropped its head and stopped dancing. Marilana leaned against the horse, both of them breathing hard.

"Wise choice, missy. You're lucky that horse didn't drag you and trample you. I won't have you trying any more of stunts. Boys, get the rag," growled their leader.

Staring at the bear, it suddenly dawned on Marilana; she knew him.

"You! You are Prince Dansho's man. You competed in the tournament," she said definitively. "Why would you do this?"

He shifted uncomfortably and looked away from her as the tiger brought him a bottle and a rag. He gave the cheetah the reins of her horse and doused the rag. He met her eyes sadly.

"I have my orders," he said quietly.

She studied his eyes as he placed the rag over her nose and mouth. She held her breath for a moment, and then breathed the herbal tincture without struggling.

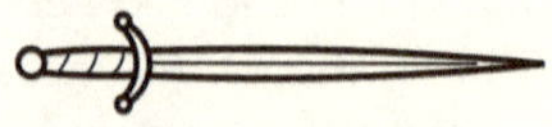

Marquiese and his guards followed the horse tracks into the forest. They found a dagger along the path that indicated to Marquiese that Marilana was doing everything in her power to escape. He would have expected nothing less.

When they heard shouting up ahead, Marquiese led his two guards to the edge of a clearing. They found cover behind a slight ridge that offered a view of Marilana and her kidnappers. Marilana was spurring her horse, trying to keep the men at bay, and Marquiese nearly let out a shout when she was thrown from the saddle. He sighed with relief when the horse calmed down and Marilana was no longer in danger of being trampled. He could see her arms were twisted in a way that did not allow her to regain the saddle on her own. He growled softly when the leader of the group poured something from a bottle onto a rag and placed it over Marilana's nose and mouth.

"Do we attack?" his personal guard whispered.

"Not yet! Not yet!" Marquiese hissed. *Why did Marilana choose not to fight the rag?* he wondered. *Something convinced her otherwise, something she saw or heard. But what?*

Marquiese was easing his sword from his scabbard and preparing to attack when he heard the cheetah say to his leader: "Prince Dansho is not going to like your decision to use the herb to subdue her, Captain."

"Prince Dansho would have liked it even less if she had gotten away," replied the brown bear as he mounted the chestnut mare and pulled Marilana up into the saddle in front of him.

"Dansho," Marquiese hissed, his anger tensing every muscle in his body. But even as his anger spilled over, he slipped his sword back into the scabbard and stared after the men as they rode north into the forest.

"Your Highness! They are on the move again. Should we not follow?" Urdan called quietly.

"No," the Crown Prince said through clenched teeth. He sprang to his feet. "We will return to the road and wait for the legion. We know where they are going. They will not harm Marilana any more than they already have."

"Your Highness, please forgive me for asking, but what does Prince Dansho want with your friend?"

"He wants to prove that I dishonored Princess Clara by having a peasant stand as a great-lady at the tournament," Marquiese replied as they turned and set out at a jog back to the road.

"Sir, I have been in your service a very long time, so I feel it my duty to speak," his guard continued.

"Speak, Urdan. I have long trusted your counsel," Marquiese replied.

"Highness, is a peasant posturing as a noble not the greatest dishonor against a lady of royal blood, and is it not against the law to claim a higher caste?" Urdan said. "I mean no disrespect, but your friend could be sentenced to death for this."

"No," Marquiese said darkly. He saw the road up ahead. "Dansho is acting without all the facts. You will understand soon enough. Everything will be told at King Carloth's Palace, which is exactly where they are headed."

Marilana slowly opened her eyes. Her body ached. Her head spun from the strong tincture of Callie leaves, an intensely strong dosage from what Marilana knew of the herb. She looked around and found herself in a dungeon cell. Oddly, it smelled of clean straw and the fresh breeze filtering through two barred windows. The cot she had been deposited on was also clean. Her gray dress was wrinkled and dirty, but still intact, signs her kidnappers had not abused her. The sunlight streaming through the windows showed clean walls and a tidy room outside her cell bars. She sat up and paused to let a wave of dizziness pass. *If this is a dungeon*, she thought, *it's the cleanest and most comfortable one I've ever seen.*

She heard footsteps pounding in the hall outside the dungeon's heavy door and a raised voice saying, "I told you, no herbs! I told you, do not hurt her!"

"Your Highness, forgive me. She was difficult. Not to mention skilled and tenacious," responded a baritone voice that Marilana recognized as the leader of her captors.

"She is a girl! A peasant girl! How difficult can she be?" sneered the first voice.

The door burst open, and Marilana rolled to her feet, still weakened by the herbs.

"So you are awake. Good," said a muscular lion who was clearly of royal bearing.

"I demand that you release me at once," replied Marilana swaying slightly. She glared at her captors though her vision was slightly blurred.

"Who do you think you are to make demands? Your position is tenuous at best," said the lion with a touch of amusement.

"I am Marilana, friend to His Highness Prince Marquiese and ward of Lady Annabella. I demand to know why I have been drugged, and inexpertly so at that . . . ," she threw a daggered look at the huge bear standing in front of the door to the hallway. ". . . captured like a common thief, and locked in a dungeon," Marilana replied curtly.

"I, my dear Peasant, am His Royal Highness Prince Dansho. And you are no longer in Redsands where Lady Annabella's protection might do you some good," he replied, his amusement now spiced with contempt.

"Prince Dansho!" she said, suddenly recognizing his eyes. "You! You are behind my capture. Why? I demand to know."

"All in good time, imposter." He looked at her with growing interest, saying nonchalantly, "I hear you created some difficulties for my men. I admire your spunk. And I would understand if you feel offended by their rash use of herbs."

"I am offended by my capture far more than your Captain's rash use of herbs, as you call it, Your Highness. Under the circumstances, however, if they had not used the herbs, their lack of knowledge about Callie leaf aside, I would have found a way to escape."

"Hmm!" The Prince studied her. His previous anger replaced not by contempt, but rather curiosity. He indicated her cot and said, "May I sit?"

"It is your dungeon."

"Yes, I suppose it is," Dansho opened the cell door, leaving it open behind him, and stepped further into the dungeon. He eyed the lioness as if weighing his options.

Suddenly he sprang forward, grabbed her by the elbows, and pushed her none-too-gently against the cell wall. Marilana stared at him, her eyes calm but still slightly bleary from the herb they had used on her. She pushed down an impulse to strike back, knowing her strength had not completely returned and that attacking royalty would gain her further punishment. *Patience,* she told herself. *Be passive. Wait for a chance to escape.*

"You see, Captain, she is not so difficult." Dansho smirked.

The lion roughly released her, then turned his back, and took a step toward the cell's one stool. In that instant, Marilana instinctively moved forward. She locked her foot against Dansho's ankle and gave the lion a forceful shove. Dansho crashed face first onto the cot as Marilana dashed out of the cell, throwing the door closed behind her. She clung to the cell bars as a wave of dizziness threatened to drop her to her knees, and her brief thought of escape crumbled. She was still too groggy from the herbs, and the element of surprise was gone. By then, Dansho's Captain had drawn his sword, and the blade was aimed steadily toward her.

While Marilana's body was weak, her mind conjured up a lie she only hoped Dansho would buy. *Appear strong, don't let them see your weakness. I don't think Dansho is the kind to kidnap without cause, King Rylan spoke highly of him. I need to know what is going on.*

"I hope you've learned your lesson, Prince Dansho," she said quickly. She pushed herself away from the cell door, stepping away from the huge brown bear's sword. "Now you see that I could easily have escaped if given half a chance."

Marilana threw back her shoulders, hoping to hide the fact that her knees were still wobbly. She blinked carefully, trying to clear her vision.

"Do not just stand there, Captain! Get me out of here!" roared Dansho.

"Don't misunderstand," Marilana said with as much bravado as she could muster given her weakened condition. "That was merely a demonstration. Yes, and perhaps a warning."

"A warning? You dare to warn me?" Dansho said as the bear threw open the cell door.

"You have abducted me, and it is my duty to escape. Or at least to make the attempt. And given a fair chance, I will."

"Why would you give us fair warning of your ability to escape and summarily ruin your chances?" Dansho spat angrily.

"You had me captured for a reason, and I want to know why. I watched you at Princess Clara's tournament, and King Rylan spoke highly of you. I have enough sense to know that you did not abduct me without cause. I am willing to wait for answers, but you will not discredit me. Your men were wounded during my capture. You should not dismiss their assessment of the encounter. They did what they felt was necessary, and know full well that they had good cause."

Dansho seized Marilana roughly by the arm and ushered her back into the cell.

"I can see now that they were in the right to incapacitate you. You may have saved them from punishment, but you have not helped your own predicament."

"I have shown you that I have chosen to stay as your captive," she said coldly. "I could have escaped, but I let your man drug me. Now I want answers."

"She is speaking truly, Highness," spoke the brown bear quietly. "She fought like a devil until she recognized me. After that she breathed the herbs without resisting. I think she still would have tried to escape had I not used the drugs, but she gave in to me by choice."

Dansho turned his anger on his Captain. "Take up a watch outside the dungeon. Admit no one until Princess Clara announces King Carloth's visitor," the lion growled dangerously.

The bear did as he was told, scurrying out the door, and leaving Marilana and Dansho alone in the cell. A tendril of fear rippled down Marilana's spine; she had the skill to incapacitate the lion, but not in her weakened condition and the law demanded she allow him to do as he willed with her. This was a far more precarious position than having the bear outside the cell with his sword drawn. She stared defiantly back at the Prince. Suddenly he grabbed her other arm, pulled her to him, and pressed his lips hard against hers. An instant later, he pushed her away so violently that she fell hard onto the floor. He took a step forward and towered above her as she tried to regain her breath. Unrelenting, she glared back up at him.

"Am I supposed to be impressed?" she said in a remarkably calm voice.

"Let that serve as a reminder to you that I am a prince and you are but a peasant. I could take you to my bed for a night of pleasure if I wished and you could do nothing. You may be strong and smart and fearless, but I have power over your life. My reasons are my own, and I will do as I wish," he said in a cold menacing whisper.

"You did not bring me here for your own pleasure. That much is clear," she said with a challenge in her voice. "Why did you? What do you want with me?"

"You amaze me, lioness. I show you my strength of will and body yet you defy me still. Why do you try so hard?"

"Try, My Lord? I do not try, I must. I am a peasant, grown up in a land of troubles. I have battled more bandits than you have enemy soldiers and defeated far more than you can imagine. I have learned to take care of myself. Without a will to live, even the strongest die. I have made the choice not to fight you. Now I want answers. Why am I here?"

She came to her feet, fighting another wave of dizziness, and struck a pose that spoke clearly of her defiance. They locked eyes for a long moment. Finally Dansho relaxed and smirked.

"I like your spunk, lioness. I can see why Marquiese likes you," he said with grudging admiration. He motioned her to the cell's one stool. "Sit and I will answer your question. I suppose even a peasant of your position knows that it is a high insult, punishable by death, to impersonate a great-noble?"

Marilana positioned herself on the stool, breathing deeply.

"I know the law," she said, her heart sank knowing he had the law on his side.

"You know, and yet you still performed such at the tournament."

"Let us not mince words, Prince Dansho. I was asked to attend by Prince Marquiese and introduced as a lady by His Majesty King Rylan."

"In Redsands, King Rylan and Prince Marquiese may make the laws as they see fit, but they cannot change the conditions agreed upon by the allied nations," Dansho said. "You insulted many a lady as well as Princess Clara, my bride-to-be. Unless it is found that there was given consent before the tournament by Lady Annabella, you will be sentenced by a court of the allied kingdoms."

"So be it," Marilana said coldly.

"And so your defiance wilts," he said, projecting disappointment.

"Not at all. Defiance has its place among injustices. You have accused me of an action that I cannot deny. Although I must say it would have been easier to send a summons and have me justly arrested rather than brutally abducted."

"A summons you would have fought, just as you have your capture. Apparently you now see the error of your way. Which may speak well of your character, though we have another agenda to meet before passing judgment on that. Princess Clara has been dishonored. Your ward, Lady Annabella, has been informed of this dilemma and is on her way—"

"In fact, she has arrived," came a stern proclamation from the cell door.

Prince Dansho's head snapped to the lioness standing in the door. Marilana recognized the visage of Princess Clara.

"Clara. What are you doing here in the dungeon? You could have sent word," he said in a voice that was at once accommodating and submissive.

"I chose to come myself to see my orders carried out. When your Captain informed me that you were locked in private conversation with our prisoner, I thought I should see for myself," stated Princess Clara in a disgusted voice. "And now we are wanted in the courtyard."

"In the courtyard?"

"Yes. And there is quite the crowd gathered." She snapped and turned to go. "Bring the peasant."

Marilana walked between Dansho and his Captain through the halls of King Carloth's Palace, down a set of stone stairs, and finally through wide doors into the palace courtyard. The crowd that Clara spoke of was indeed prominent: King Rylan, King Carloth, Lady Annabella, her escorts, and Marquiese, who was storming toward them with outrage clearly written on his face. "If she has been harmed in any way, Dansho, I promise I will make you—"

"Marquiese! Enough!" King Rylan interrupted sharply. He put out his paw, stopping Marquiese from advancing further.

Marquiese may have been momentarily subdued by his father's warning, but it was only when he saw that Marilana was unscathed and unshackled that he planted his feet firmly.

"Are you alright?" he said across the space that was forced between them by the law of the allies.

"I am fine." Marilana met his eyes, suppressing a smile. Marquiese's defense of her made her feel slightly giddy. It took an act of will, but she pushed down a brief thought of falling into his embrace and focused instead on the seriousness of the situation. She was the "accused." The law required her to remain at Dansho's side, he being her accuser.

"This is all a mistake," Marquiese said, addressed the gathering of royalty.

"Of which we are all a party to," his father said, turning to the King of Precinlia. "King Carloth, the charges you have placed on this girl are made moot by facts you are not as yet aware of. I wish to speak to you privately before the Allied Court is collected."

"Rylan, do not be hasty. It is apparent that both you and your son hold this young lioness in high regard. You were not asked here, however, to defend her or yourselves in this matter," King Carloth replied. He gave his attention to Lady Annabella, whose escorts had by now led their horses to the corral and were standing at attention some ways off. "Before the Allied Court is summoned, there is only one person who has the right to come forth and give counsel. And that is why I requested your presence here, Lady Annabella. And I must say it is truly good to see you again."

"Perhaps." Lady Annabella acknowledged his pleasantries with a curt nod and a frown of displeasure. Her bright green eyes took in the royals gathered before her. "Your Majesties. Your Highnesses. Let me get straight to point. I am very displeased by the lack of courtesy shown with regard to this predicament, not to mention the unscrupulous treatment of my ward. I was hoping to make a rather important pronouncement at a great feast in the Royal Palace of Maefair, but that plan has been waylaid by these actions."

She turned her gaze on Marquiese. "His Highness Prince Marquiese, wanting Marilana to attend Princess Clara's tournament and offer the Red and Blue of Redsands as Great-Lady of the Southern Tip, committed a slight oversight in his eagerness to do so. As a keeper of a particularly important secret of mine, he should have brought the tournament hosts into his confidence and this situation could have been averted."

"But it is not my secret to disclose, My Lady," Marquiese said slightly abashed. He glanced in Marilana's direction. "Not without your consent."

"Yes, Your Highness." The noble lioness offered him a small smile. "Perhaps we could have both communicated better on the matter."

"I apologize to you both," Marquiese said, his eyes moving from King Carloth to his daughter, Princess Clara. "It was disrespectful to have left you out of my confidences or at least to have prepared you more fully." Then he glanced from Marilana to Lady Annabella. "And I apologize further for placing your ward in danger. That is the very last thing I have wanted."

"Of course." Lady Annabella took a step forward, her glance falling with affection upon Marilana.

"My desire was to keep my secret from you most of all, my child, so I could bestow honor on you in front of a multitude of highly respected guests. Obviously, that is no longer possible, and I must reveal my secret here today."

Marilana watched Lady Annabella with shocked comprehension dawning on her face and a warmth growing in her heart.

"You mean ... you knew ... you have chosen ...." Marilana stammered brokenly.

Princess Clara gave a loud snort of disapproval, but no one noticed; they were all waiting for Lady Annabella to continue.

"Yes," said the noble lioness, beaming at her ward proudly. "I have finally chosen my heiress, she who will forevermore be hailed as Great-Lady of the Southern Tip. You, Lady Marilana, will take my place and inherit my estates and will, from this moment forward, be a noble in my house. King Rylan approved my decision the fifnight before the tournament, and I am arriving in Maefair today in order to make preparations for my official decree. The feast and decree will still happen, but the surprise for you came a day earlier than I had planned. I hope you are no less pleased."

Marilana felt a quiver run down her spine. Her knees nearly buckled. "But ...."

"There is no 'but,' child," King Rylan said. "A better choice could not a royal make. We congratulate you, Lady Marilana."

"Thank you," Marilana said, managing a graceful curtsey. Her eyes traveled from King Rylan, to Lady Annabella, and finally to Marquiese, whose smile could not have been broader nor more proud. He shared a brief bow.

"Well that settles things then," King Carloth proclaimed in a brisk tone, an open palm hailing Marilana's soon-to-be-announced position. "You are indeed a lady as King Rylan had introduced you."

"Thank you, Your Majesty." Marilana curtsied again, her eyes bright.

"What's more," King Carloth continued, "there is, consequently, no disgrace to my daughter, and therefore the Allied Court need not be notified of any indiscretion."

"Save one," Lady Annabella interrupted sternly. "Since when is it appropriate to abduct anyone for anything, much less an unsubstantiated crime? Yes, I have heard people calling the Southern Tip less than civilized, but honestly, I would never condone capturing someone before charging them of a crime."

"You are correct Lady Annabella," King Carloth conceded. "We were wrong. I should have known better than to act in anger." He bowed shortly in Marilana's direction. "I apologize personally to you, young lady." Then he turned in Lady Annabella's direction. "And to you for forcing you to impart your secret before you wished."

"If I may interject, Father." Princess Clara said with an air of superiority. "If I remember the succession laws correctly, Lady Annabella must prove to attending witnesses that the heir is indeed the person standing before us."

"Clara, please," Marquiese said, stepping next to Marilana. "You know that is not a test to be performed in front of a general audience; it should be kept to a trusted few witnesses."

"Nevertheless an heir's identity must be proven by a test or demonstration that only she, as is the case here, can perform correctly, thus discouraging imposters from imposing themselves on the rule of law."

"Quiet presumptuous, Princess Clara. But you are correct," Lady Annabella said, sighing deeply. "Marilana has studied for nearly a month at the Royal Palace of Maefair, as King Rylan can attest."

"Indeed she has," King Rylan replied.

"As to the demonstration?" the Princess demanded.

"But of course." Lady Annabella made a magnanimous gesture in the direction of the nearby paddock and Storm, the fiery white stallion upon which she had arrived. "Storm was not named on a whim. I have always maintained that he will carry none save myself and his trainer. Marilana is his trainer. To prove that this is the same young girl that has been my ward and part of my household for the past twelve years, and as the last step of conformation of the choosing process before the decree, I propose a small test of skill."

"And that would be?"

Lady Annabella ignored the Princess in favor of her father. "Storm responds rather drastically when someone unknown tries to control him. King Carloth, do you have a groom who would volunteer to attempt to ride Storm?"

"Wait just one minute," interrupted Clara. "I believe that your horse simply responds to a lady's touch rather than that of a male. Therefore I shall ride Storm as a way of disproving your theory."

Clara turned and set out for the paddock before anyone could say a word.

"I recommend that you call your daughter back at once, King Carloth," Marilana pleaded, searching King Carloth's face. "Storm will do her harm! She must not try to control him! I implore you."

"She is as fine a horseperson as we have in Precinlia," King Carloth said levelly. "And I believe she has a valid point."

"Your Majesty, if you do not take heed of what Marilana says," Lady Annabella said hastily, "I cannot be accountable for what happens."

"So be it." King Carloth acknowledged Lady Annabella's words with a curt nod and turned his attention to the paddock where Storm paced back and forth stomping and throwing his head at Clara's approach. Clara put her paw on the gate and called Storm by name, her voice calm and reassuring. When the snow-white stallion approached the gate, Clara took hold of his reins and unlatched the gate.

As soon as the gate began to open, Storm reared up and kicked it with his front hooves. The power of the kick sent the gate flying. Clara was nearly yanked off her feet as she tugged on the reins and called to the horse in her most urgent voice. Storm's only reaction was to bolt forward, and Clara only managed to release the reins at the last second. The horse raced from the paddock. He charged around the courtyard overturning carts and crashing into carriages.

Lady Annabella hurried forward, whistling and calling to the horse. All to no avail.

Then a voice wafted across the courtyard, calm but stern. "Storm! Come here at once. You have caused enough damage."

Marilana had not moved even a step, yet the result was instantaneous.

The rampaging stallion spun around and galloped full speed across the yard straight past Lady Annabella and halted in front of Marilana. Timidly, the horse stretched his nose toward the lioness and she responded with an outstretched paw. When the two touched, the effect was palpable. The muscles of the horse, taut and vibrating only moments before, relaxed. His head drooped. Marilana began to stroke the horse's ears and forelock. "Aren't you the troublemaker," she whispered affectionately. "Not that I blame you."

"Well, I never!" exclaimed King Carloth, "I have seen many a horse and many a trainer, but never I have seen that level of control."

"Storm is a very unique animal. Many talented trainers tried to tame him in his youth, but it was the paws of a young lioness that finally captured his spirit." Lady Annabella smiled at Marilana as she spoke. "Why had it not been for Marilana, Storm would have remained untrainable and far too dangerous. He would have been destroyed long ago, I am afraid."

"What I do not understand is how Storm is your horse, Lady Annabella, when Marilana has so much more control of him?" asked Prince Dansho skeptically.

"It is precisely that fact that has allowed me to ride him," the noble lioness replied. "You see if Marilana had not insisted that Storm carry me, I would have had as little control as anyone else. Storm responds to me because Marilana trained him to do so."

Lady Annabella took her place next her ward and her horse and smiled proudly. "Which reminds me. Now that you are a lady, borrowing another's horse is out of the question. From here on, you will have your own horses. And you will start with Storm."

Marilana looked aghast. "You are giving me Storm? As my own? But, My Lady . . . !"

"He has always been your horse truly. Time for you to claim him. And no, you cannot argue this with me. I know in your heart of hearts that you want him."

Marilana said nothing. Instead, she smiled in response to Lady Annabella's knowing smile. To be made Lady Annabella's heiress and then to be given Storm, all in a matter of minutes, seemed a dream that would surely come to an abrupt end.

"Well if matters are settled here, then we really must be heading back," said King Rylan briskly to the King of Precinlia. "There are feast arrangements to be settled and arriving guests to be greeted."

"Yes, indeed, it does seem to be a very busy time at Maefair, and I am sure you need to get back to the affairs of the present," replied King Carloth. "May your travels be safe, my friend."

While Lady Annabella had a word with her escorts and Marquiese said his goodbyes to Princess Clara, Prince Dansho fell in next to Marilana. The statuesque lion lowered his voice and said, "I owe you an apology, Marilana. In fact, I owe you more than one. My behavior in the dungeon was inappropriate, and I am sorry I acted that way. I do not wish you to think that I normally go around forcing myself on peasant maids. I was angry and let my anger dictate my actions. I—"

"Say no more, Prince Dansho. That is between us and in the past," Marilana said calmly. She met his gaze.

The Prince of Lentier breathed a noticeable sigh of relief. "I have greatly underestimated your character, it seems," the lion said. "For one so young you speak as though a lifetime of wisdom were behind your words."

"I am no younger than you, and while you are learning something from me, you might pass on a word of advice to your Captain," Marilana said lightly. "He would do well to use a Callie leaf tincture dilution of one to ten. It will have the same effect, but will leave his prisoners a bit less groggy in the morning."

Dansho looked at her in surprise. "All this time you have been out of sorts?"

"It is getting better, but I will be glad to ride a while," Marilana replied levelly.

"I have not only underestimated your character, but your skills, knowledge, and wits as well."

"Welcome to the club," Marquiese said as he and Clara joined them.

"Clara has chided me not to make assumptions," Dansho said with a smile to his bride-to-be.

"We might all be well-advised to never judge someone by his or her station, Your Highness," Marilana added.

"A lesson I will not soon forget, Lady Marilana," Dansho said with a slight bow. Then he glanced mischievously at Marquiese. "I am sure you have a wealth of stories to tell about this one, Marquiese."

"That is another understatement, Dansho," Marquiese laughed. "Even Clara would no doubt get a good laugh at my expense."

"I have no doubt got a good laugh at your expense on many occasions, Marquiese," Clara replied with a sour tone that the Prince of Lentier took note of.

"Clara, what has gotten your hackles up?" he asked. "You usually find our bantering tolerable if not laughable?"

"I am sure Princess Clara would enjoy your banter better without competitive intrusion," Marilana remarked gazing at the Princess. Clara returned an emotionless gaze. Marilana smiled slightly to ease the tension. "Perhaps we shall get to know each other better and start on better terms the next time we meet. We might even have a private discussion on the subject of roving eyes."

The two princes glanced at one another with confused expressions that caused Clara to smirk slightly and say, "Yes, and perhaps we can add obliviousness to the discussion as well."

"Until next time then." Marilana curtseyed.

"I look forward to it." Clara laughed shaking her head and started away. Dansho shared a last look of confusion with Marquiese and hurried to catch up. Marquiese and Marilana watched them go.

"That was an interesting exchange," the regal lion said, gazing at her.

"Well, it seemed better to defuse the situation than provoke it."

"Then you are alright?" Marquiese asked, a paw touching her lightly on the arm.

"I will be fine. Now that you are here."

They shared a smile, and then Marquiese grew serious. "You do not want reparations for your abduction? No one would be surprised if you did."

Marilana shook her head, then grinned. "I think Storm did enough damage on my behalf to satisfy my injured pride."

"I think you may be correct." Marquiese surveyed all the destruction the courtyard had suffered and smirked. "We had better go before we get left behind. Not that that would be such a bad thing, mind you. There is going to be a lot of pomp and ceremony over the next few days and little time to ourselves."

Marquiese winked at her and hurried off to join King Rylan. The King and Lady Annabella were already mounted and waiting as Marilana led Storm into the center of two legions of guards; on one side were the Royal Guards from Maefair and on the other were the green and silver clad guards of the Southern Tip.

She saw Earek jogging her way, and he fell in step with her.

"Are you alright? No one will tell me anything," he said in a low whisper.

"Everything is fine. Thank goodness Lady Annabella took care of everything," she replied quickly.

"So, in other words, you are not going to tell me anything either," the black leopard said sarcastically.

"Not now, silly." Marilana nodded toward the royal party. "Marquiese is mounting. We have to go. We will talk later."

Earek gave her a suspicious look before jogging back to his horse. Marilana vaulted into the saddle and felt Storm frisk slightly.

"It is alright, my friend," she whispered to the horse as Marquiese commanded his guard to form up. "We are going to be together from now on. Promise."

The white stallion dropped his head and snorted as the King and Prince of Redsands started off down the road at a good pace. Marilana fell in next to Lady Annabella. Earek and Master Castant reined up behind with Lady Annabella's Captain-General. Two columns of guards filed in behind and the advance riders spread out ahead.

"So, Marquiese, did you offer an apology to Clara and Dansho about your lack of communication at the tournament?" King Rylan asked once the walls of King Carloth's Palace were well behind them.

"Yes, Father, I did," the Prince said even though he did not seem convinced that an apology was absolutely necessary. "Clara will probably feel disinclined toward Marilana for a time, although Marilana seems to have made her own progress on that front."

"Good for her, she is wise to not hold a grudge. What about Dansho?"

"He seemed much more at ease with the situation. I expected him to accept my apology with his customary curtness, but he actually said that he too needed to apologize for doubting my judgment. I am not entirely sure what he meant by that, but I have to admit he has matured considerably since the last time he and I spent much time together."

"Good. Very good," the King said. Then looked over his shoulder and caught Marilana's attention. "Marilana, I hope you will not judge King Carloth and the Prince and Princess too harshly. They are good rulers. Clara can be hotheaded and sometimes Dansho does not think before he acts, but what Marquiese said is true of them both. They have grown up a lot in the past few years. In time, I believe they will be worthy to take Carloth's place."

"I shall take that under advisement, Your Majesty. And no, I do not judge them harshly. They may have acted rashly, but they also did not know how I would react. I was an unknown factor to them and they acted as they thought best, I suppose," she replied diplomatically.

"If all nobles had your calm logic and wisdom, the world would be a much easier place to live," the King mused.

Lady Annabella chuckled appreciatively. She then glanced inquisitively at the young lioness next to her and said, "Yes, but what did Prince Dansho have to say to you before we left?"

Marilana smiled knowingly at Lady Annabella. "He apologized to me for my capture. He said that he had misjudged me and that he was sorry for any inconvenience or hardship."

"How very mature of him," the noble lioness replied with well-crafted sarcasm.

Marquiese twisted around in his saddle and looked at Marilana with an expression of considerable contrition. "It would seem that I owe you an apology as well," he said to her. "I should have told you how insulted Dansho and Clara were at the tournament, and I should have warned you about the possibility of being charged with impersonating nobility. Then you would have been prepared had anything come of it. Which, obviously, it did. Forgive me."

"It would seem that Clara and Dansho are not the only ones that have done some growing up in the past few years," King Rylan interjected sagely.

"I defy anyone to live closely with Marilana and not learn to think faster, act with more humility, and have the good sense to apologize when needed," replied Marquiese with a smile. All four of them laughed.

"Yes, and now, if you do not mind, Your Majesty, Your Highness, I would like to speak privately with Marilana," Lady Annabella said.

"Of course, Lady Annabella," King Rylan replied.

Marquiese called Master Castant and Earek forward, and the two lionesses fell back slightly.

"I saw you speaking with Earek," Lady Annabella said quietly. "Did you tell him that I had named you my heiress?"

"No, My Lady. I simply told him that I was fine and that you had fixed everything."

"Very good. And what do you think of my decision?"

"To name me heiress? I think in a way I always knew that you would, but I had convinced my conscious mind to never consider it possible. I dreamed of it, but I never let my heart get set on it," Marilana admitted. "I have to agree that you have trained me well. You have guided my thinking and my honor all these long years to be the person I am. I am grateful.

Thanks to your tutelage, the past few fifnights in Maefair have not been nearly as overwhelming as they might have been."

Lady Annabella nodded as if she had expected nothing less, and then said, "And what would you think of Earek as an heir, as well?"

"Earek?" This caught the young lioness completely off guard. "You will name a second heir at the same time?"

Lady Annabella chuckled. "Most people I have asked this question of think that I am either uncertain of you or that I plan to have you wed even before you can blink," she said lightly. "Yes, I would be a fool, I think, to name you heir and not have a second heir already chosen. You are beautiful and desirable. You already have one suitor wanting permission to court you, and there will be many more."

"If you mean Master Arndt, I am not interested," Marilana said directly.

"Master Arndt wanted to court you as my ward, now as my heiress, he will pursue you even more ardently. Rest assured, many more suitors will step forward the moment you are named a lady. You will have to watch yourself over the next few months and dance carefully, or you may find yourself being courted by suitors from Maefair to Lentier and back again. And of course we cannot forget the most desirable bachelor in the realm."

"What do you mean?" Marilana asked with a puzzled smile.

"I am speaking of Marquiese, of course." Lady Annabella studied the young lioness. "You have not been in Maefair long enough to realize how deeply politics runs when it comes to matchmaking. Young daughters are thrown into the Royal Court to try to attract political suitors. It happens constantly. The highest suit of all is the Royal Suit. Your dear friend up there knows better than anyone that a dance with a girl in court could cost him months of back tracking if not done properly.

He is of courtship age. Yet, he has not made any suit proposals. He knows that all the young ladies in the court are waiting. Most of them have banned all other suitors until he has chosen one of them. Since he has come back from his 'three years of silence,' as his stay with us in Mystillion is now called, the number of successful suits has dwindled to near zero. All the nobles want their daughters to become queen, so they delay suitors or refuse courtships."

"All because of him," Marilana said with remarkable calm.

"All because of him."

Marilana sat staring at Marquiese's back for a long time, wondering about his intentions, and thinking back to those blissful moonlit walks through the garden. She allowed herself a pleasant, if slightly frightening, thought. *I thought at the time that such moments would have to end with my return to peasant life. Yet he knew the whole time that I would become a lady. What does he intend to do now that we have lost the restraints of caste and gained the politics of the Royal Court?*

8

The preparation began that afternoon and filled every waking hour of the next day as well. Marilana and Earek spent much of this time in the tailor's rooms with Lady Annabella. Marilana pretended to be puzzled by Lady Annabella's insistence that they have new clothes for the coming feast. Even though Earek was the son of a tailor himself and had dressed countless patrons for countless events, he did not know what to make of the entire affair. The Royal Palace seemed to hum with excitement as retinues arrived at the gates bringing guests that had accommodations in the palace itself or maintained manors in the city proper. Servants bustled everywhere cleaning and polishing so that the palace seemed to glow in its own light.

Rumors spread thick and fast that some great announcement was forthcoming. What that announcement would be varied in the telling from one listener to the next, but the whole city became alive with festive energy. Garlands of summer flowers were strung everywhere and musicians played merry tunes on every street corner. Wonderful smells drifted from open windows where cooks made their best meals and delicate summer desserts. The kitchens in the palace were manned by laughing cooks swinging long spoons. Lunch the day of the feast was light and early and the smells of the wonderful feast foods filled the hallways. Wagonloads of fresh produce and flowers arrived one after another, and streams of servants carried armloads throughout the palace.

An hour before the feast, Marilana stood freshly bathed in a silk dressing gown staring out the windows of her room at pastures full of horses and the grooms and drivers lining the path to the stables. She was trying, without much success, to calm the fluttering of her stomach. Serving maids bustled behind her preparing her garments and accouterments. Her gown had arrived fully finished just moments ago, and the maids were murmuring and laughing happily as they brushed off stray threads and imaginary lint.

Altia stepped up next to Marilana and lightly touched her arm. "We are ready for you now, Marilana."

Marilana turned from the windows, anticipation and apprehension sweeping over her. It was the most beautiful gown she had ever seen. And it was truly hers, not on loan from Lady Annabella as all of her other gowns had been over the years. The sight of the dress made the butterflies dancing in her stomach multiply. Nervousness had always plagued her before performing in front of large crowds, but this, this was not a performance; this was real. She would forevermore be Lady Marilana. She would accept the responsibility, the demands, and the authority as part of the noble caste, but she could not ignore her anxiety. She had hunted killers without a single flutter of nerves, but this . . . this scared her to death.

Altia took her arm and stood her in front of the dressing table. The young caracal slipped the dressing gown from Marilana's shoulders, the maids surrounded her, and began to dress her in the undergarments and petticoats. She felt in a fog as she lifted her arms and bent and turned according to the maids' directions. She could have done all of this herself, but Lady Annabella had insisted that the maids dress her. Marilana found it almost a relief to have someone else make sure that she had all her garments arrayed properly. Finally the undergarments were on and they directed the lioness to sit before the mirror while they applied paints and powders to her face and fussed with her paws, claws, and feet. Marilana watched her transformation from the Peasant that she knew to the Lady she did not. When the application of delicate powders was perfect, the maids directed her to stand again and carefully slid the finished gown over her head and secured the veil with its heavy circlet.

The many lengths of fabric seemed to float on every breath as Marilana stood before the mirror staring at the grand lady that was revealed there. She could not believe her eyes. She had always known she was beautiful, but this was beyond her wildest imagining.

Her deep amber eyes looked out from under dark lashes with glints of silver. Slight hints of green and silver touched her lids. Rosy highlights lit her cheeks and lips. The light silver lace veil framed her sculpted face, held secure with a dark green band embroidered with tiny silver flowers. Matching silver material floated over her shoulders and halfway down her arms from the v-shaped neckline. The main body of the dress was the dark green of the Southern Tip embroidered in tiny wandering vines of silver flowers. The skirt was hemmed with a silver ruffle, and the waist was cinched with a thin silver band. The tails of a bow in the back streamed down the skirt as subtle as a calming breeze. Silver slippers peeked out from under the hem.

She stood in front of the mirror for a long time trying to reconcile the image with what she was feeling, while her maids stood around her smiling and admiring their work. They all jumped as a knock sounded on the door.

"I believe you have a feast to attend," Altia said with a wide smile.

"I nearly forgot," Marilana replied. "Thank you all for your help."

Carrying herself as Lady Annabella had taught her took on new meaning as Marilana moved to the door. Stepping into the hall she found Earek frowning at the cuffs of his dark green suit.

"I feel a fool," he said without looking up. He tugged on the silver embroidered cuff and then lifted his head to straighten the silver under shirt. He stopped when he caught sight of Marilana. "By The Goddess."

"Well, you look a fool standing with a claw in your collar and your mouth hanging open," the lioness said, shifting nervously under his gaze. "Will you please stop staring? I am nervous enough."

"You look fantastic." The black leopard straightened and grinned. "I know what is going on now."

"Well, I am glad you do. You would look doubly a fool wearing that to anything but a ball," she replied, slightly annoyed.

"I know you know what is going on, but I shall voice my suspicion anyway. I had thought, after seeing you ride Storm yesterday, that perhaps Lady Annabella had finally decided to declare you as her heiress. Now I am sure of it."

"And what, might I ask, makes you so sure? Your suit is also cut in great-noble style as Lady Annabella requested. This ball could be a celebration of anything, and you and I just two of many guests."

"Did you look in a mirror?" he replied simply.

She blushed. Earek's staring suddenly took on deeper meaning, and she found herself feeling awkwardly shy.

"I cannot wait to see Marquiese's face when he sees you. His eyes might pop right out of his head." Earek laughed and took her paw in his. "You should blush more often; it enhances your already stunning beauty, My Lady."

He bowed and gently kissed her paw.

"Thank you, Earek. A fool can always rely on her friends to make a situation less lonely," she replied ruefully.

"Every fool needs a fellow fool," he replied lightly offering his arm to her. "I will gladly swear fealty to you, but I will also gladly still be your friend."

"You better. I value your friendship and loyalty higher than any publicly sworn fealty."

Just then the door to Lady Annabella's apartments opened, and the noble lioness stepped out with Captain-General Zariff by her side. She eyed them both critically, then nodded as if the results were satisfactory.

"You will do. Come. We have a feast to attend," she said before turning and sweeping down the hallway toward the entrance hall. Marilana smiled at Earek and together they followed.

The Great Hall was already full of people when they entered. Most of the nobles were taking their seats already. Marquiese stopped in total surprise when Lady Annabella's entrance was announced. He seemed for a moment not to recognize the pair following the noble lioness. Marilana blushed furiously when she caught him staring at her. He blinked, straightened, and smiled as Lady Annabella approached him.

"Ah, Lady Annabella. May I do the honor of escorting you to your seat?" he asked, his voice slightly higher than normal.

"Why yes, thank you, Your Highness," she replied taking his proffered arm and used a gentle tug to get him moving.

He cleared his throat slightly, appearing to use every ounce of will power that he had to not look at Marilana, and led the way to the head table. Marilana noticed the many heads turning their way as they progressed through the hall. All the nobles knew, of course, that Lady Annabella was naming her heir tonight; and most of them were not hiding their shock that it was one of Prince Marquiese's visitors. Many began to whisper and mutter as they watched the procession make its way to the King's table.

Marquiese held Lady Annabella's chair for her, showing her every courtesy as the feast was at her request. As he did so, he very carefully turned a blind eye to Marilana and Earek. Ignoring the would-be heirs until they were formally named was protocol, not disrespect, and certainly not disinterest. Still, Marilana wondered if his care was more a way to prevent his gaze from lingering on her than it was out of respect for the formalities. She hoped as much.

Earek helped Marilana into the seat on Lady Annabella's left. His was the one next to hers.

Marquiese seated himself to the right of Lady Annabella and engaged her in conversation, taking great care once again to avoid Marilana's eye. The relief was plain on his face when the trumpets announced King Rylan's arrival, and he was able to turn his attention elsewhere. In contrast, Marquiese's stepbrother Frishka stared pointedly at Marilana, his cold smile never touching his lifeless eyes. It was Marilana's turn to feel a wave of relief when everyone took their seats, and the tiger was forced to look elsewhere.

The feast was wonderful; she and Earek talked quietly as the rest of attendees avoided looking at them for anything longer than a quick glance. Many of the men, Marilana noticed, kept sneaking glances, and she had fun pointing this out to Earek.

"Are all males so weak willed? It's like they cannot resist the temptation to look at us."

"I cannot imagine why they would be drooling over you," he said dryly. "One half of them are still boys and the other half are old enough to have grandchildren twice your age."

"Thank you for ruining the moment," Marilana said with a chuckle.

Eventually, King Rylan stood to address the hall, and Marilana felt her insides turning somersaults.

The King raised his paw, and the hall went silent.

"My Lords and Ladies, it is my great privilege to welcome you all here tonight at Lady Annabella Ranat's invitation. As you are all aware, the Great-Lady of the Southern Tip has not yet named who will rule that province after her. I am pleased to announce that tonight she has called us here to bestow that great honor on a very worthy individual."

He turned to Lady Annabella and bowed his head to her. "My Lady, if you please."

Lady Annabella acknowledged the bow with a nod of her head, then came to her feet. Her eyes moved with a practiced calm over a now rapt audience, and she shared a warm smile. "My fellow Lords and Ladies. I am honored that you came to hear my announcement. I do not like to make long speeches, so let me get right to the subject of this magnificent feast. After due consideration and by the laws of succession set down by our forbearers, I am glad to name my Noble Ward, Marilana, as heiress to my estates and titles." Lady Annabella turned and drew Marilana to her feet. Marilana curtseyed to Lady Annabella and kissed her signet ring as the assembled nobles applauded politely. When the applause diminished, Lady Annabella turned her gaze upon Marilana and said, "Marilana, do you accept the rights, privileges, and responsibilities that would be yours as my heiress?"

"I do, My Lady," replied Marilana clearly.

"Then let it be known throughout Redsands and all lands, that Marilana is forever more, Lady Marilana of the Southern Tip, my heiress," Lady Annabella called out to the assembly. The nobles applauded again. While protocol called for the ladies and lords of the land to greet Marilana individually, Lady Annabella was not yet done. The noble lioness raised her paw again and gained silence once more.

"My fellow Lords and Ladies. I thank you for your patience," she began again, and murmurs ran through the crowd. "I have one more announcement, and I am honored to share it with you. After due consideration and by the laws of succession set down by our forbearers, I am glad to name my second heir tonight as well."

More whispers swept through the nobles at this and Lady Annabella waited for silence once again. Earek's face was set in a smile, but his eyes now had a nervous cast that had not been there during the feast. "With Marilana's agreement, I am glad to name Earek, as second heir to my estates and titles." Lady Annabella drew Earek to his feet. The black leopard bowed and kissed her signet ring as another round of polite applause filled the hall. "Earek, do you accept the rights, privileges, and responsibilities that would be yours as my second heir?"

"I do, My Lady," replied Earek for all to hear.

"Then let it be known throughout Redsands and all lands, that Earek, is forever more Master Earek of the Southern Tip, my second heir," Lady Annabella called out to the assembly.

The nobles applauded once more and this time Lady Annabella escorted both Marilana and Earek down to greet Redsands' nobles. Earek leaned close to Marilana as they walked down the steps and whispered, "You knew. You knew all of it."

"Of course I did. But at least Lady Annabella managed to surprise one of us." She laughed and turned to greet the first of the waiting nobles.

Lady Annabella had been right about the males of the court. They swarmed around Marilana as soon as the introduction of the nobles was finished. Marilana danced almost constantly, ending one dance just to be swept into the next dance by a new partner. The young men were the most insistent, but many older bachelors asked for a dance as well. Even one old widower, a wrinkled badger long past his prime, pushed his way in among the much younger lordlings and took his turn.

It was a relief when she turned to find Marquiese asking for the last dance.

"My Lady. May I?" he said, holding out his paw.

"You may," she answered.

Music filled the hall, and Marilana laughed as the Crown Prince spun her around the dance floor. It was just like old times dancing in her small house or the open meadow, only better. Much better.

"Well, thank goodness you have gotten over your initial shock," she teased. "At least you are not tripping over your own feet."

"Could not help myself. You are stunning, and staring would have been terribly rude," he said, leading her with ease around the floor. For Marilana, it was by far the most enjoyable part of the evening. When the dance ended, she was startled to find that they were the only dancers left on the floor. Everyone else had stopped to watch and many even applauded. Blushing, she curtseyed to Marquiese. He returned a most regal bow and a thinly disguised smile meant only for her.

The end of the music also signaled an end to the feast, and as part of her final duties of the evening, Marilana joined Lady Annabella in bidding good night to their many guests. Before she knew it, Lady Annabella was leading her and Earek back to their rooms. "I know you are both probably exhausted, but there is one more bit of ceremony that I would like to complete. In my rooms if you please."

They followed the noble lioness into her guest suite, and stopped next to a table on which sat a covered tray. Marilana was pleasantly surprised to find that Marquiese and King Rylan had followed them.

"Lady Annabella," Earek spoke quickly before their Lady could tell them what was to come next. "Before you continue, please, I must ask of you why you have chosen me as your second heir. I have no standing. My family cast me out, disowned me. I was only ever a merchant son, I was proud to hope that someday I could serve as Chamberlain to your house. You have shown me more kindness than I deserve and now this, being named your second heir. I accept, and I am honored beyond words. But, why?"

"Earek, I have long watched the children of the Southern Tip for potential heirs. Standing means nothing, it is all about character. You learned from a young age to be diplomatic. You treated your friends as equals and respected the lower castes. It is true that for a time I did not think you would make a good heir, you spent almost all your time fawning on Brittia. However, you grew, and when difficult choices were placed before you, you did not shirk from the difficult path. I have spent the past seven months testing you and preparing you. In short, I chose you because you made the right choices and are possessed of exemplary character."

Earek blinked speechless for a time before finally bowing to Lady Annabella. Marilana smiled at him and then watched curiously as Lady Annabella turned to the royals.

"King Rylan. Prince Marquiese. Thank you for agreeing to pay witness to this most important moment," Lady Annabella said solemnly. She took her place next to the table and the glistening silver tray. She glanced at the black leopard, who, much to Marilana's surprise, was now smiling expectantly. "Earek, I believe you understand what is next. Would you please inform Marilana."

"Yes, of course, Lady Annabella. Thank you." Earek looked at the puzzled expression on Marilana's face and his smile broadened. "It is called the Ceremony of Adoption. Lady Annabella has declared us as her heirs. Now she wishes to adopt us as family."

Marilana looked back at Lady Annabella with wonder, a glowing smile spreading across her face. "Truly, My Lady? We will be family?"

It obviously took considerable will power, but Lady Annabella managed to suppress the smile that threatening to override the seriousness of the ceremony.

"Marilana," the noble lioness intoned solemnly. "I have declared you my heir before the lords and ladies of Redsands. You have accepted. Will you now bind yourself to my family as my Daughter?"

Tears pooled in Marilana's eyes as she clasped her paws together and replied, "Yes! Oh, yes."

Lady Annabella shared a brief nod before turning her attention to Earek and saying, "Earek. I have declared you my second heir before the lords and ladies of Redsands. You have accepted. Will you now bind yourself to my family as my Son?"

"Absolutely!" he replied firmly.

"Marilana. Earek. Please repeat this pledge." Lady Annabella filled her lungs and said, "I pledge my loyalty and love to the Family Ranat. I pledge my life to the protection of her honor and swear to uphold her nobility in the face of all opposition. I swear to support the head of the family even if I stand in opposition. I accept the name of Ranat as my own and will strive to bring good fortune to my family in all my endeavors. I name Annabella Ranat as Mother and look upon her with love and respect."

Marilana and Earek repeated the pledge each in turn. Lady Annabella then turned to face Marilana.

"Marilana," she intoned again. "I have declared you my heir and named you Daughter. You have accepted and named me Mother. Will you now accept a Brother?"

"Yes!" she replied joyfully.

"Earek." She turned to face the black leopard. "I have declared you my second heir and named you Son. You have accepted and named me Mother. Will you now accept a Sister?"

"Most definitely!" he declared.

"Please grasp each other's right arm," Lady Annabella instructed. "Now please repeat this pledge in turn. I, Marilana, accept you, Earek, as my Brother and acknowledge you as second heir to my Mother, Annabella, of the Family Ranat. I swear my loyalty and love to you and will endeavor always to uphold the honor of our family. I will endeavor to be fair and just and support you in your own actions, deeds, and doings. I will protect you as best I can and will listen to your counsel even when we stand in opposition."

Lady Annabella paused to let Marilana repeat the lines and then recited a similar pledge to Earek. "I, Earek, accept you, Marilana, as my Sister and acknowledge you as heir to my Mother, Annabella, of the Family Ranat. I swear my loyalty and love to you and will endeavor always to uphold the honor of our family. I will furthermore endeavor to bring fortune and prosperity to our family and support you in your own undertakings. I will respect your decisions and provide you with honest counsel even when we stand in opposition. I swear my fealty to you and upon my blade to protect you from harm."

When Earek had made his pledge, Lady Annabella placed her paw on their joined arms. She said, "I declare before these witnesses that the oaths have been sworn and that I accept your pledge. Welcome to the Family Ranat, my Daughter, Marilana, and my Son, Earek."

The noble lioness hugged them each in turn and the warmth of her smile was filled with love and light. Marilana embraced Earek tightly, and they all laughed as Lady Annabella uncovered the tray and presented each of them with a slice of perfectly cooked honey cake.

"Congratulations," Marquiese said, shaking Earek's paw and sharing a warm hug with Marilana. "This has been a remarkable day."

"You can say that again." Marilana dabbed tears from her cheeks, careful not to smudge the colors around her eyes, and munched her cake.

After congratulations were shared and cake eaten, Lady Annabella hugged them both again and said, "It is late. We all need our rest. I will see you both in the morning, and we can discuss your further studies." Then she smiled warmly at the King and his son. "My thanks to both of you for bearing witness to this joyous event."

"It was our pleasure," King Rylan replied bowing slightly.

"Most definitely." Marquiese beamed in agreement. "Rest well."

Marquiese led the way out the door, and Earek and Marilana turned directly to Earek's door. Marilana ignored the activity behind her as the guards sorted themselves to their respective escorts. She smiled warmly at Earek.

"Goodnight, my dear Brother," she said, testing the words on her tongue.

"Goodnight, my beautiful Sister," he teased.

"And so the sibling rivalry begins," she replied with mock severity, "You will have to excuse my inexperience, but I will do my best to keep up."

"And I shall endeavor to make this family the best it can be and lead you in those popular and traditional family pursuits such as nagging and bantering," he said with an exaggerated bow.

"I think I can contend with those well enough on my own, thank you," she said with a wry grin.

They said their good nights once more, and Marilana turned to find, much to her surprise, that three palace guardsmen were stationed in front of her door and looking particularly serious. A moment later, they parted, and Marquiese stepped from their midst.

"Marquiese!" she gasped, her pulse jumping. "Is everything okay? I thought you had left for your own rooms."

"I know it is late, and I know you have had a very long day, but I was wondering if you would like to go for a walk in the gardens," he said sheepishly.

"I would like that very much," she replied warmly.

A thick crescent moon accompanied them as they wondered among the palace gardens, and the scent of lavender and jasmine scented the air. A gentle breeze danced through the leaves of slender birch trees, and the music of a gurgling stream whispered in the dark. Marilana felt more relaxed than she had in many days, and the warmth of Marquiese's company was all she could ask for in that moment.

The guards stayed close, but not too close. The Prince led her over a cobbled walk to a fountain carved of marble.

"I wanted to tell you how glad I am that you have finally been adopted. I know how much that means to you," he said softly, his eyes fixed on the dark water.

"I can hardly believe it is true. I have prevented my thoughts from considering the possibility for thirteen long years. It is hard for me to accept even now that it has really happened. Lady Annabella's daughter and heiress, Marilana Ranat. Titles I never thought would be mine." She glanced at the side of his face and let a teasing smile lift her lips. "Of course you have known this was coming for some time now and did not tell me. Thank you very much."

Marquiese didn't laugh. He fidgeted with one of his gold cufflinks and she took the opportunity to sit on the coping of the fountain. He still could not look at her, and Marilana smiled at his discomfort.

"I gave Lady Annabella my word that I would not tell you any of it until she gave permission. Annabella used to talk about her possible heiress at parties I attended before hiding in the Southern Tip. When I first met you and learned that you were her ward, I suspected her intentions. You refused to acknowledge the possibilities that being a Noble Ward gave you. When Lady Annabella cornered me at your house, she told me that she was not yet sure what her decision would be and I promised not to give you too many clues.

"Later when I was hesitant to leave the Southern Tip, she told me that she had decide she would name you her heiress, but that you were not yet ready to be named. I asked her to let you come to Maefair for your month of study. She agreed on the condition that Earek could come as well. I happily agreed. She kept my secret and I kept hers. Now you know both…" He hesitated a moment, then added in a softer tone, "…who I am and who you are."

"Is that why there is now this strangeness between us?" she asked. "I seem to remember you telling me that our friendship was more important than our differing social status. You convinced me not to run from our friendship. Must we now stand on formality when before we could just be friends?"

He glanced down at her briefly. He opened his mouth, but the words seemed to stick in his throat. He swallowed and tried again.

"I seem to be having some difficulty ordering my thoughts tonight," he said with a slight croak to his voice. "I am glad that you have finally gained your title and family. I have been waiting for over a year to celebrate this day."

She waited patiently for him to find the words he wanted to say. He sat next to her, staring at his clasped paws in his lap. She laid her paw gently on his and he finally turned his eyes her way. She said, "You seemed so at ease yesterday and so happy. So now what? Now that the ceremony is completed you are having second thoughts? Is the Lady Marilana you see before you such a terrifying beast?"

Finally, he laughed and seemed to relax a little. And now that their eyes had met, he seemed unable to look away. He took hold of her paw.

"I have known you for almost four years. I have seen you in so many different situations. I have no doubt that you deserve the honors that have been bestowed upon you today. I have no doubt that you will be a good ruler, as good as Lady Annabella, if not better. I could not be happier with the way things have turned out," he said seriously.

"So your discomfort comes from a different source," she suggested.

He laughed again and continued in a lighter, more hesitant tone. "Oh, yes. The same source that had all those jack fools, young and old, tripping over their own feet at the ball tonight. I was a little afraid that I would make a fool of myself too. It took me all evening to get the courage up to ask you to dance the last dance."

"Ah! I see. So it must be that you fear my wrath for keeping secrets from me all this time?" she teased softly.

He was able at last to take a deep breath, and they sat looking into each other's eyes for a long moment.

"I want to thank you, Marquiese," she said, suddenly serious.

"Thank me? For what?"

"I would be a very different person if it were not for you." She looked away from him, feeling exposed as she voiced her past faults. "When you befriended me, I was a hard person, caught up in the sorrows of life, pushing for justice and freedom from the terrors of peasant life. You took that young girl and opened a door for her. You showed her a whole new world. You showed her a bigger picture, a picture of what life could be. A life filled with kindness and honor. I have grown much during our friendship, and I thank you for that."

He placed his paw on her cheek and turned her face back to his. "That young girl is still with us. It is she who has the determination and strength to fight for what is right. That girl would have been a good ruler without my intervention."

"Yes," she said seriously. "But she would have been mortified by the proceedings of the evening. To have all those males watching her, fawning over her, she would have faltered. She would not have been ready to step into court politics; she would have been lost in the intricacies of political matchmaking. I can see the maneuvering for power and position; I can see the shrewd analysis behind those star-stunned eyes. I was ready for the proceedings and politicking because while I tutored you in math and grammar you unknowingly taught me politics and a host of other worldly things."

He studied her eyes for a moment before speaking again. "I am glad that I could help bring you to your inheritance ready to face the nobles' world. You would have gotten here on your own eventually, but I know the changes in your character that occurred as a result of our friendship. Not the least of which I see before me."

"What do you mean?" she asked frowning.

He laughed. "Most of those young men tonight had not a thought in their heads except their desire to be introduced to a beautiful young heiress. As you said, they were star-stunned. True, the girl I met four years ago may have indeed faltered before all those hunting, hungry men. And yes, the girl I saw at the feast tonight may have blushed. And she may have been shy. But she was also very much in control. You knew your beauty was the cause of their behavior, and instead of trying to hide it, you let it shine true."

"And you?" she said.

"And me? If there is a more beautiful creature, I have yet to see her," he added in a whisper.

She blushed fiercely at his words and was acutely aware that one of his paws still cupped her face; still, she did not pull away. The warmth of his touch and the light in his eyes seemed to hold her captive, and she was unable to look away or move. Not that she wanted to.

And then, suddenly, the spell was broken by the sound of one of the guardsmen clearing his throat. Marquiese blinked, withdrew his paw, and took a shallow breath. "Yes?"

"Forgive me, Your Highness, but I have a message," the guard said.

The Crown Prince of Redsands sighed. "I am sorry. Please excuse me for a moment," he whispered to her. He arose and stepped into the shadows.

Marilana looked into the dark waters of the fountain and felt as if something had been torn loose inside her. She was surprised to find, now that the moment was gone, how disappointed she was that it had ended.

Marquiese returned and touched her lightly on her shoulder.

"I am sorry. But I must tend to a matter. Can I escort you to your rooms?" he asked softly.

"Is everything alright?" she asked, rising to her feet.

"Yes. Fine. Master Castant is leaving, and I wish to see him off."

"Master Castant is leaving now?" she asked.

"He has been given a mission by my father. He is one of the King's advisors after all, and occasionally takes on missions that my father trusts to no one else. He is making an early start and will not return for some few days, possibly even a few fifnights. As he is my friend, I like to see him off," he replied quietly.

They turned in the direction of the palace, her paw resting on his arm. Then he stopped suddenly. "Would you like to come? I am sure that Master Castant will find it amusing that we have not gotten any more sleep tonight than he has. And he is genuinely fond of you."

"I would like that. And I do not seem to be very tired anyway," she replied with a smile. "Is his cause for a long evening similar to ours?"

"In fact it is. You see, Castant has his heart set on a certain young lady, and she returns the feelings. Her father would gladly see them married, but her mother is rather more ambitious and had a ban published that her daughter would accept no suits until certain ..." he cleared his throat and glanced at her, the color rising in his face, ". . . other matters are decided."

"Other matters. Meaning she desperately wants her daughter to make the Royal Suit," Marilana said calmly.

Marquiese cleared his throat again and glanced aside. "Uh, well, yes, as do most nobles with eligible daughters."

He gave her another glance, this one slightly embarrassed.

"So Castant and she slipped out to the gardens tonight to spend some time together before he left," Marilana surmised. "I would not like to think how hard it would have been on her had he left without saying anything to her. I can only wish them all happiness when they are finally allowed to be together."

They reached the stable yard to find it bustling with grooms and carriages. The stable staff was already busy getting the lords and ladies conveyances ready for departure later that morning. They spotted Master Castant and his horse in a cleared area next to one of the paddocks. He was whistling merrily as he settled his saddlebags in place and tied a full quiver of arrows to his saddle. He looked up and smiled broadly as they approached.

"Why, My Lord, My Lady," he said in mock surprise. "Dawn is upon us and yet you come still in your court finery. Have you not yet retired to your beds?"

"Why should we retire to our beds when the night offers such wondrous opportunities?" Marquiese replied lightly.

"And, as I hear told, young Master, you did not spend much time in your own bed this night either," Marilana said teasingly.

"Ah, indeed, tis wondrous what opportunities one can find in the night. Why should I have passed the chance to spend my time in fair company? I ride forth this day to a future unknown and could not in good conscience leave without saying sweet farewells," he said pompously.

"She must be a beauty to inspire such fortitude," Marilana said with mock wonder.

"Ah, how can one compare fair to one such as you?" he teased. "She, who is like a candle, to the radiance of the sun. Ah, see, even in the night the sun burns brightest," Castant added seeing her blush. "Shall I ride out to find you a fair suit, My Lady? Or perhaps just to bring gifts of nature's attempts at beauty?"

"Enough, dear Castant," she said, shaking her head and blushing more. Acutely aware of Marquiese standing next to her. "Save your pleasing words for your fair maiden. Her beauty shines through your words and I know where your heart lies. Dawn is approaching and you stand ready to ride forthwith. I wish you a pleasant journey and fond return."

He laughed, "It is not often that I get to make such a beauty as you smile and laugh, but you speak true. My heart lies with a fair Mistress and her true beauty shines from within. I am glad for you that you have gained the titles and family that you deserve. Perhaps when I return we might spend more time pitting our wits against each other, although I think on the subject of your beauty I will always be the victor."

He bowed to her and she laughed. Marquiese stepped up and they clasped forearms.

"Safe ride and return soon, my friend," Marquiese said warmly. "And we shall see this battle of wits play out. She is not so easy a target as you will find."

"If she were an easy target, I would not expect to see her in your company," the leopard said with a wink.

Marilana's blush may have deepened even further had she not seen the broad smile spread across Marquiese's face.

*

They did not hurry on their walk back from the stable yard, and the sky was notably lighter by the time they entered the palace. Marquiese bowed low to her when they finally reached the door to her rooms. "Here the new day has already begun and we with duties that will surely not let us rest long," he said with a smile. And then more seriously "I must say this to you. Castant was right. The other noble daughters will not be pleased to have such a beauty to contend with. You will have to be careful now that you have made your debut in court as a lady."

"I know," she replied simply. "I need to discuss the matter with Lady Annabella and decide how to proceed."

"I will see you soon." He reached out and touched her cheek.

"I enjoyed our walk," she said simply. "Thank you."

"Castant was right about something else too," he said almost whispering. "You are radiant in your beauty."

He smiled and turned away. Marilana stood watching him, her heart beating fast. She stumbled slightly as she entered her rooms and leaned back against the door breathing deeply. It took her a moment to realize that Altia was waiting for her in the room, a wide, mischievous smile on her face.

"Altia! My goodness. Have you been waiting all night for me?"

"Oh, Marilana, I'm so happy for you!" she said and hurried forward to hug the young lioness. "I offered to wait for your return and sent the others to their beds. Come let me help you out of that gown. You must tell me. Was it so wonderful?"

Marilana smiled as the girl chatted on without pause and let her help her out of the gown. She listened as Altia went on at length about the gowns the other women wore and the gossip in the servants' quarters about who danced with whom. She had apparently spent much of the night assisting the undercooks keeping the wine pitchers full and clean glasses ready. A job Marilana knew many of the serving women did during festivities to get the gossip fresh from the wine servants as they made their rounds among the nobles. Marilana had never been one to really care for gossip, but she found herself listening intently, storing away the many rumored tidbits to discuss with Lady Annabella later. She reminded herself that rumors could provide certain avenues of information that could prove extremely vital.

"You must be exhausted after such a long night," Altia said, helping Marilana wash the colors from her face and wrapping her firmly in a dressing robe.

Marilana didn't response to this. Instead, she asked about something Altia had mentioned earlier. "Did I hear you say that Lady Kenhol left rather abruptly?"

"Oh, yes. She was seen pushing her daughter Ailse out the door well before the evening ended and ordered her carriage to be fetched immediately. She and Lord Kenhol said a hurried farewell to King Rylan and rushed out," the young caracal said happily.

"This young woman, Ailse, what do you know of her?"

"Ah, well, now there is a kind one. She is a sweet girl, soft spoken and pleasant. Not at all like her mother. Takes after her father."

"Is Ailse the heir of the Kenhol family?"

"No, there is a son, Master Banol Kenhol. He is well liked and rides with the Knights of the Realm. He doesn't attend many festivities these days. He apparently prefers to stay away from the city now that he is married and his wife is expecting. Isn't that wonderful?"

"Where was Ailse during the course of the dancing?"

"No one knows. She does have a reputation among the servants for disappearing rather without notice. She just disappears after the first dance and then is suddenly back before the last."

Marilana smiled. "I will have to meet this Ailse sometime. She might make an excellent ally."

Altia laughed and clapped her paws, "Oh, I do hope so! Or, at the very least, not a rival."

"A rival?" Marilana laughed, though she was beginning to understand why Altia would say such a thing. "I have no desire to attract rivals."

"But you already have. Every girl in court has an eye on Prince Marquiese. Rest assured, now that you're a noble, well, a rival you have become. They will do everything in their power to drive you away from him."

Marilana sighed. "I keep forgetting that I am a true contender now. I may wish I were back hunting bandits before all is said and done."

Altia smiled. "Don't be silly. You will make a great noble. Now you should get some rest. Lady Annabella has plans for you, and they begin in a matter of hours, I am afraid."

"So I will not be allowed to sleep in. How disappointing." Marilana smiled ruefully.

"Well, from what I know, Lady Annabella has not gotten much sleep either," Altia said conspiratorially.

"What do you mean?"

"King Rylan only left her rooms an hour or so ago. He remained with her after your adoption ceremony and was in a very good mood as he made his way back to the Royal Family Apartments."

"Is that so?" the young lioness mused. "I wonder what Lady Prinka would say if she knew."

"That one," Altia said with disgust, "hasn't spent a night with the King since her son came of age. Not that she beds her own son, mind. She doesn't bed anyone at all, just stays in her suite, she has never even attempted to enter the Royal Family Apartments. The poor King has been alone for a very long time, and it doesn't help that he is bound by marriage to that female."

"That is terrible," Marilana said sadly.

"Ah, well, now don't you mind. King Rylan takes good care of himself, and, I shouldn't say it, but I don't think he minds her ignoring him most of the time. Good night, Marilana. I'll see you in a few hours," Altia said briskly, then paused before turning away. "My Lady."

Marilana did not think she could sleep. So much had happened over the past few days and her thoughts were chasing themselves in circles. She sat on the couch watching the sky grow lighter and thought about Marquiese. Soon enough, however, she drifted off to sleep and her dreams were filled with songbirds and the pleasant music of moving water.

9

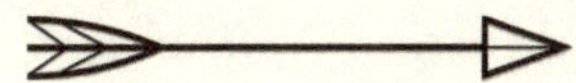

"Marilana!" Altia shook the young lioness awake. "I'm sorry to wake you, but it's time get up. Lady Annabella requests that you dress and join her for breakfast in her rooms. Rise and shine, sleepy head."

Marilana yawned. "Alright, Altia, I am awake now. Thank you."

Marilana stood up, performed a series of quick stretching exercises, and stepped in front of the water basin. She washed the sleep from her eyes and felt completely awake. As a bandit hunter, she had always been an early riser and needed far less sleep than the average lion. This morning she felt more restless than rested, but then last night had been special in many ways.

Altia helped her into a simple green dress. Together they stepped out into the hall. Altia hurried away with a basket filled with laundry, while Karndel, Marilana's ever-present guard, tipped his hat and prepared to follow her. She turned toward Lady Annabella's rooms and, much to her surprise, found a handsome young leopard standing guard outside the door.

"Jarek!" she called, her excitement genuine.

"My Lady Marilana," he said with a deep bow.

"What a pleasant surprise. I did not know you were here."

"I would not have missed this occasion for anything," he said just as the door to Earek's room opened, and another, equally handsome leopard stepped out.

"Master Earek." Jarek bowed to his brother. "A very good morning to you."

A wide smile creased Earek's face. "I am glad to see you here, brother."

"Believe me, there was a lot of competition among the guards to be the first to address you this morning," Jarek said, trying to keep his voice casual. "I suggested drawing straws, but when all was said and done, everyone agreed I deserved to be the first."

Marilana smiled. "I am so glad you are."

Jarek's expression took a considerably serious turn. "I wanted to say how proud I am of you, Earek. You chose to follow your heart. You remained friends with Marilana in the face of our parents' protests. You showed the true strength of your character. You did not shy from the right road even when it was the hard road. I know you will make a fair and effective lord."

"Thank you, brother." Earek embraced Jarek warmly. "And we will always be brothers despite my allegiance to a new family. You know that, right? Even if I cannot say the same for the rest of my relations."

"Well, I feel better knowing that I have not lost you. I also know I have no claim to any favors of state," Jarek said. "But I do have a message for you from said unmentionable relations."

"Really? So they know already."

"Of course they know," replied Jarek. "After you left for Maefair, word spread like fire that Marquiese was really the Crown Prince. Most people doubted the rumors until Lady Annabella came to the market square and announced his true identity. She also proclaimed her choice of heirs, and you can imagine the reaction."

"Oh, I can most definitely imagine." The black leopard raised an eyebrow in Marilana's direction and grinned. Then he looked back at Jarek. "And your message."

"Adrek wants you to know that he is proud of you for making your own choices and not letting others direct your life. Losing two brothers has never sat well with him."

"I am sorry for Adrek. Losing two brothers could not have been easy for him. And though he will make a good merchant, I will not give him any honor. He will have to make his own way, just as we have." Earek waited a moment before saying, "And our mother and father?"

"They wanted you to know how misguided they were. They see now that you were right to make friends with Marquiese and Marilana. They recognize your foresight and are proud that you are now a noble."

"They are looking to gain my favor, nothing more. I will not recognize them," Earek said calmly. He laid his paw on Jarek's shoulder. "I thank you for delivering their messages. You did your duty, and I expect you to continue to serve well."

Jarek nodded. He looked from Earek to Marilana and said, "My fellow guardsmen are ready and willing to serve you as Lady Annabella's family as well. We all are."

"I expected no less," Marilana said quietly. "However, I doubt that everyone is happy about Lady Annabella's choices."

"Oh, indeed, no. Already petitions have been circulated encouraging her to change her mind. Mostly from Mystillion. So far, the Lords of the Southern Tip have applauded the choices."

"Thank you for greeting us, Jarek," Marilana said, "but I think it is time we meet with Our Lady."

Jarek smiled and rapped the door smartly. Marilana and Earek went inside and were greeted by a stoic and serious Captain-General Zariff. The graying lion stared at Marilana with intensity. She stared back, unblinking. The silence stretched longer. Finally Zariff blinked, and a wide smile spread across his face. He swept Marilana into a hug and swung her around in a circle.

"You did it, girl," he said, laughing. "You held on and I blinked first. Well done. And well done for last night, too. I could not be more proud of you."

He set her down, took a step back, and bowed low. He added, "My Lady."

"Zariff," Marilana said sternly. "You have been like a father to me. Please do not stop now."

"I wouldn't dream of it." He chuckled. "You two youngsters still have a lot to learn, and I intend to teach it to you, nobles or not."

Earek stepped forward and clasped arms with Zariff. "And a better teacher we could not ask for, Captain-General."

"You'll get no argument from me, young Master." Zariff turned and led them to where Lady Annabella awaited them.

"Good morning, Mother." Marilana curtseyed politely, but she couldn't hide her smile.

The noble lioness swept her into a warm embrace. "I have been waiting to hear you say that for twelve years, Daughter."

"I dreamed of saying it in my deepest, most secret dreams and of hearing your response," Marilana replied, wiping away her tears.

"I know," Annabella said simply. She held her at arms distance and studied her face before turning to Earek.

"Good morning, Mother," he said warmly.

"Good morning, Son." She smiled and embraced him as she had Marilana. "We have much to discuss. Come, let us sit."

They turned to the dining table where, Marilana was surprised for a second time to find King Rylan and Prince Marquiese awaiting them.

"King Rylan! Prince Marquiese! What a surprise. Good morning to you both." Marilana curtseyed.

The King and Prince arose, each bowing slightly. "Good morning, Lady Marilana," King Rylan replied warmly. He turned an equally warm gaze at Earek and said, "Master Earek. Welcome."

"My Lady," Marquiese said to Marilana, his tone respectful and his smile genuine. And then to Earek, "Master Earek."

"My King and Prince. Good morning." Earek bowed.

Zariff held the chair out for Marilana, and Earek did the same for Lady Annabella. Marilana looked across the table and returned Marquiese's warm smile.

They ate a pleasant breakfast. Marilana listened to the good-natured, but always insightful gossip from the previous evening. Everyone had something to add, and the news came from as far away as Lentier and Coandor. Marilana said little and was particularly careful not divulge the gossip Altia had shared with her last night; that she would hold close to the vest.

"You are very quiet this morning, Marilana," Lady Annabella mused as a servant refilled her tea.

"I really do not have anything much to add." Marilana looked up from her plate and laughed. "I must admit, I was rather preoccupied during the evening."

"Surely at least one of your dance partners said something of worth, even if by accident," Annabella teased.

"As Earek was quick to note, most were too busy drooling to do much else." Everyone laughed, though Marilana was too self-conscious to look in Marquiese's direction.

"Come now," King Rylan chided lightly. "I seem to remember one dance that caught everyone's attention. Surely he had something worthwhile to say."

"You are correct, Majesty," replied Marilana, struggling to keep her expression serious and unreadable. "There was one dance in particular. Though it seems the young gentleman in question always chooses his words with particular care in case someone might overhear."

"A wise young man." King Rylan smiled at his son, while Earek, Zariff, and Annabella chuckled. Marquiese blushed slightly in the face of this good-natured ribbing, but Marilana looked away before the heat could rise in her cheeks.

"What about your dance partners, Master Earek?" Zariff said, leaning forward. Though he was clearly teasing, he said it as if expected a wealth of pertinent news in reply. "Surely they had something more interesting to say than Marilana's infatuated lot."

"They all seemed uncommonly hesitant about being too open," the black leopard answered. "I suppose that is to be expected for now."

"Was there one among the noble daughters that you particularly liked?" asked Annabella lightly.

"I . . . I could not say after just one dance, Mother," Earek fidgeted.

Marilana glanced at Marquiese again. Their eyes met, and Marilana was quick to note the Prince's mischievous smile and the glint in his eyes.

"Well, perhaps you will know them better after a few more dances," Lady Annabella said behind narrowed eyes and a wry smile. They waited as a wave of servants removed their breakfast dishes and refreshed their tea, and then Lady Annabella looked spiritedly at the newest members of her family. She said, "Now we must leave the gossip behind and discuss matters of more importance. You two have a lot to learn with not a lot of time to learn it. I want you both to take advantage of the Royal Library while you are here. The books of law are precise and well kept. You should study them and the records of disputes managed by the Royal Court of Law. King Rylan has agreed to allow you to study the Family Annuals as well. Those are the records kept regarding all the noble families, their genealogies, adoptions, inheritances, and holdings. Also their disputes. Never forget their disputes.

"Now that you are family, your names will be added to these books too. It is a good place to learn about the other families and where allegiances and political lines lie."

"Yes, My Lady," replied Marilana and Earek together.

Then the noble lioness' eyes settled on her former ward. She said, "Marilana, Sir Libor informed me that you made a strange inquiry of him, but he did not say what exactly it was."

Marilana took a deep breath and met her mother's gaze. She said, "I asked if he had access to any records regarding the Hungdie."

Marquiese and Earek exchanged inquisitive glances. King Rylan stiffened. Zariff leaned back in his chair and waited. Annabella moved not a muscles, saying simply, "And?"

"Sir Libor said he was not familiar with any references to the myths, so I asked if I might study the histories. I looked for any strange deaths, disappearances, or assassinations, anything that might indicate Hungdie involvement."

"The Hungdie are a myth meant to scare children, girl," growled Zariff. "You were wasting time better spent on other studies."

"Peace, Zariff," said Lady Annabella without looking away from Marilana. "Marilana, I am going to insist that you refrain from pursuing this search any further. Is that understood?"

"If you insist, My Lady," Marilana replied calmly.

"You will both continue to study the histories, however," Annabella said looking from Marilana to Earek. "With your new positions, you are entering the political arena, a field you are unfamiliar with, and one with some sharp claws. The laws, annuals, and histories are good places to begin. You need to learn what motives drive the nobles, what problems the merchants and peasants have faced, and what choices previous royals have made, good and bad. Hear this: When you are done, I want you to be able to read the motives behind every word someone says and every gesture anyone of any caste makes. Clear?" She waited.

"Yes, My Lady," Marilana said. Earek nodded emphatically. He said, "Absolutely."

"Earek, you already know the merchant caste, and you have made good progress with the peasants. Marilana, you know the merchants, bandits, mercenaries, and peasants better than most. You need to share what you know and take in what you do not. Prince Marquiese has offered to help you learn about the nobles and royals, and you could not have a better resource. I will only be here for two more days, but I will also be available to you for questions while I am here, if need be."

"Two days?" Marilana heard something in Lady Annabella's voice, and it set off an alarm. "But you have only just arrived. Why are you leaving so soon?"

Their eyes met, and Lady Annabella smiled thinly. "You have a unique gift for reading people, Marilana. Cultivate it." The noble lioness tried to change subjects. "Do you wish to remain here at the Royal Palace for another month? I encourage you to do so."

"I do," Marilana answered firmly. "However, I also want to know what you are not telling us."

"Very well." Annabella sighed. "The bandits are behaving strangely."

"Strangely how? Are they attacking? Are they gathering arms? Have they kidnapped anyone or made demands?"

"That is why I am returning early. To learn more about their activities."

"I should return with you," Marilana said flatly. "I, better than anyone else, can find out what is going on."

"Marilana!" Marquiese interrupted sharply. "You are a noble now. Your days as a bandit hunter are behind you."

"The oaths of a bandit hunter are for life and do not change by caste," Marilana replied without looking at him.

Lady Annabella raised her paw, silencing them both. Marquiese sat back in his chair, angrily crossing his arms, a scowl painting his face.

"Knowledge is power," Annabella said calmly to the newly ordained Lady Marilana. "Your knowledge and the knowledge you would seek would be helpful, of course, but it is not needed right now. I would prefer you to remain here. Continue to study as I have directed. Concern yourself with gaining the knowledge you need to be safe here at court and to navigate the pitfalls of politics. I have high regard for your skills and knowledge. Trust that I will call for your aid when it is needed."

"Yes, Lady Annabella." Marilana sighed, concern and unhappiness touching the corners of her mouth. "But will you at least tell me what you know so far?"

"We have other people reporting to us now, young lady. Capable people," Zariff growled. "Indications are that the bandits are withdrawing beyond the southern border into the mountains. We do not know why. It is not something for you to worry about."

"Thank you, Zariff," Annabella said sternly.

Zariff ground his teeth and sat back.

"Further reports are coming in now, and we need to be there when they arrive," finished Lady Annabella.

"Is The Phantom involved?" Marilana asked, her concern obvious.

"Yes," the noble lioness said gently. "It was she who first alerted us to the situation. We have sent out trackers and they have also confirmed the situation. We sent out a second wave just before we left. We will know how concerned we need to be when they report back. Meanwhile, I need you to devote your thoughts to your studies while you have the time."

"Yes, My Lady," Marilana said, her sigh audible.

"Very good," King Rylan said briskly. "I had Sir Libor open the annuals to Marquiese before he left this morning. You may start your studies as soon as you wish and Sir Libor will be able to help you when he returns in a few fifnights. If we are done here, I need to see to other business yet this morning."

King Rylan rose and everyone else followed suit. Marilana curtseyed as the King started toward the doors. She met Marquiese's eyes and could see the anger smoldering there. She drew her shoulders back, her eyes calm. Lady Annabella must have seen an encounter brewing, because she stepped between them.

"Your Highness, I have some matters of importance I would like to discuss with Marilana in private. Would you be so kind as to assist Earek in starting his studies in the library?" Annabella asked pointedly.

"Of course, Lady Annabella," Marquiese said drawing a deep breath. He glanced at Earek, then nodded toward the door. "Shall we?"

"I think we should, yes," Earek said, sharing a quick wink with Marilana.

The young lioness watched the pair leave. Zariff followed them out without a word and closed the door. Marilana looked at Lady Annabella and waited. The noble lioness studied her newly anointed daughter critically for a moment, then gestured toward the couch. Marilana sat, her posture rigid, her eyes calm.

"Firstly, I want to know what you determined in your search for the Hungdie," Annabella said quietly.

"I found several instances that I am confident were the work of the Hungdie," Marilana said evenly. "But Sir Libor is correct; there are no direct references to them."

"I understand your need to search for such information, but you should not have asked Sir Libor directly. There is too much fear in the stories. And if you are right that they target royals and nobles, then there could be restrictions on who knows about them. King Rylan was not pleased that you had asked about them. I told him it was just a curiosity, and I know Earek and Marquiese would support that assertion. You need to be more careful here. Rumors of your interest could be used against us and could draw unwanted notice."

"I understand. And I will be more careful in the future," Marilana said.

"Secondly, I know how important your vows are to protect the innocent from the predation of bandits." Lady Annabella said this gently but with total conviction. "I want you to know that I have no intention of making you forsake your vows or to prevent you from performing your duties as a bandit hunter."

Marilana saw the warmth in her mother's eyes. She also saw her strength. "Thank you," she said simply.

"I will ask you to think carefully about how you will proceed, however. As a bandit hunter, you vowed to protect, though not necessarily to kill. You have gained considerable knowledge, and, as I said, knowledge is power. I will not tell you what to do. As a lioness with her own view of the world— a view I deeply respect—you need to come to your own conclusions and live according to your own heart."

"I have devoted my life to the pursuits of a bandit hunter; it will not be easy for me to change."

"I know. Change is never easy. I am glad beyond words that you accepted my invitation to be my heiress. I was concerned that your lifelong devotion to the hunting of bandits might cause you to refuse."

Marilana shook her head. "In my heart I have been prepared to become a noble for many years, even though I refused to let myself hope too strongly for it. It has been four years since I set out in pursuit of any one bandit's head. The fact that I am not troubled by this should have indicated my changing passions, although I did not acknowledge my feelings. I have abdicated this role to The Phantom and am content with that. As for my other duties, I hope to balance my vows as a hunter with those of a noble and make you proud."

"You have already made me proud, Daughter," Annabella assured her. "I will not pressure you one way or another, although there is another who seems to have a very firm opinion about it."

"Yes." Marilana sighed. "He did seem quite angry. Well, I will have to try to calm the Crown Prince down enough to at least talk sensibly about the subject."

"I wish you luck with that." Annabella vouchsafed her a smile. "Which brings us to our last topic of discussion."

"That being?"

"Just how you wish to proceed with your dear friend Marquiese."

"Honestly, Mother, I do not know." Marilana laughed and blushed and shook her head all at the same time. "I get butterflies just thinking about it. The fact that he is the Crown Prince and the most sought suit in the kingdom hardly concerns me. When I was just Marilana the orphan and he was just Marquiese the merchant's son, I daydreamed of his courting me. I always had the feeling that it was a pointless fantasy since his secret lay between us and prevented him from getting too close to anyone. Then I found out he was royalty, and I knew nothing could come of our friendship. Now, I am nobility and do not know what I want. Should I jeopardize our friendship by pursuing him on that level? I have known him for four years and there were times when I thought he would willingly open courtship with me. Other times I felt a resistance to a closer relationship. I am at a loss as to what to do."

"That is one benefit to a family," Annabella said, gently laying her paw on Marilana's. "I can see plainly that you care a great deal for him. Even in your questions just now, I can see that you would allow him to court you. That you are willing to find out if you are right for each other. This is what I suggest. Stay here this month with him and see what comes of it. Do not press him. Let him come to his own decision. Time will tell what road lies before you."

"Thank you, Mother," Marilana sighed. "Your words have calmed my thoughts. You are right. I do want to find out if he shares my affection and if it will grow into something more. I must be honest with myself if I am to be honest with him."

"Very wise, Marilana. Now, what gossip did you hear from your serving girl that you did not wish to discuss with the others?"

"How do you know about that?" asked Marilana curiously.

"Because I know you, Marilana." Annabella laughed. "You would have quickly made friends with the servants upon your arrival. You would have thought of them as your equals as you think of most people."

"I promised Altia that our friendship would be kept secret. It is not that I do not trust the others, but I do not want to betray Altia's trust."

"Caution is good," said Annabella, nodding her approval.

"Mother," Marilana said with great hesitation. "I have a question. A rather personal question."

"That is another benefit to family. The right to ask personal questions."

"Do you love King Rylan? Is he why you never married? Altia said that he was here for a rather long time last night."

Annabella studied her for a moment and then sighed.

"I suppose you should know my heart, now that you are fully my daughter," Annabella said quietly. "Yes, I have loved him since I was your age. I have told you before that he is my dear friend, and that I am one of his closest supporters, but I should give you a better account so that you understand my position more fully."

She took Marilana by the paw, as if doing so gave them both additional strength. "Queen Sahry was my best friend long before she became queen. She was a high-noble of Maefair and an absolute joy to spend time with. I cared so much for her. And she me. We both sought Rylan's favor, and I dare say he had a hard time choosing. In the end, however, he chose Sahry. I was happy for my friends and pushed aside my disappointment. Throughout it all, Sahry and I remained close, almost like sisters.

"When she died, I was heartbroken. So was Rylan. So much so that he pushed me away."

"But why?"

"Because I reminded him of her. Of all the wonderful times we shared. Then Prinka entered the picture, and he married her. I was furious. I could see that Prinka was infatuated with him. And perhaps he thought for a time that he loved her. I knew he could never love her like he had Sahry." Annabella shrugged, but there was sadness in the gesture. Then she filled her lungs and was calm once more. She said, "At first, Prinka saw me as a threat and restricted my visits to the Royal Palace. Later, she stopped caring what I did, or anyone else for that matter. Now she takes notice of Rylan only for public ceremonies."

"And yet you have remained loyal to King Rylan," Marilana said.

"Yes, though we have had our disagreements over the years. I finally forgave him for marrying Prinka, and I have been a source of comfort to him, especially when Marquiese was in hiding. Like anyone, Rylan needs to relax once in a while and talk with someone he can trust. I provide him that. Also an outlet for his frustrations.

"I have never shared his bed, however, no matter what the rumors say," Annabella said firmly, holding Marilana's eye. "And I will not, not as long as he is married to another."

"If he were no longer married to Prinka would you consider marrying him?"

"Oh, Daughter," Annabella said, smiling ruefully, "marriage is a pursuit of the young. He and I have spent many nights in each other's company, and we are happy just to be close to each other. I doubt that he will marry again if Prinka finally loses her hold on him. It might be possible for me to share his bed as a lover, but mostly he and I have found shared enjoyment in games of strategy. He is an avid chess player, and

I am hard-pressed to beat him at backgammon. We have accepted our relationship and uphold our responsibilities."

"But you do love him," the young lioness said.

"Yes, Marilana, I do love him. And yes, he is the reason I never married. But his friendship is worth more to me than any mere act of passion. I will not risk losing his regard just to say I once shared his bed."

"Okay then. What about Zariff? Where does he stand in your affections?" Marilana persisted.

"Ah, yes, dear Zariff." Annabella smiled. "He is my right paw, my sword, and my shield. He was a Knight of the Realm, a peasant that achieved high honor and was accorded rank equal to a high-noble. He rode with King Rylan and my father in the last kingdom war and was named a Hero of the Realm. Back then, I frequently visited the war camps to learn strategy and carry messages. Zariff fell in love with a serving woman I had in my retinue and chose to move to the Southern Tip after the war. My father was very impressed with him, so he offered Zariff a post in the Southern Tip guards. Zariff accepted, and he and I got to know each other well. He and my serving woman married and lived many happy years together, but never had children. When I took over the running of the province, I needed a Captain-General I could trust. I offered the position to Zariff, and he accepted. He and I have grown very close, especially after his wife died nearly twenty years ago now. He is like a brother to me. Similar to the relationship you have with Earek, a trusted friend and confidant."

"I thought as much."

"You know, of course, that he has always thought of you as a daughter. He took you under his care and training the day I took you in. He has looked after you and loved you all these years. He would have adopted you himself, but I asked him not to."

"Because . . . ?"

"Because I wanted to adopt you myself one day. I did encourage him to treat you as he would a daughter, though he needed no encouragement. I know you think of him as a father figure. He is your family too, even though he does not share our family name," Annabella said. "I expect you to take care of him when he is aged and weakened."

"And I will dote on him like only a loving daughter could," Marilana said with fond amusement.

"I know you will. And, I expect you to keep every word of this conversation to yourself," Annabella admonished. "Zariff would hate for me to be talking about him in such an intimate way, although he would admit every word is true. Also, my feelings for King Rylan, were they confirmed, could be used as leverage against us. Tell no one, even Earek. I will tell him if he asks, but only when I feel he is ready."

"I understand." Marilana smiled. "Thank you for telling me, Mother. I feel better knowing the truth."

"And I feel better knowing that you know my heart. Thank you for being brave enough to broach the subject." Annabella smiled. Then her eyes narrowed. "Now, what else did your maid have to say? I want to know it all."

The two lionesses spent the rest of the morning discussing news and gossip both had heard recently. Where background was needed, Annabella filled Marilana in. Where gossip, rumors, and facts overlapped, the two gleaned what facts they could.

Marilana held back only one piece of information, that being her suspicions involving Ailse Kenhol and Master Castant. She wanted to test her suspicion with the one creature who she knew could confirm it.

Later, Earek joined Marilana and Annabella for lunch. The trio then went back to the library and spent the afternoon studying the Redsands' history and law books. Annabella directed them to specific events in the histories and then showed the laws that resulted. Marilana enjoyed the discussions and engrossed her thoughts fully in her studies. The time flew as it often did when she was hunched over a book, and it was late afternoon when their session ended.

"Time to ready ourselves for dinner," Lady Annabella said.

In very little time, Altia had Marilana cleaned, dressed, and ushered out the door. The young lioness felt a nervous flutter as she and Earek followed Annabella into the dining hall. She was a noble now, and these occasions would never be the same.

Marilana saw Marquiese watching them from his seat at the head table, and she realized with regret that the chairs that had previously been her's and Earek's were no longer there. Since becoming Lady Annabella's heirs, they were no longer present at Marquiese's request. They were there in their own right representing the Southern Tip. They would now sit with the rest of the assembled visitors.

When King Rylan entered the room, all stood. It was only then that Marilana realized there were no place settings in front of Prinka and Frishka's empty chairs, and no sign of the tigers. *Interesting. I wonder where they have gone.*

Dinner wasn't the same. She missed her conversations with Marquiese. Yes, a number of nobles engaged her in small talk, but it wasn't the same. He looked lonesome sitting by himself at the table of honor, and she felt lonesome sitting so far away.

However, she was once again drawing the attention of many of the young males in attendance, and she was glad Altia had helped her with her face paints and powders. *If they want to look, let them,* she thought.

When dinner was finished, Lady Annabella led Marilana and Earek to say good night to King Rylan and Marquiese.

Then together they made their way to the palace entrance hall where many of the visitors stood around talking.

Annabella turned casually to her in the middle of the hall. "Marilana, I have a few things I need to discuss with Earek. Your evening is your own. You may continue your studies or pursue any other activity you wish."

Earek shared a puzzled look with Marilana before quickly following Annabella toward the guest rooms. Marilana watched them go as she thought about what she wanted to do. It was the first time that she was not joining King Rylan for an after dinner talk, or going on a walk with Marquiese. In fact, she did not know what Marquiese was doing this evening. A quick glance around the entrance hall was enough to make her decide she could not just stand there. Many of the young men were watching her and waiting to see where she would go. Calmly she motioned to Karndel and headed toward the library. Several of the young men smiled as they watched her walk out of the entrance hall. She nodded politely to them but continued to walk briskly on her way.

As she and Karndel reached the turn to the hallway leading to the library, she glanced back the way they had come. No one was in sight. She made a quick left into the servant stairs and descended to the lower level of the palace. Karndel chuckled.

"You find something humorous, Guardsman Karndel," Marilana asked quietly.

"You've spent the last month acquainting yourself with the lower level of the palace, and now I know why. Those young lordlings are going to have a difficult time keeping track of you."

"Thank you for that very astute assessment," Marilana said with a thin smile. "And thank you for bearing with me."

"Prince Marquiese warned me that you might make my job difficult, but so far joining in your adventures has been an absolute delight."

They made their way past the dungeon and the armory, up the servant stairs on the far side of the palace, out the doors to the stable lane, and into the gardens below Marilana's balcony. Marilana found a secluded bench at the far end of the gardens.

"I need to collect my thoughts for a while," she told Karndel quietly.

"As you wish." The guard took up a position that honored her privacy without impeding his vigilance.

It was peaceful and quiet and afforded her a perfect view of the stars. She had always loved staring up at the stars, though usually laying on her back in a field of tall grass far from everyone and everything. It was the perfect setting for thought and musing, and tonight she spent it thinking about her future and the best way to balance newfound responsibilities with old ones.

A soft sound caught Marilana's attention—footsteps growing louder with each passing second—and she arose and moved silently into the shadows. She looked in Karndel's direction and saw him come to attention, saluting in the direction of the approaching steps. Marilana relaxed.

A moment later, Marquiese rounded the corner and stopped a dozen paces from her, his scowl obvious.

"So here you are," he said coldly. "I do not mind you giving your admirers the slip, but I would rather not search high and low when I want to find you."

"Had I known you were looking for me, perhaps I would have chosen a less secluded bench." She stepped from the shadows. "Is there a reason for your scowl, Your Highness, or should I guess."

"Yes, in fact, there is."

"In regards too?"

"This morning. Your tone."

"My tone! I see. Well, then, I should apologize," she said, her voice even and measured, her posture still and poised. "Perhaps I should not have been so harsh. I do, after all, value your opinion. Perhaps I should not have been so quick to stop you from voicing it."

"Marilana," he replied, his voice quiet now in an attempt to control his anger. "I am glad you value my opinions. Please listen to what I have to say. Hear me out and think about what I am about to say."

"I am listening, Marquiese," she replied, her face serene and watchful.

He turned away from her and looked up at the stars. He took several deep breaths before facing her again. She did not back down, she wanted him to know she was being open and honest. Although she cringed inwardly facing his powerful, angry eyes. She hated to be the source of his ire.

"Marilana, you are a noble now," he began seriously. "More than that, you are heiress to a great-lady. You have accepted the responsibilities of that station. You have to remember that you now have many people, peasants, merchants, and other nobles, relying on you to uphold the laws of the land, settle disputes, and direct their lives. Your every action and every decision affects others. You can no longer risk your life for no more benefit than to satisfy your sense of revenge. You killed the men who hurt you; you have had your revenge. It is time for you to move on. You must stop being a bandit hunter and start devoting your life to being a noble worthy of your people."

Marilana turned away. She took her seat on the bench once again, her back straight, shoulders back, paws crossed in her lap. She looked up in to his eyes, holding his gaze, and said, "Marquiese, I am afraid that you do not understand. The vows of a bandit hunter are for life. I cannot simply stop being a hunter just because my caste has changed. I have spent most of my waking hours fulfilling my oath, and I will not stop now. I did not become a hunter for purposes of revenge. I became a hunter to protect others from harm. I killed the men who hurt me, because they beat, abused, and killed the two maidens who were with me, not because of what they did to me. I thought you understood that. The oath of the bandit hunter is not to kill, but to protect. I thought you understood that too."

Marquiese sat down next to her. He lowered his voice and said, "I did not mean to suggest that being a bandit hunter is not a worthy vocation. And I know how much your vows mean to you. I only meant that as a noble you cannot afford to run off into the forest whenever you choose to gain some shred of information or to deal with a bandit personally. You have to be protected."

"I seem to remember saying something similar to you," Marilana reminded him.

"Yes, you did. And now you need to follow your own admonition. Your life before others."

"We clearly look at this differently, Prince Marquiese," Marilana said, calmly still holding his eye. "As a noble, I am responsible for protecting my people, exactly as I am as a bandit hunter. The two vows are not conflicting. As Lady Annabella said, knowledge is power. I intend to use my knowledge of bandits to help me with the choices I make as a noble."

"I suppose that is true," said Marquiese looking aside. "I may have assumed wrongly that one could not be both bandit hunter and noble. I should have known you would not take your new responsibilities lightly. There are, however, many dangers that the upper castes face, and you have not yet learned to see them. The intricacies and intrigues of court may not be the bloodletting fight of your past, but it is still dangerous. The entire population of the Southern Tip could be affected by your decisions. The Southern Tip is the largest province in the kingdom, and although it is not the most populous, you still wield considerable power now. Knowledge is indeed power, but knowledge is also the road to making the best choice possible, whatever the issue. Please be careful."

Marilana shared a smile. She said, "Your words mean a great deal to me, and I am touched that you care enough to say them. I am learning to be a noble, but I also do not want to be ruled by caste alone."

Marquiese looked back and smiled. Marilana could see that his anger had been replaced with concern.

"You are my dear friend," he said warmly. "I do not want you to be hurt, but I cannot protect you if you put yourself in danger."

"You are repeating my words to you back at me. Not fair."

He chuckled. "You were wise and right to say them to me when I was in your domain. Now you are in my domain."

"You want to protect me? I see." She smiled. "For that I thank you. But, as it always has been, it is still my duty to keep you from danger, by choice and pleasure."

Marquiese chuckled softly. "Perhaps we can agree on our mutual duty to protect each other. How does that sound?"

"As you decree, My Prince, so shall it be."

Marquiese threw his head back and laughed heartily. "Come along, oh cunning one." He stood and offered his paw to her. "We got very little sleep last night, and tomorrow is another busy day. May I escort you to your rooms, or do I have to make a decree for you to walk with me?"

"If it is my choice," Marilana teased, laying her paw in his, "then I would say you must decree that you will escort me to my rooms."

"I think perhaps you should not be allowed to study the law. You already twist words around dangerously."

Together they walked back to the palace, laughing and teasing, their argument set aside, but not forgotten.

*

The next day was indeed spent in long study. Annabella tutored Marilana and Earek again in history and law. Marquiese joined them in the afternoon so that they could study the Family Annuals, Sir Libor having entrusted the Prince with the key. That evening, Lady Annabella again announced in the entrance hall that Marilana was free to do as she wished for the rest of the evening. As she had the night before, Marilana acted as if she were heading for the library. Only this time she actually did. She peeked out the library window and watched a group of young lordlings on the front steps of the palace looking perplexed and shaking their heads. She couldn't help but smile.

"They are actually working in teams tonight," Marquiese said as he closed the door behind him. "After you gave them the slip last night, they were determined to find you tonight before I did. Unfortunately for them, I knew you would be here."

"Yes, you did have an unfair advantage," Marilana teased.

"Actually, I had an unfair advantage last night too," Marquiese laughed. "Altia saw you go into the garden and clued me in. She would not tell the lordlings, though."

"The maids in any household can be a good resource if one treats them well," Marilana said with a grin.

"Even with that hint it still took me half the night to scour all the garden paths before I finally found you."

"But am I worth the effort?"

"Most definitely worth the effort."

"Which reminds me," the young lioness said with a playful laugh. "I have a question for you."

"Really? I cannot wait. What about?" Marquiese asked smiling.

"Mistress Ailse Kenhol."

"Oh, Ailse. A kindhearted girl. Have you met her?"

"Unfortunately, I have not yet had the good fortune," Marilana said watching his face. "But I am wondering how Master Castant sneaks her out of the great hall without anyone making the connection?"

The Prince's eyes widened. "How would you know about that?"

Marilana laughed. "One plus one. Altia tells me that Ailse has developed a reputation for slipping out after the first dance of a gathering and then suddenly returning before the end, and that no one knows where she goes. You told me the other night that Master Castant had slipped out to spend time with a secret lover. And you just confirmed my suspicion."

"You tricked me, Lady Marilana." Marquiese plopped into a nearby chair. He shook his claw at her playfully. "And after I promised Castant his secret was safe with me."

Marilana sat in the chair next to his and laid her paw on his. "Don't worry, his secret is safe with me too."

"We were careless," he replied seriously.

"Not at all. You trust me, and he trusts you."

Marquiese looked up and met her eyes. They smiled at each other.

"You are right, I do trust you," he said with a nod.

Just then the door to the library opened and one of the young lordlings, a lean and strapping puma, hustled in. "Ah, ha! Found you ...," he proclaimed. And then he saw Marquiese. His eyes snapped to Marilana's paw, resting on Marquiese's as she leaned close and smiled. The young puma stammered his apology. "Ah, Your Highness, please excuse the interruption."

He bowed, backpedaled, and closed the door behind him.

Marilana blushed fiercely, but Marquiese laughed. They both looked out the window. A moment later, the main palace doors opened, and the interloper hurried out. He spoke rapid fire to the lordlings out front, and every eye glanced up at the library windows as he spoke. One of them, a fierce looking brown bear, threw his hat on the ground and stomped away. Soon enough, they all dispersed.

Marilana looked back at Marquiese and they laughed. He said, "Two nights in a row you have eluded them. They will be harder to trick in the future."

"There are many suitable hiding places in this palace, and I can elude them far longer than they think. And besides, two nights in a row you have found me first."

"Yes!" Marquiese brightened. "And with luck, I will find you first every time."

"Luck!" Marilana proclaimed, teasing him. "You mean inside information."

"I will consider myself lucky then if I continue in your good graces so that such inside information remains available to me."

"You will need luck if you strain my favor, young Prince." Marilana blushed.

"Then I should refrain from noticing the flush of color blooming in your cheeks," he said with mock formality.

"Restraint seems beyond your grasp." She laughed and slapped his paw playfully.

10

"I am not sure I should leave," Annabella said worriedly. "You have been a noble for only three nights and already you have resorted to eluding the lordlings."

It was an overcast morning and Marilana and Earek were saying their farewells to Lady Annabella as she prepared to return to the Southern Tip and her estates just east of Mystillion.

"What difference would it make if you were here?" asked Marilana with a touch of irony. "You announce that I have no duties to attend to and that I am therefore available for pursuing."

"The lordlings are more cautious and less forward while I am close," Annabella stated with a deep frown.

"Mother, do not worry." Marilana laughed. "I may be new to this whole match-making business, but I am well trained in courtesy and evasion. I can cope with the lordlings for at least a month. Besides, I am not alone; I am sure that Earek and Marquiese will help me, if need be."

"I promise to look out for my sister come hook or crook," Earek announced calmly.

"Alright," Annabella said, sighing. "Be cautious at dinner too. The lordlings may try to engage you in conversation hoping to get you to agree to continue the conversation after dinner. I wish some of my allies were here, but they will not come to court for a while yet. Try to sit next to some of the older married nobles, but beware of introductions they may want to make. I may be back in a fifnight anyway. If the reports are good, I will return to spend the National Day of Worship with you. Take care of each other. And be careful."

"We will," Marilana said, smiling.

"That is what brothers and sisters do, Mother. They take care of one another," Earek assured her.

Annabella embraced them and then climbed into her carriage. Marilana waved as the carriage moved down the drive with escorts front and rear. Together, Marilana and Earek turned and made their way to the library for another day of study.

"Her concern is endearing," the young lioness said.

"Her concern is genuine, and I share it," the black leopard replied. "And I intend to act as such."

Marilana hooked a paw through his arm, smiled, and said, "Thank you for both your concern and your presence. What new noble could ask for more?"

That evening Marilana sat between Earek and an elderly zebra couple. Lord and Lady Bostwik had yet to meet Lady Annabella's heir and were pleased to converse with her. A pack of eager lordlings sat close by, but they dared not interrupt the elderly high-nobles of a county in Abdshar.

It was a pleasant dinner, though Marilana was disappointed to see that Prinka and Frishka had returned to their customary seats. Frishka's gaze frequently settled on her, but Marilana ignored him as best as she could. After she and Earek said goodnight to King Rylan, Earek escorted her to his room for a quiet evening together. Marquiese joined them after he was done with his duties.

"The lordlings watching the hall were not very pleased to see me join the party," Marquiese said, laughing. "I think they were hoping Earek would invite them to join the after dinner conversation."

"How rude of me. I will try to make amends tomorrow night." Earek tipped his head back and laughed.

Earek served them tea, and the friends fell into a spirited conversation. Marquiese enlightened Earek on the merits of the various noble daughters who seemed most interested in him. Marilana shared the gossip Lady Bostwik had bestowed on her at dinner. Earek talked about the food, fashion, and sports that he had discussed with the lordlings.

When the night grew late, Marquiese escorted Marilana back to her room.

Altia was waiting for her.

"I must say that you have been doing a fine job eluding the lordlings seemingly in hot pursuit of you," Altia said, giggling brightly. "Almost as well as Prince Marquiese is doing eluding nearly every noble daughter in Maefair."

"He is?" It was, of course, a silly thing to say, but Altia responded as if Marilana was a complete novice in the war of the matchmakers.

"He is the most eligible bachelor in the kingdom, is he not?" she said. "The daughters have been positioning themselves around the dining hall exits every evening since your elevation to nobility. He has lots of practice at the eluding game, however. He has been doing it ever since returning from his years of silence. The daughters are not as forward as the lordlings, however, so he can usually walk past them with a polite nod. You will have to be careful whenever you visit Maefair unless you publish a ban. I think things will get easier once His Highness makes a suit. My guess is that he will ask you soon enough."

"Do you really believe that?" Marilana asked nervously.

"Let me think!" Altia struck a sarcastically thoughtful pose. "He has spent time with you every day since you came here, including the past three evenings when you were no longer his guest. He has avoided spending any extra time with any of the daughters for the past year. You and he are close friends, but he is sometimes lost for words with you. He is helping you study and learn how to stand for yourself among the nobility. And just this evening King Rylan sent this invitation for you and Earek to join Marquiese and he for breakfast while Lady Annabella is absent. Correct me if I'm wrong, which I am not, but I dare say that not one of the other daughters have ever received such invitations."

"Has it ever occurred to you, my nosy friend, that perhaps he sees me as just a good friend."

"Well then I suggest you take your own advice," Altia said gently. "Be seen, push not, and let time take its course."

"That I will do." Marilana smiled. "I will see you in the morning. I have a breakfast to attend."

"Goodnight, Marilana." Altia curtseyed, turned on her heels, and closed the door behind her.

*

The next morning dawned bright and sunny; it was as if the day were expecting something extra special. Altia helped Marilana wash and dress for breakfast. When she was ready, Marilana left her room and greeted Karndel, her ever-present guard. Earek emerged from his room, offered her an arm, and escorted her to breakfast with Saffon, his own guard, following behind with Karndel.

"Good morning, Majesty. Good morning, Highness," Marilana said as she entered the breakfast room, and Earek echoed her. She curtseyed. He offered a deep bow.

"Ah, and a good morning to you both," King Rylan said warmly. "Come sit with us and have something to eat."

It wasn't until after their meal that King Rylan came to the business of the moment, saying, "Today, as you know, is the first day of the new month. It is the day I hold Open Court. Anyone can bring his or her petition to me to be heard. As is our tradition, nobles are allowed to sit and listen to the petitions. I would like it if you both would come and learn something of the proceedings. Lady Annabella agreed it would be beneficial."

"I would be honored," Marilana replied seriously.

"I too would like to see how you judge such petitions," Earek agreed.

"Good. I am pleased you see the value in watching such proceedings," King Rylan stood. "Follow me."

They followed the King and his son to the great hall. Rylan took his throne on the dais, and Marquiese sat behind and to his left. Marilana and Earek took chairs along the side of the dais to the King's left that were set aside for any nobles viewing the proceedings. There were only a few other nobles in attendance, and they sat far enough away so that they might converse among themselves without being overheard.

When everyone was seated, the doors were opened. A long line of petitioners followed a steward into the hall. The steward stopped, bowed, and read the name of the first petitioner.

Actually, it was rather dull sitting there listening to people of all castes complain about their lives and their neighbors. Marilana spent most of her time studying King Rylan and Prince Marquiese. She was quite impressed. Both acted as if the petitioner in front of them was the most important business they had at that moment. Even when there was nothing that they could do about their plight, they always had some bit of advice or another to give. King Rylan was fair and just in his rulings no matter how honorable or petty the petition was. He never awarded anyone with gold or treasure or anything of a monetary measure, but he always advised them where they could get help in the city or how to better their lives.

The last petitioner of the day was an old puma, obviously a poor peasant, who twisted his cap in agitation as he entered the room. Marilana watched with great intent as he approached the King. The old puma bowed awkwardly and swallowed several times before he could speak.

"My Lord, Your Majesty, My King," he stammered, "I . . . I'm just a humble farmer see, and well, I uh, I need your help. It's my daughter, see, she, um . . . she's been taken."

"Take a deep breath and calm yourself," King Rylan said gently. "Who has taken your daughter?"

The man took several deep breaths before continuing.

"My daughter was taken by bandits, Sire," he said hoarsely. "She was berry pickin' in the forest, see, and she never came back. We got a note for ransom. We got no money to pay a ransom, Sire. I don't know what to do."

Marilana fought to hold her face emotionless as she watched the old man pleading for help and a wave of anger swelled her chest. King Rylan turned toward Marquiese as he did some times to consult with him, but instead of meeting Marquiese's eyes, he locked eyes with Marilana.

"I wish to consult with one of my nobles, if you don't mind, sir," King Rylan said to the puma. The King stood and motioned for Marilana to follow him into his private sitting room. He studied her for a moment before saying, "What would you advise our dear farmer?"

"His pleas are heartfelt, but the girl is more than likely already dead," she replied sadly. "You cannot afford to pay every ransom, nor should you. It would embolden the bandits to try for more. I would tell him to procure the services of a qualified bandit hunter. If there is any chance the girl still lives, a skilled bandit hunter would her best bet."

"And what about you? Would you hunt these bandits for him?"

"No, Your Majesty," Marilana said without hesitation. "I do not know the area well enough. He should go to the local magistrates; they will know the local bandit hunters and be able to put him in contact with one."

"Clearly he has no money to pay for such a hunter," King Rylan reminded her.

"Some of the hunters will try a rescue without pay," she replied calmly. "The magistrates will know which ones."

"Very well," he said laying his paw on her shoulder. "And thank you."

She nodded and followed him back out. The old man watched Marilana nervously as she resumed her seat.

"I cannot help you with the ransom," King Rylan told the old man gently. "You should go to your local magistrates and ask them to put you in contact with a bandit hunter who is willing to attempt a rescue without charge. Tell them I sent you. I cannot promise that your daughter will survive, but that is her best chance."

"Yes, Your Majesty," the old man said tearfully. "Thank you and blessings on you."

When the hall was empty of both petitioners and nobles, they retreated to King Rylan's sitting room.

"So," he asked Earek and Marilana seriously, "what did you learn from your observations?"

"You are just and wise, Majesty," the black leopard said promptly. "You devote your full attention to each petition, and give honest responses. I respect that highly."

"And do you know why, Earek?"

Marilana watched Earek without interrupting.

"I assume that you want to provide the best assistance to your people and hear what their greatest concerns are," the black leopard said. "By listening to these petitions, you can get a feel for the condition of your people."

"Very good. And what would you add to that answer, Marilana?" King Rylan said, glancing her way.

"By allowing the people to bring you their concerns, you create the impression that you care for all of them. They have the chance to hear your words personally, to see your concern, and visit your home. It strengthens the bond between you and your people. They love you all the more for it. It also gives you an avenue of information other than your nobles. You have a chance to hear from the people if what the nobles and soldiers report is accurate."

"Precisely!" King Rylan smiled. "While I trust the reports I receive, I know that if I hear something that contradicts those reports, I have an idea of where to look for the problem. Remember this: a ruler can never strengthen his or her bond to the people enough. Every chance to show the people that you care, even if you cannot help them directly, is a good way to secure their loyalty."

"Sire, why did you ask for my advice regarding the last petitioner when you already had your answer ready?" Marilana asked quietly.

King Rylan sat back in his chair. He studied her with a slight smile. Marquiese frowned darkly. Earek looked surprised.

"I wanted to know what you would say," King Rylan finally said. "I knew the man's story would touch your heart. I wondered if you would want to help him yourself."

"You would not have let her go hunt these bandits, in any case," Marquiese stated firmly.

"What would you have said to the man, Marquiese?" King Rylan asked.

"I would have said very much the same as you did," Marquiese replied, his frown still pronounced. "He will have better luck with a local bandit hunter; they know the terrain; they know the trade. We could not pay the ransom, of course, because it would set a poor precedence and make the situation worse."

"And you, Earek, what would you have done?" the royal lion asked the black leopard.

"I do not know what I would have said," Earek replied honestly. "I understand why you and the Prince responded the way you did. My first reaction, though, would have been to consult with Marilana. There is no greater bandit hunter in all Redsands than The Ghost."

"Very good. Consulting with an advisor when you do not know what choice to make is both prudent and wise." King Rylan nodded. "I consulted Marilana for that very reason. I have never consulted with a bandit hunter in person, and I would have been amiss to ignore her experience. She is correct though; I had already determined a course of action. You always have to have a plan in case you cannot consult an advisor and be willing to adapt your plan as more information reaches you."

"So her words did not change your decision," Marquiese said flatly.

"I considered her words very carefully." King Rylan frowned at his son. "Marilana, please repeat your advice for Marquiese's sake."

Marilana did, word for word, her voice calm and assured.

"So you did not offer to hunt the bandits yourself?" Marquiese was surprised.

"I did not. I do not know the local area well enough. If I had to hunt this area, my first step would be to find a local hunter to act as my guide," she replied, meeting Marquiese's eyes.

Marquiese sat back and studied her for a moment. "Your advice was sound," he said finally. "Though I am not surprised in that."

King Rylan pressed his palms together, smiled, and sprang to his feet. "Come now. Petitions have taken most of the day, and we have missed lunch. We all need to get ready for dinner, because I, for one, am quite famished."

Earek and Marilana parted company with the King and Prince and walked to their rooms.

"So, truth be told," Earek said as they paused in front of Marilana's door, "why did you not offer to go on the hunt?"

"I was honest," she replied earnestly. "I do not know the local area. Aside from that, I am heiress to a great-lady; I have to consider that situation in my choices now as well."

"I noticed that Marquiese seems to think you need to be reminded of that."

"Yes, he has a firm opinion on the matter," Marilana said without emotion.

"I happen to agree with him, but I also know you can make your own decisions."

"Thank you, Brother." Marilana shared a crooked smile and went into her room.

*

Only an array of compound torches and the yellow-gold of a waxing gibbous moon lit the archery range.

"I doubt the lordlings will think to check the practice yard to find you," Marquiese said, approaching Marilana from behind. "Especially at this time of night."

Marilana loosed her last arrow. It arced through the dark night and struck solidly into the center of the target. She lowered her bow, and they watched a young recruit collect her arrows. All twelve were perfectly centered, and the soldiers watching the display murmured appreciatively.

"Nice shooting. And I am not the only one who thinks so," the Crown Prince said with a nod toward the crowd of soldiers. "You have not lost your touch."

"I had not practiced for a while, and there is no excuse for not practicing," the young lioness said matter-of-factly. "Archery helps clear my thoughts, and shooting at night is a good challenge."

They walked toward the armory. Marilana returned the bow and quiver to the armsmaster, a huge black bear with a knotted face. The bear snatched the weapon with a grimace and turned away without a word.

"I think my father and Lady Annabella will both be hearing about this from our rather gruff armsmaster," Marquiese said in a low, conspiratorial voice, "and I doubt he will be complementing your skill."

"Meaning?" asked Marilana.

"You came out here alone, in the dark, to shoot arrows in your evening finery. Rest assured, the old bugger does not think it proper," Marquiese replied, laughing.

Marilana looked down at her light blue evening gown and shrugged.

"Obviously I did not think about how it would look to a gruff, old black bear," she admitted. "However, I had a lot on my mind and needed to clear my thoughts."

"Only you shoot arrows under a waxing moon to clear your thoughts," the royal lion said with obvious admiration.

"Oh? And do you not focus on the moment when you practice sword play or jousting?" she asked lightly. "Shooting arrows does the same for me; it allows me to focus on the moment and pushes aside any stray thought that might try to distract me."

"Yes, I suppose I do understand that," mused Marquiese.

They entered the kitchen gardens and strolled along the path at a more leisurely pace.

"You are thinking about that farmer's daughter, are you not?" Marquiese said gently.

"I just wish I knew if she was one of the lucky ones who survive unscathed. Unlikely, but that does not stop me from wishing."

"You cannot help everyone," Marquiese said, gently placing his paw on her shoulder and stopping on the path.

"I know that, Marquiese," she said, looking up at him. "Something about it bothers me, though, and I cannot stop thinking about it. What bandit sends a ransom note for a simple farmer's daughter? The answer is obvious. They do not."

"You think something else is going on, and they sent the note to cover up her disappearance?" Marquiese frowned. "What else could it be?"

"I do not know," Marilana replied with frustration. "I would bet my last arrow that something is wrong, but I cannot find a plausible alternative."

"Whatever it is," Marquiese said reasonably, "you gave good advice to my father. I know it must have been hard for you to resist going on the hunt and using your skills to help."

"Not as hard as you think," Marilana said, her eyes moving elsewhere. "To tell the truth, I have not hunted any one specific bandit since the summer before you came to the

Southern Tip. I still patrolled around Mystillion and protected the town as needed, but I was content to let The Phantom do the head hunting."

"Well, that was easy. Lady Annabella asked you to stay close to protect me," Marquiese pointed out.

"Yes, and while I was protecting you, I discovered, that I did not have the urge to do more," she replied. "After you left, I still did not go out on the hunt. I helped The Phantom and I patrolled the area around Mystillion. I protected the county from raids, and I escorted the children to and from school. But the need to do more was gone."

"What about Lady Annabella? You were her prized bandit hunter," Marquiese reminder her.

Marilana shrugged. "She never asked me to hunt during that time. She seemed happy to keep me closer to home. Now I know she wanted to encourage the feelings so that I can more easily leave the hunt to others."

"If you feel this way, why continue to call yourself a bandit hunter?"

"Because I still am a bandit hunter. And always will be," Marilana said firmly, meeting his eyes again. "I will not stop protecting my people. I will just do it in different ways."

Marquiese sighed irritably, but let the subject drop. They started walking again. Frishka slinked past, smirking as always, and they both ignored him.

"I was thinking," Marquiese said in a brighter tone, "that tomorrow we could go for a drive. I have not shown you the seacoast yet, and I thought you would like to see it. Such uncompromised beauty. You will love it. My father needs to do some work in the library and said he would be happy to help Earek with his studies while we are away. I think we could both use a break from the Royal Palace."

"That sounds nice." Marilana smiled. "I have never gotten to see the seacoast up close, only glimpses from inland as I traveled. The only opportunities I had to visit any of the coastal villages were in service of Lady Annabella, and kept me way too busy to stroll on any beaches, I am sorry to say."

"It is settled then. Tomorrow morning after breakfast. With one caveat. I need to review part of the guard, so we will have to be accompanied by a half legion of cavalry, if that is alright."

"That will be fine." Marilana chuckled. "After what happened on our last outing, I will be comforted to have as many guards as possible with us."

"I doubt anything like that will happen again." Marquiese flushed slightly. "I learned my lesson about offending tournament hosts."

One of the lordlings walked past with a sour expression, and Marilana laughed softly.

"Perhaps we should be worried about offended lordlings."

"Perhaps we should." Marquiese smiled and offered her his arm.

11

It was the pitch black of night between moonset and dawn when Marilana awoke to a quiet thud in the hall outside her room and the sound of her door latch quietly opening. She was moving before she was fully awake, rolling to the edge of the bed closest to the wall and crouching, poised and ready. Having had no reason to use the healing trance tonight, she had been sleeping deeply, and it took several seconds for her thoughts to completely clear. She listened intently, her eyes searching the darkness. The last thing she wanted to do was hurt some maid or guard who had come to fetch her, but something about the depth of this silence caused her hackles to rise.

Fool! She chided herself. *You know better than to grow complacent. You should have suspected something like this would happen and taken better precautions. Marquiese warned there was danger here.*

Marilana knew that her guard, Karndel, and Earek's guard, Saffon, were the only ones on duty in the guest hallway since every other guest had departed the palace earlier. She also knew how easy it would be to overpower two men, especially if they were taking turns sleeping.

The lamps in the hallway must have been intentionally extinguished. Even so, Marilana caught the movement of darker shadows moving silently toward her. Her thoughts raced: *There are at least two, maybe more. Probably more in the hallway. Not maids and not guards.*

Marilana chastised herself for not learning the tricks of the secret door in her bathroom. She could not directly see the French doors leading out to the balcony but knew that unlocking them and climbing down would take too long.

So, get past these in my room, surprise the ones in the hallway, and escape down into the servant quarters. At least there you can lose them long enough to get back up to the Royal Family Apartments.

Unfortunately, with Master Castant away from the palace, she didn't know who among the guards she could trust.

The first shadow rose up at the head of the bed. Another approached at the foot. Now that they were closer, she could make out four distinct shadows. Marilana threw one of the pillows toward the foot of the bed and launched herself toward the head. She caught the canopy post, swung into the air, and planted her feet in the stomach of the shadow. He grunted as the wind burst from his lungs. This one was large and strong and recovered quickly, evidently a bear, and clearly well trained. Instead of flailing back, as Marilana had hoped, allowing her momentum to carry her past him, he doubled forward and wrapped his huge paws around her legs. Together they crashed to the floor. Marilana twisted and struck at the bear with blows that would have rendered a lesser creature unconscious. But not this one. He rolled and pinned her legs under him. Three more shadows descended on her, restraining her arms, and holding her fast against the cold stone floor. A paw clamped down over her mouth and a second on her throat. Marilana stilled, knowing that one wrong move could crush her windpipe and kill her immediately.

The unpleasant fish smell of the emaciated tiger told her it was Frishka well before he spoke. And when he did, his voice croaked, hoarse and guttural.

"You are spirited, I like that. Do as I tell you or I will kill you." Marilana felt the paw at her throat flex slightly and knew it was Frishka's paw. "Today, when you are driving along the shore, you will invite Marquiese to go down to The Beach with you. You will know the place when you see the well-worn path dropping over the edge of the cliff. It is an easy decent to the sandy shore at the bottom. You will tell no one. If you do, your dear friends will suffer the consequences."

He was so close that she could feel his lips and teeth against her ear as he whispered and was nearly overwhelmed by the fish stench in his breath.

Marilana strained against the paws pinning her down, but Frishka's grip tightened, cutting off her breath. Her last thought as she lost consciousness was that she should have just killed them. Killed every last one of them.

*

When she awoke again, she was in bed, and the sun was up. Marilana took a deep breath and felt her neck where Frishka's paw had been. There was a slight soreness, but less than she had expected. Getting up she went to the wardrobe and examined her reflection in the mirror. No bruises, no cuts, no marks at all were left from her early morning visitors. Marilana's hackles rose as she realized Frishka had skills that made him far more dangerous than she had suspected. She hurried to the hall and threw open the door. There was no sign of Karndel or Saffon. She rushed back into the room, threw open the balcony door, and sprang to the rail. She surveyed every inch of gardens and the paddocks beyond. Nothing, all was quiet in the immense palace grounds within the walls.

Marilana dressed quickly, pushing aside her anger and calculating her next move. By the time she left her rooms she had decided that the best course of action was to discuss the events with Marquiese and King Rylan.

She knocked briskly on Earek's door and waited. There was no answer. Turning away, she walked quickly through the hallways and knocked softly on the door to the breakfast nook. She went inside and froze when she found Marquiese and his father and two empty chairs. Where was Earek?

"Good morning, My Lady," Marquiese said standing up and smiling at her.

"Good morning, Your Majesty. Good morning, Prince Marquiese," she said much more formally than intended. "Will Earek be joining us?"

"We were hoping so. We expected him to be with you," the King replied.

"He was not in his room and his guard was not at his door. He must have gone out early," Marilana said by way of explanation, a very flimsy explanation at that.

"It is not like Earek to go off without informing someone," Marquiese protested.

The lioness shrugged and went to join them. "Perhaps it is a girl."

"I can think of no better reason," the King said as breakfast was served. "And are you excited to see the seacoast today, young lady?"

"I cannot wait. It will be a first for me," she replied. All through breakfast she tried acting normally, making small talk, and hoping against hope that Earek might hurry in, filled with apologies. That didn't happen.

When breakfast was over, the King excused himself, saying he had a full day ahead. Marilana and Marquiese got to their feet and bade the King farewell. Then the Crown Prince turned his attention to the lioness beside him. "Are you ready for a buggy ride?" he said with a warm smile.

When Marquiese saw Marilana's hesitation, he frowned. Concern etched his handsome face, and he said, "Marilana, is everything alright? You have been distracted all morning."

More than anything, Marilana wanted to confide in the Prince, tell him how she had been attacked, tell him that she knew Earek had been taken prisoner. But Frishka's words echoed in her ear. *You will tell no one. If you do your dear friends will suffer the consequences.*

Marilana forced a smile. "Oh, yes," she lied. "I am fine. I just realized I forgot my scarf. I will meet you in the entrance hall as soon as I find it."

"Do not be too long," Marquiese said. He also forced a smile. "The seacoast awaits."

They parted in the hall, and Marilana hurried toward her room, her feet barely touching the ground, even as her heart beat fiercely in her chest. She burst through the door and was relieved to find Altia cleaning.

"Altia. Oh, thank goodness," she said to the caracal. "I need to write a letter, and I need you to deliver it to King Rylan personally."

"Yes, of course, but . . . My Lady? Are you all right?" her maid asked.

Marilana drew parchment and pen from the writing desk, sat, and began composing a formal letter.

"Do you know any of the guard accompanying me this morning?" she asked Altia, her pen still moving across the page. "Anyone you would trust beyond a shadow of doubt is *not* one of Frishka's men?"

Startled, Altia paused and then answered, blushing as she spoke, "Captain Lorne. He is a cheetah, a good man, and loyal beyond doubt to King Rylan and Prince Marquiese. I have spoken with him and he commonly voices his dislike of Frishka and his traitorous ways."

"Lorne? He is the one I advised you about?" Marilana asked gently.

"Yes," Altia admitted. "He is."

"Thank you, Altia. Please deliver this message to the King an hour after our convoy leaves. And I need a scarf to match this dress, quickly," Marilana said putting the final touches to her letter.

When she was done, she folded the parchment, sealed it in an envelope, and gave it to the maid. She tied the scarf around her neck and hurried through the palace to the Entrance Hall. She saw Marquiese waiting impatiently by their buggy.

Marilana stepped outside, but didn't immediately join Marquiese. She first identified Captain Lorne and approached him quickly. She did not know the place Frishka had called "The Beach," but she hoped the guard captain knew the local area well enough that she wouldn't have to describe it.

"Captain Lorne," she said quietly. "A word please."

"My Lady. At your service," the guard said, tugging the reins of his horse.

"I need to trust you with a very dire situation, and I have but a moment to explain it. At some point during our ride today, I am going to take a walk with Prince Marquiese along the seacoast."

"Yes, My Lady."

"As we move down the path to the place called The Beach, I require that you and your men surround the area as quickly and silently as you can. Wait for my signal before acting, no matter what you hear or see. I will shout a name. It will not matter whose name. That will be your signal to arrest everyone on The Beach. Everyone. Myself and Prince Marquiese included. Do you understand?"

"My Lady, what is this about?" he asked cautiously.

"I am placing you in charge of springing a trap meant to capture individuals I know to be guilty of treason. I was told by one who I trust that you are loyal to the King and can be trusted with this. Do you agree to act as I have instructed?" she replied firmly. "Yes or no?"

"Yes, My Lady. I will act as you have said," he replied gravely.

*

It was a pleasant morning and a beautiful drive. Or it would have been had Marilana not been so distracted. She managed a less-than-inspiring conversation with Marquiese even as her mind played through every possible scenario once they arrived at the seacoast. In the end, she decided that following Frishka's instructions and taking a walk along a beach was the only way to save Earek, and she would do almost anything to save her newly anointed brother.

"If you were anymore distracted, I would accuse you of wanting to be taking a carriage ride with someone else," Marquiese finally said as Marilana spotted the entrance to The Beach. Most of the shore was a jagged line of steep cliffs, but one spot had a clear path over the edge. She could not see the sandy bottom from the road. It was, she realized, a perfect ambush site, and Marilana could only hope that Captain Lorne had sufficient skills to pull off an ambush of the ambushers.

"I would want to take a carriage ride with no one other than the company of the most handsome lion in the kingdom," she said, touching Marquiese arm and painting a solemn smile on her face. "Can we walk a bit and talk privately?"

"Yes. Of course. I can think of nothing better," the Prince said.

Marilana felt as if someone had just twisted a hot poker in her insides when Marquiese called a halt to the driver and their guardsmen. She looked Marquiese straight in the eye as he offered his paw and helped her from the carriage.

"May I hold your arm?" she said, not waiting for a reply before placing a paw firmly by his elbow. "Am I being overly bold?"

"Not at all," Marquiese said, a shadow of concern crossing his face before placing his paw on hers as they set out for the path.

Marilana quickly scanned the rocks around the beach. She did not see anyone, but she knew they were there.

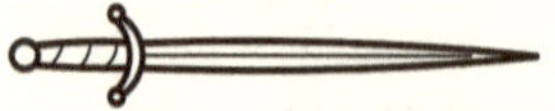

Marquiese was uneasy. It was not like Marilana to conceal her thoughts from him, and, despite her attempts at conversation and levity during their trip to the coast, she was visibly agitated about something. She had smiled at him, but even her smile was laced with distraction. She met his eye, but it was the eyes of a bandit hunter staring back at him. Something had definitely put her on edge.

Marquiese watched Marilana closely as they descended the path and moved across the sand. As they neared the water's edge, Marilana spun suddenly to the side. "Look out!" she hissed, letting go of his arm.

The Prince wasted a moment of precious time glancing inland, and his reaction was an instant too late. A heavy, entangling net dropped down over him. All around them, creatures of all types, all heavily armed, menacing, and traitorous, swarmed from hiding places across the beach and stepped forward creating a half circle blocking him from the path through the rocks to the road. Earek stepped from behind Marquiese to stand next to Marilana, both avoided looking at him.

"Well, what have we here? A little princeling caught in my net," Frishka called. He stepped out of the shadows of a large boulder, stopping a dozen paces from his captive. He looked from Marilana to Earek and snorted. "You two have done very well. When I am King, I shall show you the gratitude you deserve."

Earek hunched slightly as if to protect himself from the power of those words. Marilana's reaction was quite the opposite. She looked up sharply and struck an impervious pose. Marquiese recognized the rage and focus in her eyes. He struggled against the strands of the net, but it was heavily weighted and several of Frishka's men were stepping on the edges.

"And now what, snake?" Marilana shouted forcefully. "You have accomplished nothing."

"The Prince here will be charged with treason. Trying to undermine the King," the tiger said cunningly. "That is hardly nothing."

"You traitors!" yelled Marquiese. Fury rose in him. He tried to draw his sword, but the net prevented it. "Guards! Guards!"

Frishka laughed as two of his accomplices twisted the net and pinned Marquiese's arms to his sides.

"You should pick your friends more carefully Marquiese," Frishka sneered. "It was so thoughtful of you to bring a black leopard into the Royal Palace who can be so stealthy. It was also so good of you to place your trust in such an undeserving peasant maid."

Marquiese glared at Earek and Marilana, and she in turn glared at Frishka with pure hatred in her eyes. She stepped up onto one of the many low, broken boulders that littered the beach.

"Frishka!" Marilana yelled, her voice full of rage and echoing across the beach. "You will not get away with this!"

"Silence her," Frishka snarled. But even as he turned to signal his band of traitors, Marilana lunged at him with all her considerable skill. Her attack took the tiger fully by surprise, and she flung him from his feet. They rolled across the sand, Marilana's skirts flying wildly. The force of her attack caused her to roll off him and back onto her feet. She crouched low, preparing a second attack. Frishka sprang to his feet and drew his sword. "How dare you attack me, wench!"

The tiger froze as a short sword suddenly crossed in front of him, coming to rest on Frishka's sword arm.

"What is this? Do you know who I am?" Frishka sneered.

"I do, sir," Lorne said as his men appeared all around, taking one and all prisoner.

Marquiese stared in total shock at the scene unfolding in front of him. An instant later, he recognized the Captain of the Guard as the very one Marilana has spoken to out in front of the palace. Cold fury burned in his gut. *She planned this.*

Marilana assessed the scene on the beach. It had gone as well as she could have expected. Her attack on Frishka had done its job, allowing the royal guards to sweep in unnoticed. As she had commanded, every creature within sight of the beach had been subdued and disarmed. The captain had indeed executed the trap perfectly.

"Your Highness," the Captain of the Guard called to Marquiese with the upmost authority and respect. "I am afraid I must take you under arrest and escort you back to the Royal Palace."

His eye fell upon Frishka. "The same goes for you, Your Lordship, and all here present."

"Me? Have you lost your mind?" Frishka demanded. "I have charged Prince Marquiese with treason. Why am I under arrest?"

"I do not know who is charged with what here. Only that everyone found here on this beach at this time is involved with treasonous acts in some way and so I will arrest everyone and take them to the King to let him sort out the charges."

"Very well, Captain. I will allow this for now; but know this, you will never again hold the rank of captain once I am done with you," Frishka growled.

"Be that as it may," Lorne said calmly, relieving Frishka of his weapons. "Please allow yourself to be escorted back to the palace peaceably."

"Captain, I commend you on the measures that you are taking. Your service to my Father will be rewarded," Marquiese said coolly, as two guards helped remove the net. When he was free, Marquiese gave a guard his own weapons, turned sharply on his heel, and accompanied them up the cliff.

"Lady Marilana, I hope that you also approve of my actions," the Captain of the Guard said in a quiet voice as he turned to her.

"Yes, Captain. You have done very well. I hope that it is enough to get this whole mess started down a path of truth finding. Now as I am also under arrest, we should speak no more of it until the King is fully apprised of the matter."

"Yes, Lady."

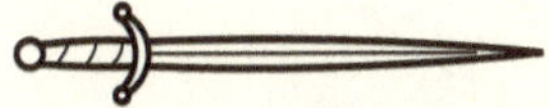

Marquiese eyed Marilana as she climbed over the top of the cliff and was pleased to see that a pair of guards also accompanied her. He was sure that she had instructed the captain to take everyone on the beach under arrest. He was also sure that her attack on Frishka had been a diversion to prevent any of Frishka's men from noticing the guards until it was too late. What confused him was Frishka's assertion that she and he were in league. Could that possibly be? *Not even if the heavens opened above them and The Goddess herself proclaimed it so,* he thought. Yet she had led him down to The Beach knowing it was a trap. His fury turned to ice in his stomach as doubts intruded into his trust.

Marquiese and Frishka were asked to ride in the buggy together. The captain rode next to the driver and the buggy was paced on either side by a guard on horseback. The rest of the prisoners were made to walk two by two behind the buggy.

Marilana and Earek were the last two prisoners. They walked a pace behind Frishka's men, side by side, but did not appear to be talking. A single guard rode behind them and the rest of the guards were spread out around the column of Frishka's men. After initially glancing back to make sure of the guards' placement, Marquiese refrained from looking back at Marilana and Earek. Frishka never looked back at all; he simply stared straight ahead, hardly even blinking. Marquiese watched for movement out of the corner of his eye, he never trusted Frishka sitting next to him, however, the journey back to the palace was uneventful.

When the convoy reached the palace, they made for the stable gates. There, the gate guard hailed them.

"Captain Lorne," he called from his station. "I have orders to place Prince Marquiese under arrest."

"Prince Marquiese and the rest of this party are already under arrest. I am conducting them to the King," Lorne replied from atop his horse. "Who issued that order, Lieutenant?"

"The order comes from the King himself, Captain."

"Very well," Lorne said dubiously. "You and one of your men will accompany us to the King."

"Yes, Sir."

King Rylan and his guards stood waiting on the palace steps as the legion moved solemnly up the lane from the stables.

"Lieutenant, my orders were to place my son under arrest," the King called. "Explain yourself."

"Forgive the Lieutenant, Your Majesty," called Captain Lorne before the gate guard could reply. "I took Prince Marquiese and Lord Frishka's party under arrest on The Beach as all are apparently party to treasonous dealings in one way or another. I brought them all to you to manage whatever charges may be dealt."

"Very well, Captain Lorne," King Rylan intoned gravely. "Marquiese, you have been charged with treason against me. Your accuser is Lord Frishka. You will be confined in the tower dungeon."

"That is ridiculous, Father. You know that," Marquiese called.

"Be that as it may, my order stands." The King turned to the gaunt and lean tiger, the misbegotten son of his Lady-wife. "Lord Frishka, you have been charged with treason against Prince Marquiese."

"But Your Majesty, how—"

"And the next person to interrupt me will be tied to the stake and flogged. Please do not force my paw," Rylan said. Then he began again. "Because your charge against him stands first, by law, your treason is dependent on his treason being proven false. You are hereby restricted to the grounds. You men that followed Lord Frishka are like-wise charged with treason against His Highness Prince Marquiese. You will be escorted to the lower dungeons. Lady Marilana and Master Earek you have been charged as conspirators to both treason charges. You are under arrest and restricted to your quarters. According to the laws regarding conspirators of your standing, you are placed in the direct custody of Lord Frishka. All of your chambers have already been searched for any incriminating documents."

Marquiese heard the entire pronouncement before being led away to the tower. It had sounded to him as though every word was causing his father pain. He hoped that it was the pain of being forced to do this by law, and not the pain of believing Marquiese was guilty. He was surprised however to find that someone had already placed the treason charge against Frishka. Marquiese had fully been ready to claim the charge, but someone else had already done so. The fact that his father had not acknowledged who had placed that claim was also surprising as the law stated that the person charged with treason should be told who placed the claim. The only way around that is if the person who placed the claim would be in danger if it were told. That left only two possibilities in Marquiese's mind. Marilana or Earek. The King was trying to protect them while they were in Frishka's custody.

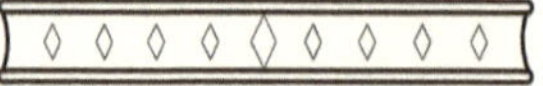

King Rylan stood on the steps as his orders were carried out. Marquiese passed him without meeting his eyes. Frishka's men were escorted away without emotion. Frishka yawned and stretched and shot a glance at Marilana before sauntering off toward his rooms.

The King had watched Marilana closely as he stated the charges. She had held an emotionless face, meeting his gaze eye-to-eye. However, what he saw looking back at him was a complicated and intriguing blend of bandit hunter and noble. It was full of focus, determination, and regret. It was a look Rylan had never seen before, and he wondered seriously if he could trust it.

The only change in her expression happened when the King pronounced that Frishka would have direct custody over Marilana and Earek. It seemed then that a challenging spark flashed in the lioness' eye before her gaze turned down in resignation. Even as the young noble was led past him, she refused to meet his eye, yet the set of her shoulders suggested strength and poise.

King Rylan was furious at Frishka for the flawlessness of the setup. The King was not sure even now on how to judge Marilana and Earek. He had accepted them, trusted them, and now Frishka was toying with them. Had Lady Annabella's heiress and second heir changed loyalties? Rylan could not tell. He would have to wait for the trials.

In the meantime, he needed to speak with Marquiese.

12

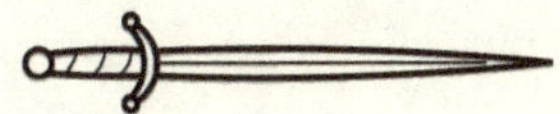

The door to the tower dungeon opened, and three guards escorted Marquiese inside. The tower dungeon may have been reserved for prisoners of noble standing, but this did not stop the guards from locking his wrists with manacles and securing the chains to an iron peg protruding from the wall.

The chains were long enough that he could lay comfortably on the straw mat on the floor, or at least as comfortably as one can be on a hard, stone floor with only a thin layer of straw. Marquiese sat brooding on the mat thinking of the events on The Beach. The dungeon door opened again, and he was only slightly surprised to see his father step onto the landing at the top of the dungeon stairs. Marquiese had assumed that Frishka would first want to engage the King in lengthy discussions to determine the course of the trials and the proper protocols for dealing with the "accused," but his father had obviously sidestepped that conversation for the moment.

King Rylan stood looking around the large, circular room. This was not a place for long confinement. The door was placed above the floor to discourage any foolish attempts at escape. The stairs divided the room into two areas, but guards looking in from the observation room could see what could not be seen from the door. Sunlight streamed in through the two barred windows. The smell of fresh clean, straw was prevalent.

"I wish to speak to my son privately," King Rylan said without looking at the guards.

"Your Majesty, that is not allowed according to the laws governing prisoners accused of treason," the guard responded timidly.

"Am I not King?"

"You are, Sire, but—"

"Then I will speak to my son alone," King Rylan raised his voice just slightly, but still did not look at the guardsman.

"Yes, Sire. My apologies." The guardsman bowed his head and retreated back out the door, closing it and locking it behind him.

King Rylan descended the stairs, bringing with him one of the guards' stools. He positioned the stool in front of Marquiese and sat.

"Forgive me for not standing up," Marquiese said bitterly.

"And forgive me for having to follow the laws in this matter, my son." King Rylan kept his voice low so that the guards at the door could not hear what was said between them. "I assume that you have already guessed that Marilana has accused Frishka of treason against you. Unfortunately, her charge was delivered to me an hour *after* you left this morning on your coastal ride. Frishka's charge against you was delivered thirty minutes earlier. By law, I must consider the charges as they came to me."

"I am aware of the law," the Crown Prince said bristly.

"Marilana signed the charge of treason against him, but also included her own name and Earek's as conspirators to the treason. I am unsure what to make of this."

"If she did so, then it must be true."

"Well, as I said, I am not quite as certain." The King paused. "I need to ask you if you would sign your name to the charges against Frishka. By doing so, I could name you as having placed the charges against him and could leave Marilana and Earek unnamed. I am concerned that Frishka may harm them both if he finds out."

"Why would I want to protect traitors?"

"My son, listen to your heart in this matter," the King said gently. "Marilana and Earek may be the only witnesses able to condemn Frishka. He has set this trap up so well that I am forced to put you on trial. By placing the charges against him, Marilana has allowed suitable doubt to be placed on his testimony and any evidence that is brought before the magistrates will be carefully examined for the smallest of errors because of that doubt. She may well have provided the only flaw in his plans. It will make the trials condemning you extremely hard to prove. Why she is doing it, I cannot say. All I know is that this act of hers is in direct conflict with Frishka's plans for you, and he cannot be happy about it."

"I would have thought my so-called stepbrother would have prevented you from coming and telling me all of this. I expected him to have lengthy conversations with you about the protocols and regulations for the upcoming trials." Marquiese looked away from his father as he spoke.

"Of course. But I have not given him that chance yet. I had to speak to you before he could interfere. He also seemed a bit preoccupied by thoughts about Marilana, if I read his mannerisms correctly as he left the courtyard a few moments ago. Which leads me back to the point about protecting her if I can."

"Yes, I will sign my name to the charges against him," Marquiese said at last.

His father unrolled a sheaf of paper listing the charges against Frishka, and Marquiese scrawled his signature across the bottom. He dropped the pen, shook his head, and said, "Though I must say that I do not like being indebted to a traitor for saving my life. Her actions might protect me, but she is also betraying me. I have to place charges against

Marilana and Earek for direct treason against me. I do not know how long they have been on Frishka's payroll, but they have played me like the biggest fool there has ever been."

"My son, I do not wish to believe this of them. I also trusted them. I trust Lady Annabella's faith in them. She has known them far longer than we have. We must wait to pass judgment on them until we have heard their testimony."

"I will leave the sentencing up to the Court, but I have no doubts that they have betrayed us. That she has betrayed me."

King Rylan sighed. "Very well. I must leave you now. I know not when we will be able to speak again, but I will do everything I can to get you out of here and be rid of Frishka for good."

King Rylan rose with these words, turned to the stairs, and left the cell.

Marquiese did not watch his father leave. It was good to know that the trust was not broken between them, and that the King did not believe a word of Frishka's charge of treason. However, it weighed heavily on his mind that Marilana and Earek had been used against him. Marquiese had always known it was a risk having them in the palace, but this was not a possibility he had considered even in his wildest dreams.

As much as their actions against him angered him, it pained him even more that Marilana was risking her life by charging Frishka with treason. Would it not have been easier for her to tell him of the trap awaiting them at The Beach rather than the charade of leading him down to the shore? What purpose could that possibly have served?

Marquiese understood Frishka's ultimate purpose, of course. He intended to eliminate the Crown Prince either by death or banishment so that he could become King. That obsession had always driven Frishka's plots. Involving Marilana and Earek was devious beyond words. It was brilliant using Earek to throw the net that entrapped Marquiese given his heightened sense of stealth. Using Marilana to lure him down to The Beach made perfect sense because he trusted the lioness explicitly. But how had Frishka gotten his two friends––though he now bristled at the word *friends*––to cooperate?

Marquiese had believed in Marilana and Earek's loyalty with his whole heart. Believed with total conviction that they would defend him at all times no matter the cost. Had he been so wrong in his judgment of them?

◊ ◊ ◊ ◊ ◊ ◊ ◊ ◊ ◊

Frishka looked up as King Rylan made his way down the last curve of the tower stairs.

"Your Majesty, I assumed you were checking on the condition of the prisoner, so I waited here for you." Frishka spoke smoothly, bowing his head in King Rylan's direction.

"Yes, everything in the tower has been taken care of. I assume you have made arrangements for the prisoners under your care as well?"

"Not yet. I wished to speak with you first."

"Speak then."

"I must ask, first and foremost, who charged me with treason." Frishka fell in step with King Rylan, who headed in turn for one of the palace's private conference rooms.

"Marquiese did."

"Marquiese! He arranged for the charges to be issued while he was away from the palace?"

"You charged him with treason. Should he not reciprocate that charge against you?"

"Indeed I did expect him too, yes. I simply find the timing *odd.*"

King Rylan did not miss the tiger's emphasis on the word odd. Whatever Frishka found "odd" was not good for Marquiese or, in this case, Marilana. The King wished that he could claim the charges himself, but, as the initial charges involved his son, the law forbade him to make countercharges. He was keenly aware that the deception was an inadequate defense for Marilana and worried that she would pay whatever consequences Frishka had in mind. The King had to try and protect her, if he could.

The King of Redsands and his stepson by way of his ill-advised marriage to Lady Prinka spent the next several hours debating and finalizing the protocols for the trials and the arrangements for the prisoners. Frishka had insisted that no private conversations be held with prisoners, and they finally agreed that all conversations must be witnessed by at least one individual willing to provide testimony, in court if needed, to the subject and extent of the conversation. The prisoners would have ankle manacles at all times and would have wrist manacles chained to their ankle manacles whenever they were outside of their confinement areas. The prisoners were also to have wrist manacles whenever someone was with them. Instead of being chained to the wall, Marquiese would have a heavy ball chained to his ankle, granting limited movement inside the tower dungeon. Frishka insisted that none of the prisoners be allowed in the courtroom for any testimony except their own, a requirement King Rylan wanted as well, though he feigned an argument in opposition before relenting.

As for Marilana and Earek, the tiger was adamant that they should be allowed to move about the palace grounds as long as properly chained and escorted. King Rylan disliked the idea of Frishka taking the prisoners for walks like prize pets, but could see no way to prevent it. When Frishka was satisfied with the arrangements, he left to go dress for dinner. King Rylan remained alone in the conference room, contemplating their arrangements and looking for any loop holes he could use.

The law stated that individuals charged of treason could only be trusted in the custody of the one who had filed such charges, with the exception of members of the royal family who could only be in the custody of the Monarch. The law had its roots in the fact that the full extent of a conspiracy was never known, and the only one who could be positively identified as not part of the conspiracy was the one who had charged the other. It did not take into account, however, that it provided the accuser with an excellent way of ridding himself of his own enemies.

King Rylan had always disliked that law, but had never had reason to have it changed. Now he was fully regretting it.

Marilana couldn't help thinking how badly her plan had backfired. She and Earek now found themselves at Frishka's mercy within the confines of the palace. Had she only instructed Altia to give King Rylan the charges against Frishka sooner. Yet the timing of the trap she had planned at The Beach was critical to Earek's safety. She had made sure no word of her treason charges could reach Frishka on The Beach before his arrest, securing Earek's safety. Earek's and Marquiese's safety were her primary concerns.

The sound of the lock clicking in the door alerted her to the emanate arrival of someone with authority. She turned from the balcony windows to see Frishka and three of his men entering her rooms. She had been expecting him—it was his job to explain the protocols in which she would live during the trials—but it still did not make it any easier for her to see him standing in her rooms, smirking at her in a truly evil way. Anger and fear clawed at her insides as he stopped to allow the door to be re-locked behind him.

"So you thought you would get away with that stunt, did you? Did you think I would not know that it was you who placed the charges against me? I know everything that happens at this palace. Well, it seems that I have out done you and am now in a position of greater authority over you. I can overlook the stunt, as it has done nothing to hinder my plans, but I cannot overlook the fact that you disobeyed my orders."

He strutted deeper into the room, sneering. "From now on, you will do as I wish. You will kneel when I tell you to kneel, eat when I let you eat, speak what I tell you to speak, and even dress according to my whim. You are nothing more than dirt on my boots."

He spoke with a slow menace that settled Marilana's insides to a solid mass of ice; she would have to deal with this one someday soon, and that thought would help sustain her during the time she could not harm him. "You dared to cross wits with me," he spat. "Now you will learn how wrong you were to even think you could outdo my superior intellect. I have the knowledge, the experience, and the power to quell any thought that comes into that pitiful peasant mind of yours."

"You will find that task considerably harder than you think." Marilana fixed a haughty expression on her face and spoke lightly as if his words were below her notice.

His back-armed slap was not unexpected. It was forceful enough to cause her shoulders to twist. He followed through with his other fist, hitting the back of her shoulder, and hooking her ankles with his foot. The lioness spun and fell hard. The back of her head slammed into the stone floor. Stunned, she turned her eyes up at him, pinning him with an unreadable gaze. She propped herself up on her elbows but made no move to rise or to roll sideways. He made a twitching motion to his men and one of them moved forward carrying a heavy chain.

"You will learn to speak with respect when addressing me." The tiger's expression was twisted with rage and his voice was harsh with anger. "From now until the end of the trials, you are in my custody. You will wear manacles on your ankles at all times. When you leave your rooms you will have your wrists manacled together and chained to your ankles. You will be chained likewise when you have visitors. I can escort you anywhere on the grounds at anytime I want to."

The man with the chain finished locking the manacles on Marilana's ankles and made sure that the chain was secure. When he was done, he rose and returned to his place with the other guards. Frishka took one satisfied look at the chain then spun on his heel and left.

Marilana listened for the locking of the door and the drumming of footsteps as they moved down the hall. She knew that Earek would be next. She listened but heard no raised voices, no cries of pain, no signs of a commotion. Not that she expected too. The stone walls were thick and designed for privacy. She also expected that most of Frishka's anger would be directed toward her and that Earek would not purposely provoke his anger as she planned to.

She sighed, then rolled to her feet. Pain shot down her arm. She was still slightly dizzy from the blow to her head, but managed to make her way to the couch and sit down on it. She was regretful that her analysis of the ill-bred tiger was so stunningly accurate. He was spiteful, malevolent, and relished cruelty. She was sure before all was finally finished between them that she was going to have to endure much worse at his paws. She wished she could fight back—oh, how she wished— but she also knew that her success in this campaign would be on the mental battlefield not the physical one.

Just then, a movement from the bathing room caught her attention. She looked up and Altia came forward with two bottles in her paws. She sat down next to Marilana and pulled a soft cloth from her pocket.

"For your shoulder," Altia said softly.

Marilana nodded. The caracal helped undo the laces of her bodice and eased the fabric over her shoulder. Then she opened one of the bottles, poured a sweet smelling liquid onto the cloth, and applied it to a bruise that was already becoming evident. She then poured a little liquid from the second bottle into a cup and gave it to Marilana.

"For the dizziness."

Again Marilana nodded and swallowed the liquid. "Thank you."

Altia put another dose of the first liquid on the cloth and began a very gentle massaging of the bruised shoulder.

"What made you say that to him? He was furious. I thought he was going to kill you," Altia whispered. Marilana looked her in the face and saw tears brimming in her eyes.

"An act of necessity, my good friend," the lioness answered calmly. "If he continued to think about the consequences of what I had done, then he would have seen the danger to his plan. Instead he will now only think of ways to punish me for what I tried to do and the words I use against him now. He will believe himself invincible against me, that I can never do anything to hurt his plans. But in fact, he will be unable to think beyond his anger at me to the truth. To the fact that I *can* stop him."

"But what if he does," her maid fretted. "Then he will kill you. I'm sure of it!"

"Yes, he will eventually see the truth, and he will eventually try to kill me," Marilana admitted. "He will almost certainly reach the point where killing me will be his only goal in life. But he will not kill me outright. He will want to torture me first; that is the way his mind thinks, and we can use that to our advantage. Even now he sees me as a challenge he wants to overcome. He wants to break my spirit and make me his obedient slave. That is good news. It has bought Prince Marquiese time to formulate a proper defense. And it has given King Rylan a means to break apart Frishka's carefully laid evidence. It will also make the magistrates wary and cautious."

"But it places you in great danger, My Lady."

"Yes, it does. I am accepting that danger and all the pain that will come with it. There is no alternative. This is the only way I can help Prince Marquiese, and that is my only goal now."

"I could get you out of the palace. I could help you escape," Altia said with growing urgency. "We could escape the borders. We could . . . could . . . ."

Marilana turned and took Altia by the shoulders. "Yes, we could. But can you leave the Crown Prince knowing he might lose his life? Can you run away from King Rylan, knowing he needs your help? Can you ignore the damage that Frishka will do to the other servants and to your friends and family if he finds out that you smuggled me out and ran away? Of course you cannot, my dear friend."

Tears began to stream down Altia's face, and she looked down at the rag in her paws. "No, I couldn't live with that knowledge. I also can't live with the knowledge of what he is doing to you. How can I? You took me in, made me more than I was, accepted me as your friend, and I care for you as a sister. Is there no place in your heart for that now?"

"Altia, you are my friend. I care for you and my heart will always have a place for you. I know it will be difficult. But I need you now more than ever."

"We could go to King Rylan," Altia blurt out.

"And we will. But it is too early yet to go to the King. Eventually, that is what you must do. When it becomes evident that the magistrates are in a position to accept your evidence of Frishka's treatment of me is when you must go to King Rylan. Until then you must be strong. I will need you to tend to my injuries, just as you are now, but late at night, when there is little fear of Frishka finding out. You are my witness. You are my hope." Marilana wrapped her arms around the weeping caracal and held her close. The dizziness was past and the pain in her shoulder greatly subsided. Altia's remedies were good ones. Marilana knew them as well, and had used them many times in the past. She knew she was in good paws and that the girl she was trusting in was strong and capable. She could ask no more.

Altia pulled back from Marilana's embrace and dried her tears. "I know we will survive. That's what we peasant maids do, isn't it. We do what we can for others, and we survive."

"Yes, dearest, that is what we have done, and will continue to do. It will be hard. I do not know how it will end, but end it will. Now you must go before you are missed. Remember, our time will come. Be strong."

They embraced again, and Altia bustled through the bathing room and through the secret door, her self-control firmly reestablished. Marilana wished that more of the rooms had the secret doors; it would have been easier to get messages to Earek if his room also had one. Frishka obviously did not know about the secret door in her bathing room, or he certainly would have taken action against its use. This was a bit of good luck.

Marilana got up and walked to the balcony. She scanned the area. If there was anyone watching, she couldn't detect it. She stepped out and left the door ajar, leaving a paw-width gap so she could hear if anyone entered. She inched her way to the edge of the balcony and stood in the shadows created by the approach of twilight. She scanned the palace grounds as far as she could see. Again she saw no one. She watched and waited. She had been teaching Earek signals for silent communication over the past six months, and on the way back from The Beach she had made three signals—private, twilight, and balcony— she only hoped he remembered them.

Shortly, she caught movement out of the corner of her eye but resisted the urge to look in that direction.

"We're clear." Earek's soft voice drifted from his open window.

"Do not look my way," Marilana whispered.

"I won't," came his answer. "Are you alright?"

"Yes. You?"

"Yes. Frishka paid me a visit. He seemed furious. Also distracted. Was that your doing?"

"Yes. I hope to divert his attention as much as possible from the trial proceedings. I assume we will not be allowed to hear anyone else's testimonies."

"None of the accused will be allowed hear anyone else's testimony. Which means Frishka will not be allowed to hear our testimony. I don't think he meant to tell me that part, but, like I said, he was rather distracted."

"Yes, I gave him a lot to think about. He wants to break me. He wants to make me his obedient slave."

"How can I help?"

"We tell the truth, no matter what he tells us to say, Earek. He will have his revenge for our disobedience, but we have to stay strong. It is the only way to help Marquiese."

"I had hoped you would tell Marquiese and King Rylan what was going on before bringing Marquiese down to The Beach."

"I am sure he had spies watching the activity of the palace, and people placed to relay to him if his trap had been betrayed to the King. If I had alerted them, then you would have died. I was not going to let that happen."

"I know. You are pitting yourself against him, and you need to learn his ways. I just wish you had spared yourself all the beatings that Frishka will visit upon you. When will you tell the Court about his punishments?"

"It will be his word against mine, and the Court will not believe me without proof. At some point, my maid will go to

King Rylan and offer witness to my injuries. I do not know when exactly, but the right time will present itself."

"I wish it weren't too late to talk you out of this plan, but I also hope that it works."

"It has to work, for our sakes as much as for Marquiese's."

"I know. Get some rest. I don't think that Frishka will be back tonight, but he will definitely want to wake you up in the morning. Good luck, Marilana my Sister."

"Take care, Earek my Brother. We will see each other again soon."

Earek waited for a few moments after Marilana had gone. Then he closed the door and turned to face his room. It was empty. He stepped sideways and peered back out the window. He saw no motion. They had escaped detection this time. He wondered if they would be as lucky in the future.

Earek cringed as he thought about Marilana's plan. He absolutely hated that they were both going to suffer at Frishka's whim. *Marilana, I know you are doing what you feel is best, but I wish you had just killed him on The Beach. I will follow your lead. I will be strong for you and for Marquiese.*

13

Marilana was fully awake when she heard the clicking of the lock in the door. She had slept, but only the shallow sleep of the healing trance. She would not resist. As difficult as it was to succumb to the insane bullying of a creature worthy only of her contempt, she would not resist.

She waited a few more seconds before pretending to give a start and to get up hastily. A well-muscled arm hit her across the shoulders. The force of the blow threw her back on to the bed and knocked the air from her lungs. As she gasped, four strong paws grabbed her arms and pinned her down to the bed. Frishka's weight settled across her shins. A true wave of terror swept over her. She had hoped that Frishka would refrain from taking pleasure from her body until she was obedient and compliant. She had been sure, in any case, that he would not want his men to be attendant on the act. Had she been so wrong?

"When you are my queen we will consummate our union properly. I will not take you by force out of wedlock as I have taken so many other peasant maids." He smiled down at her, certain he had caught her off guard. "At least as long as you still appeal to me as a future queen. If I ever decide that you no longer deserve such an honor, I will do as I wish with you and then dispose of you in whatever fashion I feel appropriate. Do you understand me?"

Marilana drew a deep, slow breath, controlling the pounding of her heart. She refused to look away or to nod, despite the sour smell wafting off the tiger and his men. He took her lack of response as an affirmation, crooning, "Good. Now, you will learn the lesson I did not have time to teach you yesterday. Respect is of vital importance to your continued survival. You will kneel to me every time I enter this room unaccompanied by witnesses other than my men. You will avert your eyes at all times. You will answer my questions promptly. Shall we practice?"

He stood and walked away from the bed. Four pairs of exceedingly strong paws launched her into the air. She curled into a ball and crashed down on her already bruised shoulder. Her momentum carried her into a roll that stopped at the feet of another one of Frishka's men, a huge and unkempt brown bear. His paws circled her upper arms in a vise-like grip and lifted her effortlessly off the floor. Frishka slammed his fist into Marilana's stomach causing her to pull her legs up into a curled position. The bear dropped her to the floor. She landed on her knees at Frishka's feet, clutching her stomach and gasping for breath, her nightdress askew. She concentrated on slowing her breathing, a process that took less than three seconds. The pain receded. She straightened her back, laid her paws in her lap, and kept her eyes on the floor. She fixed an emotionless, wooden expression on her face and said nothing. Frishka's slap barely caused her head to turn. At the edge of Marilana's vision, Frishka's men exchanged a look of surprise.

"Well, well, well. You do learn fast. You are resigned to doing my bidding without question. Curious." Frishka's voice sounded pleased with her apparent lack of resistance.

"I am resigned to your treatment of me," Marilana replied in a steady voice.

"So you will kneel to prevent being struck, is that it?" He spoke with a rumble of anger. "And what will you do to avoid pain, I wonder?"

Marilana didn't so much as blink. "I do not avoid pain. I will not try to avoid your anger."

Frishka lashed out with a side-angled kick. Marilana took the blow on her arm and rocked sideways. Frishka growled with rage. He grabbed her arms, pulled her to her feet, and slammed her back into the wall. She kept her gaze to the side so as not to look Frishka in the face.

"Even your submission reeks of defiance. I will not have it. I will break your spirit; it is only a matter of time." He spat the words at her as he pinned her to the wall. His paw came up hard under her chin; she felt a sharp explosion of pain to the back of her head and knew no more.

◇ ◇ ◇ ◇ ◇ ◇ ◇ ◇ ◇

King Rylan narrowed his eyes as Frishka entered the courtroom, followed by Earek and six guards. There was no sign of Marilana.

"Lord Frishka, all prisoners were required to attend court this morning. Where is Lady Marilana?" asked Lord Komph, the red fox Head Magistrate, with equal parts irritation and surprise.

"Yes, forgive me, Your Honors, but Lady Marilana seems to have had an accident in her room this morning," Frishka replied as if reporting the weather.

King Rylan leaned forward in his chair, his breath caught in his throat. Had he underestimated Frishka? Had the worthless excuse of a tiger killed Marilana and made it look like an accident? Marquiese had been brought into court moments before and had been standing proudly, staring emotionlessly at the raised Magistrates' Bench. Now he turned slightly, staring hard at Frishka, a frown tugging at his entire face. Earek, for his part, projected a resigned look, his eyes staring at a point beyond the Magistrates' Bench.

"Forgive me, Lord Frishka, but what do you mean an accident? How badly is she injured?" asked Lord Komph, also leaning forward in his chair.

"I do not know the full extent of her injury, but it appears that she tripped and hit her head rather hard. I had a servant run for the Royal Head Healer; he is caring for her now with the servant's help."

"Your Honors, I will look in on Lady Marilana after our session here today. But I think we can proceed a few days while she heals," King Rylan said from his seat behind and slightly above the magistrates' seats. He noted that Frishka's smile stiffened in response to this statement.

Lord Komph and the other two magistrates, Lords Hunmis and Quinre, nodded in agreement.

"Very well, Your Majesty," Lord Komph said. "We will continue for now."

"We now open the case of Lord Frishka versus Prince Marquiese, where the former accuses the latter of treason against his father, His Majesty, King Rylan of Redsands. All participants are present, excepting Lady Marilana, for this first session in order to hear the formal charges and the explanation of the trial proceedings. His Highness, the Crown Prince, Marquiese Mercurer, son of Rylan Mercurer of Redsands, is charged with attempting to undermine His Majesty, the King, Rylan Mercurer, son of Coryan Mercurer of Redsands, by conspiring with murderers unknown and Lady Marilana and Master Earek of the Southern Tip to force the premature retirement of King Rylan and the subsequent succession of Prince Marquiese to the Throne of Redsands."

Lord Komph looked up from his recitation to fix Marquiese with an evaluating look. "Do you, Prince Marquiese, deny these accusations?"

Marquiese met the Head Magistrate's look levelly, his eyebrows slightly raised. He said, "Yes, I deny these accusations."

"Very well. This trial will proceed in order to determine the guilt or innocence of His Highness Prince Marquiese as charged. The subsequent sessions of this court will be held with only one of the accused in attendance to obtain testimony for cross-referencing and verification of evidence presented. Lord Frishka Ebnic-Mercurer, second son of King Rylan Mercurer, you have been countercharged with treason against both King Rylan and Prince Marquiese for attempting to undermine their authority resulting in their removal from power. As this trial shall provide evidence about your involvement in treasonous actions as well as Prince Marquiese's actions, you are restricted from hearing witness testimonies. Also you are restricted to the grounds until further notice. The Royal Court of Law, consisting of His Majesty King Rylan, and Magistrates Lord Hunmis, Lord Quinre, and myself, Lord Komph, will determine legality and authenticity of all evidence presented. I declare this court session adjourned."

*

King Rylan waited outside Marilana's door as Frishka escorted Earek back to the confines of his room. When Frishka returned, the guard unlocked the door and let them in. Inside, the Royal Head Healer was giving instructions to the young maid as to the continuing care of Marilana, who was, at that moment, lying with eyes closed on her bed. When the healer was finished, he turned his attention to the newcomers.

"Ah, King Rylan, Lord Frishka. Good. I was just finishing up here." The healer smiled in his usual sad anteater way.

"What can you tell us, Healer Strunt?" asked King Rylan.

"Well, Your Majesty, Lady Marilana has a moderate concussion resulting most likely from a fall. There." He pointed one long claw to the far wall. "From the bruising I found on her arm and her shoulder, I would say she tripped, hit her arm on this chair-back, spun, and hit her shoulder as she fell. I would suggest that her head snapped back and hit the wall with more force than it might have had she not hit with her shoulder first. It may be several days for her to fully recover."

"Has Lady Marilana been unconscious this entire time?"

"The patient has showed limited signs of consciousness, but has said nothing coherent as of yet."

"Thank you, Healer Strunt."

When the anteater was gone, King Rylan stepped up next to Marilana's bed and looked down at her face. Frishka stepped up next to him. The King vouchsafed a sideways glance and caught a truly greedy look as it flashed across the tiger's gaunt face. An instant later, one of mild interest replaced it.

The King returned his attention to the bed as Marilana stirred. She opened her eyes and blinked, making a feeble attempt to focus on their faces.

"Ma . . . jes . . . ty . . . he . . . Frish . . . ka . . . hit . . . head," her words came out broken and slurred, barely audible in the quiet room.

"We are here, Lady Marilana. What are you saying?" Frishka nearly shouted the words, and Marilana winced at the uproar.

"Marilana, you need to rest. Do not try to talk now," King Rylan said softly.

"He . . . lies." Marilana struggled with the words, but there was no mistaking what she had said.

"Do not worry, child. Just sleep." The King placed his paw gently on the lioness' cheek and felt her drift back to unconsciousness. He glanced in the direction of the young caracal. "Take good care of her."

"Yes, Your Majesty," she replied.

The King and his second son left the room then, the maid having settled into a chair with a basket of mending.

"Given that interaction, Your Majesty, I would say you care a great deal for Lady Marilana?" Frishka fell into step beside King Rylan as they made their way toward the King's chambers.

"As for you, Frishka, your bedside manners are appalling," Rylan said. "You might try to remember that when dealing with someone with a concussion, they are highly sensitive to sound, light, and touch. Putting even one sentence together is difficult. The more they try, the more frustrated they become and the faster they become exhausted. Sleep is the best antidote. Now if you will excuse me I must prepare some correspondence before dinner."

He opened the door to the Royal Family Apartments and closed it behind him, leaving Frishka alone in the hallway. He walked to his study and paused, replaying Marilana's words. Had she conveyed her message correctly? What she said, that Frishka had lied about what had happened and the possibility that he had intentionally slammed her head against the wall, made startling sense. But why?

It took King Rylan a moment to realize that he wasn't alone. Someone was standing in the shadows watching him. He backpedaled a step and nearly shouted, "Who's there?"

"Your Majesty, forgive me for startling you. Your chamberlain let me in to await your return. It seems there have been many changes since I left only a fifnight ago," the young leopard said, bowing.

"Master Castant! You scared the daylights out of me, young man." The King shook his head and then smiled. "You have no idea how very glad I am to see you! We have a lot of work to do, my boy. A lot of work. Sit."

The King poured tea for them both and then spent the next half-hour describing all that he knew of the events of the past few days.

"Well, what are your thoughts?"

"I do not, and never have, trusted Frishka. Marilana and Earek, however, I came to trust explicitly. Marquiese's friendship with them, and my own interactions with them, led me to like them both very much and to consider them friends. It disturbs me to find so many mysteries surrounding their activities," Master Castant said thoughtfully.

"My thoughts exactly."

"However, I find Frishka's timing as perfect as ever."

"His timing?"

"Yes, he chose to attack at a time when all of your advisors were off on errands or missions. You had no one to consult nor anyone to help sort out all the possibilities."

"Indeed, yes, even you were not supposed to return from Lord Arndt's for another fifnight."

"Yes, and Lady Annabella was certainly not supposed to arrive back the first day of the trials."

"Lady Annabella? She is here? She just left a few days ago."

"Upon learning of the treason charges, she and her entourage chose to camp on the tournament field. She wished to be here for the Day of Worship Celebration, but returned early. She said she had a strange feeling, like she usually got when Marilana was preparing for a hunt, and decided she needed to spend time with her heirs. We were both shocked to find that they had been arrested. Marquiese as well. Lady Annabella's testimony on their characters may help once their parts of the trial commence."

The King shook his head. "Hmm. Her testimony may be thrown out as biased. Much as my own will be. However, it would still be good for the magistrates to hear it."

"Majesty, you spoke of Marilana seeming distracted at breakfast yesterday."

"Quite."

"And what of Earek's behavior?"

"Actually, Earek was not at breakfast. Which I thought a bit odd given that I had offered to help with his studies after breakfast. Marilana mentioned the possibility that he might be visiting a girl, but I assumed he was just taking the morning to rest while Marilana and Marquiese were out."

Castant jumped to his feet. "That is it, Your Majesty! Marilana was distracted because Earek was missing. She must have known or guessed that Frishka was also using Earek, perhaps even taken him hostage."

The young leopard paced from one side of the room to the next. "Of course! How else could Frishka have convinced Marilana to do what she did. He had to use a level of persuasion that she could not ignore. He had taken Earek hostage and was using his life as leverage. Conversely, Frishka almost certainly used the threat of *her* life as leverage against Earek as well."

"So Lady Marilana betrayed Marquiese to save Earek?"

"Not at all. She had to get Marquiese down to The Beach without telling him why, but she did so to save both Earek *and* Marquiese. While they were away from the palace, Marilana had her maid deliver to you the treason charge against Frishka. Then she arranged to have everyone on The Beach arrested, including herself and Earek. It would have been perfect to catch Frishka in his own trap had he not also sent the treason charges against Marquiese at the same time."

"Of course. Arresting herself and Earek was meant to remove them from Frishka's retaliation. Unfortunately it placed them in his custody. Her plan backfired."

"To some degree, yes." Castant stopped and gestured with a pointed claw. "But you also said that Frishka has been acting rather distracted since their return. He is usually very much in control of his emotions. If he is having trouble controlling his emotions then it is possible that Marilana is purposefully pushing him to his limits. That she is purposefully distracting him from his efforts toward the trial and exposing his true intent before his plan is complete."

The King arose as well, his feet taking him to the fireplace. "It makes sense, Castant. And it is in perfect keeping with the Marilana we thought we knew. So now it is really up to us to decide if we can trust her or not."

"Begging your pardon, Sire, but personally I have no doubts of her loyalty to you or Marquiese."

"It may not end well for her or Earek in any case. If Marquiese is proved not guilty of the treason charges, then he will probably banish them both or have them killed for their suspected betrayal of him. And if Frishka prevails, they will only live so long as they are useful to him." King Rylan paused, his eyes landing on the young leopard. He said, "One thing still troubles me, though. Why is Marilana out of court with a concussion?"

"If we think about it from her standpoint, then it may have been that she provoked Frishka a little too severely this morning. He may have been teaching her one of his notorious *lessons*. I still remember the lesson he tried to teach me. Apparently, I was disrespectful to him, so he and Confidante cornered me in an alleyway and gave me a thorough beating. The same fate has very likely befallen Marilana as well."

"That very well could be. Frishka did not seem happy with the fact that Marilana would be out of court for several days and that the trial would not be postponed. He may have made his first mistake. He may have lashed out at her and is now racing to cover it up. But we need solid evidence, Castant. Other than Marilana's word."

"If I know Marilana, she is well ahead of us in that respect. It is the only way she can influence the outcome of the trial. To provide evidence that directly opposes Frishka's claims."

Marilana's head throbbed. She let out a moan. Every muscle in her body ached, and her shoulder sent spikes of pain down her arm when she tried to move. It felt as though a horse had trampled her. She had succeeded in provoking Frishka, and now she was paying the price.

She opened her eyes as a shadow cut across the light, and she flinched involuntarily. "It's okay," a soft voice whispered. "It's just me, Altia."

"Al … ti … a." Marilana managed the caracal's name, but the words were broken and slurred. "How … am … I?"

"I've seen better," her maid answered with a reproachful shake of the head. "I have remedies and broth for you. You have a concussion."

"How … bad?"

"The healer called it moderate. I don't believe it is as bad as he says, though. Not with my remedies at work anyway."

Marilana let herself relax. She had to allow her body to heal before provoking Frishka again. That would take several days given the healer's prognosis. Her thoughts were clear, which meant the blow was to the back of her head, so controlling her body would be difficult. She mumbled, "Will … play … up … to … rest … ex … tra … day."

Altia nodded. "I understand. You are going to act like it is more severe than it is, so that you can rest an extra day. I like that plan."

"You … good?"

"Yes, they know I am here, but they don't know about the secret door or about my helping you, of course. The healer gave me instructions to stay and watch over you and to administer his medicines."

"Do . . . they . . . know?"

The caracal nodded again. "King Rylan and Lord Frishka were here. The King covered for you saying that he was used to concussion victims speaking gibberish. You kept repeating the words 'he lies,' and 'Frishka hit head.' I think the King understood. At least I hope he did."

"I . . . re . . . mem . . . ber . . . some."

Altia seemed surprised. "Good. Then your concussion may not be as hard to heal as I thought. But no more talking for now. Just drink this and sleep."

Altia tipped liquid into Marilana's mouth, and she quickly drifted back to sleep.

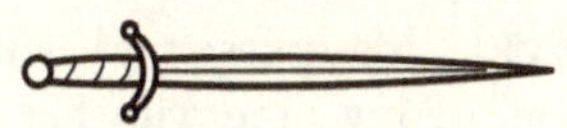

It was still early morning when the dungeon door opened and two sets of footsteps descended the stairs. Marquiese did not bother to open his eyes, expecting it to be a maid removing the tray that had brought his meager breakfast an hour earlier. He was surprised then to hear a stool scraping the cell floor and a heavy sigh as someone sat down.

"Good morning, Marquiese," King Rylan said.

Marquiese hastily raised himself to a sitting position, glancing up as he did at the towering form of Master Castant.

"Good morning, Father. And to you, my good friend Castant." Marquiese acknowledged them both with a brusque nod, and the young leopard returned it.

"According to my agreement with Frishka, we are to have no private conversations with any of the prisoners unless we have a witness who can testify in court as to the content. I figured that if his men qualified as his witnesses, then Castant here qualified as mine. Of course, Frishka did not expect any of my councilors to be back before next fifnight, so we are one up on him in that regard."

"Especially this particular councilor," Marquiese suggested.

"Precisely," the King replied. "Now Castant and I have been talking over the facts of the case as we know them so far, and we believe we know how Marilana is trying to help you."

"I do not think she is trying to help me at all," the Crown Prince replied. "Why should we believe a word she says?"

"She is not acting like she is trying to talk her way out of this. In fact, she has a moderate concussion that I think Frishka gave her. The healer said that he thought she tripped and hit her head against the wall, but I would be willing to bet that Frishka inflicted the wound."

"Of course he did," Marquiese said as if nothing could be more obvious. "In all of my time with her I have never seen her accidentally trip, even when someone tried to play a rather nasty joke on her and tied her boot laces together. In fact, she got up and walked on her toes to a chair with perfect ease before untying herself in a matter of seconds. What I cannot figure out is what advantage it has given him?"

"In that case, I am sure that we are correct to assume that she is provoking his anger on purpose. She is trying to force him into making mistakes, and lying about what happened was his first one."

Marquiese thought it over for a time. It made sense. Frishka would have been furious at her for placing the treason charge against him and used any excuse to beat her, especially if she were shackled and bound. Such a coward.

"Did she have other injures that seemed odd for someone who had tripped and hit their head?" Marquiese asked.

"Yes, in fact she had rather severe bruising to the back of one shoulder and another bruise halfway between the shoulder and elbow. Why do you ask?"

"Because that is what Frishka does. He beats anyone who shows the slightest disrespect and does so without witnesses. It is his favorite method of obedience control. If someone does not act properly according to his definition or show him the respect he thinks he deserves, that is how he responds. With violence."

"That is indeed what I thought," Castant stated quietly. "He hides his punishments by targeting areas that do not bruise easily or that are covered by modest clothing. I speak from experience."

"I know you do," Marquiese said, shaking his head and remembering well the time Castant had returned to his father's house with terrible bruises on his thighs and stomach. It had made riding a horse unbearable for a full fifnight. The memory struck Marquiese hard, and it hurt him now to think that Marilana was bearing Frishka's wrath in order to give him a way out of the treason charges.

"If her plan succeeds, then I will be indebted to her and Earek for saving my life, again. They will still have to face conspiracy charges. However, I will not push for their deaths. I would be content to let them leave the kingdom," Marquiese said, sighing heavily. He still felt the sting of their betrayal, but they did not deserve the injustice of Frishka's persecution.

"Very well, my son," King Rylan replied with resignation. "You will not be summoned for court today. Today's session is to be devoted to Frishka's testimony and his presentation of evidence. Tomorrow we will receive your testimony. Then we will break for The Day of Worship and Earek and Marilana's testimonies will be heard the start of next fifnight. We will speak again after that. I have brought you my personal copies of the books of law dealing with treason. The library copies have been moved to the deliberation chamber for the magistrates. I thought you might wish to refresh your memory on all the points of the law." Master Castant set a parcel of books on the floor.

"Thank you, Father, I appreciate how hard this is for you. We will see Frishka finished. That I promise."

When the King and his counsel were gone, Marquiese sat staring at the far wall, lost in thought. *I still cannot understand why Marilana did not confide in me before taking me down to The Beach. I could have trapped Frishka just as effectively as she. What leverage did Frishka have on her to make her betray me? Or is this another part of Frishka's plan? To make everyone believe Marilana is innocent in order to . . . what? Frishka has no alternatives now; he has to either banish me or take the throne by force. Marilana's part in those plans was first to bait the trap on The Beach, which is done, and now what? What is it that Frishka wants? To become King is obvious, but to be a successful King he will need more.* Marquiese's blood began to boil at the thought that began to form in his mind.

A successful King needs heirs.

It will not matter to Frishka if Marilana fights against his plans. If she remains loyal to me and fights to prove me innocent of treason, then Frishka will have to take the throne by force. If Frishka manages to break Marilana's spirit, then he can win the court case and take the throne by right. Either way, once Frishka is king, he can hold Marilana up as a good and loyal peasant-turned-lady, making the populace love her and love her children. It will not matter that they do not love the king, because they will love the queen and her heirs.

The thought made Marquiese's skin crawl.

If Frishka can plan this in such detail, what else can he plan out? What other use could he have for Marilana in the mean time? How much time is Frishka spending on thinking about Marilana? She is definitely very effective at distracting him. That part of her plan will work well.

Distracting Frishka? She is distracting me! That is what Frishka is doing. By having her and Earek play such prominent parts, they serve to distract me from my own defense, from thinking out Frishka's arguments. I need to stop thinking about Marilana's betrayal and begin thinking through how to put the lie to Frishka's evidence. Master Castant and Father have already started doing just that. They gave me just enough information to start doing it on my own. And because of Marilana, Frishka himself is being distracted from thinking through the rebuttals that we will present. Good then, I will use this to my advantage.

A slow smile spread across Marquiese's face as he sat alone in the dungeon. He blocked all thoughts of Marilana and Earek from his mind and began to systematically think through everything he could remember of what Frishka had ever done or said during the seven long years they had been stepbrothers. He turned to the books of law with renewed determination.

King Rylan listened as Frishka provided his testimony and presented his evidence. Overall, it was well done and well thought out.

The fifnight previous, according to the gaunt yet immaculate tiger, an errand rider had been given a message from Prince Marquiese and had been instructed to go to a certain place northwest of Maefair, leave the scroll in a small hole, and cover it with a large flat rock. The errand rider, Frishka testified, had been uneasy with the instructions and had come to him for help. Frishka had read the letter, which he presented now to the magistrates.

"I then went myself to see if such a place really existed," he said to the magistrates. "And indeed it did. Upon returning to the Royal Palace, I secretly entered Marquiese's readying room, searched it, and found two more incriminating letters. These letters outline a plan to waylay the King, wound him, and have Marquiese ride in to drive off the very attackers the Prince himself had commissioned."

Rylan frowned. He had expressly forbidden Frishka from entering the Royal Family Apartments, however, Marquiese's readying room was outside the restricted area. Marquiese would never have left important documents lying around there.

"Such a plan would have set the King up for early retirement so that Marquiese could ascend to the throne as soon as possible," the tiger continued.

"Forgive the interruption, Lord Frishka, but do you remember this errand rider's name?" asked the large boar, Lord Hunmis.

"Of course, Your Honor. Rider Hektor. He is loyal and dependable. I have myself sent him with occasional missives in the past."

"Then you know him well?"

"As well as any of the men."

"And where is he now? His name is not on the list of witnesses under guard."

"I beg your patience. I knew that if Prince Marquiese saw Rider Hektor while he was supposed to be on errand that the Prince would surely get suspicious. So I sent Hektor to the Northwest of the kingdom to try and locate several known bandits' camps. He is one of the best of the palace trackers. I have full confidence that he will return before the fifnight is out."

"Thank you. Please continue."

"The first letter is a letter of inception, asking if the recipient is willing to undertake a contract with Prince Marquiese to waylay and injure a wealthy traveler. It states that any correspondence should be directed to Lady Marilana to avoid detection. The second letter outlines a plan to ambush King Rylan, and the third discusses payment for such a treasonous act including a pardon promised by the future king. I thought about just confronting Marquiese with these letters, or making it known to the King and Your Honors, however, these letters prove that Marquiese has a penchant for secrecy. The first letter was enough provocation to give me legal cause to search for more evidence. The second two letters gave me cause for the treason charges; however, letters alone would not convince Your Honors of his guilt.

"I decided that it would be better if I had more evidence. As nobility, I have the authority to arrest someone in the act of a crime. So I decided to set a trap for Marquiese. I wrote a letter and delivered it to Lady Marilana's room. In it, I described a place to have a meeting the following day, The Beach off the eastern seaside. If Marquiese showed up, then I could arrest him and have the evidence that he had gone to The Beach specifically for the purpose of meeting the King's attackers. If these murderers also arrived due to some further correspondence with Marquiese, then I could arrest them as well," Frishka said with confidence and certainty.

"Lord Frishka, if you knew the method of communication between Prince Marquiese and said attackers, why did you not leave a letter to have them come to the meeting place as well?" asked the eland, Lord Quinre, interrupting Frishka's presentation. "Please explain."

"Well, My Lord, I could not be sure to catch these people with such a trap. They might have sent scouts. Scouts who knew nothing of the setup so that if they were caught they could betray nothing. Or they might have some arrangement that prevented them from being caught by Marquiese himself; many bandits are suspicious of dealing with people who hold power. I was not even sure that my trap would catch Marquiese. I took the risk that it might not work, in order to catch him in the act of treason."

"Would it not have made your case against His Highness stronger if you had apprehended these would-be murderers at the same time?" insisted the eland.

Frishka's voice took on a hard edge as he replied, "Yes, My Lord, it would have. As King Rylan can attest, I am gathering information from my sources in order to locate these murderers even as we speak."

"A feat made harder by the arrest of His Highness, which no doubt caused these unknown murderers to change hideouts and discontinue use of established lines of communication," interrupted Lord Komph.

"No doubt, My Lord" replied Frishka with a slight bow of his head, "Shall I continue with what *has* been done?" Frishka forced his voice back into polite tones, but King Rylan did not miss the stress the exchange had caused.

Another small crack to exploit.

"Before you continue, might I ask why you chose The Beach as the site of your ambush?" asked Lord Quinre.

Frishka relaxed a bit as he turned again to the eland. "Of course. I chose The Beach for several reasons. For one, it has many places for my men to hide that are not easily seen from the cliff edge or the beach floor. For another, it is only accessible by one easy descent down the cliff or by boat through a shallow channel. Additionally, it is not in view from far off. Travelers along the road or boats out at sea would not have seen the events taking place."

"Thank you, please continue."

"An hour prior to the arranged time, I took a force of men and hid around the edges of The Beach. There we waited and watched. A few minutes prior to the agreed upon arrival time, a dark figure crept down the cliff and began to search amongst the rocks. I had some of my men quietly apprehend the person. It was Master Earek. I was not surprised to find that Marquiese had sent him ahead to look for signs of a trap. I had him bound and gagged. Then we returned to our hiding places and waited. At the appointed time, two more figures appeared and descended the path."

"Two more figures? Do you mean Prince Marquiese and Lady Marilana?"

"Yes, though I did not recognize them at the time," the tiger said stringently. "One of my men cast a heavy net at my signal, snaring one of the two. As I approached, I recognized Prince Marquiese in the net and Lady Marilana standing nearby. His Highness tried to draw his sword, but it became entangled in the net, so he resorted to yelling at me. Up to this point, Lady Marilana had shown no signs of aggression so my men let her be. As I got closer, she began to accuse me of treason and attacked me. We struggled for a few moments before she managed to knock me backward off my feet, a difficult feat. As I stood back up, I realized that Marquiese's guards had encircled my men, and their captain had his sword on me. He arrested everyone on The Beach and escorted us all back to the palace. King Rylan was waiting for us; he read the charges I had placed against Prince Marquiese and then the countercharges that had been placed against me presumably by His Highness. So here we are now in court."

"Thank you for your presentation. We will deliberate on what we have heard and recommence tomorrow afternoon." Lord Komph spoke briskly and rose to leave.

Frishka's brow rose in surprise at the sudden dismissal, but he bowed with everyone else and said nothing.

All of it was of course ludicrous in King Rylan's mind. However, Frishka had set it up so that there were few witnesses on either side. It was down to the word of Marquiese and his conspirators versus the word of one absent errand rider and three letters all apparently written by Marquiese himself. It made it look like Marquiese had covered his tracks very well. It might be possible to prove that the letters were forgeries, then again depending on how Marquiese responded to them, the Court might have them thrown out as unreliable. As for the attackers that Marquiese had supposedly hired and the errand rider, they were probably dead in some ditch somewhere. It was a simple scenario, yet it was impossible for the magistrates to make a simple ruling. Both sides had to be examined before any such lies could be unearthed.

Frishka was in high temper by the time he left the courtroom. He had presented his case perfectly and yet the King did not seem to take any of it seriously. He would have to prove somehow that the King was blinded to the facts by his devotion to his son. That was a problem that could be dealt with. It was not the court case that had his temper up though. No, he was in a temper because the maid watching Marilana reported that there was no change in Marilana's condition. The healer had examined her again, too, and reported only minor improvements. He wanted to have her up and about the grounds where Marquiese would see them together. If he did not do something soon, the Prince's sense of betrayal would cool and he would begin to think about the matter at present.

Frishka paused in front of Marilana's room, and the guard opened the door for him. He entered and almost swore when he saw the maid making her curtsey to him.

"What is her condition?" He spat the words at the little caracal and felt only a little better at the look of terror that fixed itself on her face.

"She is still mumbling in her sleep. She has eaten only minimally. I have continued to administer the medicine left by the healer, M'Lord," the maid stammered and curtseyed again.

Frishka had noticed this maid before. She was quite attractive. If it weren't for his policy of never taking any of the staff, he would have enjoyed her body. He was in the mood for some female distraction, but maids were expensive and easily missed. He would send one of his men into the city later to bring him a worthless girl. But for now, he had other matters to attend to. He approached the bed and glared down at Marilana's sleeping face. He had suspicions that she was faking. He reached out and gripped both shoulders.

"Marilana, can you hear me?" he kept his voice soft, caressing.

She did not stir.

"Marilana?" He shook her slightly and spoke softly again.

He used the action to hide the fact that he was digging his fingertips hard into the bruise on the backside of her shoulder. She winced slightly and began to mumble, but did not awaken. He removed his paws and stepped away from the bed.

"You will inform the healer if you notice the slightest change in her condition," he told the maid.

"Yes, M'Lord." The maid curtseyed again.

Frishka left then, satisfied that the lioness was not faking. *No one in their right mind,* he thought, *could have ignored the pain of my claws digging into the bruise on her shoulder; she has to be truly oblivious.*

When Frishka's footsteps had completely died away, Altia moved quickly to Marilana's side.

"Are you alright?" the caracal asked with open concern. "He tried to conceal what he was doing, but I was not fooled."

"I'm fine." Marilana sighed and opened her eyes. She tried to smile. "Now then, out with the bruise tonic. Had we not been treating the bruise all afternoon, he would have caused a tremendous amount of pain."

"The coward."

"A fiend and brute indeed, but not a coward. He is sly, devious, and bold enough to work this plan of his. And he definitely knows how to inflict pain. If he were a coward, I would have been able to force him to submit. Instead, I must play this deadly game of wits."

Altia helped Marilana sit up. She fetched her rag and tonic from her basket of mending. She tended the bruise and then gave Marilana more broth and remedies.

"I know my business with herbs, My Lady, and you are healing far faster than any one rightly should. Also you fall asleep in an instant," her maid said. "Do you not intend to share your secrets? Even with me?"

Marilana smiled gently.

"Has Aunt Gwina not told you stories about the old ways of healing?"

"That some people can control the energies of the body? Even heal their bodies by controlling their sleep?"

"Correct. It is called the healing trance. I can enter the trance at will, and, in that state, the energies of my body focus primarily on healing. It is an ancient secret that the healers unfortunately forgot long ago. I read about it in an old book in Lady Annabella's library and trained myself how to use it when I was still a very young girl. This was when I first began to study healing herbs. I also learned ways to direct the healing of another so that the worst injuries may not be fatal."

"Can you teach me?"

"Some, but not the healing trance. That must be learned at a very early age. The energies of the body are not to be tampered with, Altia. Without proper training, tampering with the body can itself be fatal."

"I understand," Altia said simply.

Marilana lay back down and fell quickly to sleep.

Altia was glad that Marilana knew how to use these energies, yet she was slightly jealous of the ability. Upon reflection though, she was even more relieved that she had never been in a situation to have the need for such an ability.

15

The next morning Marilana sent Altia running for the healer. When the knurly old anteater came in, Marilana turned her head slightly and blinked blearily up at him. When the healer saw this, he sent Altia to fetch Lord Frishka and King Rylan.

By the time the royal lion and his second son arrived, the healer had finished his examination of Marilana.

"How is she, Healer Strunt?" asked King Rylan as he entered the room.

"She will be fine." The anteater touched Marilana's cheek, then her forehead. "She has improved remarkably over night. This is a normal pattern for concussions. Very little healing at first and then a much faster rate toward the end. She will be back on her feet tomorrow almost certainly. However, I want her to take it slow for a few days."

"Wonderful news! Thank you," exclaimed Frishka with a rather uncharacteristically happy smile on his face. King Rylan frowned. He looked down at Marilana. She was, in turn, watching him, while blinking furiously and squinting the way one might in strong sunlight.

"Marilana, the maid will stay for the rest of today. You are forbidden from talking to her or anyone else, unless you need something and have no other way of expressing it. Do you understand? I want your word," King Rylan said sternly.

"I . . . un . . . der . . . stand, . . . your . . . Ma . . . jes . . . ty. You . . . have . . . my . . . word." Marilana slurred the words softly.

"Very well." The King turned to Altia. "You, girl, are to tend to Lady Marilana's every need, and you are to do so without undue talking. And please see to it that she is bathed. Perhaps during dinner, when you've finished your other chores."

"Yes, Your Majesty," replied the young caracal with a deep curtsey.

"Come, Frishka, we have other matters to attend to," King Rylan said as he swept out the door. Frishka vouchsafed Marilana a dark look before following King Rylan out the door.

After Healer Strunt had shared his final instructions with Altia and closed the door behind him, Marilana let a smile spread across her face. The caracal came and sat down on the edge of her bed, the excitement coloring her face.

"We did it!" the lioness said.

"You tricked the healer. How did you do that?" asked Altia, looking amazed.

Marilana laughed quietly. "I knew what he was looking for. Or maybe I should say, I knew he did not know how to tell if someone was faking, so I played the part. It was a risk, but it worked. I think King Rylan knew, however. Which I hoped he would. I could tell he was thinking ahead, too. He found a way for me to bathe without Frishka watching."

"During dinner, of course."

"Yes." Marilana managed a thoughtful nod. "I think he still trusts me!"

"Of course he does. He is a wonderful king," Altia said confidently.

King Rylan led the way back down the corridor to one of the conference rooms. Frishka followed him inside and struck a pose of regal impatience.

Finally, the King faced him and said, "I am wondering who the 'murderers unknown,' as you put it in your testimony, could have been. 'Murderers unknown.' They could have been either bandits or mercenaries, I suppose. I know you have been using the resources available to you to follow any leads, however, there are more avenues we might consider." Frishka tried hard to mask the irritation he felt as he met King Rylan's observant gaze. With a wave of his paw, King Rylan gestured to the dusty stacks of files weighing down the conference room table. "I have asked the archivist to pull all reports of mercenaries known to have been working in the northwestern areas in the past ten years. I would like you to go through all of these reports to find any that might have done business in the manner you described in your testimony. I expect your report in court on the third day of next fifnight."

King Rylan didn't wait for a reply. He turned on his heels and left the room.

Frishka swore under his breath. The King had indeed found a research trail that needed to be followed. They both knew that the archivist could have done it as easily as Frishka, of course, and certainly faster, but the King wanted to keep him busy. *The troublesome old fool. I will be stuck working through all these for at least five days, but he has given me only four to complete the task. Clever. Very clever. It's a good thing I don't participate in the blasted Day of Worship.*

Before getting started, he called one of his men and ordered him to go into the city and find him some female entertainment for later. He was in a towering temper again and needed something on which he could vent his frustrations. Then he pulled up a seat and set to work on the reports.

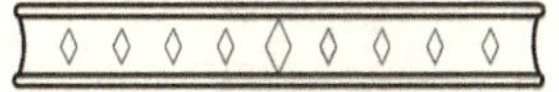

King Rylan listened intently to Marquiese's testimony.

His son did not try to flatter the magistrates with praise nor did he insult Frishka. He was not overly dramatic nor was he cavalier. He stood firmly, made his statements with an air of indubitable fact, and yet invited scrutiny and questions. He recounted the events of three days previously as though he were presenting the gravest evidence. He recounted how he and Marilana had planned to go for a pleasure drive along the coast. He spoke of something bothering Marilana and how, when asked, Marilana changed the subject. Nor would she give him an answer when he voiced his concern at the absence of her guard.

"When we arrived at the seashore, Marilana suggested that we take a walk down on The Beach. It would give us an opportunity to talk privately while enjoying the beautiful scenery, she had said. I agreed and so we made our descent to the sand. We had not walked more than a few paces before the trouble started. Without even a hint of warning, we were attacked. A net came out of nowhere and dropped over my head," the Crown Prince said. "And then we were surrounded.

"Earek appeared from behind me. He had not been present at breakfast, and I wondered why. Now I knew. He took his place next to Marilana and both refused to make eye contact with me. I had been betrayed."

"So, Master Earek was close by. Very close," interrupted Lord Quinre with a slight expression of surprise.

"Yes, Your Lordship." Marquiese held the eland's eye and said, "He was in fact the only one close enough to have thrown the net."

There was a murmur of surprise from the gallery, and the magistrates expressions ranged from disconcerted to deeply concerned.

"Please continue," Quinre eventually instructed.

"Thank you. My first reaction was to draw my sword to defend myself, but even as my paw closed around my hilt, I knew that the net was too heavy to permit the extension needed for the sword to leave its scabbard. I called out for my guards, but they did not respond. I looked around for help as my attackers drew close, but I was alone among adversaries.

"Finally I understood what was happening when Frishka stepped from his hiding place. He came forward, taunting me. He said that I was to be charged with treason and that he would become king."

"And how did you respond to this."

Marquiese did not so much as blink. "I told him that he would not get away with it. He laughed. He also said that Marilana and Earek had done their jobs very well and that they would have the gratitude of the new king.

Marquiese took pause, and the magistrate urged him on. "And?"

"And it was then that Marilana took action. She called Frishka out, shouting his name and saying that he would never get away with his plan. Then she attacked him. While they fought, my guards suddenly appeared, as if hailed by an unknown source, subdued Frishka and his men, and arrested everyone on The Beach under the pretense of treasonous dealings. We were all escorted back to the Royal Palace where my father read the treason charges presented to him by Frishka. I was escorted to the tower and here we are now."

"Thank you, Prince Marquiese, for that account," said Lord Komph formally. "We have a few questions for you at this time."

The red fox nodded in the direction of Lord Quinre, who took up the questioning. "Highness, have you ever communicated with or made arrangements with bandits or mercenaries with the intent of waylaying travelers anywhere within the borders of Redsands?"

"Never, Your Lordship," replied Marquiese without emotion.

"Have you ever planned an attempt to attack or harm travelers anywhere within the borders of Redsands?"

"I have not," was the Crown Prince's reply.

"Do you know an Errand Rider of the Crown named Hektor?"

"I do. I have often sent messages with Rider Hektor. He is a trustworthy errand rider and a very talented tracker."

"When did you last see him?"

Marquiese did not hesitate. "I sent him with a private communication north to Prince Dansho nearly a fifnight and a half ago. I expected him back long since. It is only a two-day ride there and back. And although I gave him permission to visit his mother—she lives to the northeast of the city—he still should have returned by now."

"Do I understand that you allowed Rider Hektor to take pleasure time while on the job?"

"No, Magistrate. Once he had delivered the message in question, his job was done. Had there been a reply message, in this case from Prince Dansho, then Hektor would have come straight back. However, he and I have a standing arrangement. If he rides the North Road and does not have a return message or finishes the task given without need of quick return, then, with my prior approval, he may stop to visit his mother. She is elderly, and he is her only child. He takes care of her as best he can. She receives a portion of his wages each month directly from the palace. He visits when he can and takes her trinkets or sweets."

"Most mothers appreciate flowers."

"Yes. In this case, however, she is allergic to flowers."

"You seem to know a lot about this woman. Why would that be?"

"I consider it my duty to know about my errand riders and their families," the Crown Prince said with an abundance of sincerity. "They have very dangerous jobs. There are many individuals who would like nothing better than to read the messages of the royal family or those of our nobles. These riders could die on any mission, peace time or not. It is my duty to guarantee that their families be taken care of in the event of their death. I know all of my errand riders very well."

"I see. What was this private communication about?"

"That is private and my privacy is well-guarded. However, it will do no harm to share a brief summary. Prince Dansho won a tournament two fifnights ago, and I sent him my congratulations and my continued good will."

"If your privacy is so well-guarded, then why would you leave private correspondences in your readying room for anyone to find?" asked Lord Hunmis quite unexpectedly.

"I would not." Marquiese fielded the query calmly. "As part of my ongoing education in matters both political and societal, my father has charged me with certain important aspects of State. With that in mind, I am well aware of the necessity to guard any and all private correspondences."

"Very well. Where in your rooms would you keep such secret missives?"

"That is not information for you to know," Marquiese answered calmly.

King Rylan leaned forward. "Please answer the question, Marquiese. I am fully aware that there may be documents that should not be exposed. I will personally look through all such documents, and no one will see anything that they should not."

Marquiese looked disgruntled, but nodded nonetheless. "I want the Court to realize that by telling this information I will be forced to change my methods and will never again use this location to conceal anything."

He paused and waited for all three magistrates to nod in acknowledgement before continuing. "In my study in the Royal Family Apartments, not in my public readying room, I have a locked drawer of my writing desk. The bottom of the drawer is a false panel that can be removed. Beneath the panel is a flat case that I keep locked. I keep the only key to that case on my person at all times. All missives in the case are rolled and sealed with my personal seal. No one could get into these documents without forcing both locks and breaking the seals on the letters. My father has a key to the drawer so that he can leave me messages without doing so in the open."

"Thank you, Highness," Lord Komph said, and nodded briefly at the King.

"Marquiese, if you would please join me and one of my guards in the deliberation chamber, I will receive your key," King Rylan said. He stood and walked to the smaller chamber used for non-public court dealings.

Marquiese followed. Once inside, he very discretely removed a delicate gold chain from a pocket hidden inside his shirt. Attached to it was a tiny key, which he placed in King Rylan's paw. The King used equal discretion and tucked it inside his coat. The guard then escorted them back to the courtroom, and the proceedings continued.

"Thank you, Highness," said Lord Hunmis gravely when Marquiese and King Rylan had taken their places.

Lord Komph looked across the courtroom to the witness standing confidently before them. Marquiese calmly held the Head Magistrate's eye.

"Have you ever contemplated forcing King Rylan into early retirement?" the magistrate asked bluntly.

"Never in my life."

"So you have no knowledge of three letters outlining such a plan?" Lord Komph held up the three letters submitted by Frishka the previous day as evidence of Marquiese's treasonous plans. "One, given to Lord Frishka by Rider Hektor the first of last fifnight, and two more taken from your readying room here in the Royal Palace. All three appear to be written by your paw and sealed with your personal seal."

"I have no knowledge of these letters, and I certainly did not write them," Marquiese replied without blinking.

"Well, someone wrote them."

"Yes, Your Lordship, I do not deny the documents existence. I am merely suggesting that forgery is a strong possibility. If I might make a suggestion to the Court? Sir Libor, the Royal Librarian and my tutor, knows my writing better than anyone," Marquiese said with a slight bow to the magistrates.

Lord Komph sat back in his chair and fixed the Crown Prince with a contemplative gaze. Lords Quinre and Hunmis mirrored this reaction, though both seemed expectant of further explanation. Marquiese did not accommodate them. He crossed his paws and waited patiently for the next question.

After a moment of silence, Lord Hunmis cleared his throat and said, "Highness, have you ever heard of a method of passing secret messages in which the message in question is left in a pre-determined hole, a hole that is then disguised by a stone? Most commonly, I would imagine, a flat stone?"

"Yes, Your Lordship," the Crown Prince replied, his surprise at the question quite genuine.

"You have?" King Rylan exclaimed suddenly.

"Yes, I have." Marquiese waited for the King and the magistrates to regain their composure and told them the story. "A number of years ago I discovered Lord Frishka in the iris garden on the west side of the palace. He was bent down and seemed to be replacing a stone seemingly at random in the middle of the path. But he also seemed rather suspicious in his movements, so I hid. After he left, I surveyed the place where he had stopped and discovered that one of the stones had a neat hole under it in which lay a neatly folded piece of paper. It was a note from Frishka to someone he called Confidante and was very disturbing." Marquiese glanced in the King's direction. "If you recall, Father, I showed the note to you, and you confronted Frishka about it."

"I remember, now," replied Rylan. "It described a plan to drive Lord Castant and his son out of the Royal Court. Frishka denied the whole thing, but a fifnight later this so-called Confidante attacked Master Castant, beating him badly, and then the following fifnight attacked you and broke one of your ribs. He was subsequently banished from the allied territories."

The magistrates listened intently, then exchanged dark looks.

"Thank you, Highness. That will be all for today," said Lord Komph.

Marquiese bowed respectfully to the magistrates before being escorted out of the courtroom by his guards.

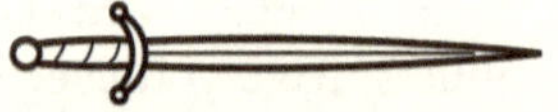

An hour after dinner, King Rylan and Master Castant entered the tower dungeon. The King was in high spirits.

Marquiese had been reading one of the books of law by the last light of the sun streaming through the bars of the cell's lower window and turned to greet them.

"Good evening," he said in a low voice, he had expected them earlier. His father had said they would not talk again until after Marilana and Earek's testimonies, but Marquiese knew that staying away was very hard, especially given his performance in court today.

"This was a great victory today!" exclaimed King Rylan, sitting on the stool Master Castant placed for him. "The magistrates deliberated in chambers for two hours after court recessed. When I spoke to them, they seemed inclined to call into question everything Frishka has said to date. You did wonderfully."

"Slow down, Father," Marquiese replied calmly sitting down on his pallet and setting the book on the pile of others on the floor. "It was a victory, but a small one. We have a long way to go, and they still have to hear from two more key participants. After that, they have all the supporting witnesses to question. Then they will have to call everyone back to ask questions that were raised from the other testimonies. The magistrates will be swaying across the line many times before we are done, I think."

"You cast a lot of doubt on Frishka's story when you recalled his use of the very method of contact he accused you of employing."

"No doubt Frishka will say that is how I knew to use such a method or why I chose bandits who use the same," said Marquiese in disgust.

"That is what I thought as well, Your Highness," said Castant, standing beside the King and blocking the view from the cell door. "But you brought it up in court and the King validated your story. This puts Frishka on the defensive when it comes to the magistrates' questioning. This is an advantage to you."

"Did the magistrates call for Sir Libor to validate the letters?"

"Not yet, no," said King Rylan. "Sir Libor is traveling on business and will not yet return for three more days. They will call on him then."

Marquiese sat forward suddenly, his face taut with concern. "Father, Sir Libor is in grave danger. Frishka will do whatever he must to prevent Sir Libor from identifying the forgery and providing evidence that Frishka is the forger. Even if it means waylaying him."

"Or worse," Castant said with equal concern. "I should have thought of that. I will send out riders immediately."

"Do so quietly, Castant," Marquiese said. "We do not want to alert Frishka."

The young leopard paced nervously. He said, "Frishka cannot risk attacking Sir Libor while he is in the company of others. To do so would be to show his intent. He does not know exactly where Sir Libor is; his errand was secret. Frishka will have to wait to attack him on the road and make it look like bandits. We must get to him first."

"You must also send riders out to track Rider Hektor."

"You are right, Highness. Hektor should have been back long since. I will send riders to Prince Dansho as well as to Hektor's mother to find out if he has visited her yet." Castant drew up. His brow furrowed. "Frishka testified that he had sent Hektor on a mission in the northwest region. I will also send some of my best trackers to see if they can find any clues as to his whereabouts."

"Good, Castant. Would you also get me the personal accounts from the Royal Chamberlain, Head Maid, and Royal Seneschal? They may have seen something of Frishka's activities over the past seven years that could lend weight against him. I remember the Seneschal added an attendant to track the movement of arms from the palace armory shortly after Frishka and Confidant arrived, and I think the Chamberlain did the same for the storerooms. I would like to confirm their reasons for the added security."

"That should not be a problem; they have all been inquiring if there is anything they can do to help you."

"Good. Give them my thanks." Marquiese nodded, a sense of urgency spicing his words.

"But Frishka does not know of the testimony that you gave today in court," the King argued.

"No, Father. Frishka almost certainly has his spies in court. At the very least, Lady Prinka will tell him everything. And I am sure he has others as well," Marquiese said with conviction.

King Rylan nodded soberly. He glanced at Castant. "Make it so, Castant."

"Yes, Majesty."

The King arose, his eyes on his son. "I will see you one hour before noon tomorrow. The magistrates have granted me permission to escort you to the Royal Chapel for a private worship. It will just be you, the priest, and a witness of my choice. I will see you to and from the chapel myself to make sure there are no problems. Lady Annabella has likewise been granted permission to have a private worship in the Royal Chapel with her heirs."

Marquiese straightened. "Marilana is better then?"

"She awoke this morning from her concussion-induced sleep. She will make a full recovery. She will probably still be weak tomorrow, but she has the option to worship with Lady Annabella and Master Earek if she chooses."

"Frishka allowed that?"

"Well, he did not have much to complain about; he set the rule regarding one witness to any conversation, and insisted they be allowed to be escorted around the grounds. Not surprisingly, Lady Annabella slipped into the loophole with considerable skill. Frishka does not understand how important the National Day of Worship is to the people. And he surely does not understand how such support ingratiates a leader to his or her people, a lesson Lady Annabella and I know too well. That is why you must be seen to worship tomorrow. For the people's sake."

It was just before noon on the National Day of Worship when footsteps sounded in the hall outside Marilana's door. She had prepared herself mentally and physically for a visit from Frishka, so she laid back, allowing her face to twist uncomfortably and blinking her eyes with confusion. The lock clicked, and she mentally braced herself. *Remember why you're doing this,* she told herself. *Think only of Marquiese.*

The door opened. She was stunned to see Lady Annabella, Altia, and a coterie of maids entering her room.

While the maids set about drawing a bath and laying out clothes, Lady Annabella approached the bed. She spoke quietly. "Time to get ready for service, my dear. I have gained permission to worship in private with you and Earek. I think it will be good for the people to see you both in chapel today, sway their liking of you a bit. The healer said that you would still be weakened from your recent accident. I am sure you will play that part well enough."

Marilana smiled slyly, "Yes, My Lady."

With the maids' help, the young lioness ate, bathed, and dressed. She was shackled and leaning heavily on Altia's arm as she followed Lady Annabella out of her room. Earek was likewise constrained and appropriately dressed as he exited his room with Captain-General Zariff. There was a smoldering anger in Zariff's eyes as he looked at her chains. Marilana gave him a look asking for patience, and he sighed heavily in return. They took the stairs slowly to the entrance hall. The hall was crowded with people waiting for the King to commence the day's celebration. All eyes turned to follow them. Some nodded. Others whispered greetings. Most were somber.

From the entrance hall, the entourage moved slowly down the long hallway, around the corner, past the library, and finally arriving at the Royal Chapel. Everywhere, people watched, exactly as Lady Annabella hoped they would.

They reached the chapel just as Marquiese and King Rylan were exiting the room. Marilana studied the Crown Prince, searching his face for any signs of emotion. When their gazes met, hatred flared in his green eyes, a hatred so strong that she could almost feel the heat of it.

Marilana turned her face away quickly. Color rose in her cheeks, and tears welled in her eyes. No matter how she tried, she could not stop them. With eyes downcast, the young lioness allowed Altia to guide her into the chapel. She fell to her knees on a pillow on the top step.

The ceremony began, and Marilana let the words of the priest flow over her, hearing only bits and pieces. When the priest's attendant moved among them with a basket of flower petals, Marilana took several in her paws and felt their cool softness. The Head Priest, an elderly leopard, saw her anguish and knelt in front of her. He took her paws in his.

"You are deeply troubled, my dear," he whispered. "I am Father Iscoot, Head Royal Priest of The Goddess. How can I help you relieve this burden on your soul?"

Marilana knew the words were ceremonial, spoken to every person who knelt in this place, but she could not help feel that this priest truly meant them.

Her whisper was hardly louder than a sigh. "Do you serve the King-to-be or his enemies?"

"I serve King Rylan and his son, loyally. I ask you to trust this with faith," he whispered back.

"His Highness hates me for what he thinks I have taken part in."

"He is unsure of where you stand, my child," the leopard replied. "He hates what the traitor has done to you."

"May I have sanctuary here from the traitor if the need arises?"

"I will arrange it, yes. Blessings on you, Fairest One."

Then he was gone. Marilana was hardly aware when the worship ended, only that Altia was guiding her back to her room. Lady Annabella did not speak as she watched the maids put her back to bed, but embraced her firmly before she left. Marilana could think of nothing but Marquiese's eyes as she lay staring at the late afternoon sunlight slowly moving across her room, tears leaking from her own eyes, fighting off the despair that threatened to take hold of her heart.

*

The click of the lock again woke her from her sleep, a deep sleep plagued with dreams. She did not open her eyes, but remained still with sudden fear. For a moment, she could not think of what that meant. As reality of her situation reasserted its self, she listened to the sound of heavy footsteps entering her room. A tray was set on the bedside table, and then one set of light footsteps left the room, and the lock clicked again. Silence stretched.

"Open your eyes and look at me."

Frishka had finally come to call.

Marilana blinked several times and turned her head weakly to look the tiger full in the face. He towered over her as she lay in her bed. All but one of his men, a stout brown bear, walked out on to the balcony and stood with their backs to the doors looking out into the twilight. Fear grew stronger in the pit of her stomach.

"The healer said that you will be back to full health by tomorrow evening. I think you have been faking the severity of your injuries. Perhaps not all, but some," he hissed. "Truth be told, I think you have been well for at least a day. Yet, weak you may be, and this is to my benefit. Why? Because you need not regain your full strength for what I have planned. From this moment on, you will walk on your own and present yourself as if you were full of strength. Do you understand me?"

Marilana nodded. She knew what he was planning. But did *he* know what she was planning? If so, he would have killed her now while he thought she was still weak.

The tiger let his eyes settle on the tray of food they had brought in. He said, "This is an excellent dinner. A rich vegetable stew for the healing patient. Warm crusty bread, and even a fresh sliced plum."

He snapped his claws and the bear retrieved the tray and took it to the table on the opposite side of the room. The man sat and began to eat with exaggerated enjoyment.

"Watch him."

Marilana did. When the bear had finished, Frishka spoke again.

"You will eat with your medicines in the morning, but that is the last time until I say otherwise."

He spun on his heel, snapped his claws again, and he, his men, and the empty tray were gone. Marilana sighed heavily and knew that tomorrow would be back to business as usual, back to the painful fight to save Marquiese's life.

16

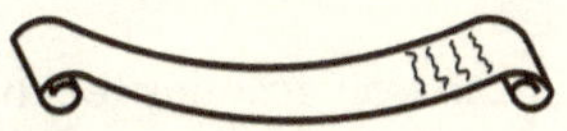

Earek braced for yet another blow to his stomach. "You will tell the Court what I tell you to tell them, is that understood?" Frishka sneered, his paw clenched in anger.

Earek straightened, sucked air between clenched jaws, and said nothing; he stared stonily at the wall over Frishka's shoulder. This earned him another punch to the stomach and a fist to his kidney. He dropped to his knees and caught his forward fall with his paws. His arms shook with the pain coursing through his body.

"Is that understood?" the tiger asked again, this time in a quiet voice.

"Yes." Earek gasped for a breath that he could not draw because of the pain.

"Good. You will tell the Court that on the morning of your arrest, Marquiese came to your room in the early morning hours and ordered you to go down to The Beach at the quarter-hour before noon. There you were to look for any indications of a trap. Once there, you were knocked down and tied up. You could not warn Marquiese that it was a trap, and you watched as one of my men netted him. Everything else is the same as it really happened. Can you manage that? Or should my man here help you to remember?"

"I will remember, Your Lordship."

"Good. I will escort you to court an hour after noon."

Frishka punctuated his orders with a swift kick to Earek's side, knocking him to the ground. He heard the door to his room close, and he was once again alone.

"Master Earek, can you account for the Court the events of the day of your arrest?" Lord Komph asked.

"Yes, Your Lordships," Earek said with a humble bow. "I was woken early in the morning by, Saffon, the guard who had been assigned to watch over me. He seemed panicked and told me to dress quickly. A dark suit had been lain out for me, and I dressed quickly and quietly, all the while wondering what was wrong. Shortly thereafter, I heard hasty footsteps outside my door. The door burst open and five large creatures charged in. Two bears, a boar, a tiger, and a huge elk.

"They spread out, and I tried watching their movements as they checked the windows and the bathing room. The next thing I knew, one of them—the boar, I think—jumped me from behind and knocked me to the ground. They gagged me, tied my paws behind my back, and covered my eyes with a scarf. They hurried me out of the palace and on to a horse. We traveled some distance before they took the horses away and hurried me down a steep incline to some sand. I heard the waves and knew we were at the seashore. I could not imagine why. There, they removed the gag and blindfold, but left my paws tied."

"And then?" the red fox asked.

"And then I was surrounded by Lord Frishka and at least a dozen of his men. A single torch provided what light there was, and I could see nothing beyond the light of this torch.

"Lord Frishka stepped forward and said, 'I am implementing a plan to capture Prince Marquiese, and you are going to help me. When your charming lioness friend leads the Crown Prince down here . . . .'"

"Please clarify. Here meaning The Beach?" Lord Komph asked.

"It was a beach, yes, but I do not know if it is The Beach you are asking about. I am not familiar with all the places in this area. It was a stretch of white sand strewn with many boulders and surrounded by tall cliffs. Many large rocks lay off shore that I believe would have made a boat approach difficult. Is that the place you mean?"

"Thank you for the description," Lord Komph said emotionlessly. "Please continue."

Earek nodded and continued his narrative. "Lord Frishka held out a net and said, 'You will take this net and ensnare him.' I asked, 'Why should I?' He responded by saying, 'If you do not, you will die. Not only that, but your charming friend will also die.' I knew, of course, that he meant Marilana. Then he added, 'I have archers here who will be aiming their arrows at her heart. If you do not do as you are told, I will give them the order to fire.'"

Earek shook his head. "I knew I could not condemn Marilana to death. And I knew by the way Frishka had said, 'When your charming lioness friend leads the Crown Prince down here,' that she was being forced to participate in Frishka's treachery as well; I also knew that if she and I died there on that beach, we would never be able to give testimony to this treachery. So I agreed to throw the net over His Highness. When I asked Lord Frishka why one of his own men could not do this, he laughed and said, 'You are much more skilled at being silent and stealthy. You can get closer to Marquiese and thus will be so much more accurate. But more than that, you are his friend and hers.' After that, I was again gagged and dragged toward the surrounding boulders."

"And then, Master Earek?"

"And then everyone hid," Earek continued. "As the time drew near, I was untied. When Prince Marquiese and Marilana were climbing down toward the beach, the gag was removed. I was given the net and a meaningful shove. I slipped out behind His Highness and threw the net over him. An instant later, Frishka's men made their presence known. His archers took aim at His Highness. Prince Marquiese called for his guards, but none came. He glared at me, but I was too ashamed to meet his eye."

Earek paused. He drew a deep breath and shook his head. Then he continued, saying, "Just then, Marilana growled at the top of her lungs. She yelled Frishka's name and proceeded to attack him. While all eyes were fixed on Marilana and Frishka, I glanced up and saw the palace guardsmen suddenly appear. In the blink of an eye, they quickly disarm Frishka and all of his men. Everyone on the beach, including the Crown Prince, Lord Frishka, myself, and Lady Marilana, was declared under arrest and were led back to the Royal Palace. Shortly thereafter, I was placed under guard in my room and shackled as you see me now."

Earek bowed to the magistrates once again.

"Thank you, Master Earek. You may go." Lord Komph dismissed him without asking any questions, and Earek was led away.

King Rylan watched him go. He was glad to hear that Earek's account matched Marquiese's to the word, but he realized that there was plenty of room for Frishka to dismiss the account as a fabrication. Saffon, the guard assigned to Earek was missing. Frishka's men would tell no other story than the one Frishka told them to tell. It was again Earek versus Frishka with no reliable witnesses. Frishka was making this trial very frustrating.

The King arose and led the magistrates out of the courtroom. He passed through the deliberation chamber, out to the hallway, and back toward his rooms. Master Castant was waiting for him as he had hoped, but it took him a moment to realize that another person was in the room as well.

"Sir Libor!" The King smiled broadly at the spindly snow leopard. "I am delighted to find you safely back from your errand."

"My liege, Master Castant sent one of his men to fetch me. When he explained what was happening, I knew I needed to hasten back here and quietly."

"We have much to speak about."

"Yes, Master Castant has been filling me in on all the details. I quite agree that Marilana and Earek are being coerced and performing against their will." Sir Libor fell into the nearest chair and waited for the King to join him. He said, "So tell us about Earek's testimony this afternoon."

King Rylan took a seat and smiled. Sir Libor, for all his formality around others, was one of the few creatures with whom Rylan did not have to conform to protocol and tradition. When the three of them were settled, he gave them an accounting of the day's session, and they proceeded to debate how it all fit together.

"It will be very interesting to hear Marilana's words tomorrow. She has a presence of mind that is quite astonishing. She learns quickly and studies hard to learn everything she can, and she already knew much when she came here." Sir Libor came to his feet and prepared to leave. "I will keep the guards close tonight and every night until this is all over. Rest well my friends, we will need our strength."

He left with two guards that waited outside the door. King Rylan turned to Castant.

"I was not surprised that the magistrates did not ask Earek questions today, but nothing was said that provided any new light on the matter either. I hope Marilana has some more to give."

Castant nodded in agreement. "Frishka has done a very good job of compartmentalizing the information. It appears as if no one individual can present anything more than he wants. On the other side, he is trying to juggle a lot of balls at one time. It remains to be seen whether he can keep them all in the air without a serious misstep."

Earek heard the rattle of the lock and turned away from the garden windows. He didn't wait for Frishka and his men to march into his room before kneeling. He showed no signs of emotion; he had been expecting this visit. He had, after all, told the truth in court this afternoon and by now Frishka would know that he had disobeyed his orders. He expected to be punished harshly.

Frishka entered the room and stood before him, contemplating.

"You did not do as you were told," the tiger growled eventually. "Did you not understand the lesson you were taught this morning? Do I need to reinforce my authority by different means?"

"I understand your authority over me, and I learned my lesson just fine this morning," Earek replied with no change in his expression. Frishka spun and kicked Earek just below his rib cage. Earek sprawled sideways, caught unprepared by the sudden attack. Two of Frishka's men—a huge eland and a foul smelling boar—hoisted Earek between them and the second son of King Rylan threw several punches into his mid-section. Earek fell with a dull thud onto the stone floor, filled with too much pain to catch himself.

Frishka rolled him onto his back by prodding him with his foot, and then leaned close.

"Until I say otherwise, one of my men will be eating your morning and evening meals. This punishment will be replicated for Marilana's benefit as well. Every time you disobey me, I will punish her as well. Do you understand?" whispered Frishka, his voice thick with disgust.

"As you wish," slurred Earek.

Frishka didn't like this answer and drove a fist into the young leopard's ribs. "Do you understand?"

"Yes, M'Lord," Earek managed to say.

"Good." Frishka stood and his entourage followed him out the door.

Earek lay on his back for what seemed like hours before he could draw even a shallow breathe without pain. Slowly, he rolled on to his side and struggled to his feet. He trudged across the room to the garden windows and opened them. The cool evening air mitigated the pain somewhat. He leaned heavily against the balustrade and waited.

After a long while, Marilana's voice drifted softly to him. "Earek? Are you alright?"

"I'll live." Even his whisper sounded slightly hoarse. "I'm so sorry. I know that sadistic varmint beat you. It's all my fault."

Her soft laughter made him smile in spite of his pain.

She said, "What part of this situation is solely your doing? Was I not the one who convinced you that the truth was our strongest weapon? Is it not Frishka who caused this whole situation in the first place? Not that it will make you feel any better, but when Frishka left my rooms, he was no longer thinking about your disobedience. He was obsessing over my declaration that he could rip out my tongue and I would still tell the truth. And that came even after he painfully beat me."

Earek could not suppress a grin caused by the lightness of her words, knowing, as he did, the cost she had surely paid for her obstinacy.

"Marilana, you shouldn't provoke him so," he said with the utmost conviction. "He may just decide to kill you and make it look like another accident."

"Do not worry about me, Brother. He is not nearly mad enough to kill me. If my suspicions are correct, he has many more plans meant to break my spirit before he will give up and kill me. Let me take the brunt of his punishments. I know the arts of healing and I have been through worse in my life."

"Yes, I know." Earek sighed heavily. "Marilana, Sister, why is he in such a position of authority over us? I'd have thought the King would have custody of those charged with treason."

"It happened a long time ago," Marilana replied softly. "Many generations ago a prince of Redsands married a Queen of Tanzamell. He became her consort and they had two sons. A loyal lord discovered that a group of lords were plotting against the royal family. The lord arrested them and brought the matter before the Tanzamell High Court. The court placed the traitors in the custody of a different lord. By the next day all the prisoners were dead. The loyal lord attacked the custodian of the prisoners, accusing him of treason. By the end of the fifnight noble houses all across Tanzamell were accusing each other of treason and civil war erupted. It all ended a year later when the loyalist nobles won, but the royal family had been slain during the fighting.

"The king of Redsands had been unable to help his beloved brother. As a result, he vowed never to allow such a thing to happen in Redsands. He wrote the law so that all those accused of treason are placed in the custody of the accuser. He assumed that the accuser would protect the prisoners so that they could stand trial and be publicly sentenced even if the accuser was the one committing treason. The only amendment to that law since its creation is the exception for members of the royal family, making it impossible to place royalty into the custody of anyone except royalty. That was added by a queen who was worried that a treason charge could lead to an assassination."

"So we have been charged with accessory to treason by Frishka, placing us in his custody. He has the right to treat us however he wishes in his custody."

"Correct. Most people would have morals preventing the abuse of prisoners, but as we know, he likes to cause pain and he is the real traitor. If I had gotten my charges of treason to King Rylan first, we would have been placed in Marquiese's custody. I am sorry I had Altia wait too long."

"It is not your fault, Marilana. You could not have known he was going to have his treason charges delivered in letter form. Now it is late, and we have risked talking too long. Good luck tomorrow."

"Thank you. Good night, Earek."

The young leopard stood statue-still long after Marilana had withdrawn. Nothing in his line of sight moved. Twice they had gotten away with it. He knew that eventually they would get caught; it was just a matter of time.

Marilana heard the soft patter of footsteps and was fully awake in less than a second. She was hungry and sore and the night was pitch black, but she knew at once that it was not Frishka or his men. He had made his mark at dinner time, forcing her to watch one of his guards devour her meal and then viciously taking out his temper on her. Her stomach muscles ached and the inside of her legs burned, but he had left unsatisfied, his obsession growing with every passing visit.

Altia's voice whispered in the darkness. "M'Lady, I brought you what food I could. I am not allowed to take much from the kitchen, but I saved some bits from my own meals."

Marilana winced as she sat up in her bed. Her eyes adjusted to the darkness, and she could make out Altia hovering at the foot of the bed.

"He beat you real bad, didn't he?"

Marilana sighed. "Gentle heart, I will be fine. It looks worse than it is. He does not want to damage his prize beyond repair. I will survive even without your help, but I cannot defeat him alone. Now come closer. I will not bite."

Altia moved to the edge of the bed and sat down. She uncovered a small bundle containing part of a loaf of bread and some strips of dried meat. Marilana ate quickly while Altia mixed remedies and applied tonic to her bruised legs.

"I'm sorry I couldn't bring you more food."

"Do not worry, Altia. And please, do not go hungry on my account. Your mistress will get suspicious if you are hungrier than normal or if you ask for food from the kitchens. I do not need much. Just a bit of bread, even half of what you brought me tonight will give me what I need."

Altia gave her a cup with water and tonic. "I must go; I don't have a lot of time."

"Thank you, my friend."

Altia paused, looking at Marilana, then tucked everything she had brought back into their hiding spots and left. Marilana lay back on her bed and concentrated on the healing trance that she was so skilled at.

17

Marilana woke at dawn. She got up and dressed quickly in a somber green dress. Then she sat on the couch and studied the gardens as the sun climbed into the sky.

She did not have long to wait. When she heard footsteps in the hall, she slid off the couch, knelt facing the door, and kept her eyes on her paws. The lock clicked. Frishka and three of his henchmen filed into the room. The lock clicked again.

The tiger stared at her. "Perhaps I should leave you moaning and gasping on the floor every day. It seems to have brought on the attitude that I have been seeking all along. For that I will let you wear the dress that you have chosen. It is appropriate for the occasion. Anger me again, however, and I may have your wardrobe removed."

He paused to let the words sink in a bit. Marilana still did not move.

He put his paws behind his back, straightened, and assumed a lecturing tone. "Today in court, you will be asked to recount the details of the days prior to your arrest as well as the events leading up to and including your arrest. You will tell the Court that Prince Marquiese had confided to you a plan to waylay the King, injure him, and have Marquiese ride in to the rescue. This action, Marquiese confided, was meant to put the King into early retirement so that he, the Crown Prince, would become king. You will confess that Marquiese promised you grand rewards, even hinting that you could become his queen. Your part in the plan was to be an interim step for the bandits to send letters to in the Royal Palace. They send letters to you and you deliver them to the Crown Prince. Understand?"

"Yes, Your Lordship."

"Good. The day before your arrest, you received a letter indicating a meeting between the bandits and Marquiese on The Beach. That day, you and he made it clear to anyone who might hear that you wanted some private time on The Beach; you did this so as not to arouse the suspicion of the guards that were accompanying you. As you approached The Beach, you watched for a signal from Master Earek, who was there to scout for any traps. Not seeing the signal, you and Marquiese made the descent. A net was cast over Marquiese by one of my men and everything else happened just the way it did, including your ill-advised attack on me. Now do you think you can remember all of that and present it flawlessly in court, or do I need to remind you that I control your life?"

"I will remember every detail, Your Lordship."

"Very good. See that you do. For the consequences will be severe if you do not," Frishka said, turning on his heel and marching his men back out the door.

Marilana did not move until the lock clicked and the footsteps moved off again. Then she let a smile that she had been holding in during the interview spread across her face.

The foolish tiger had told her his entire lie, and she would not forget it.

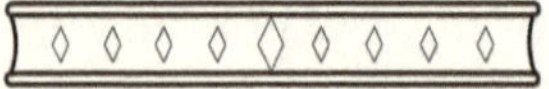

King Rylan watched Lady Marilana walk sedately to the witness box and noticed that it was not the humble walk of a peasant, but the calm self-assured walk of a noble. He glanced at the magistrates; they too had noticed.

For a brief moment, Rylan wondered if the young lioness had been wise to assume this attitude for her first appearance in court, although her dress spoke of humility and modesty.

When she had taken her place on the stand, Marilana looked up at the magistrates with an air of calm interest.

Lord Komph seemed taken aback by Marilana's attitude, and he addressed her with a slightly hostile tone, saying, "You have been brought before us in this matter of treason to provide witness to events that have occurred and for which Prince Marquiese has been accused. Do you intend to answer our questions openly and truthfully?"

Marilana looked back at the red fox, her mien calm yet emotionless. She said, "Yes, Your Honor, I do. I swear to The Goddess on my soul that I will answer openly and truthfully."

The magistrates looked at each other with evident surprise. No witness had yet been asked to swear to tell the truth—it was just accepted as law—yet Marilana had offered the oath freely. She had clearly been in trial proceedings before.

Now Rylan knew why she had chosen this attitude. She had no intention of being hostile. Nor would she allow her testimony to be used against her in any way. Lord Komph nodded his head slightly. When he spoke this time, there was no trace of the venom he had demonstrated previously.

"Lady Marilana, can you please relate to us the events that led up to your arrest?"

"Of course, My Lord. Early in the morning of the day in question, still in the black of night, I heard a slight commotion in the hall . . . ." Marilana spoke for a long while recounting the events of the day of the arrests. She spoke in detail, and easily answered the magistrates queries for clarification or additional details. "My plan to save Earek and Marquiese had succeeded, or so I thought. I allowed myself to be escorted back to the Royal Palace. When we arrived, King Rylan read out treason charges, but they were not the ones I had sent to him. Frishka had gotten his charges against the Crown Prince in before mine."

Marilana shrugged ever so slightly. "And that is the full of my testimony of the day in question."

She curtseyed low to each of the magistrates and waited. King Rylan was amazed at the detail of her narrative. It seemed more real to him than any of the other testimonies so far. She had left hardly anything out: her thoughts, her observations, and her rational conclusions. She had even admitted to the treason charges against Frishka. Surely she knew he had spies in the courtroom, but she seemed indifferent to what could happen to her if he knew. Perhaps he had already confronted her on that point, and thus she did not fear discovery.

The magistrates studied her. Finally Lord Quinre leaned forward, and Marilana calmly met the eland's gaze.

"Did you receive a letter the day before you went down to The Beach?"

"No, Your Honor. I have not received any correspondences since I arrived at the Royal Palace little more than a month past."

Lord Hunmis spoke up next. "You said that you knew that Lord Frishka would not hesitate to kill His Highness or Earek on The Beach. Why would he not also kill you?"

"He would have," replied Marilana, again calmly meeting the boar's eyes. "But that was not part of my reason for acting the way I did. I do not fear death for myself. If it comes to my death, I have either failed and deserve death or I have succeeded and died in the process. If Prince Marquiese and Earek were killed on that beach, I would have failed and if Lord Frishka had not killed me, I would have attacked him and his men and killed as many of them as I could. They would have had to kill me to stop me."

The courtroom became so silent at the end of this pronouncement that King Rylan felt as if all the air had left the room. No one moved; no one seemed to breathe. He sat and gazed down at her and saw again the girl who had asked for a guard not to protect herself, but to protect Marquiese. Where was that guard now? Here was Marilana showing her great heart before the entire Royal Court and his own attempt to protect her seemed drastically inadequate.

Lord Komph eventually broke the silence, saying in a quiet, remarkably respectful voice, "Thank you for your testimony, Lady Marilana. We will deliberate and call you back for questioning as needed. Court is adjourned."

Marilana followed Frishka into her room. As the door locked behind them he turned to face her, and she dropped immediately to her knees. He lashed out with a kick to her chest. The force of it threw her backwards into the legs of one of his men and knocked the wind out of her. The man reached down and grabbed the chain that still linked her wrists and ankles. He lifted the chain and twisted Marilana so that she lay on her belly, her arms and legs pulled tight behind her back, her skirt falling around her knees. Frishka knelt down in front of her and pulled her head back so that she stared back at him.

"You did not do as I instructed you to do. You said you would remember everything I said this morning. Did you lie to me?"

It was difficult to talk with her head pulled back so sharply and her reply came out as a gasp. "No, I did not lie. I still remember every word."

His face twisted with rage.

"Then you will remember every punch of my fist."

He moved around behind her. A gag filled her mouth. A blindfold covered her eyes. He shredded her skirt and then he began. He was methodical and skilled in the way he caused pain. He pummeled the area of her inner thighs sending waves of pain through her body. Marilana strained against the chains bending her backward and bit down hard on the gag to prevent herself from making any sound. She could not, however, stop the tears streaming from her eyes and soaking the blindfold, the pain was terrible.

When, at last, he seemed satisfied, he had her wrist manacles removed and left her on the floor, still blindfolded and gagged. She heard the door open and the men march out. Even after the door was locked and silence had been restored, she did not move. She was weak from fighting the chains and pain throbbed in her shoulders, legs, and back. Tears continued to soak the blindfold, and she lay on the cold stone and cried silently until sleep gratefully took her.

*

Marilana was woken by the touch of soft paws removing the blindfold and gag. Altia helped her to her feet and into the bathing room. Together they removed the torn and dirty dress, and Marilana stepped into the low cold bath that the caracal had prepared. The many bruises on her legs ached and throbbed, but gradually the pain numbed and finally disappeared.

"I didn't have enough tonic to make you a full bath," said Altia apologetically.

"Thank you for what you have done. I am already feeling better," replied Marilana softly.

"I heard what you said in court today. I knew he would be furious at you for telling all those details." Altia moved around behind Marilana and began a gentle massage on her shoulders. "He's insane. This has to stop, My Lady. This has to stop now."

Marilana ignored this. "Did he pay Earek a visit after leaving here?"

"He didn't. I was delivering the dinner trays. He sent yours back to the kitchen saying that you weren't hungry, and then he stormed off down the hall. Earek looked worried when

I delivered his dinner. I'm sure he is wondering what has happened."

"I am sure he is. But I am in no condition to talk to him. I will need to be very careful the next couple of days. Frishka will be watching and hoping for any reason to teach me another lesson."

18

The next morning, Frishka walked into her room without a word. He stared at her. She looked at him with eyes so calm that it was impossible to read any emotion in them. The tiger clamped his jaws shut so hard that Marilana could hear his teeth grinding together. She braced herself for another unprovoked attack. It didn't come.

The same scene played out at mid-day, when he spared her a bowl of soup, and again in the evening.

Marilana chose the hour after sunset to slip out onto the balcony. She leaned on the railing, scanning the grounds for any signs of movement. Seeing none, she called softly in the direction of Earek's adjacent window.

"Earek. Are you there?"

"Marilana. Thank The Goddess!" His voice was full of relief. "I've been so worried about you. Two nights I've waited. Are you safe?"

"I will be alright," she answered simply. "How are you?"

"I get one meal a day, but at least I have not been beaten since my testimony."

"Good. He is noticeably pre-occupied. I will try to keep it that way."

"Are you getting enough to eat?"

"Enough to survive."

"We will see an end to this," the black leopard whispered.

"Oh, indeed we will, my brother," the heiress to Lady Annabella said in a low menacing voice. "Indeed we will."

"And I will never forget your courage."

A moment passed as Marilana regained control of her anger. "Take care as best you can, Earek."

"I will. Sleep well, Marilana."

King Rylan groaned as he dropped onto the stool. His eyes played upon the walls of the dungeon. His sigh filled the room. Master Castant added another parcel of books to the pile of law books on the floor.

"We've heard multiple testimonies the last two days," the King told his son. "Frishka made a brief appearance to say that his search of the archived records detailing known bandit activities has resulted in no useful information."

"What a surprise," Marquiese said sarcastically. He studied his father and realized the ordeal of the trial was taking its toll.

"The Court ordered him to widen his search," Rylan said without much hope. "We heard from all of Frishka's men."

"And let me guess," the Crown Prince said. "They all gave the exact same account as Frishka."

"Like they were reciting a play. Even to the point that none of them are claiming to have thrown the net over you. Lord Komph picked up on that and tried to get them to identify who it was, but none of them could. It might lead to more questions, but I doubt it will crack Frishka's case."

"And what about you, Father? You look exhausted." Marquiese sat on the pallet and watched him with a worried expression.

"I am just tired."

"Like I said: exhausted. And that is not going to help you think straight, Father. You need to get better sleep."

"No argument there," the King said. "Tomorrow, the magistrates have called the captain of the palace guards and finally Sir Libor. These are the only two witnesses that are being called on your behalf. After that, Frishka will be called to present any further information he has found and will begin cross-questioning."

Marquiese sat up. "Have you seen Marilana and Earek lately?"

"No, I have not. I know that Marilana was escorted to the chapel yesterday. I do not know why."

Alarm spread across Marquiese's face. "Frishka? Frishka took her? But, surely he did not wed her?"

King Rylan smiled slightly. "No, the chapel was not his idea. He was far too angry for that. He did not enter the chapel. He and his guards remained outside the doors. I asked Father Iscoot about it, and he said only that he was granting Lady Marilana her request for private prayer and that anything she had to say there was between her and The Goddess. Apparently Father Iscoot sent for her. Frishka could find no reason to deny the request, so the Court granted her time for private reflection with The Goddess. Nor could he get any more out of the good Father than I could."

Marquiese's face split in a wide grin, "She is working around Frishka's restrictions. She has found a way to limit the amount of time he can spend with her in her room. Even if it is in a very small way, it will irritate him that she was able to do it. Things are not going too badly. At least what we can see of the hidden parts."

"I am not so optimistic. The story that Frishka has put together has been repeated by all of his men so as to ingrain it in the minds of the magistrates."

"Yes, but that was to be expected. It will do us no good to dwell on it. We must try instead to put cracks in it and make it crumble under close inspection. If everything goes well, the testimonies tomorrow and the cross-questioning will accomplish that."

King Rylan arose. He put his paws on his son's broad shoulders. "I am glad that you are not giving way to your anger. Stay strong, Son."

"Stay strong, Father."

Frishka entered Marilana's room followed by a maid carrying a lunch tray. Marilana waited until the maid had left before dropping to her knees in front of him.

"You will eat your lunch with me today. Get up," he spat at her. Marilana hid the smile that tried to slide onto her face. Obviously he was still upset that she had managed a summons to the chapel the previous morning. Father Iscoot had done well to achieve her visit and had said that there would be more visits in the future.

They sat and ate quietly for a time. Marilana ate daintily, trying to act as if she were starving but trying to act as though she were not. It was a good thing that Altia had been able to bring her food in the night. Frishka ate only a few bites before he just sat watching her.

If he keeps brooding like this his ears will burst into flame. There must be something going on that is bothering him more than just my visit to the chapel. I wonder if I can get him to start ranting. It might be worth the beating to know what is going on.

"Surely you will eat more, Your Lordship? It will not look good for your case if you appear to have stopped eating out of nervousness or uncertainty." She spoke softly and dipped her head submissively. She turned one of the bowls so that the spoon was in easy reach of his paw.

"You are getting food from somewhere."

It was not a question, but Marilana heard an inflection of doubt.

She sniffed disgustedly and her voice hardened. "The only food I eat is what you give me. I am sure King Rylan would not approve of your methods to loosen my tongue. If obedience is what you want, look elsewhere." She pushed the tray of food away from her; she had eaten most of it. "I would rather starve."

He stood up and towered over her as she sat staring forward, her arms crossed angrily. "Yes, Marilana, you will starve."

His slap across her cheek barely moved her head. He grabbed both her arms as they were crossed in front of her and yanked her up. He made to throw her to one of his men to hold, but she took the opportunity to twist the chain between her feet around his legs and they both toppled to the ground. As she came down on top of him she twisted her arms so that she drove one elbow into his stomach. He grunted with the impact. She rolled sideways; her attempt to scramble to her feet foiled when he hooked her chain with his foot and pulled her feet out from under her. One of his men grabbed her arms as she sat up on the floor. She did not bother to struggle any further. She knew fighting here in this place under these constraints would get her nowhere, but it felt good to have knocked the wind out of Frishka for a change. If he had been furious before, now he was livid. Rage showed plainly on his face, twisting his mouth into an evil snarl as he got to his feet.

"Do you think you are invincible? You are no more than flesh! Weak and pliable! You are mine. You will learn respect or die in the process!"

A kick to the stomach sent her and the wolf holding her sprawling backward. His other two men did not wait for the wolf behind her to get up. They seized her arms and lifted her to her feet. Frishka's punch landed as soon as they were set.

"You and your games. Do you think you are smarter than me? Do you think that Marquiese will win just because you tell your story of events? He will fall. I will see him finished! All the time I have put into this trial, and he thinks to have Sir Libor invalidate the letters. Well, I took steps to make sure that the letter writer would not be identifiable, not by Sir Libor or anyone else. They might not prove anything, but they cannot be used against me."

He punched her in the stomach again. She retched slightly, but swallowed quickly to keep her meal down.

Gasping, she managed nonetheless to speak. "So you think you have thought of everything? Are you really that stupid?"

His punch hit her before she could say any more. He landed three more blows in quick succession.

"You foolish girl! Why can you not just give up? What are you trying to accomplish? All this act of yours is doing is getting you hurt. Not that Marquiese is in any better condition." He punched her again. "He might have remembered that I exchanged messages with Confidant the same way that he was supposed to be contacting these bandits, but I can counter that." Two more punches landed. "The errand rider cannot confirm or deny anything if he cannot be found. Now can he? I made sure of that, and your guard went the same way." Another punch. She retched again. "If you would just submit! Why won't you submit?"

He screamed as he punched her twice more. She could not stop the retching any more. Frishka jumped back as his men dropped her to the floor. Her stomach contents splattered on the stone.

Frishka moved around behind her even as Marilana struggled to control her heaving stomach. He stepped between her legs, gripped the lower part of her skirt and tore it off. Stepping to her side, he dropped the pile of cloth beside her.

"You really shouldn't wear your cleaning rags, Marilana. They are not very becoming," he said, sounding smoothly arrogant and triumphant once more. "Clean up that mess. Quickly now; I have more desirable things to do today."

He stood with his back to her at the balcony doors as she used the remnants of her skirt to clean the floor. When it was spotless again she bundled the reeking fabric in more of the torn skirt, and a boar took it. Turning from the windows at a slight cough from the wolf, the tiger stormed out without looking at her.

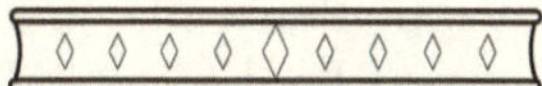

King Rylan watched as Captain of the Guard Lorne marched out of the courtroom doors, and Sir Libor appeared in his place. The Captain's testimony gave backing to Marilana's story, just as the King knew it would. *Good,* he thought, watching as Sir Libor took his place in the witness box. *Marquiese needs all the support we can get.*

"Sir Libor, it has been suggested to the Court that you can verify Prince Marquiese's writing. Is this true?" Lord Komph began without preamble.

Sir Libor's expression held no emotion. "Yes. I was his tutor for the last ten years, excepting the years he spent away from the Royal Palace. I have watched his writing take shape and know his individual touch as well as my own."

"We have here several letters that were taken from Prince Marquiese's personal study. We have also copied those letters in an attempt at forgery." The magistrate held them up. "Could you please tell us which of these letters are truly written by the Crown Prince?"

Several pages were given to the wiry snow leopard. The Court waited quietly as he scrutinized the letters. Finally he separated two of the pages and held them up.

"These two are the originals written by His Highness' paw. These others are the copies." The supposed copies were passed back to the magistrates without further comment.

"You are correct. These are the copies we ourselves made. We have here three letters that we have been made to believe that His Highness wrote. Can you tell us what you think of them, please?"

Three different pages were passed to Sir Libor, and the snow leopard studied them with narrowed eyes. When the librarian looked up, his expression was grave. "These three letters were not written by Prince Marquiese," he said simply. Then he looked directly at Lord Komph. "However, I would ask to speak with you privately to elaborate on the writing."

King Rylan was taken aback by this response, but nodded to Lord Komph when the magistrate glanced to him for guidance. The red fox drew his shoulders back and said, "Very well, we shall take a private session in this case to confer regarding the evidence."

The magistrates followed King Rylan toward the deliberation chamber door. Sir Libor brought up the rear, clutching the papers as though a ghost might snatch them from his grasp. Once the door was closed, the King turned to face Sir Libor.

"Well? What can you tell us?"

"Your Majesty, Your Honors, I beg your forgiveness, but this probably should not be said in public at this time." The librarian laid the letters he had identified as belonging to Marquiese on the sideboard. "As I said, these two letters are written by the Crown Prince. These slight flourishes here on the g's and here on the d's are very indicative of his style."

Then the old snow leopard nodded in the direction of the three letters that Marquiese, according to the librarian's testimony, had not written. "See here. Those distinguishing marks are missing from these three letters. However, there are marks here on the r's and here on the t's that I have only seen one person make."

"Lord Frishka?" asked Lord Hunmis.

"No." Sir Libor took a deep breath. "Lady Prinka."

"Lady Prinka?" King Rylan could feel his stomach twist into a ball of ice.

"Yes, Your Majesty. Forgive me, but I do not think that this evidence should be presented at the present time," Sir Libor said, bowing deeply.

King Rylan could only stare at him.

"Yes, you are quite right," Lord Komph said, looking toward his fellow magistrates as he spoke. Both the boar and eland nodded. "We must first deal with the charges at present, those against Prince Marquiese. Once we reach a verdict, then we will look at potential conspirators. Although, we should most certainly place Lady Prinka under arrest at once."

"No!" King Rylan roused himself from his shock and looked at each of the magistrates. "She has other conspirators as well. If we place her under arrest, then we alert them to the fact that we suspect others. I will have additional guards placed around her under the pretense that I am concerned for her safety. They will be ready to arrest her when the time comes.

In the meantime, the evidence stands that Marquiese did not write the letters that Lord Frishka found."

"As you wish, Your Majesty," said Lord Komph bowing. "It stands to reason then that doubt is cast as to who the traitor is. The letter writer could have been under orders by Prince Marquiese or by someone else, or could have planted the letters to cause Lord Frishka to challenge Prince Marquiese, leaving the true traitor in the background."

"You are quite right. We cannot rule out anyone just yet," agreed Lord Hunmis, his statement eliciting a nod from Lord Quinre as well.

"Very well, Your Honors. The questioning will continue as you have directed," King Rylan said, nodding a single time before turning away.

"So Sir Libor said Prinka wrote the letters." Marquiese shook his head, though hardly in disbelief. "We should have known she was more deeply involved."

"Indeed. We knew that she would spy on the court proceedings for Frishka. Why did it never occur to me that she might have had a bigger part in the plotting? I have been blind. Forgive me, my son."

The royal lion sagged on the stool, his head in his paws.

"Father, not one of us could have guessed what part she has played. We all knew that she would do anything for her precious son. Without proof, however, we could not have charged her with anything. Now we can. Sir Libor can testify to her paw as the one that wrote the forgeries. Frishka must have suspected that Sir Libor would be called to examine the letters, and that his writing would have been readily recognizable by his tutor no matter how close it looked to mine. Lady Prinka's would not have been. Frishka must have had her practicing my writing style for a long time to pull off such a difficult forgery."

"Yes, it was just a good thing that I have had Sir Libor analyzing my correspondences with Prinka over the years. He knows her writing as well as yours and mine."

"Then you have suspected previous forgeries of her letters?"

"It was a necessary precaution. She is close to me. If anyone wanted to strike at me through her, a forged letter could be sent to set up an ambush. I have actually had him analyze your letters the same way. I just did not think about it when Frishka presented those letters in court. I have no excuse."

"You have had a lot to think about recently," his son said.

"Thank goodness you brought it to the attention of the magistrates. They have accepted Sir Libor's analysis, but they want to be certain as to who ordered Prinka to write the letters before going public. They agree that none of this can be discussed in court until after the verdict against you is decided."

"I will gladly add her name to the list of Frishka's conspirators when the time comes," the young lion said. "I am sorry that Prinka has betrayed you."

"She stopped loving me long ago. I just had to realize that I had stopped loving her as well," the royal lion admitted. "At first, I was ready to deny Sir Libor's statement about her forgery, but, as I thought about it, I realized that what I was most angry about was the fact that I had let her deceive me. I was a fool, and it almost cost me my son. That would have been the greatest loss of all."

"Thank you, Father."

"Have you found anything in your reading?" King Rylan asked indicating the piles of books now littering the floor of the dungeon.

"Not against Frishka directly," Marquiese sighed. "There are many accounts of Confidant trying to steal from the armory or storerooms. There are even accounts of Confidant threatening the servants and maids, but no direct evidence that I can use against Frishka."

"Why did they never mention these encounters before?" King Rylan asked concerned.

"The interactions among the servants are kept among the servants," Master Castant said quietly. "Your palace servants considered Frishka's Confidant to be a servant, and so did what they felt was necessary. He never pushed them far enough for it to reach your ears, according to what the Royal Chamberlain told me when I spoke to him about his personal accounts."

"I wonder what else that young man was doing when he was here," King Rylan mused darkly.

"I do not know, but I am glad he is gone," Marquiese sighed.

19

Frishka stood frowning at the magistrates; he had found no additional evidence to present against Marquiese or to indicate who the murderers could be.

"We have determined that the letters that you presented to us are forgeries and were not written by Prince Marquiese," stated Lord Quinre.

"If he did not write them, then who did?" Frishka asked angrily. "I acted on false information? That cannot be!"

King Rylan thought Frishka's reaction was extremely well played. The tiger was acting angry at finding out that he had acted on false information.

"We do not know, at this time, why those letters were placed for you to find," Lord Quinre replied calmly.

"Well if he did not know of the letters before, why did he so blindly walk into my trap?"

"That is a very good question, Lord Frishka, one that we intend to find an answer for," Lord Komph said. "Why do you think the palace guards arrested everyone on The Beach, and why did they not come when Prince Marquiese called for them earlier?"

"I cannot fathom what the palace guards were thinking, Your Honors. From what I have seen of the Captain in charge, he seems to be a man of duty. I feel that he would have followed orders no matter what he heard as long as he was told to do so. It could have been an order from Marquiese to wait for a signal before taking a specific action," he replied heatedly.

"Thank you for your speculations on the Captain's character. Lady Marilana claims that you threatened her life to get her to lead Prince Marquiese down to The Beach. There is no evidence that a letter was received by her, appointing the time of the meeting on The Beach, or that Prince Marquiese knew of the meeting."

"I would assume that the letter that I wrote, and had delivered to her, fed the fire in her rooms. All I know is that they arrived exactly on time."

Lord Hunmis spoke next, asking, "Lord Frishka, what cause would Lady Marilana have to eliminate the guard that was assigned to protect her?"

"I would not know. Perhaps he overheard something about the meeting and threatened to expose her. She is unpredictable and wild. She exhibits many of the traits that we expect from the peasants of the South, very close to the mindset of dumb wild animals. She can behave properly when she wants to, but really she can be quite dangerous."

"Yet you seem to be spending a lot of time alone with her."

"Only as alone as I can be with three guards around at all times. I have been attempting to convince her to tell the truth. To leave her wild ways and live in a more civilized manner." The tiger grinned slightly, then added in a much calmer voice, "She is quite beautiful. I have told her that if she would confess to her crimes, I would try to persuade the Court toward a more lenient sentence. Beauty and honesty should be preserved, should they not?"

Lord Hunmis nodded, "I have always said that both traits are admirable."

"Lord Earek said you ordered him to throw the net over Prince Marquiese on pain of death," interrupted Lord Komph. "You claimed that you had him tied up out of sight, yet by all accounts when Lady Marilana attacked you he was standing unbound not far from His Highness."

Frishka looked slightly annoyed at the interruption and answered in a tight voice, "I saw him standing unbound and ungagged under the swords of the palace guard after Lady Marilana attacked me. I would assume that one of the guards untied him so that he could walk back to the Royal Palace. As to throwing the net, I do not understand why he would say such a thing. He does tend to fabricate stories regarding past events. I have tried to persuade him to tell the truth as well, but have not had much success. He is prone to violent outbursts, as it turns out."

"Do you remember the name of the man who *did* throw the net? No one seems to remember who it was."

"I had a full half squad of men with me," the tiger replied. "I cannot be expected to remember all of them, surely."

"Can you tell us the exact location of the message depository that you spoke of; the place where Rider Kor was to leave the letter sent by Prince Marquiese?" asked Lord Quinre without pausing.

"I believe you misspoke, your Honor. Rider Hektor is the one who brought the letter to me. That said, the location can be found with these directions. Follow the North Road north for five miles. Turn west at the lightning struck oak. Follow the cart track for two miles. Turn north again and cross a large meadow to the point where three boulders sit. On the backside of the boulders, there is a flat rock slightly wedged beneath the largest boulder. Removing the flat rock reveals the hole where messages can be stored."

"Very precise, Lord Frishka," Lord Quinre said with narrowed eyes. Then the eland pushed his glasses up the bridge of his long snout and asked, "Prince Marquiese said that he granted Rider Hektor time to visit his mother after delivering the message. Did Hektor say anything about that to you?"

"He said nothing of it. I would not have granted such a request. He had duties to perform." The tiger looked perturbed. *The consummate actor,* King Rylan thought. "Although he did have some flowers with him; I thought that odd at the time."

"Why would you suppose Hektor came to you rather than the King with Marquiese's purported treason?"

"I assumed it was because he knew that Marquiese and I have had our disagreements over the years and that I would, therefore, see that justice was done." Frishka struck a thoughtful pose. "I am sure that he thought the King would be biased and confront Marquiese privately, therefore allowing the Prince to escape any retribution."

King Rylan frowned; it was a valid concern, no denying it.

"Speaking of Rider Hektor. Has he returned yet?" asked Lord Hunmis.

"No, not yet, and I fear greatly that something terrible has happened to him." Frishka frowned as he spoke, a display of sorrow and concern that may have been contrived, but, as King Rylan could see, the Court seemed to accept it.

"Lord Frishka, where exactly in Prince Marquiese's readying room did you find the two letters in question?" asked Lord Komph breaking the mood created by Frishka's last statement.

"I found them mixed in with a stack of papers on his desk," the tiger answered at once. "Amongst a number of directives for servants and staff."

"Why would someone leave incriminating documents in a place that almost ensures that someone will read it?"

"Perhaps the letter writer left them there so that Marquiese would find them and then distribute them as he wanted."

"So you think that Marquiese ordered the letters written? Is that what you are inferring?"

"It seems logical. If he had someone else write them and then, by chance, another found them, then it could be proven that it was not his writing, thereby removing him from suspicion." Frishka's eyes narrowed, as if following a marked path. "He could then proceed cautiously for a while before making contact with the bandits again. Whoever found the note would look a fool, and the treason case would be dropped. I am just glad that I went ahead with my trap and caught him on The Beach so that the charges cannot be dismissed solely on the evidence of the letters."

"That does seem to have worked in your favor after all," Lord Komph said, his voice touched with curiosity.

Lord Hunmis said, "Earlier, Prince Marquiese recounted a tale for the Court evidencing the fact that you had left a message under a pathway stone in the gardens many years ago. It seems an odd coincidence that this is the same method that he used to communicate with the bandits now. Do you remember the circumstances of the event?"

"Now that you mention it, I do indeed. He seems to be targeting me as his fool. I find the false letters. He copies a childhood method that I used to exchange a secret message with a long forgotten friend, and his conspirators say I coerced them." The tiger looked from one magistrate to the next. "It would seem that he is doing his best to prove treason against me. Why else would Lady Marilana have sent King Rylan her treason charges while they were out at a meeting with bandits? When they got back and found out that I had placed my charges against them first, Prince Marquiese must have insisted he be named as the one placing the countercharges. I am sure they are not feeling as confident in their plans now that I beat them to the punch."

Frishka finished with a smug smile, but Lord Hunmis ignored him.

The boar said, "How is it that you know Lady Marilana placed the charges?"

"She told me. Obviously she did not know that Marquiese had placed his name to the charges, as that was not announced at the time of the arrests. Then she had her accident and could not attend the first day of court. She claimed the charges to me privately. She was still confused by her concussion and I was doing as King Rylan had instructed me. I was speaking softly to her and trying to comfort her. She was resentful and told me that the charges she had placed against me were going to end my rein. I understood then why the timing of the charges and the naming of who had placed the charges was odd. She could not claim the countercharges as I had claimed she was a conspirator to treason. Prince Marquiese had to do that."

A thoughtful silence fell on the courtroom, and then the Head Magistrate said, "Thank you, Lord Frishka. That is all the questions we have for you at the present time. Court is adjourned."

Frishka inclined his head slightly to the magistrates as they rose.

Marilana knelt quickly as the door flew open. Frishka and his three guards entered at a quick pace. She remained frozen in place until she could determine Frishka's current attitude.

"You and your friends are going to lose the trial," the tiger gloated. "Today's questioning played right into my paws. All of the little annoyances that you have caused have only helped make me look a victim. The evidence is tied up in confusion, and the magistrates are spending most of their time chasing dead ends. They will grow tired of going around in circles, but I will play the victim convincingly and they will find Marquiese guilty."

He moved closer to her.

Without looking up, she smirked and spoke lightly, "Well, I am pleased to see you are setting yourself up for a fall. Your overconfidence is going to make your defeat so much easier."

His kick to her stomach, while not as hard as some he had dealt, never the less left her gasping.

"Get up," he hissed at her, and then turned to his men. "Chain her. We are going for a walk in the gardens.

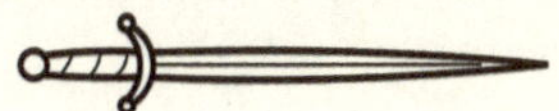

Marquiese stood staring down into the gardens from the dungeon window. King Rylan and Master Castant joined him.

"My son, do not be discouraged. Today did work in Frishka's favor, but we must not lose hope. Tomorrow you will have the chance to discredit what he said. You must think carefully about what to say."

"Father, everything I have said has done what was intended. The magistrates are at least in doubt. He is just staying one step ahead. We are dancing to his tune, and there is no way for me to change that. If Lady Prinka is called to testify, I am sure that she will say I forced her to write the letters and to keep quiet. I have to stay to the truth. They do not."

"What about the accounts of Frishka's Confidant trying to steal from the palace? Could those help shed light on Frishka's character and penchant for law breaking?" King Rylan asked.

"No," Master Castant sighed. "I spent some time asking for more details about those accounts, but everyone involved agreed that it was just Confidant and not Frishka causing those problems."

"Even if it was done under Frishka's orders, he would deny it, and there is no proof of his orders," Marquiese added. "Most of the staff fear Frishka, and many would testify to his nature, but again, it is not solid proof that he plotted against us. The law books are clear that testimonies of character are important, but must be reserved as a last resort in a determination."

They stood in brooding silence for a while, watching people moving about in the gardens. Gardeners tended to the plants, servants and stable staff walked to and from the stables, and groups of nobles enjoyed the last of the sunshine for the day. One group of five people came into view around a tall hedge and Marquiese froze.

"It seems the chapel is not the only place Frishka takes Marilana these days," the Crown Prince said dryly.

"It seems he finally made good on his statement that she could move around the grounds if properly escorted," replied Rylan also studying the entourage.

They watched as Frishka and Marilana approached a bridge over a water garden. Frishka seemed to take Marilana's arm to help her up the steps. She jerked away and marched across the bridge unaided. Frishka hurried to catch up to her. When he did, he stopped and seemed to be speaking urgently. She thrust her chin up and spoke back to him. Marquiese recognized her posture as one she took when angry and defending herself. Frishka gestured with one paw toward the guards. Two of the big brutes stepped up on either side of Marilana. Frishka spun on his heel and marched off on the most direct path back to the palace doors. The two guards hurried Marilana along while the third guard took up the rear.

King Rylan smirked. "It would seem that Marilana does not like the idea of being escorted politely around the grounds."

Marquiese frowned. "Frishka probably hoped that I would see them strolling along, the two of them having just the nicest time. Marilana took offense at something he said or did and made him change his attitude. He might not be dancing to her tune, but she is not dancing to his without a fight."

He sighed and moved back away from the window. King Rylan followed and sat down on his stool. Master Castant took his customary stance against the wall.

"Marquiese, I would suggest that you take the message she just sent you to heart. That display showed you that she is still fighting; she has not given up on the truth. We must think of how we can throw more doubt on his story."

"I think at this point I will just have to wait to see what questions the magistrates ask. I trust them to try to put holes in everyone's stories. They are fair and will not let anything go unsaid."

"If that is the path you chose, I will trust in it." King Rylan arose. "I must go. I have other business to deal with yet tonight. Rest well, my son."

Marquiese sat trying to push the image of Marilana's defiance from his mind, but he could not focus his thoughts. He wondered what was happening to Marilana now. Frishka was clearly furious, and he was not the kind to let such an affront go unpunished.

More likely than not, she will not get supper tonight. Surely he considers her too valuable to consider a more severe punishment than that, he thought without much hope.

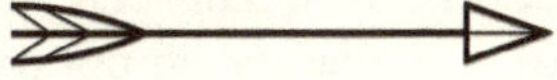

Marilana lay gasping on the floor as Frishka left. She had known that open defiance in the gardens would not go unpunished, but she had to do something. Frishka had been watching the dungeon window. When he was sure someone was looking, very likely Marquiese, he ordered her to look as if she was enjoying her walk. Not a chance.

She struggled into a sitting position against the wall, wincing at the pain, and swallowing to gain control of her stomach. She focused on her breathing, wondering if Marquiese really had seen what happened in the gardens. She hoped not. She knew it was Frishka's intent to distract Marquiese from the proceedings in court. Marquiese's testimony had already stretched Frishka's limits, though the tiger still seemed to have the advantage. She had learned Frishka's plan for the trial, she had kept him distracted, and was learning how to manipulate him without him realizing it. As of yet however, Marilana had nothing more to offer the Court except the evidence of the many beatings she had endured. She was not sure the magistrates were ready to accept such an accusation. She had to wait until she was sure, but she could not wait too much longer. Her life depended on it, she could not afford to continue to expend her energies on so much healing with lack of food and proper sleep.

She struggled to her feet and made her way to the balcony. She leaned back against the wall, breathing the cool evening air. After a time Earek poked his head out of his room and checked to see if anyone was lurking beneath the balcony.

"I was worried that he would come to see me after he got done with you. He did not. I saw your performance in the garden. I know you had to do it, but I am sure that the results in your room were not nice," he spoke softly to the gathering night.

"I will be fine. I just do not want you to worry. He has had some setbacks from things Marquiese remembered from their childhood times. I am hoping that Marquiese can pull a victory from tomorrow so that we do not have to continue this way much longer. Frishka still seems to have the advantage though."

"We will win. I trust you. It is just a matter of time. Stay strong, Marilana my Sister."

"Stay strong, Earek."

They had talked for less than a minute before Marilana slipped back into her room and laid down. She was weaker than she would admit, least of all to Earek, but not nearly as weak as she could become without giving in.

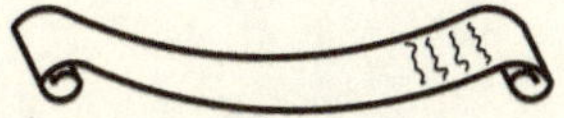

Earek closed his windows and stood watching the dark shadows in the garden. After a time, a man moved out of the shadow beneath a tree and walked down the path. Earek had seen the man moving from shadow to shadow as he and Marilana bade each other goodnight. He had no way of knowing if the man had seen them or not, but something in Earek's stomach writhed with sudden foreboding. They were in trouble. He had no way of warning Marilana. He had no way of telling her not to come out tomorrow night for their pre-arrange chat. If he did not appear, she would worry that something terrible had happened. Of course, if they did speak again, something terrible would happen.

Next time they spoke could be their very last; he had no way to make certain that did not happen.

20

◇ ◇ ◇ ◇ ◇ ◇ ◇ ◇

King Rylan, Master Castant, and the three magistrates rode out early the next morning following the directions Frishka had provided. They found the meadow and the boulders easily and, when they moved around behind the boulders, found the flat rock that signaled the message depository. It had some leaves and dirt on it, but the vines working their way across the other rocks did not cover the flat one.

Master Castant pointed this out and said, "This place has been disturbed recently. And then someone placed leaves and dirt to conceal the disturbance."

"Let us have a look," the King said.

They dismounted, removed the rock, and examined the hole underneath.

"By what I can tell, I would say this has been used as recently as a few days previous."

"How can it have been used that recently? His Highness has been in the tower for well on a fifnight now," said Lord Komph.

"I never said that His Highness had used it. As far as I know, he has never been here," replied Master Castant. "Nonetheless, someone has used it. It may have been a spy of the true traitor warning that the location was about to be compromised, or just some local kids leaving love letters. I have no way of knowing."

"Yes, of course not. Thank you, Master Castant. Your knowledge and help are most appreciated."

As they were mounting to ride back to the city, several riders approached. Master Castant gave them a wave. "These are my men. I have had them scouting the area for the past several days," he said to King Rylan. "If I may, I will speak with them a moment."

When he was done, Master Castant returned with news.

"One of my men just returned from Prince Dansho and brought Prince Marquiese's letter back," he said to Rylan and the magistrates. "We can have Sir Libor validate it."

"Good. What else?" the King implored.

"Prince Dansho sent word that Rider Hektor checked in with the south gate guard mid-afternoon, delivered the message, and logged out a replacement horse. He checked out with the south gate guard before dinner. One of the gate guards said he remembered Hektor saying something about getting to his mother's for supper. One of my other riders went to Rider Hektor's mother's place. She has not seen her son since last month."

Lord Quinre looked to the riders, saying, "Perhaps one of you should take Hektor's mother some flowers and reassurances that we are trying to find out what has happened to her son."

One of the riders moved a step closer. He said, "I'll gladly take the reassurances to her, but flowers are more likely to get thrown back in my face. She is allergic to flowers, Your Lordship. I grew up around her place. Hektor was my best friend as a child. She won't let flowers closer to her house than fifty paces. The reassurances, though, those she will welcome."

"Thank you," Quinre replied. "Please share those, if you would."

Master Castant nodded to his men and they bowed to the King and lords before riding off into the trees. "I have sent them to backtrack Hektor's route and to look for any signs of what might have happened."

"Very good," Lord Hunmis said. "So we know at least that His Highness did send Rider Hektor with a message to Prince Dansho. However, the Crown Prince may actually have sent both letters; the one to Prince Dansho as a means of covering for the other. If I understand Rider Hektor's sense of duty, however, he would not have told Lord Frishka about the letter to Prince Dansho; it would have compromised that part of his errand."

"If that is so, then Lord Frishka would not have known about it," Lord Quinre added.

"In which case, Rider Hektor would have delivered the letter and then set off to fulfill his assignment set by Lord Frishka."

"Yes, to look for the bandits," Quinre responded.

"Very logical conclusions *if* everyone is telling the truth about those events. We cannot yet rule out the possibility that some of the testimonies are outright lies, although it seems His Highness was telling the truth about knowing his riders well," added Lord Komph.

The magistrates continued to debate this new information as they turned and rode back toward Maefair.

As they did so, Master Castant fell in beside King Rylan.

"Sire, the magistrates are right to question everything, but these new facts will likely not help," he said quietly. "The only thing I can think of now that would prove Marquiese's innocence beyond a doubt would be finding Rider Hektor alive and hiding. He could testify to the truth of the matter."

The King shook his head. "I am afraid that even that would not prove anything. So much doubt has been cast by the conflicting stories that the magistrates have begun to look for coercion around every corner. If Hektor agreed with Frishka, the magistrates could say he had been threatened; just as they might if Hektor agreed with Marquiese. It is becoming much more difficult to prove the truth of anything, I am afraid. What we need is solid undeniable physical proof."

*

Marquiese entered the courtroom with a look of determination on his face.

The magistrates would be looking for signs of worry or stress, so King Rylan did the same. He fully expected his son to tell the truth without equivocation, but with the trial leaning in Frishka's favor, he might try to sway the judges by manipulating the facts in some way.

When Marquiese stood in the witness box, Lord Komph opened the questioning, eyeing Marquiese with notable intensity.

"Prince Marquiese, we know that the three letters in question were written by someone else. The question then is who did you order to write them?"

Marquiese's expression darkened, but his tone was level. "I did not ask, coerce, or command anyone to write letters ordering an attack on my father, and I resent the insinuation. Moreover, I had no knowledge that such letters ever existed. They were certainly not in any of my rooms when I left on the morning in question. In fact, Magistrates, I had not known of the existence of these letters until you told me about them during my first appearance here in court."

Lord Komph pressed the matter, saying. "Who are your conspirators?"

"I have no conspirators."

"Lady Marilana and Master Earek; those we know. Who else?"

"Marilana and Earek are not my conspirators. They betrayed me on The Beach on the day in question. If they support my claims now, it is for reasons unknown to me. I most certainly did not ask it of them. In fact, I have asked no one to stand with me. I stand alone."

Lord Quinre leaned forward, his voice sharp. "Why would you have The King attacked?"

A little more heat entered Marquiese's voice. "I have never in the past nor would I in the future plan an act of aggression against my father. I would put my life before his even if he ordered me not too. What would my motivation be for such an act? There is none. I will be king when I am king, and I have no intention of becoming king soon. I wish a long life and sustaining good health for my father. And I wish for myself to enjoy the time I have with him."

"You could enjoy that life with him when you are king just as easily as with him as king."

Marquiese's chin rose defiantly as did his voice. "When I was a boy, I swore to The Goddess to defend my father against all who would do him harm, foreign and domestic, without prejudice. I have never forgotten that pledge."

The Crown Prince dropped to one knee and fixed his eyes on Rylan. "I swear again now, on my life to The Goddess that I will honor, obey, and defend my father, King Rylan, son of Coryan of Redsands." His gaze shifted to the magistrates. "I also swear to The Goddess that I have told and will tell nothing but the truth to the Court."

He rose and stared silently at the magistrates.

"Words of desperation?" Quinre said, more a statement than question.

"If that is the only way you will hear my words of truth, then that is what I must do."

All three magistrates leaned back in their chairs and contemplated Marquiese for a while. Finally Lord Hunmis spoke. "Why did you go down to The Beach that day at that exact time?"

Marquiese took a calming breath, the heat less noticeable in his voice. "Marilana asked me to walk with her. The time of our arrival on The Beach was not planned. Leaving the Royal Palace when we did placed us at The Beach at noon. It was not my plan to stop at all, and we would surely have been back to the palace by noon had Marilana not taken so long retrieving her scarf before we left."

The magistrates exchanged a look. "You mean that Marilana delayed your ride by long enough to place you at The Beach at noon?"

"Yes."

"It has been suggested that you made promises to Marilana in order to secure her assistance in the matter of your betrayal. What promises did you make?" asked Lord Quinre shrewdly.

"I promised her nothing."

"Then why did you bring her here to the Royal Palace in the first place?"

"She was my friend when I was in the Southern Tip. I had spoken to Lady Annabella about the situation because it seemed to me that she was training Marilana to be her heir. Lady Annabella said it was her dearest secret. I asked her to send Marilana to the Royal Palace of Maefair to study for the month required by succession law. I offered to send an invitation when Lady Annabella was ready. When the time came, Lady Annabella told me that she was going to name

Earek as her second heir and asked if I would invite him as well. I agreed willingly as they were my dear friends."

"So you had no intentions of offering Marilana marriage, of making her your queen?"

"Marilana needed to study away from the Southern Tip in order to fulfill succession law. As she was my friend I offered a safe place for her to study. I had no further intentions than to help Lady Annabella and her heirs to establish their position among the Nobility and the Royal Court," Marquiese replied. If his voice had been hot before, now it was ice.

Lord Hunmis leaned forward. "It is said that Marilana is both wild and dangerous and that her intent was to harm Lord Frishka that day on The Beach. It is said also that Master Earek tends toward violence and has a propensity for lying."

Marquiese's voice was flat and disdainful when he said, "If you listen to lies rather than learn the truth then I cannot expect a different opinion. The people of the Southern Tip are just as civilized as anyone in this room. They may place even more emphasis on truth and honor than most people in Maefair. Earek is one of the least violent people I know and I cannot recall a single lie he has ever told. Is Marilana wild? Not in the slightest. Is she dangerous? Most assuredly so. She could out shoot and out swordplay anyone in this room. She is a bandit hunter, one of the best I have ever known, and has been since she was ten. She has saved my life on several occasions. She could have killed Frishka that day on The Beach. Quickly and easily. Instead she tackled him high so that her momentum would carry her away from him. Her attack was nothing more than a distraction."

"A bandit hunter!" exclaimed the boar. "That beautiful child? Capable of killing people? Surely you jest? She could no more be skilled with a sword or bow than I with a needle and thread!"

"On the contrary, Lord Hunmis." Rylan spoke calmly. "She is more than skilled in the arts of war; she is deadly. She is a highly acclaimed bandit hunter, known to some as The Ghost, accredited with more than thirty heads. She has ridden for me twice in the past at Lady Annabella's behest.

"Years ago, I asked Lady Annabella to arrange for her best bandit hunter to take on a particular job. In response, she pointed to a young girl mucking out stalls and offered to introduce me. In my disbelief, I said no. Lady Annabella went over to the girl and spoke to her of the bandit I wanted hunted down. The girl nodded and left quickly. I felt sure that she simply worked for some bandit hunter, perhaps as a messenger. But the next day, she arrived back with the bandit's head in a sack. She was dressed in hunter garb and was grim with determination.

"Later I saw her practicing her bow with Lady Annabella's Captain-General. She hit every target dead center. He had even set a series of covered targets, nearly impossible to see much less hit, and she hit them all.

"Needless to say, the next time I asked for a bandit to be hunted in the Southern Tip, I asked for her. She returned again the day after with a head in a sack."

Lord Hunmis had gone pale and Lord Quinre looked disapproving, but Lord Komph nodded slowly.

"I have heard of The Ghost," he mused. "I have heard rumors that she was young and that she never failed. I have talked to magistrates in the Southern Tip who have dealt with her. It is no wonder to me now that Lady Marilana has such a presence about her when most others are uncomfortable in court."

"And we just let her walk around the palace! She could have killed anyone she wanted!" Lord Hunmis was outraged.

King Rylan cleared his throat, stopping Lord Hunmis in his tracks.

"You have not dealt much with bandit hunters, have you, Lord Hunmis? They have a very strict code of conduct. Marilana has not been in the role of bandit hunter here. She has been Lady Marilana." He emphasized the title carefully. "She would not have killed anyone unless she had perceived a threat to someone's life. Even then she probably would have taken the individual into custody rather than kill them. But we have traveled a long way away from Prince Marquiese's questioning. Might I suggest we return to it."

Lord Quinre frowned in thought, and Lord Hunmis continued to mutter and shake his head. Lord Komph, in contrast, nodded briskly and turned to Marquiese. He said, "Thank you, Highness, for offering your knowledge of Marilana's and Earek's personalities. You claim that you would gain little by acting against King Rylan and that Lord Frishka would gain much by acting against you. Please explain for everyone why you make these claims."

"Certainly, Your Honor." Marquiese's voice was level and calm, his face showing no emotion. "I am the Crown Prince. When my father steps down from the throne, I will become king. If I were to act against the King, I would at best become king sooner rather than later. At worst, I would be banished or killed. It is a foolish choice to risk everything I have ever known to gain the possibility of becoming king a few years sooner than if I simply waited. Frishka instead will never become king unless something happens to me. He has tried in the past to change that. When he first came to Maefair, he tried to convince my father that because he is the older, that he should be first in line for succession. Later, he tried to best me in a battle of swords in an effort to prove himself a better choice for the future king; he failed. In a more recent and even more desperate attempt to eliminate me, he had his cohort Confidant attack me; the attack failed. I see his direction plainly behind this trial as yet another attempt to take the throne for himself."

"Do you think it possible that someone else is manipulating the events so that both of you are victims?"

"It may be possible, but Frishka did taunt me on The Beach, saying that I would not get out of this as easily as I have in the past," the Crown Prince responded. "And because all of our past encounters have always been by his design to gain the throne for himself, it is clear to me what his motivation is."

"Thank you, Prince Marquiese. Court is adjourned for today."

Marilana and Marquiese crossed paths as they were both escorted through the palace. Frishka was escorting Marilana back from a long visit in the chapel. Three guards were returning Marquiese to the tower dungeon following his testimony. Marilana had been forced to wear a dress chosen for her by Frishka, with a plunging neckline that left her feeling embarrassed. They were both shackled and chained.

Their eyes met. Hatred burned in his, and his face tightened to a scowl. Tears sprang to Marilana's eyes when she saw this, but she did not look away. She stood frozen until he turned down the hall and was gone.

Only then did she realize that Frishka was standing next to her, holding her arm in a pseudo-protective fashion. She jerked her arm out of his paw and started down the corridor, furious, even as Master Castant turned down the hall in arrears of the palace guards, his eyes watching the interaction carefully.

Frishka caught up to her. He pushed her into her rooms and locked the door behind her. The condescending tiger had not even bothered to unchain her.

She made her way over to the couch and sank deeply into it, the tears still tinseling her cheek. All she could think of was the look on Marquiese's face.

Oh, Marquiese, what would I give to see you smile at me again? I did what I had to do to save us all. Please believe me. I have no choice how you see me. I must do what I must. I cannot stop Frishka from touching me or dressing me as he will. Please forgive me.

She looked down at the dress she was wearing. Frishka had become obsessed with her attire. For his most recent punishment he had removed all of the dresses and accessories from her wardrobe. Every dress he had brought her since had necklines far lower than she thought decent and tight enough to accentuate every curve of her body. She knew she was a beautiful lioness. She had been the recipient of many compliments over the years, and much jealousy. Marilana felt dirty wearing gowns far more appropriate for the local brothels, even more so that they were Frishka's choices. He had even taken her sewing kit so that she could not alter any of the dresses. Marilana laughed at that. He was, in many ways, firmly in her grasp.

Then she shook her head in disgust. She hated manipulating creatures.

She stared out the windows, her eyes coming to rest on the palace horse pastures. She longed to be among the horses. She longed to be back in the forest. She longed for a time when her life wasn't filled with complications, most of which she had no control over.

She leaned her head back and closed her eyes, the afternoon sun warmed her. She drifted off to sleep and dreamed of the Southern Tip, her friend Child, and the peace of a meadow she might never see again, a meadow where she and Marquiese had created some of her most enduring—and most endearing—memories.

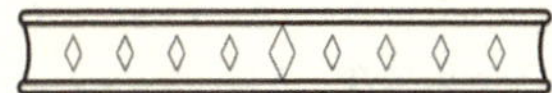

Marquiese was furious. He paced the length of the dungeon cell, oblivious to the heavy ball impeding every other step. King Rylan and Master Castant watched this display of temper in muted silence.

The King had sent the guards down to the lower guardroom so they would not be privy to anything the Crown Prince might say or do.

Now he waited. When the silence grew unbearable, Master Castant broke it, saying, "I will say that court went well today, in my opinion."

Marquiese spun around. "Went well? How can you say that? I lost my temper. I said things I should never have had to say. And all Lord Hunmis seemed to care about was the revelation that Marilana is a bandit hunter. He will have to be watched."

"Hunmis will not be a problem," the King assured him. "He will voice his opinions, but the others will not be swayed. Quinre may not like women fighting, but he recognizes skill where it is due. And Komph was as impressed as I have ever seen him." He turned a stern gaze toward his son. "That is not the reason you are riled up. Would you care to share the real reason?"

Marquiese sniffed and resumed his pacing.

"He was holding her arm. Protecting her. Protecting her *from me*. And she just stood there. It was as if she was so shocked to see me that she had forgotten how to move. A nice little show for the fallen prince. So much for her fighting him. Clearly she has given in to him. He has become her protector." He spat the words.

"That was hardly what I saw," Master Castant said, his voice unconcerned.

Marquiese spun on him.

"Not what you saw?" He spat heavily, then growled. "What did you see?"

"I saw pain when she looked at you. Excruciating pain, my friend. I saw tears. Tears in response to the hateful gaze you vouchsafed her. And when she realized whose paw was resting on her arm, I saw her jerk her arm away and storm down the hall." Castant held his good friend's eye. "The show was there for you, but it was Frishka's doing not Marilana's."

Marquiese turned his back on them both and stared out the window.

"Did you see her dress, too, oh great observer? I would say she has certainly changed her attitude about a great many things."

"Again you are wrong, my son," King Rylan said quietly. "She has not changed."

Marquiese turned, his stance aggressive, a retort fast upon his lips. His father silenced him with a raised paw. He said, "I have been monitoring Frishka's activities. He sent a man to a tailor into the city last night and collected an order of eight dresses. All silk, all in a style that no noble would ever wear in the Royal Palace. Nor, in fact, would any decent peasant. I imagine this to be his way of punishing Marilana's little display in the gardens. If she is not dancing to Frishka's tune, which she clearly is not, then he will restrict the tune until she has no choice."

Master Castant nodded. "I think you are right, Your Majesty. Frishka is in a position to control what she wears, what she eats, where she goes, and, to an extent, who sees her. Frishka was not upset by the chance encounter in the hallway. I think he was quite pleased, at least until Marilana jerked her arm out of his paw. He did not look so confident after that."

Marquiese turned back to the window and leaned against the sill.

"I just cannot stand this," the young lion said, leaning against the sill. "I feel so helpless. I want to know what he is doing, all that time he is spending with her alone." He paused again. "I want to rip his throat out."

King Rylan exchanged a worried look with Master Castant.

"I just want her out of his grip," Marquiese hissed.

"I understand," the King of Redsands said. "I want the same thing. But you have done everything you can. It is truly up to the magistrates now. Unfortunately, I think the trial still has a long way to go. The magistrates are as unsure of the truth as if night has suddenly become day. I do not want to think what condition Marilana and Earek will be in if this continues much longer. I do not know what Frishka does with them, but I know they are not eating as well as they should. Too many trays of food have been sent back to the kitchen or been carried out by Frishka's men.

Rylan arose, put a comforting paw on his son's arm, and turned to go. "Trust your heart, Marquiese."

Marquiese did not look back. He did not move, his eyes fixed on the fast approach of evening.

Marilana woke to the sound of her name. She was still lying on the couch; the sun was little more than a red glow in the distance. It had been hours since she had returned to the confines of her room. Confused she looked around and saw an empty dinner tray sitting on the table. Craning her head around further, she saw one of Frishka's men sitting back in a chair watching her with a crude smirk on his face. How desperately she wanted to remove that smirk, permanently. *Be patient,* she told herself.

"Marilana," crooned Frishka from above her. "Did you have a nice nap? We have had a nice time ourselves, watching you sleep while eating your supper. You are most pleasant company when you do nothing but breathe deeply."

"To bad for you that a sleeping woman is the best company you can enjoy," she said with great calculation.

His eyes widened in mock surprise, and he walked around to the front of the couch.

"Tut, tut. What a nasty tongue you have. Maybe someday I will do you a favor and remove it for you, and then you won't be able to offend all your friends."

He paused and looked her up and down slowly. She was still wearing the gown he had chosen for her, and she could not stem a wave of embarrassment and revulsion.

"You were quite difficult to rouse out of your sleep. Could it be that you are weaker than you are letting on? Perhaps we should test your true strength?"

"Is that the only thing you can do, test a woman's physical strength against your own? Perhaps your limited strength fails you at the most inopportune time? Then you would be left with only your weak intelligence to bore her to death," Marilana remarked sarcastically.

She had done it, provoked him once again. He struck his fist down into her stomach. She tried to curl her body around the pain, but two of the tiger's men grabbed her, pulling the chain tight between her ankles and wrists, letting her skirt slide up to expose her knees. She focused on her breathing. Slow and deep. *Focus. Hold his eye.*

"You are truly pitiful, but not as pitiful as you will become. Oh no, I will break you," he said, his confidence overwhelming. Then he had to boast, just as she knew he would. "You see the magistrates are leaning heavily in my favor. The next time I speak with them they will be pulled even more to my side. Nothing you or Earek can say will change that."

He drew his long thin dagger from his belt and began lightly trailing it through the fur of her exposed legs, not hard enough to draw blood, but enough to send shivers up her spine. *Breathe,* she thought.

"I cannot wait to introduce you to a dear friend of mine, Marilana," he said with great fervor. "He knows how to inflict physical pain like no other. And the mental pain he inflicts is even more noteworthy. You will learn to appreciate his skills. When I have won this joke of a trial, it will be easy to eliminate the King and any of the lords and ladies that oppose me," he spat. "I will be king and you will be my queen. You will have no power, of course. You will be nothing more than a vessel to bring forth my children. Of course, you are a lion and I a tiger, and while you could bear my child, that child would not be able to have children of his own. That is a problem. Instead, my dear friend, who just happens to be a lion, would only be too happy to plant his seed in you. He has already agreed to bed you as many times as it takes to get a good number of male heirs, all of whom I will adopt.

"You see, my friend is this moment gathering my army so that if I do by some slim chance lose the trial, I can come back and take over by force. I trust him the way Marquiese used to trust you. After I have taken Redsands, I will conquer Ankenhun, my homeland. My grandfather has unfortunately died, but my uncle rules there now as king. I will make him pay for my suffering and humiliation when they disowned me and took my name from me. You will have to bear heirs for all the kingdoms I conquer."

His blade never stopped moving as he spoke, like a serpent choosing where to strike. Marilana moved not a muscle. She took in every word he was saying, amazed and please at how loose his tongue had become.

"Why do you even want to be king?" she sneered. "It's not like you care about governing people or leading others in life."

He chuckled with amusement. "I would have thought that obvious to a girl like you. Power, my dear, I want the power of the throne. The power to send others to fight and die for me. The power to have everything I want—armies, females, food, followers, slaves. My mother once tried to tell me I don't need more power, that Rylan was a good king, but my friend showed her it was better to help me get what I want. He will show you the proper way to behave as well."

Frishka used his blade to slide her skirts up her legs another inch.

"Of course when my friend is not bedding you, I will be. I will not pass up the opportunity to enjoy myself, especially at your discomfort. Perhaps I will even grant you the lives of your friends. I am sure Earek will enjoy watching me bed you. I would even consider letting Marquiese watch the show, if I was willing to let him live long enough."

Marilana's breath caught in her chest at the thought of Frishka torturing her in front of Marquiese. Luckily Frishka thought it was because he had slid her skirts up some more. He smiled at her fear and slid her skirts up even further. She began to tremble with fear and anger. If he learned her weaknesses, it would be the end of her, and if he won, it would be the end of peace for more than just Redsands. She had to stop him, she could not fail. His grin widened showing his pointed teeth.

Marilana forced her voice to work; it was dry and croaked as she spoke. "I would kill myself before you managed to get me to your bed."

His face twisted with rage and the dagger blade pierced the skin of her thigh. Marilana clamped her teeth shut to stop the gasp of pain.

"I am smarter than you. I will prevent you from killing yourself. Do you think that I would not have taken steps to keep you from harming yourself? You little fool. You will not touch a knife or a rope or anything I deem even remotely damaging. You will be chained and under guard except when I am with you." He forced a smile back on his face and his voice back to coolness. "You will enjoy the times we will spend together."

Marilana took a deep breath. "You are the fool. Do you truly think I need a blade or a rope? I can use anything.

Clothing, bed sheets, cushions, chains, even the wall you chain me to. You will not stop me, and you are too stupid to break me. I will never give up until I win. And the moment a chance avails itself, I will kill you."

She was pushing hard now, but she needed to redirect his thoughts and it was necessary to learn if he would accept her skills as the truth.

His smile became a sneer, and a fanatic light shone in his eyes. "You will be mine. I have all the resources I need to stop you from killing me, but that goal is what will keep you alive until you break. You will not kill yourself as long as you think there is a chance to get your revenge on me. I will use that to keep you on the brink as long as I can, to make you suffer for as long as possible before you break. You are already starting down that path. I will see you suffer. I will see you live in the palm of my paw."

Pulling all the moisture she could, she spat in Frishka's face as he bent over her. His fist slammed her down into the couch again. His face twisted in rage again as he slapped her across the face and then began to pummel her stomach. She could not draw breath; stars began to pop in front of her eyes. Darkness was crowding her vision. She could see Frishka's face getting closer, felt his paw grip her chin then his lips pushed on to hers. Hot air flowed into her lungs. Again and again hot air flowed into her. She took a breath of her own, cool air flowed through her nose and her lungs expanded more fully. Vision began to return.

Frishka knelt holding her head back slightly. He pushed his lips to hers again in a fierce kiss. She tried to pull back but he had a strong grip and she was weakened by the lack of breath. He pulled back smiling.

"You see, I know enough to keep someone on the brink of death and pull them back so that I can do it all again. You will learn that I am your world."

He stood back and motioned to one of his men. The chain and wrist manacles were removed, and they left. Marilana lay crumpled and gasping on the couch, unable to lift herself. She focused on one thought, reminding herself that her plan had to work.

The stupid fool was so close to the truth, so close to my weakness. He hates Marquiese too much to keep him alive. But if he does keep him alive, I will do anything, anything, to stop him from harming Marquiese. He never saw it though. If he had, I would not have a chance.

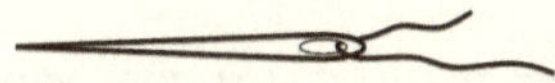

Altia was crying silently as she bent over Marilana's crumpled form. *She always seems so sure, so strong. Now look at her.*

"It's not right, M'Lady," she whispered. "You should never have to suffer this way."

Marilana moaned. Her eyelids fluttered.

"M'Lady, it's me, Altia. I have to get you into your bed."

Marilana grunted, and the caracal helped her sit up. She got under Marilana's arm and pulled her to her feet. Haltingly, they crossed the room and climbed the few steps to the bed. Marilana sank weakly back onto the pillows.

"This has gone on long enough," the maid said firmly.

"No," Marilana uttered. "I will be alright. Please do not say anything to anyone. Not yet."

Altia shook her head, tears streaming down her face. "No! Please! Let me go to the King. You are too weak to go on. You need his help. Please let me do something."

A thin smile worked its way across Marilana's face. "I am not as weak as you think."

"You did not rouse when I came with the dinner tray. You always wake at the slightest sound, but you did not. I coughed a little to try to wake you. Frishka just smirked and sent me away. He was here a long time. I didn't dare come to you until I knew he was in his rooms. Why must you make him so angry? Why can't you just obey him for the little things? It surely won't matter to the trial?" The caracal sobbed even harder.

"I cannot give in to him. I am sure that he had every intention of torturing me again even before he saw how deeply I was sleeping," Marilana said softly. "Do you expect me to take torture without fighting back?"

"Do you expect me to watch you being tortured without trying to do something?" Altia responded.

Marilana raised her paw and gently brushed the tears from the caracal's face. "I know it is hard to watch me becoming weaker and gaining more bruises, but we must be smarter than Frishka. Think, Altia. What would the magistrates say if you went to them and claimed to have tended my injuries? They would say I inflicted them on myself and that you were my conspirator. Or, at the very least, that I lied to you. We must find a way to make them see the truth. We must wait for them to be ready to see the truth. If not, all my suffering will be for nothing."

Altia sobbed harder. "I know the truth. I know the wisdom of your plan. It is just so hard to do this by myself. I need help. Please, let me go to someone."

Marilana thought for a moment. Then she tipped her head and said, "Go to Father Iscoot and tell him everything. Do not let him tell anyone else, however. Bring him to me if you must. He can help you with what you need."

Altia nodded, jumped up, and scurried out.

Marilana woke from the healing trance as soft footsteps approached the bed. Earlier, she had mistakenly allowed her body to enter a deep sleep at the wrong time, and she could not afford to make such a mistake again. Through the darkness, she could make out two people approaching the bed.

"M'Lady, I have brought Father Iscoot," Altia whispered.

"Father, thank you for coming," Marilana replied, her senses fully alert.

"Is it true what this young one says about the beatings and the torture at the paws of Lord Frishka? About her helping you? Bringing you food? Tending your wounds?" Father Iscoot uttered in a stunned voice.

"It is."

"But King Rylan would be furious if he knew. How dare Frishka treat you this way? It is an outrage!"

"Father, please listen to me. If I had gone running to King Rylan the first time, Frishka would have gotten his paw slapped, nothing else. Now his cruelty can be well-documented. The magistrates must know the quality of my character before learning about this. They must see the true battle going on; my refusal to accept Frishka as My Lord and King; my refusal to abandon Prince Marquiese and King Rylan; and most importantly, my ongoing attempts to lead Frishka into costly mistakes and to reveal his true plans. The magistrates must see these things of their own accord and not at King Rylan's urging. I am sorry to involve you in this and to ask for your silence, but Altia does need help."

Of course I cannot tell you the rest of the plan. Marilana added to herself. *You would not approve of my taking on the burden of these beatings in order to learn about my opponent. I learn his mannerisms, thoughts, plans, everything about his life, so that I can learn to manipulate him. He may think he is training me, but I am training him. Neither of you would understand how or why I do this, but when the time is right, he will tell the magistrates everything they need to know to proclaim his guilt.*

The priest pondered Marilana's words for a very long time, pacing the room with a paw to his whiskered chin. Finally, the gnarled and graying leopard drew a deep breath and said, "Very well, I will give you my silence."

"Thank you," Marilana sighed.

"But not if your well-being is at stake, young lady," he said firmly. "Now what can I do?"

Altia set about telling the priest what her limits were and what assistance he could offer. Father Iscoot listened, took notes, and made several suggestions. In very little time, they had a plan and he departed. When Marilana and Altia were alone again, the young maid pulled bottles from her pockets and laid a bundle of food on the edge of the bed. "You eat, M'Lady," the caracal said and began mixing tonics in earnest.

Marilana ate a half loaf of bread and a few strips of cheese while Altia administered her remedies. The cut on Marilana's thigh was deep, but the thinness of the blade let the skin close nicely. It had missed the major blood vessels and tendons. Altia washed it and then made a bandage from the ruined dress Marilana had been wearing.

"Why were you able to waken tonight when I brought Father Iscoot, but not earlier?" Altia whispered.

"I let myself become too comfortable this afternoon. Too relaxed. It was my mistake," the young lioness said simply. "I will not let it happen again."

"If you don't sleep deeply enough, you are naturally draining yourself of more energy. You are not eating enough to lose that energy." Altia's tone was part awe, part accusation.

"I am use to it. I have not let myself sleep more than a few hours at a time since I was ten. But you are right. I have not been getting enough sleep. I will do better from now on, I promise."

Altia nodded, then gathered her supplies and left. Marilana focused her thoughts and let herself drift into a deep, controlled sleep. She really did need it.

21

Earek stood in the witness box and fidgeted. The three magistrates sat silently and watched him fidget. King Rylan observed the entire interaction and knew that this was part of the magistrates' plan. The idea was to make the witness so uncomfortable and confused that he or she would blurt out the truth just to put an end to the staring and break the silence once and for all.

When this didn't happen, Lord Komph took matters into his own paws and leaned well forward in his seat. Earek was so startled by the sudden movement that he almost jumped out of the witness box.

"What were your exact instructions from Prince Marquiese?" the red fox asked without preamble.

"What? I mean . . . I . . . I . . . had no instructions from His Highness," Earek stammered. He drew a shallow breath and added, "I have not spoken to His Highness since the day before our arrests."

"So you claim. The fact is that your story and that of Prince Marquiese do not match up. We know what really happened. We know that you have a history of telling lies, and we demand that you tell us the truth at once," Lord Komph snapped, his voice aggressive and accusatory.

It was a common tactic. Tell the witness that you know the truth and that you know they are lying. Most of the time, if the subject is lying, they amend their story accordingly or simply blurt out the truth. Rylan was not sure how Earek would respond, but his expression changed slightly when told he had a history of lying.

"Excuse me, but you are mistaken. I have not lied to Your Honors," Earek said in a far more forceful voice. The young black leopard drew his shoulders back and straightened. "Not a single word. Not a single phrase."

It was almost like seeing a different Earek standing where the more timid one had been moments before. King Rylan recalled his son saying how the creatures of the Southern Tip placed high honor on telling the truth, and clearly Earek was responding to the slight to his honor.

Lord Komph pressed the matter. "Do not lie to us, Master Earek."

"I swear my life to The Goddess that I have never and will never lie to the Court. If there are inconsistencies between the stories you have heard, it is not my doing. I am willing to guess that the inconsistencies are not between my story and Prince Marquiese's or mine and Lady Marilana's, but between my story and Lord Frishka's. I am even willing to go so far as to say that of the four stories, the only one that differs is Lord Frishka's." Earek looked from one magistrate to the next. "I am also willing to go so far as to bet that he is the one who conjured up, as you put it, my history of lying."

Earek's face took on a rather thoughtful, brooding expression. Lord Komph leaned back, but his eyes never left the witness. Lords Quinre and Hunmis had moved not an inch throughout the exchange and still stared at the black leopard. One moment of silence stretched into many, but this time Earek defiantly stood his ground, his eyes fixed on the magistrates.

"Very well," Lord Quinre said with a look at his fellow magistrates. "Tell us why Lord Frishka would have chosen you to throw the net over Prince Marquiese."

Earek's voice never wavered. "I believe Lord Frishka chose me for two reasons. First, I am highly skilled at moving in complete silence. This was necessary in order to preserve the element of surprise. The net was heavy and Prince Marquiese would have been able to dodge the net had he been forewarned by even a second.

"Second, and more important, I am Prince Marquiese's friend. Lord Frishka would want as much doubt placed on this trial as possible and, as he planned, I am now here in court responding to accusations of lies and doubt is thick on everything I say. Also, as Lord Frishka surely planned, you can rest assured that Prince Marquiese is spending far too much time considering my apparent betrayal rather than considering his own defense."

Lord Hunmis leaned forward. "How long were you untied before Prince Marquiese and Lady Marilana climbed down to The Beach that day?"

"It is hard to say exactly. From my position I could not see the sun or track its position other than by watching shadows. I would say a little more than an hour before they appeared."

"An hour! In your original testimony you said you were untied only moments before they were supposed to arrive."

"I beg to differ, Lord Hunmis. What I said was that as the time of their arrival drew near, I was untied. The men around me spent the morning dozing and taking turns keeping watch. When the order came to untie me, they were all awake and fully alert. For a disciplined battle group, it was a common run of the mill ambush. You set up much earlier than the expected arrival of your target so that there is no chance of a missed opportunity. The men's sudden alertness told me that His Highness' arrival was imminent. But there was a restlessness among the younger soldiers that told me Marilana and His Highness must be running late."

"And you recognized these signs how, I wonder?"

"Captain-General Zariff. He trained me."

"Why did you not mention this before?" asked Lord Komph.

"I did not think it relevant. The detailed working of a group of soldiers waiting for an ambush was nothing extraordinary, nor was the fact that His Highness was running late as often happens when leaving the city. Is it pertinent?"

"No," replied Lord Hunmis smoothly. "Just that we would have preferred to have heard about this at the start."

"We have no more questions for you at this time, Master Earek. Thank you," Komph said. "Court adjourned."

"We have been seen," Earek said from his window when he and Marilana rendezvoused that evening.

"Are you sure? When?"

"Last time."

"Frishka has said nothing. Are you sure it was one of his?"

"He has said nothing to me either, but I am sure. We will not get away with it this time."

"In that case, how was court today?"

"Marilana, we were seen," Earek said desperately.

"Earek, my friend and brother. If he has been waiting to catch us in the act, then we are caught, and there is nothing to be gained by worrying about it. So let us say what needs saying and get on with it."

He smiled in spite of himself. Her matter of fact tone and confidence were calming and heartening to hear. She would never give up; he knew that.

"The magistrates tried some different tactics," the young leopard said finally. He described them in short and then added, "I do not think they know what the truth is, nor do they have any idea who to trust. If this goes on much longer, I am afraid that they will not even trust each other. Doubt and fear are corrosive motivators."

"That they are," the young lioness agreed. "Trust your heart, my friend. Tell the truth, no matter what. Trust that I do the same. We are the last stones of Marquiese's defense; we must not fail."

"Nor shall we," the black leopard replied.

"We had best go now. Until we meet again, Brother."

The finality of Marilana's voice chilled Earek to the bone as he spoke the ancient parting phrase: "Be at peace with The Goddess, Sister."

He stood still and heard the latch click on Marilana's balcony doors. Then, taking a deep breath, he turned to face his room. It was empty. With dread carving a hole in his guts, he closed his window and made himself ready for bed, knowing without a shred of doubt what Marilana, with her great heart and steadfast courage, would soon be facing.

22

Marilana slipped into her room and closed the balcony doors without turning to face the room. She knew Frishka was waiting for her. She suspected he had brought more than his usual contingent of guards. She considered feigning surprise, but decided against it. She took a breath trying to still her racing heart and turned.

The room was empty.

"No," Marilana gasped and clutched her paws to her mouth.

Had she miscalculated? Had Frishka turned his wrath on Earek instead? She could hear nothing through the thick stone walls. Maybe Earek had been wrong, maybe they hadn't been seen after all. Maybe Frishka was simply making her wait to let her feel relieved first. Marilana began to pace in frustration. She had to keep her hold on Frishka, she could not let his anger slip away from her. Thoughts spun through her head as she continued to pace late into the night. Altia came and made her go to bed. Marilana slept fitfully, dreaming of Frishka torturing Earek and Altia, and killing Marquiese in dozens of painful ways. Eventually she slept deeply.

*

Marilana woke late the next morning. Bright sunlight filled the room with light and Marilana's heart grew heavier with dread. Frishka had not come to wake her. He had not even let her breakfast tray enter her rooms. Marilana got up and paced some more.

She needed to push Frishka's temper today, she had hoped to do so last night as well, but he had not come. She needed to see how far she could manipulate his response. If he lost control, he would have to explain her condition to the Court, and that would be a push to the magistrates. If he said she did it to herself, she would of course tell the truth. One of them would be lying. The problem would be to convince the magistrates that it was worth listening to her. Earek had said they were confused and doubtful of the truth. She would have to be very careful in court tomorrow no matter what happened today.

Deciding quickly, she went to the washbasin. The pitcher was still empty. He would, of course, have to let her wash before her court appearance tomorrow, but his withholding of such basic privileges in order to prove his control of her life, just showed her how little control he really felt. She continued to the wardrobe and sorted through the dresses Frishka had left for her. Most of the dresses had touches of black and blue on them. None had red. She sorted through them until she found one that had blue and green in more somber shades and changed into it. The two with black and eye-hurting yellow she pulled out too; these were Frishka's favorites.

Marilana spent the rest of the morning in careful productivity. She used her claws to sever the seams of the two dresses before tearing the cloth into strips. She braided the strips together to make long cords. She tested each cord for strength before moving on to the next. As noon approached, she pushed all the scraps and cords under the bed and very carefully arranged a few bits to be poking out as if she had shoved them hastily out of sight. Frishka would see them and be struck by three possibilities: escape, murder, or suicide. He could afford none, of course, and he would act accordingly.

The young lioness then sat on the bed and waited. She did not have long to wait before Frishka and his men entered. She jumped hastily away from the bed and quickly went to her knees. She saw the suspicion in the gaunt tiger's eyes as they darted to the bed and back again. She pushed down the triumph and the smile that threatened to show on her face and covered it with a look of fear; she was becoming quite good at this theatrical act.

"What have you been doing?" Frishka asked suspiciously, then stopped, "Never mind, let us sit and eat some lunch."

He stepped over to her and offered his paw to her. She glanced from his face to the bed and back again. She graced him with a smile, took his paw, and rose. The tiger could not possibly have been more startled. The young lioness tossed her head back and stepped quickly to the table. One of Frishka's guards, a huge bear, pulled a chair out for Marilana, as automatically as he would have a member of the royal family, and she kept her smile carefully in place. She kept her breathing fast and her eyes darting about the room. Frishka sat carefully, and Marilana felt him shift her ankle chain so it was under his foot.

Frishka said nothing. He dished up their lunch, fish in a light white sauce. They ate in silence. The ever-suspicious tiger watched her closely. Marilana intentionally finished first, then shifted and fidgeted with her skirt, clasping and unclasping her paws repeatedly, her eyes darting from Frishka to his men and briefly toward the bed.

Frishka finished eating and studied her.

"Would you like more to eat," he asked slowly, the suspicion edging his voice.

Marilana turned a longing gaze at the tray and then one of nervousness at him. He waited, watching her closely. She looked down at her plate then closed her eyes and swallowed.

"I would. May I?" she asked simply.

"Your manners have been good until now. You know what I ask of you," he said coolly.

Her breath caught slightly at his words. She kept her eyes closed and rephrased her response. "May I have some more, please, Lord Frishka."

She waited; if this was the game he wanted to play, so be it. Marilana considered her internal battle. She was hungry, of course, but succumbing by calling him her lord would be a sign of subservience. He would see it as another step under his control. That was not going to happen.

Suddenly she flung herself away from the table, knowing he would step down harder on her ankle chain and knowing she would fall to the floor. She managed to catch herself with her paws, but her arms trembled under the impact. He released the ankle chain, stood, and moved around to stand in front of her. She folded in on herself. Her face became smooth and emotionless. She sank back into her customary kneeling position and folded her paws in her lap. She used all of her skills to control her breathing.

The tiger grabbed her arm.

"Why?" he shouted. "Why, Marilana, do you continue to defy me in such a fruitless manner? Is it better to starve? Would it not be easier to speak with respect? Why do you insist on making life harder for yourself? I am just trying to help you achieve all that you have ever dreamed of."

"You know nothing of my dreams," she said in the calmest of voices. "You would torture me even if I showered you with every insignificant response that you so childishly demand. You will never break me, and you will never be my lord. I know this. And you are coming to know this."

"You are strong-willed, Marilana," he said. "I look forward to your long training after the trials are complete, but I cannot let you play your little games. Did you think I would not watch your balcony to see if you attempted anything? Did you think I would not learn of your little chats with your so-called brother? You will be punished for that misbehavior, but you are doing something else today. What are you up to,

Marilana?" He enunciated her name like a parent scolding a child.

"Nothing. Nothing at all." Now the young lioness replaced the calm mask with a look of fear.

"Look under the bed!" the tiger snapped at the huge bear.

Marilana whipped her head around.

"N-No." She projected a stammer. "There is nothing of importance there. Just some rags. Just some rags."

"Lord Frishka!" the bear exclaimed. He pulled the black and yellow bundle from under the bed. "She has made ropes!"

"Ropes? Let me see," Frishka demanded. He pulled Marilana up by the arm and led her toward the bed. Marilana hung her head as the bear held out her morning's work.

"Ropes made from my dresses, if I am not mistaken," Frishka hissed. He shook her. "What, may I ask, were you planning on doing?"

"You will never break me." She said the words with utter coldness, exactly as she had planned. Then she waited.

Fury twisted the tiger's face as he threw her to the floor. She rolled onto her back, and he loomed over her. She wouldn't resist his attack. He could not afford to beat her as he surely would have liked. She had to be strong and healthy for court tomorrow, at least in appearance. He pulled back his foot to kick her but stopped suddenly. A truly evil smile spread across his face. He snapped his claws and two of his guards yanked Marilana to her feet.

Frishka walked to the door and spoke to the guard outside. He sneered at her as he returned.

"If you will not do as you are told when you are beaten, then perhaps a different form of persuasion is needed." The tiger turned and picked up one of the ropes. He used it to bind

Marilana's paws behind her. Then he tied it to her ankle chain, forcing her to her knees. Then he gagged her. He picked up another length of cord and more of the scrap material. Then he waited.

Marilana could feel true panic welling up in her. If he was not going to beat her, then what was he up to? Dread filled her as she realized she truly had pushed him too far. A moment later, the door opened, and Earek was dragged unceremoniously into the room. Their eyes met briefly, hers filling with tears of rage, every muscle in her body rebelling against the shackles. But Earek gave one firm, almost indecipherable shake of his head, and Marilana stopped. She drew a deep breath, knowing what was to be, and knowing she was powerless to prevent what she had started. They would torture Earek in an attempt to break her. Well, they didn't know the black leopard near as well as she did.

"Oh, so Earek thinks he will be brave and take whatever comes to him, does he?" Frishka laughed lightly. "This is what you get for breaking my rules."

"Do your worst," Earek spat back at Frishka.

Marilana locked eyes with Earek for one brief moment and then it began. It went on for ten minutes, yet it seemed so much longer. Earek refused to yield. And, despite the tiger's malicious taunting, Marilana did not beg for it to end. When it finally stopped, Earek hung limp and unmoving. Frishka waved his guards away. They checked that the hall was clear, then dragged Earek out and closed the door behind them. Frishka knelt in front of Marilana again, holding her gag and studying her eyes.

"You are strong. But your heart is soft. If you defy me again, your leopard friend will get more of the same. You think on that, because I promise he will not die easily."

He shoved her face roughly away. The huge bear cut the gag and the rope binding her and followed the tiger out the door. Marilana buried her face in her paws and wept for her friend, her brother.

Altia gently touched Marilana's shoulder.

"M' Lady." The caracal touched her face. Marilana's eyes opened. She had not moved from the floor and knew many hours had passed. "It's me. Altia. Why have you been crying?"

Marilana shook her head, but eventually the words poured out of her. Frishka's brutality. Earek's defiance. Her own defiance.

When the tears returned, her maid shook her head and asked, "I don't understand. Why are you so upset? You and Earek both did what you had to do. The battle was won. That's what you wanted."

"Yes, the battle was won, but that does not make me forget that my friend and brother was just beaten near death because of my actions and all I did was watch. I have killed many a creature for far less than what I witnessed today. I have spent all of my life trying to prevent the brutalizing of my people. Now today not only did I watch it happen, but I was the cause. I pushed Frishka on purpose, and he surprised me with his restraint."

"You could not have done otherwise."

"There is always a choice. I could have stopped the beating; I could have begged Frishka to stop it. I could have uttered a single phrase of submission, and it would have stopped in a heartbeat."

"Yes, but that would have meant losing everything you have been fighting for and everything Earek has suffered for, would it not?" the caracal said as if nothing could be more obvious.

"I cannot see the future. I cannot say for sure what would have happened if I had given in. What I do know is that I will do it again and again if it means Marquiese still lives and Redsands is still free from Frishka. Even so I grieve for the price paid."

Altia sat for a while and stared at Marilana as she stared down at her paws.

"Come now, it is time to focus on the next challenge," said Altia, helping Marilana to her feet. "We must get you to bed. You must be prepared for court tomorrow, and you must find a way to convince the magistrates of what is right and true."

Marilana smiled weakly. "Yes. I cannot do that with red eyes, can I?"

23

Marilana woke at dawn feeling better than she had in days. She got up and selected a blue and yellow gown. The gown was certainly not appropriate for wearing in public, much less a Court of Law, but it was slightly less unbecoming than anything else Frishka had demanded she wear. She then spent the rest of the morning meditating and focusing her thoughts on the court appearance to come.

It was mid-morning when Frishka finally came to call. Marilana regarded him coldly, speaking only when she had to. He brought with him a pitcher of cool water and wash towel. He left her bread and cheese, though hardly enough to curb her hunger. "I'll be back in one hour. Be prepared."

When he was gone, the lioness washed carefully and ate slowly.

When the door opened again, she was ready, both mentally and physically, her calm absolute. "You will tell the Court exactly what I told you last time," he said. "You will tell them that you have seen the error of your ways and have decided to tell the truth. Then, when I call for them to make their decision tomorrow, your admission will be utmost in their minds. Do you understand me?"

"Yes."

"Would that not be 'Yes, My Lord'?"

"No, it would not."

He stared. She stared in return. In time, he growled, saying, "You know what will happen if you displease me."

Prepare to be displeased, she thought.

They walked in silence to the courtroom. Frishka stopped at the doors, and Marilana walked past him without acknowledging his presence, then continued to the witness box with her head high and her expression calm.

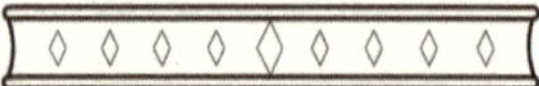

King Rylan stared at the young lioness, dumbstruck, anger flushing every vein in his body. She was dressed exactly as Marquiese had described.

The King found it hard to believe that Frishka could think that sending her into the courtroom dressed as she was would curry favor with the magistrates. His arrogance could not possibly run that deep. For her part, Marilana seemed not to notice the whispers that spread through the room as she walked confidently to the witness box.

Lord Quinre leaned forward angrily. "Lady Marilana, your attire is completely inappropriate! This is a public courtroom and I will not have you making a mockery of it!"

Marilana curtseyed to the magistrates, and King Rylan was impressed that she could do such a thing without appearing even more inappropriate.

"Please, Your Honors, I beg your forgiveness. I have no other clothes. They have been removed from my quarters and have not been returned. I will leave, if that is your wish, but I came because I did not wish to delay this trial on account of such a frivolous matter."

"No, Marilana," replied Lord Komph. "We do not wish to extend this trial any more than it already has been. You will stay and answer our questions."

"Very well."

"First tell the Court why someone would remove your clothes and leave such a shameful garment in its place."

"The answer is very simple. My clothes were removed in an attempt to humiliate me. They were replaced by indecent garments such as this in an attempt to disgrace me further."

"But who would do such a thing?"

"Lord Frishka," Marilana replied simply.

"Lord Frishka?! Is that so? Well, then, we shall look into it." The Head Magistrate sounded unconvinced. "In the meantime, let us turn to the matter of the day."

The magistrates could not stare Marilana down as they had Earek. She had already drawn responses from two of them; that trick was no longer viable. Still, Lord Hunmis stared down at her as if she were dirt under his foot, doing his best to intimidate her. He may as well have tried the tactic on a tree as ineffective as it proved to be.

Finally, Lord Komph cleared his throat, perhaps a tad embarrassed by the uncomfortable air in his courtroom. He threw out a brisk question, asking, "Lady Marilana, why did you delay the outing with Prince Marquiese for exactly an hour on the morning of your arrest?" he asked.

"Exactly is too strong of a word, Your Honor," the lioness replied with not a trace of unease. "I delayed for as short of a time as I could, but the writing of a Letter of Accusation of Treason does take considerable concentration. It has to be legal in its formality and cannot be abbreviated even if time is short. Likewise, I could not risk taking too long or else Lord Frishka's spies would know something was going on. Also, if I had delayed too long, Lord Frishka might have decided I was planning something to counter his malevolence and killed Earek before he lost his chance. I wrote hastily, but carefully. Then I also spoke quickly with Guard Captain Lorne knowing that the clock was ticking."

"So you did not plan for an hour to be spent so that you would arrive at The Beach at noon, exactly when the meeting with the bandits was arranged?" asked Lord Quinre.

"Of course she did," spat Lord Hunmis before Marilana could answer. The aging boar was still staring, his contempt on full display. "She had to delay their departure somehow. The letter requesting the meeting had arrived *after* the arrangements for their outing had been made with the servants, so something had to be done so that they did not arrive early and scare off the murderers. Do not try and deny it, Lady Marilana. We know all about the meeting at High Noon on The Beach with the bandits. Are we not correct about the rest, as well?"

Marilana studied him. He, of course, was expecting her to be nervous and shocked by his verbal aggression. Her expression instead was calm and scornful. She said, "If you knew the ways of bandits even slightly, you would never fall for such lies, Your Honor."

"Well, if you know better, please enlighten us," the boar replied, his face flush.

"I would be happy to. You see, most bandits are uneducated. Most live in poverty. They do not spend money on frivolous items such as clocks and time pieces." She shifted her gaze to Lord Quinre. "Let me explain. I did not plan to delay our ride by any specific amount of time. I was guided by necessity. I had to write the letter before I left because I knew that when we returned an arrest needed to happen legally. I did not know Lord Frishka's exact plan, but I knew he was after the Crown." Marilana let these words settle in before continuing. "Had we not come back at all, if we had all been killed, that letter of accusation was the only way I could insure that His Majesty would have some idea as to who was behind it.

"As it turned out, it took a little less than an hour for me to make my arrangements. If it were bandits awaiting us," she said, glancing briefly at Lord Hunmis, "they would not have noticed the passage of an hour by looking to a time piece. They would have calculated the time by the changing shadows. They would not have arranged a meeting at High Noon . . . ," she emphasized the words. ". . . but at the hour when the sun reached its zenith. Bandits would have arrived when the shadows were slivers on the west side of the boulders and departed when the shadows were slivers on the east side of the same boulders. Whether their rendezvous was successful or not. They never tarry. They expect every meeting to be a trap, and they act accordingly."

"So if you had received a note from supposed bandits that indicated a specific time—say High Noon—you would have suspected a trap," Lord Komph said perhaps a touch too quickly.

"Not necessarily, Your Honor," the lioness said, sidestepping his trap. "I would have suspected that the letter had been written by an educated individual. Please understand, there are bandits who were previously men of higher status who then fell on hard times. I would not trust or distrust them any more or less than any other bandit. I am always cautious when dealing with bandits.

"Know this. Mercenaries can be bought. If they can be bought once they can be bought again. Bandits are often more loyal, especially if they see you as protection from the law. Either way, I dislike dealing with them. Now consider the bandits' point of view; I am a bandit hunter of high reputation and therefore neither bandits nor mercenaries are comfortable dealing with me. They would have refused a meeting with me on The Beach for any reason less than full pardons for their crimes. Had they not known it was me they were meeting, they would have been very unhappy when I showed up. They would have assumed it was a trap. And rest assured, someone would have died."

Marilana paused a moment, allowing the magistrates to catch up with her thinking. Then she said, "As it was, however, every creature waiting to ambush His Highness on The Beach that day was loyal to Lord Frishka and underestimated me, leaving me untied and unhindered. This allowed me to attack

Lord Frishka before they could respond. If I had intended to, I would have killed him on that day, and we would never have had to have this trial."

Her last words were thick with scorn, and all three magistrates sat back in momentary surprise.

Lord Komph responded with a slight display of scorn of his own, saying, "Of course we would have had this trial. Even if Lord Frishka had died, his treason charges had arrived first and we would have had to sift through the facts all the same. I would even say that if he were dead this trial would be much harder without his evidence."

"Forgive me, Your Honor, but it is precisely because of his evidence that we are here. He has given a very convincing story and trumped up supporting evidence. All of the accounts have been plausible. What you have to decide is which set of stories and evidence is truthful and which is a fabrication. I believe that you have done a good job sorting through all the points and searching for the facts."

Marilana paused and took a deep breath before continuing in a softer voice, almost pleading. "Please consider what I say here today. I know it is not my place nor do I think I should have to say it, but I feel I must. You have heard the witnesses. You have seen the evidence. You have searched out the facts, as all good men of judgment should. Now it is time to take a step back and ask yourselves a question that can only be answered truthfully by your hearts. Who do you trust?"

Rylan felt his breath catch in his throat. The magistrates went deathly still as Marilana spoke. Now the silence stretched as Marilana waited quietly for a response. She had spoken almost word-for-word the Magistrates' Creed. *'When logic and reason fail to find the truth, one must take a step back and evaluate the character of the matter and of those involved. The answer to that question can only be answered by emotions of the heart, and, as such, one must be completely truthful to one's self.'*

These creatures of justice had not taken that step yet as far as King Rylan could tell, and they would not take kindly to someone outside the magistracy reminding them of their creed. It was a great risk to take.

Lord Hunmis rolled to his feet, his broad boar's nostrils flared and his eyes rimmed deep red. But before he could lean across the desk and shower Marilana with his rage, Lord Komph reached out with his paw, face severe, and halted him. When his colleague was seated again, the Head Magistrate leaned forward and said, "Lady Marilana, that was a very grave thing to say. Some of our order would have you punished for uttering such words. I, in this case, am not so proud as to hold your views against you; however, you will refrain from such utterings in the future. Is that understood?"

Marilana curtseyed low. "Yes, Your Honor. Thank you."

"Very well. Court is adjourned."

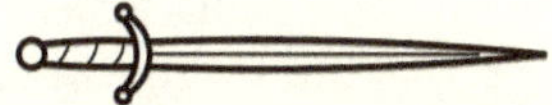

It was King Rylan's turn to pace the dungeons. "I do not know what will come from today's session," he said to his son.

Marquiese, seated on the window sill with a claw holding his place in a book of law, did not address the statement directly. Instead, he asked, "Did something happen to Marilana?"

King Rylan spoke over his shoulder as he passed. "She was dressed as you saw her last."

Marquiese clinched his free paw. "Frishka."

"Yes. The Court was unsettled. But the questioning went as expected. She lectured on the ways of bandits and mercenaries, all of which seemed to have no influence on the magistrates."

Marquiese looked at Master Castant, who was leaning against the wall near the window and had yet to say a word. "So why is my father pacing like a Wild animal in a cage?"

The yellow leopard grimaced. "Lady Marilana reminded them of the Magistrates' Creed."

Marquiese realized that his mouth was hanging open. "No one outside the magistracy is supposed to know that creed."

"Once again we underestimate her," Castant said matter-of-factly. "I thought for a moment that Lord Hunmis was going to have her flogged right there in the courtroom."

"To call him furious would be the understatement of the season," King Rylan added.

"What happened?"

"Lord Komph stepped in. He told Marilana never to mention it again. That he was being lenient and that others in his order would not be so kind. Probably right." King Rylan turned to the window. "At any rate, Marilana accepted the reprimand and court was adjourned."

"What could she have been trying to do by risking such a stunt? The magistrates live by that creed; they do not need to be reminded of it. Do you think she was threatening them?" Marquiese suggested with a frown.

Castant shook his head. "I do not think she was threatening anyone. I think she was simply telling them to do their jobs."

"No," King Rylan corrected. "She was begging them to do their jobs. Begging. I saw it on her face, and that is what I am most worried about. Why would she risk their fury? Why try something that could easily push them the other way?"

They were all quiet for a time before Marquiese said, "Marilana does not beg. She calculates."

"I would not have believed it if I had not seen it in her face and her eyes," King Rylan replied quietly.

"And Komph and the others? What have they decided so far?" The Prince of Redsands asked, his cynicism on full display.

"They were all very quiet when I left them. Each lost in his own thoughts. The only thing they did before I left them was to ask for a small private supper in the deliberation room. They will be there for many hours this evening, I think."

"Well, then, that is one thing she did achieve that none of the rest of us has yet. She made them stop and think. And perhaps even think deeply."

Marilana stood with her arms crossed, looking out at the gardens beyond the windows. The door behind her clicked and opened. She did not move; she stared out at the trees without really seeing them as she listened to the footsteps entering the room.

"You should be kneeling before me," Frishka said.

The young lioness did not move. His footsteps came closer. A paw set gently on her shoulder. "We will go for a walk in the gardens. Come," he ordered.

One of the tiger's guards chained her wrists to her ankles and Frishka led the way out the door.

The gardens were beautiful in the twilight, and Marilana soaked in the peace and quiet, not knowing when she would next be allowed a breath of fresh air. Frishka paused next to a pool and stood gazing into the depths of the water. Marilana stopped just behind him; she knew they were in full view of the tower dungeon windows. The dim light was brighter here and they would be easily seen. She did not risk looking up to see if Marquiese might be at the window.

"You made quite the stir in court today," the tiger said, his voice amused. "That dress had everyone talking. It did not sound like anyone really believed that you had nothing else to wear. Although some did suggest that the servants might be playing a cruel joke on you."

She said nothing and moved not an inch. She clutched the chain shackling her wrists to her ankles to stop herself from hitting him.

"I also heard that you threatened the magistrates with their own creed. They are simply livid with you now, of course. I congratulate you. You did quite an excellent job preparing them for me tomorrow when I will call for a final judgment. Whether they are ready or not, they will have to make a decision. In the morning, you will dress as I direct you. We will share lunch and then I will escort you to the chapel where you will wait for me. After the magistrates pronounce Marquiese's fate, I will expect you to do your best for me in your rooms. You will be mine tomorrow evening, and I will begin to break you. No one will stop me."

He chuckled again and gently rubbed her arm with his paw.

This was too much. Marilana could hold her temper no more. Tears began to run down her face. She struck fast, faster than Frishka could ever react even if he was fully prepared for the attack. She drove both paws into his gut with as much force as she could muster and tripped him backward into the bushes. She did not wait to see how he landed.

She held the chain in her paws and sprinted down the path. The surprised guard stumbled back as she burst around the corner and hit him square in the chest. She did not waste time taking him down; the other guards would not be far behind. She ran on, half-blinded by tears of rage as she charged around corners, not caring where she ended up. Of course there was no escape. This was not an attempt at escape, only a means of channeling her fury.

She could hear yells and curses behind her, the confusion left in her wake. She rounded another corner and burst out onto one of the party lawns at the back of the palace. She ran a little further then threw herself down on one of the gentle knolls that populated this side of the palace. She lay there sobbing, even as the shouting grew closer.

Marilana concentrated on her breathing, one deep breath at a time, and the tears quickly dried up. Behind her the shouts were getting closer, until suddenly one voice rose loud and clear.

"This way! The tracks go this way!"

Marilana glanced over her shoulder. She came to her feet and prepared herself for the punishment that was sure to come.

She pretended to still be running away as the guards caught up to her. A foolish gesture, but necessary to keep Frishka underestimating her. The guards knocked her to the ground and then hauled her to her feet again. Frishka was not far behind. Marilana looked into his face. He was livid. Good.

"How dare you?" the tiger hissed. "How dare you attack me? Where did you think you could go? Fool of a girl."

Marilana braced herself. He slammed his fist into her gut. She could not draw breath. He back-armed her across the face, snapping her head sideways.

"I am your master, now, and for the rest of your life."

Marilana lifted her chin to him and spat in his face. "I have no master."

His slapped her again, then wiped her spit from his face.

"Drag her," he growled, then spun on his heel and marched back into the gardens.

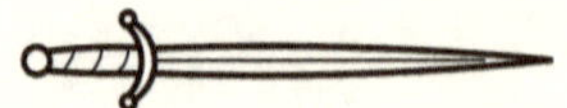

Marquiese quivered with rage and frustration. He wanted to scream; he wanted to yell for the guards to arrest Frishka, to have him thrown into the dungeon. He instead rested his forehead against his white-knuckled fist gripping the bars of the window.

He had seen it all. Marilana's fur had gleamed in the twilight, even at this distance. Watching her made him reminisce about the time he had spent with her in the Southern Tip. He missed those days of simplicity and freedom.

He had watched their confrontation, seen Marilana put Frishka into the bushes, seen her dispose of his guard, and then flee.

What could have made her do such a thing? What had Frishka said to elicit such a response? Marquiese could only imagine.

It was hopeless, of course. She could not escape the palace grounds, so why had she taken such a foolish risk? One of the palace guards might have thought she was trying to escape and taken blade to her. He had wanted to yell at her to stop. Helpless, he did not know what to do though every fiber of his being wanted to try.

Then she had stopped and dropped to the ground, her face in her paws. Even from this height, he could tell she was shaking.

He had stood transfixed, wondering what had pushed her so far that she now lay sobbing. He felt utterly helpless. He watched Frishka and the guards searching frantically through the gardens, then watched as Marilana sat up, calming herself, and preparing to be found.

The guards spotted her. When Marquiese saw them charging across the lawn, he gripped the bars with all his might. When they knocked her down, he bit his tongue to keep from screaming. When he saw Frishka and his band of ill-kempt guards dragging her across the lawn, he vowed revenge. When he saw Marilana struggling to get to her feet, he was so furious that there was no more room for thought; he simply wanted to see Frishka finished; crushed like the venomous snake he had always been.

24

Frishka's guards dragged her through the gardens, and he headed the long route for the main entrance.

"We should use the side entrance, My Lord," the huge bear at his side said. "It's the fastest way back to her rooms."

"No," the tiger growled. "We go in the front. With luck, we will run into Rylan. I will say that she tripped, and you will corroborate it."

"Yes, My Lord. If you insist."

He led them to the palace entrance and up the front steps. He schooled his face to a look of concern and pushed open the great doors. His wish was granted immediately. Rylan was just crossing the hall along the upper balcony.

"Frishka!" Rylan said sharply, his eyes glaring down on them. Frishka could see that the old fool was watching Marilana stumbling forward, her distress obvious. "What is the meaning of this? Why are your guards dragging the prisoner?"

Frishka let a look of surprise pass over his face, then he turned to see his guards dragging Marilana up the steps.

"What do you think you are doing, you fools?" he snapped with mock outrage. "You were supposed to be helping her! Not dragging her! If she cannot keep the pace you have set, I would have slowed down for her."

He crossed the distance back to her and helped her to her feet. His guards bowed their heads and murmured apologies.

"You should be sorry," Frishka spat at them. Then he turned back to the King. "Forgive my inattention, Your Majesty. I was worried, and wanted to get her back to her rooms quickly. We were out walking in the gardens, and she tripped. It was a nasty fall."

"A nasty fall. I see," Rylan said coldly. He stared. "Very well." The King of Redsands turned and walked on.

When his footsteps had gone, Frishka motioned his men to follow. They dragged Marilana up the steps to her rooms. Frishka led the way inside and turned to face her.

"You fool. You foolish little girl," he shouted at her. "Did you think you could escape me? Did you?"

He kicked her in the stomach, and she went limp.

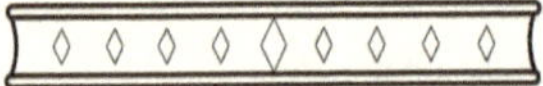

King Rylan was furious as he crept quietly back to the Entrance Hall. Of course she had not fallen. He could see it on her face. He could clearly see the red outline of a paw print through the thin fur on her cheek. He stayed close to the wall and peered around the corner. The King shook his head. He wanted to help her, but he could not see how. He knew that if Frishka proved victorious at trial, his own life would be in even greater danger. He could not risk helping Marilana and going against the law, no matter how foolish the law in this case might be. Doing so would be giving Frishka the Crown. No, without evidence, he could do nothing to help her.

A paw suddenly touched his arm, and he jumped momentarily alarmed. He turned quickly, ready for an instant to defend himself until he saw the face of the elderly leopard. "Father Iscoot!"

"Your Majesty, forgive me for surprising you," whispered the priest. He took the King's arm. "But we must hurry."

"Hurry? Hurry where?"

"Quietly, now. There is something you must see."

The old leopard scurried down the stairs and across the Entrance Hall, the King close on his heels. They hurried along the hallway toward the courtroom. But instead of turning toward it, as Rylan expected, Father Iscoot led him toward the guest rooms. He checked the hallways, then threw open one of the stairwell doors. The priest paused to listen, then ushered Rylan inside. He led the way up the stairs and then stopped seemingly in the middle of the staircase. Paused, listened, and then unhooked part of the banister.

King Rylan took a deep breath as a portion of the wall swung silently away and revealed the hidden walkway behind.

"What in the world?" the royal lion hissed.

The old priest shushed the most powerful creature in the kingdom, and then ushered him through. Rylan stood in stunned silence as the old leopard closed the hidden door. It was a few seconds before he realized that there was a dim light further down the walkway.

"Quietly, Your Majesty. Watch the steps here," Father Iscoot whispered.

The priest climbed a short flight of narrow steps and continued carefully down the walkway. As he neared the light, the King could see the outline of a waiting figure. When he was close enough, he recognized the young maid named Altia. When he opened his mouth to speak, she placed her paw to his lips.

"Shhh," she whispered. The young caracal pointed to the source of the light. It was coming through two small holes in the wall. The King put his eye to one of the holes and was instantly transfixed.

His eyes took him beyond the empty bath to a scene in the sitting room that held him still and silent. He felt his anger rising quickly. Marilana lay on her stomach, bound with her arms and legs pulled behind her back, gagged and blindfolded on the floor at Frishka's feet. Her skirt had been torn away, barely keeping her modesty. Frishka was shouting down at her, rolling his thin bladed dagger in his paw. Rylan was amazed that he could not hear what was being said. He raised his paw to the hole and found it was glass. He glanced at the maid. She raised her paw to a panel and slid it open just a fraction. Suddenly Frishka's voice filled the hidden space.

"You know what I expect from you. You know what else I ask of you. Still you deny me. After tomorrow you will be mine. I am your master. I will not tolerate your disobedience any longer. You will break. You will be my queen. You will acknowledge me as your lord."

Rylan placed his eye back to the hole and watched Frishka crouch down between Marilana's knees. The vile tiger stabbed and sliced at her, then took a liquid from one of his men and splashed it on the bleeding cuts. After a while Marilana began to tremble. As the time went on, she shook harder, moaning.

Rylan wanted to close his eyes, to close the panel, to shut out Frishka's voice. He did nothing of the kind. He watched every movement of the blade and memorized every word. He watched without blinking as one of Frishka's men pounded his fists into Marilana's bleeding thighs. Marilana's ragged breathing could be heard over the dull thuds of fist to flesh. Frishka stood cleaning his blade on a scrap from Marilana's skirt. He dropped the cloth to the floor and motioned for the pounding to stop. The man stood up and cleaned the blood from his fists on another scrap of cloth. Frishka knelt next to Marilana's head, grabbed the back of the gag, and pulled her head back cruelly.

"You know what will happen tomorrow. Your precious Marquiese will be found guilty, and I will make sure his death is not quick. You are mine, and you will watch his dying breath leave him. Then you will watch as your dear friend Earek dies even more slowly. And you will want to join them no doubt, but I will not let that happen. You will live long after they are dead, long after Rylan joins them, and you will bear my sons."

Then they were gone.

Rylan turned away from the view hole and leaned against the opposite wall. The maid was crying silently. Father Iscoot slid the panel closed and turned to face Rylan.

"I am sorry to have to show this to you without any warning," he whispered. "My hope is that you will help her. She has been fighting this way from the very first day she was arrested. That fiend does not have a kind bone in his body, and she and Earek have suffered horrible atrocities for it."

Behind them, a light suddenly flared up as the maid stuck a match to the wick of a lantern. "It is not safe yet to go in. Marilana has warned me not to enter too soon," Altia said in a hoarse whisper.

"What do you mean go in, go to her?" Rylan asked.

"This is not just a place for looking and listening," the priest said. "This is a secret door that will let us into her rooms."

Rylan looked incredulously at the view hole. "What's been going on here, Father Iscoot? Speak now."

And so they told him. About every beating. Every interrogation. How they helped. How they failed her. The secrets they kept.

"Right under my nose," the royal lion said miserably.

"You must help her," Altia said. "Marilana told us not to go to you, but…"

"Marilana is weakening," the priest said. "She cannot hold out much longer."

Rylan held up his paw. "Is it safe now to open the door?"

"Yes, Your Majesty," whispered Altia. She went in first, then called back. "It's clear."

Rylan followed Father Iscoot through the doorway and into the room beyond. Altia was already bending over Marilana and removing the gag and blindfold as the King approached. The caracal cleaned Marilana's face as gently as she could, while the old priest began to pull bottles and rags from inside his robes.

"Help me, Your Majesty," the maid said. Together they eased the battered lioness onto her back. "Thank you."

Then she eased Marilana's head into her lap and stroked her forehead. "Marilana. Please wake up, My Lady."

Marilana groaned. She choked a ragged breath. Her eyes cracked open. She blinked, and focused on Altia. The maid smiled tremulously, her relief palpable. She and Father Iscoot exchanged places, and the caracal began to clean and bandage Marilana's legs. Father Iscoot held a cup of liquid to Marilana's mouth, and she drank gratefully.

"How can I help?" the King whispered.

"A cool cloth, if you would, Your Majesty." Altia nodded toward the water pitcher.

The King of Redsands came back a moment later, knelt, and laid the cloth gently on Marilana's forehead. "My child. Forgive me for allowing this to happen."

Marilana took the rag from his paw, pushed herself to a sitting position, then looked directly at him, their eyes meeting. She answered his apology by saying, "Well now that you are here, Your Majesty, what will you do?"

Rylan shook his head. He was amazed by her strength and how aware she suddenly was.

"I suppose Altia and the good Father have told you all about helping me and slipping remedies to Earek in his food."

"They did."

"Well," she said philosophically, "I suppose I should apologize for breaking the rules of my arrest. And I am sorry that I have gotten these two involved; they are wonderful. Great friends. Loyal and kind."

"Yes, they are," Rylan admitted.

"I must also tell you that Earek and I have talked since our arrests, only briefly and always privately. From my balcony to his windows. I want you to know that I only did these things to help."

"To help who, Marilana?" Rylan said gently. "At first glance, all of these things would appear to help only you. So if they help you, then who are you helping?"

She stared at the rag in her paws. He knelt down next to her and lifted her chin gently with his paw. He looked into her eyes and again saw pain. Tears welled up in her eyes as she looked back at him. "If I were just looking out for myself, I would have left. I have stayed to help Marquiese, of course," she whispered.

"I knew that," he said with a sigh. "Thank you for saying it out loud."

He patted her cheek, then drew a breath. "This is not going to be easy, but it is the only path I can see." He looked up at Altia. "Get a long, dark cloak, please. Bring it here quickly."

The caracal nodded. She sprang to her feet and ran quietly for the secret door.

"Please do not suggest that I run away," Marilana said calmly. "I have endured a bit too much for it to come to that."

"Not at all. We are going to pay a visit on the magistrates."

"Ah. Brilliant," the old priest said.

"However, no one can know of this meeting. We must make absolutely sure that Frishka does not find out. The law, as sad as it may be, is on his side in this matter."

He looked at Father Iscoot, "Go to the deliberation chamber. Tell our courtly friends that I am coming to speak to them. Tell them it is urgent and secret. Tell them nothing else until I get there. Hurry Father."

"Consider it done, Your Majesty." Father Iscoot moved swiftly to the secret door and disappeared behind it.

"You are certain?" asked Marilana softly.

"It is time the magistrates know. I cannot say which direction it will push them, but, after hearing Frishka's threats, I know tonight is all we have."

"Frishka is going to call for a judgment tomorrow," Marilana informed him, the words coming between painful breathes. "The magistrates will have two hours to come to a verdict. That is why I reminded them of their creed. I knew it was a risk, but I was expecting the responses that I got."

"You read people very well," the King said, his eye narrowed. "But how do you know what Frishka is planning with such certainty?"

"He tells me much more than he should. By design, of course. My design, not his," the young lioness said with icy calm. "He does not see me as a danger to him."

"He is a fool in many ways."

King Rylan took a key from inside his shirt and removed her ankle manacles. "So what did you do this afternoon that made Frishka so mad?"

She smirked. "We had a disagreement about the future of our relationship," she said sarcastically. "I hit him. I tripped up his guard. I went for a short run."

"You ran away?" Rylan asked incredulously.

"No. There was no place to run. I simply put some space between us. It was either that or kill him on the spot."

Rylan was saved the necessity of replying to her comment by Altia's return with the requested cloak.

"Here," he said, reaching out and helping Marilana to her feet. She clung to his paw for a moment before easing back on her own feet. "Are you alright, Lady Marilana? Can you walk?"

She looked up into his eyes and smiled. "I will be fine."

Altia draped the cloak around her and made sure the hood concealed her face. Then the three of them made their way into the secret passageway, carefully closing the door behind them.

The King followed Altia and Marilana down the narrow passageway and to the second door. Altia slid a small panel aside and put her eye to it. Nodding, she carefully opened the door and led the way out. They made their way cautiously down the stairs and along the corridors. Rylan took the lead as they approached the courtroom guard post. The guard let them through without question. Rylan wondered briefly who the guard was loyal to and realized how the trial had distorted his thinking. He led the way into the Magistrates' Readying Room and through to the Deliberation Chamber. He held the door open and ushered the young lioness and her maid through. He turned and faced the magistrates, their expressions filled with concern and consternation, suspicion and outrage.

Lord Komph was the first to speak.

"Your Majesty, I must protest. This is most unorthodox behavior, especially from you. Unless this is some new witness to the scene on The Beach that has been evading death to reach you, I must request that everyone leave these private rooms," he said taking a firm stance in front of the other two magistrates.

"Please sit down, Lord Komph," the King of Redsands said with calm authority. "I do bring evidence that will shed new light on the trial. It is, however, of events that have taken place after the arrests. Secrecy regarding this visit is indeed a life or death risk."

"Whatever has happened after the arrests is not yet our concern, Your Majesty. With all due respect, please make a list of charges and let us cope with one trial at a time," said Lord Hunmis with scorn.

"That is not entirely accurate, Magistrate Hunmis, and you should know that," Lord Quinre said directly. "The only time it is important enough to be brought before us as evidence of the current trial is if by deciding one way or the other the new charges would also be negated or dismissed. As King, His Majesty knows our creed as well as we do, and is likewise held by it."

"True enough and even now I trust My King," Lord Komph added thoughtfully. "Very well, Your Majesty. We will hear your evidence."

King Rylan took a deep breath. He set his feet like a lion readying for a fight, "I bring before you evidence of Lord Frishka's vile nature."

"You are biased against Lord Frishka," interrupted Lord Hunmis. A boar of considerable bulk, he leaned forward and scowled. "This is a matter long since settled."

"Excuse me, Lord Hunmis, but we are listening to the presentation of evidence," reprimanded Lord Komph. "If Your Majesty has proof of such accusations, we are here to listen."

"Thank you, Lord Komph. I do bring proof." King Rylan turned to Marilana and lowered her hood.

"Your Majesty!" Lord Komph flew from his seat. He colleagues followed him. "This is completely irrelevant. We have heard what Lady Marilana has to say. We do not need you to bring her before us unasked. Honestly, I do believe you have gone too far with this."

"Indeed. We are in agreement," Lords Quinre and Hunmis intoned, boar and eland in agreement for once.

At that moment, King Rylan, as regal and powerful a lion as there was in the kingdom, turned on them, his shoulders back and his chest thrust forward, his face filled with rage. His voice growling when he said, "If you do not sit back down and listen like proper magistrates then I will have you replaced. All three of you. I am the final law in this land. If you continue to carry on in this less-than-professional manner, I will do what I must to make sure that this trial proceeds lawfully."

All three magistrates looked as if they had just been slapped, their jaws gaping. One by one, the magistrates retreated with considerable trepidation back to their seats, eyes never leaving the King.

"Very well," said King Rylan. "I call Father Iscoot, Head Royal Priest, and Palace Maid Altia to give their accounts of the pertinent events leading up to tonight's meeting here."

He opened his palm in Altia's direction. "If you would, Altia. Please be thorough."

Altia stepped up in front of the magistrates, quivering but determined.

"Your Honors." The caracal offered a brief a curtsey. "I must start at the beginning, when Lady Marilana first arrived at the Royal Palace over a month ago."

Altia held their attention for nearly a half-hour, recounting every moment in the company of Lady Annabella's heir. Every blow that Frishka wielded, every wound she treated, every breathless moment hoping Marilana had not been killed. The beatings, the starvation, the wounds left by Frishka's knife. "Three days ago, the loathsome beast nearly beat her to death. I needed help. Marilana sent me to Father Iscoot. He has since been helping me get remedies and food to Marilana. Tonight, we both agreed that we had reached the limit of our abilities to help her. She refuses to admit it, but she is growing weaker. We agreed to go to King Rylan, and he has brought us before you now."

She finished with a curtsey, her place before the magistrates taken now by Father Iscoot. The old leopard's eyes were clear, and his voice was steady as he said, "Your Honors, I too have been giving aid to Lady Marilana through this terrible ordeal."

The aging priest told the magistrates how she sought sanctuary in the Royal Chapel from Lord Frishka. He recounted the severity of the beatings Marilana endured, the remedies they used to keep her alive, the food they had to sneak into her room to fend off starvation. "Tonight I agreed with Altia that the end was near, so I approached King Rylan. He brought us here."

"Very well, Father. Thank you," Lord Komph managed to say, as the King and the priest exchanged places.

"I had believed previously that something of this sort was going on between Frishka and Marilana, but I had no proof," the King told the magistrates. "This evening, I came upon Frishka and his men dragging Marilana into the Entrance hall. Frishka said that she had tripped in the gardens. I did not believe it. Father Iscoot came to me shortly thereafter and took me to the secret room, and I watched in horror as Frishka used a dagger to slice and stab the inside of Marilana's upper thighs and then to have one of his men beat the cuts with his fists. I listened as Frishka threatened her with worse beatings and a terrible future full of pain and suffering. We waited until they had left and then entered the room. Altia and Father Iscoot revived Marilana and bandaged her legs. They told me everything you have now heard. I decided that I had to act, and so brought them here for you to hear for yourselves."

When he finished, there was silence.

Marilana stood mute, watching and waiting and fearing the magistrates would show themselves to be on Frishka's side.

"Thank you, King Rylan, for bringing this before us now in secret," said Lord Komph softly. "Torture is hardly proper treatment of any prisoner, much less a noble lady."

The red fox finally looked in Marilana's direction and said, "I call you before us now and, although I fear to hear the tale you have to tell, I am asking you to recount in full the events that these others have witnessed."

Marilana nodded. She started at the beginning, on the day when Altia confirmed the existence of the secret door. She spoke for a long time of all the interactions between Frishka and her. By the end, her mouth was dry and she was beginning to feel light-headed and dizzy. She was still weak from the events of the evening, but she forced her knees straight and held her head high.

Lord Hunmis leaned forward and said, "Why did you not bring this before us before now? Why did you wait and suffer so long? I can understand not wanting to alert Lord Frishka to your helpers, but why suffer the injustice of the torture?"

"If I came to you in court the first time I was able, even if I did not tell that I was getting help, would you have removed me and Earek from Lord Frishka's custody? By law, either good or bad, we are in his custody and no one else can make arrangements for our care. You would have reprimanded him and accepted his word that he would not do any more harm to us. The result would have been that he beat us senseless, kept us bedridden by accidents or drugs, and we would not have been able to even set foot in court without one of his people for escort; constantly under threat of more grievous injury for not complying with his wishes. I accepted the private battle between him and me in order to present my witness to Frishka's treason rather than be incapacitated by him. I accepted Altia's help, and Father Iscoot's, so that I could take even more punishment from him. To make him lose his temper. To cause him to make mistakes, as he did tonight when he struck me hard enough to leave a clear paw print on my cheek. I would gladly take all the torture again if it proves him a traitor."

"So, can you provide proof that he tortured you all the times you say he did? We have King Rylan's witness of tonight, but what about before tonight. Your other two witnesses do not have our trust the way His Majesty does," said Lord Quinre firmly.

Marilana looked them each in the eyes, eland, boar, and fox. She took a breath, reached up to untie the strings of the cloak, letting it drop to the floor, and removed the strips of cloth bandaging her legs. Their reaction to the sight of her bruised and battered legs was immediate. Lord Hunmis turned in his seat and vomited; Lord Quinre clamped his mouth shut, his teeth clicking; Lord Komph's face became redder by the second.

"By The Goddess." The Head Magistrate spoke with tightly controlled anger, his reddish fur bristling. "Some of those bruises are fifnights old, clearly."

"But how do we know they are not self-inflicted?" Lord Hunmis mouthed.

"No one has the ability to self-inflict that much bruising on those parts of the body. It takes full force swings to cause that amount of damage."

"She has a secret door to her room. Perhaps someone else used it to help her with this," Lord Quinre said through gritted jaws. "Who knows about this door?"

"Only three other servants of the royal family," Altia said quietly. "It is a very carefully guarded secret. Not even King Rylan knew of it before tonight."

"And these other three? How can we know of their loyalties?" persisted Lord Quinre.

"They are loyal beyond reproach. I am sure. They know nothing of this matter," replied Altia.

"I believe this maid," King Rylan said firmly. He looked from fox to eland to boar, holding their eyes in turn. "She has been loyal to me for many years. She and the other three are part of my personal servants, and I will vouch for them."

"I trust your word, Majesty," Lord Quinre nodded.

Lord Hunmis swallowed noisily again and could barely manage a nod.

"Thank you, Lady Marilana," Lord Komph said rising from his seat. "My thanks to you all. And to you, Your Majesty. You were quite right to bring this to our attention. Please leave us now so that we may deliberate."

Marilana leaned on Altia's arm as they made a small curtsey to the magistrates and turned to the door. Marilana replaced the cloak and hood then exited the room without assistance. She managed to walk all the way back to the stairs without stumbling. As soon as the stairwell door closed, however, Altia and Father Iscoot grabbed her by the arms. They helped her up the stairs, into the secret passageway, and back into her rooms. They helped her into bed, and Altia replaced the bandages. King Rylan stepped up to the bed and reluctantly relocked the manacles on her ankles. He touched her gently on the shoulder.

"I am sorry to have to chain you again. I keep a master key. I tell you this so that you know I can release you and Earek if the need is great enough. You did well tonight. I just wanted to thank you for everything you have done, and I want you to know that I am sorry for all the pain you have had to suffer. I cannot guarantee that you will not have to suffer more, but I believe in my heart that Marquiese's freedom will be granted tomorrow." He smiled down at her after a pause, "Please, sleep well tonight."

Marilana nodded weakly as he turned and walked away. Father Iscoot patted her shoulder and Altia gave her paw a quick squeeze before both hurried to follow King Rylan.

25

Marilana woke late the next morning; mid-morning sunlight lit the rooms with a warm glow. She moved her stiff legs around carefully to loosen them up and then swung them over the side of the bed. She removed the bandages and threw them in the chamber pot. As she stepped over to the washstand, she realized someone had already been in her room. Clean water filled the porcelain pitcher and a clean fluffy white towel hung ready on the bar. Marilana shook her head and cursed herself. *How could you sleep through that? Someone enters your room without you noticing? Are you really that weak?* She knew such a thing would never have happened in her old life in Mystillion. Never. But she also realized that she had never been put through such torture and tested so thoroughly. *No excuse. None.*

She stripped off the ragged remains of yesterday's dress and washed carefully. She felt better and stretched her arms and legs to cleanse the last of the stiffness from her muscles. The good feelings died completely when she opened the wardrobe. One dress with a matching veil hung inside the large cavernous space. One pair of clean slippers sat beneath the dress. Marilana clenched her paws, rage boiling through her.

The dress was by far the most risqué that Frishka had ever chosen for her. Humility and self-control would hardly be enough to prevent her from blushing every time someone saw her. Knowing that she had no choice, she pulled the dress out and put it on. She tied the slippers slowly on her feet before looking at herself in the mirror.

The dress was the purplish gray color of bruised flesh.

The full billowing sleeves were made of material so sheer that the fur of her arms could be plainly seen through it. That sheer material covered her shoulders to a tight collar of heavier material, which matched the cuffs of the sleeves.

The sheer material extended midway down her back and created the effect of a deep V-shaped neckline on her chest.

The same heavy material that made the collar made up the remainder of the bodice—which was far too tight—extended in spikes into the full skirt to preserve what little remained of her modesty, and had the effect of exposing her legs below her knees.

To make matters worse, the sheer material separated the front and back of the bodice and left the sides of her torso and legs fully exposed.

The slippers were sown of the same heavy material as the collar, making it appear that she had manacles on her wrists, ankles, and neck. Carefully, Marilana placed the sheer veil on her head and secured it with the circlet of heavier material, the finishing touch to the vision of Frishka's painful domination. Marilana sank to the floor; she could not stand to look at the mirror any more, and sobbed into her paws.

She hoped with all her being that this would be the last dress Frishka ever forced her to wear and hoped with equal fervor that Marquiese would never see her wearing it.

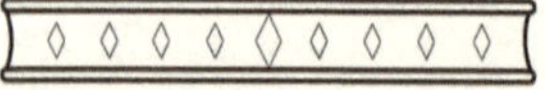

King Rylan entered the Deliberation Chamber. Frishka and the magistrates were already gathered there, and Lord Komph spared no niceties, saying, "Lord Frishka, we have gathered at your request. What do you wish to see us about?"

"Your Majesty. Your Honors," replied Frishka formally. "I have asked you here to call for your final Judgment. I feel that you have heard all the evidence that can be presented and that nothing more can be gained by delaying longer. By law, I have the right to call for your Judgment. Therefore, by law, you have two hours before you are required to declare your verdict in the case of treason by Prince Marquiese against King Rylan."

The magistrates shared a nod and Lord Komph said, "Very well. The Court will convene in two hours' time. You will arrive alone and we shall give you further instructions at that time."

Frishka bowed once more and left. When the chamber door was closed, King Rylan turned to the magistrates.

"It is as we were forewarned," he said gravely. "I will prepare to implement our plan of action. Gentlemen, I shall see you in two hours."

Marilana slid off the bed and knelt as the lock clicked in the door. Frishka and his guards entered. Frishka motioned for the man carrying the lunch tray to take it to the table, then for the guards to go out onto the balcony. Marilana did not look up at him; she stared straight ahead, her back straight and her head high.

"Stand up. Let me get a good look at you," he said quietly.

She stood, still staring blankly ahead.

"My, my, how lovely that does look on you. My heart pounds. I wish nothing more than to throw you back on that soft bed of yours and lay claim to that perfect body. That will have to wait, however, until after the magistrates name me as the new heir to the throne. Then you will scream for me. Now walk to the table. We will eat some lunch together."

Marilana stomped toward the table, her face burning with rage and humiliation. Her thoughts focused on the many ways she could kill him.

"Tut, tut," he chided behind her. "Such rage does not become you. You will have to work on your self-composure if you are to retain functioning limbs. I would hate to have to break your legs just because you annoyed me by stomping around."

He motioned for her to sit, chuckling softly as he served her a plate of food. While Marilana ate, she concentrated on slowing her breathing and gaining control of her rage. A loss of self-control could provide him a wedge into her emotional defenses, and she would not allow that to happen.

"I called for the magistrates to make a decision this morning. Their two hours are almost over. I will take you to the chapel, and you will wait for me there. When I take you back to the courtroom, they will tell you what is to happen next. I expect you to collapse into hysterics and claim repentance for your sins. I will then step in and assume control of your penance and revoke the treason charge against you. You will continue to weep quietly as I escort you back here to your rooms where I will begin your re-education. You will make me proud today. Now come."

◊ ◊ ◊ ◊ ◊ ◊ ◊ ◊ ◊

King Rylan took his chair by the magistrates and stole a deep breath. This was not going to be easy, but he hoped that there would not be too many surprises other than the ones he had planned. Lord Komph motioned for the guards to open the courtroom doors. The room filled with creatures of all types waiting to see the next scene of the drama unfold. Lady Prinka took her seat in the front row and sat with a smug smile firmly in place. Frishka entered alone and came forward. He stood facing the magistrates with an undisguised smirk on his lips.

Lord Komph got to his feet and motioned to the guards. "Bring him in please."

A moment later, the sound of many boots could be heard moving toward the door. A moment after, Marquiese, chained yet proud, entered with a large escort of palace guards. He came forward and stood equal to Frishka.

"Lady Prinka, please join your son," said Lord Komph.

Frowning and clearly a bit confused, Prinka got to her feet and stepped up next to her son.

"Very good," the Head Magistrate said, nodding. "The Court has been called to declare judgment in the case of treason of Prince Marquiese against King Rylan. As the evidence presented is the same as that in the case of treason of Lord Frishka against Prince Marquiese, we shall declare our judgment for that case as well."

Frishka's frown equaled that of his mother, while Marquiese raised his eyebrows in an expression woven of hope and uncertainty.

"At this time," the red fox continued, "the Court will take Lord Frishka and Lady Prinka into custody. Guards please chain them and escort them to a holding cell until recalled."

A wave of turmoil swept over the courtroom. Shock spread across Prinka's face as the guards surrounded them. Frishka's face darkened but he turned without a word and allowed the guardsmen to escort him out. Marquiese stood and watched the proceedings as if he were a guest actor in a previously unheard of play.

Once Frishka and Prinka were gone and the crowd had been silenced, Lord Komph stared down at the Crown Prince. He said, "Prince Marquiese, it is the decision of the Court to place Master Earek and Lady Marilana into your custody at this time. Guard, please release his bonds."

Once again, a murmur shook the courtroom, and Lord Komph gently silenced them. He watched as Marquiese held out his paws, and the manacles were removed.

"We ask you to please take the waiting guardsmen and retrieve Lady Marilana and Master Earek. Have the guards on duty taken into custody. Then return here with Lady Marilana and Master Earek for the declaration of Judgment."

Marquiese bowed with a grave expression and left.

The Crown Prince followed Captain Lorne down the hall to the chapel, where the doors were blocked by two of Frishka's guards. They straightened at the sight of Captain Lorne and the palace guards forming a gauntlet in front of them.

"You will surrender your arms to me and are hereby arrested as accessories to treason," the Captain of the Guards said quietly.

The pair stiffened. Any thoughts of escape evaporated as they looked at all the waiting guardsmen and they surrendered their swords and daggers without resistance.

"Escort them to the dungeon," Lorne told two of his men. Two others took their place by the doors and stood aside as Marquiese stepped forward.

The Crown Prince took a deep breath, then pulled open the doors. His eyes fell at once on the figure kneeling on the steps, the prayer robe on her shoulders, her head bowed. He walked forward quietly, his eyes fixed on Marilana. Her gown and the prayer robe were spread gracefully around her. What he could see of her gown appeared to be as black as the marble she knelt on. She was stunningly beautiful kneeling there with the sculpted white and black marble surrounding her, and the inlayed stained glass reflecting the light like a thousand stars. He knew she was waiting there by Frishka's order, waiting for his triumphant return to claim her as his bride, queen, and slave.

He stepped forward and stopped just behind her. She turned her head slightly. The sheer head veil shifted and he could see the side of her face. He watched spellbound as a glistening tear rolled down her golden cheek and tumbled onto the white kerchief clasped tightly in her paws.

Marquiese managed somehow to clear his throat and whisper, "Lady Marilana. Frishka has been taken into custody upon the orders of the Royal Court of Law under the charge of Treason to the Crown. You have been placed in my custody, and I have come to escort you to the courtroom to face the magistrates and hear their formal Judgment."

Marilana swayed slightly and raised the kerchief to her face. Father Iscoot stepped forward and gently removed the prayer robe. Marilana rose gracefully to her feet, but as she turned toward him he took in the dress that had been covered by the prayer robe. Fury rose in him so strong that he had to curl his paws into fists to stop from breaking something. Marilana glanced once at his face, then bowed her head meekly, her own paws clinched together at her waist, the chain of her manacles hanging to the floor. He could see the tears brimming in her eyes.

"I rejoice to know that your freedom is secure and your life safe, My Lord," she whispered, and then turned and walked toward the guards waiting at the chapel doors. Marquiese jumped again as Father Iscoot gripped his forearm.

"She prayed that you would never see that dress," he whispered. Marquiese nodded and began to turn away, but Father Iscoot held firm to his arm. Looking back, he saw the long black cloak the old leopard was holding out to him.

"Thank you," the Crown Prince said, taking the cloak and hurrying to catch up to Marilana.

She looked up at him as he draped the cloak over her shoulders. Her eyes glistened brightly for a moment, then she bowed her head again and clutched the cloak tightly closed.

Marilana kept her back straight as they walked through the palace to the courtroom. She was grateful for the cloak that Father Iscoot had provided, and even more grateful that Marquiese had placed it around her. She knew though that it would not be allowed to stay in the courtroom. She fought for composure, knowing she had to face the magistrates with calm, not tears. She took a deep breath as Marquiese paused before the courtroom doors, and then lifted her head slightly as she stepped forward and followed him inside. Earek was already there, his posture rigid as he faced the magistrates. Their eyes met briefly, and she took her place next to him.

"Lady Marilana, I am sure you are aware that concealment is not allowed in the courtroom," Lord Komph said uneasily.

She was sure he was remembering the previous night and wondering what the public would see when she removed her cloak. She began to reach up to remove it when Marquiese reached around her and lifted it from her shoulders. Gasps ran through the crowded room. Earek turned pale under his dark fur as he stared at her and his paws clinched with his rage. The magistrates faces became stony and outrage clouded King Rylan's eyes.

Marilana scanned each of their faces, trying to find the right words to explain her situation. But before she could muster a word, Marquiese stepped forward and addressed not only the magistrates, but the whole room.

"Your Honors, you see before you one more example of Frishka's cruelty," he said in a carrying voice, his paw raised in Marilana's direction. "When you instructed me to bring Lady Marilana here, my guards and I went to her rooms. I found them empty. Her wardrobe door was open, and I saw that there were no garments inside it. No scarves, no shoes, no cloaks. A maid informed me that Lady Marilana had earlier been escorted to the Royal Chapel. When I went there, I found her praying to The Goddess dressed as you see her now."

Marquiese looked from one magistrate to the next. "It is apparent to me that Frishka has forced her to wear what he chose each day, and his choices clearly illustrate how he perceives females. To him, they are nothing more than inferior vassals of his authority, to do with as he pleases. To him, they are nothing more than objects of beauty to be displayed and admired."

He paused to let his words sink in. Then he said, "Your Honors, I ask that you allow me to replace this cloak around Lady Marilana's shoulders so that she may be more comfortable. Obviously, she conceals nothing of danger. I know that I, for one, perceive women as far more than warm bodies. I, for one, recognize that Lady Marilana is an intelligent, honorable individual equal in strength of will and character to any man in this room. She should have the right to choose how she covers herself."

His speech concluded, Marquiese bowed slightly to the magistrates and waited.

King Rylan also waited, the pride he felt for his son etched on his face, his eyes studying each magistrate in turn.

Lord Hunmis moved not a muscle, staring hard at Marilana. Lord Quinre and Lord Komph both consented to Marquiese's request with precise nods. The Crown Prince nodded in return, and then gently swung the cloak back around Marilana's shoulders. She looked up at him with an expression of gratitude, but he did not meet her eyes.

"Very well," Lord Komph said, coming to his feet. Marilana looked at the red fox with as much calm as she could muster, but her stomach filled with nervous butterflies. The Head Magistrate made eye contact with the guard at the entrance and said. "Bring them in please."

The door opened, and Frishka and Lady Prinka were led into the courtroom. The gaunt and malignant tiger cast a malevolent smirk in Marilana's direction, but she kept her eyes forward, her expression cold, and her thoughts firmly fixed on providing any possible evidence necessary to prove Frishka's treason.

Lord Komph was about to address the Court when Lady Prinka called out in a voice filled with anger and arrogance. "I demand to know why I have been arrested. I demand to know why I have been placed with the accused? This is a disgrace."

"All will be told in good time, Lady Prinka," said Lord Komph calmly.

"I have been arrested without explanation," Prinka growled, her striped fur bristling. "I demand my rights. If I am accused of a crime, I demand that those crimes be named."

"And the Court orders that you remain silent until told otherwise," Lord Komph said firmly.

Prinka's eyes widened in surprise, but she held her tongue nonetheless.

"You have all been brought before us because Lord Frishka called for our verdict this morning. By law, a call for Judgment means that this is our last court session for this case." Lord Komph leaned against the high desk. "Allow me to reiterate some points we consider important. First, the witness accounts from Prince Marquiese, Lady Marilana, and Master Earek all support each other. The accounts of Lord Frishka and men following Lord Frishka's orders have some points that match Prince Marquiese's account, but leave some questions unanswered. Lord Frishka and his men all claim that one of them threw the net that captured Prince Marquiese, however, none of them can say who it was."

"Your Honor," Frishka interrupted, "if I may—"

"You may not," said Lord Komph firmly. "You will not interrupt the Court again."

Frishka clamped his mouth shut, his yellow eyes ablaze with anger.

Lord Komph continued. "Lord Frishka and his men also claim that Master Earek was tied up and hidden, but Captain Lorne stated that Master Earek was standing near Prince Marquiese when he arrested everyone on The Beach. Captain Lorne's account supports Prince Marquiese's account.

"Next point of note. Three individuals who could provide testimony to treasonous actions are missing. The guards assigned to Lady Marilana and Master Earek have not been seen since the early morning the day of the arrests. This leaves us wondering what roll they played in the treasonous events that took place that day. Also Errand Rider Hektor has not returned nor has a thorough search revealed his whereabouts. We know that he delivered a missive to Prince Dansho as ordered by Prince Marquiese, but never made it to his mother's house, which was where he told Prince Dansho's guardsmen he was going. We have collaborating evidence from a childhood friend that Hektor's mother is allergic to flowers just as Prince Marquiese said, so he was clearly not bringing her flowers. This confirms that Prince Marquiese has much better relations with his errand riders, including Hektor, than does Lord Frishka. This brings us to the question of why Hektor would have brought concerns to Lord Frishka rather than to trust the instructions of someone he knew better. Without Hektor's testimony, however, we cannot determine his true actions one way or the other.

"The last point of note is the letters supposedly written by Prince Marquiese. Sir Libor proved to the Court that he could positively identify Prince Marquiese's writing style. From his testimony, we know that the three letters Lord Frishka presented as evidence to support his treason charge against Prince Marquiese were forgeries. This leaves the question of who would want to try to frame Prince Marquiese of treason."

"Yes, most interesting," Frishka said in a voice edged with false concern. "It all comes to the same point. You do not have enough evidence to convict Prince Marquiese of treason. So just say so and release us all so we can get on with our lives."

"Indeed we do not have the evidence to convict Prince Marquiese of treason," agreed Lord Komph. "However, treason charges cannot simply be dismissed. We, the Magistrates, are charged with finding the root of the treason and placing our verdict upon the guilty parties. Two charges of treason where given to King Rylan within a half hour of each other. The events that took place definitely indicate that there has been treason committed. You called for our Judgment, so we must make a verdict here today. To that end, we have a few other pieces of evidence to make public."

A deep frown spread across Frishka's face, and his yellow eyes continued to spark with anger.

"But first a question, one the Court wishes to pose to Lady Prinka." Lord Komph swung his eyes in the aging tiger's direction. "And that is this: to what extent do your loyalties lie with your son? Would you ever do anything that could endanger him or work against his plans?"

Prinka glared back at him. "What a foolish question. I am completely loyal to my son. I would do anything to protect him and would do nothing that could needlessly endanger him or work against him."

"Very well." Lord Komph added a further note of formality to his voice. "Lady Prinka, your name has been added to the treason charge of Lord Frishka against Prince Marquiese. We have been given testimony that you wrote the forged letters that Lord Frishka presented to the Court. And since you have just told us that you would not work against your son, we must assume that writing the letters was a conscious and deliberate attempt to help him."

Prinka opened her mouth to make a retort, but Lord Komph silenced her with a look. The Head Magistrate turned his gaze to Frishka.

"Redsands has laws governing the proper treatment of prisoners and carefully outlines the circumstances that would allow for torture to be used," he stated calmly. "Lord Frishka have you followed these laws?"

"Of course I have," Frishka growled, "but I cannot prevent the prisoners from self-inflicted injuries."

Lord Komph held the tiger's gaze a moment longer. Then he gave brief study to Marilana and Earek before settling his gray eye on Prince Marquiese.

"Prince Marquiese, you have been in the King's custody," Lord Komph said. "Do you have any injuries to report from your imprisonment?"

"None, Your Honor," Marquiese said levelly.

"Would you be willing to submit to an examination by a team of healers to prove that you have sustained no injuries?"

"Of course," Marquiese bowed slightly.

"If I might suggest, Your Honors," Frishka intoned quickly, "that since Healer Strunt is already familiar with Prince Marquiese and Lady Marilana, he could give you an accurate estimate of their condition."

"Thank you, but no," replied Lord Komph. "We have already asked our personal healers to gather in the Deliberation Chamber. We know them and trust their skills. They also have no bias toward any of the accused and so will present their findings without embellishments. Prince Marquiese, if you would please join us and our healers in the Deliberation Chamber."

Frishka snarled slightly as the door closed behind the magistrates. Marilana felt suddenly very exposed without Marquiese standing between her and Frishka. From the corner of her eye she could see his smirk as he looked at her again, but this time there was more anger in his features as well. She stared at the Magistrates' Bench and knew what she would have to do.

After a few moments Marquiese and the magistrates returned. They were accompanied by a beaver wearing a healer's coat.

"Healer Nacobi," said Lord Komph. "Please tell the Court of your findings."

"Yes, Your Honor," said the healer calmly. "Prince Marquiese is in the best of health. We could find no indications that he has suffered any ill effects from his imprisonment."

"Thank you," the Head Magistrate said. He turned to Marilana. "Lady Marilana, we know you suffered from a concussion at the start of this trial. We were told by your warden that it was an accident. What do you have to say about your treatment during your imprisonment?"

"I have had no accidents, Your Honor," she said calmly. "What I suffered during the time of my confinement was torture. I have been beaten, humiliated, and starved. I have been forced to wear indecent clothing, and I have been threatened with far worse treatment, all in the custody of Lord Frishka."

"How dare you lie to the Court," spat Frishka as whispers swept through the room.

"We shall see," said Lord Komph darkly. "Please accompany us, Lady Marilana. The healers await."

Marilana curtseyed and walked calmly into the Deliberation Chamber. Three healers waited in the room. Magistrates Komph, Hunmis, and Quinre, as well as King Rylan, took their chairs. Marilana was beckoned forward by the healers.

"I am Healer Steppe. With respect, please remove your cloak," a tall goat said.

Marilana did so. When the cloak dropped to the floor, the healers looked with shock at her appearance. Healer Steppe quickly slid a mobile curtain between her and the magistrates.

"I am Healer Jellon. We must ask you to remove your garments," a tawny wolf said quietly.

Marilana nodded. She undid the laces of the gown and let it slide to the floor. She said nothing as the healers set to work examining her various wounds and bruises. All three healers wore dark expressions when they finally finished. Healer Steppe helped Marilana re-don the hated gown and gently replaced her cloak. Once she was properly covered again, the curtain was removed. Without a word, the magistrates rose and lead the way back into the courtroom. Marilana boldly met Frishka's eyes as she returned to stand between Marquiese and Earek. Frishka snarled slightly.

"Healer Steppe," Lord Komph said gravely. "Please tell the Court of your findings."

"Yes, Your Honor," the goat replied. "Lady Marilana has sustained multiple punctures along her inner thighs and has amassed more bruises than I can count along her inner thighs, lower back, buttocks, and abdomen. She is also exhibiting signs of severe dehydration and acute weight loss."

"Can you estimate a time frame for when these injuries were acquired?" asked Lord Komph.

"All of her injuries have been acquired in the past two fifnights. The oldest from two fifnights ago and the newest I would say are from yesterday."

"Thank you. And how serious is her condition?"

"Honestly, with as much damage as she has sustained and the severity of her dehydration, I cannot believe she is able to even stand up," said the healer, shaking his head.

"Thank you," said Lord Komph and turned his gaze in Earek's direction. "Master Earek, what do you have to tell the Court of your imprisonment?"

"Your Honor," said Earek with a slight bow. "I have also been beaten, deprived of adequate food, and threatened with worse beatings and even death."

"Very well," replied Lord Komph. "Please accompany us to the healers."

Marilana waited as calmly as she could for Earek and the magistrates to return. She could see Marquiese shifting slightly beside her and realized that he was actively blocking Frishka's view of her.

Frishka sniffed disgustedly as the door to the Deliberation Chamber opened again and Earek resumed his place at her right side.

"Healer Steppe," Lord Komph said to the goat once more. "Please tell the Court of your findings."

"Yes, Your Honor," sighed the healer. "Master Earek has amassed multiple bruises along his inner thighs, lower back, and abdomen. He also exhibits some minor signs of dehydration."

"Can you estimate a time frame for when these injuries were acquired and the seriousness of his condition please?" asked Lord Komph again.

"All of his injuries have been acquired in the past two fifnights. The oldest from two fifnights ago and the newest I would say are from the day before yesterday. His condition is moderate."

"Thank you," said Lord Komph.

"As I said," growled Frishka, "I could not stop them from inflicting wounds upon themselves, Your Honors. There are, after all, only so many hours in a day."

"Healer Steppe, could these wounds have been self-inflicted by the subjects?"

"No, Your Honor." The healer shook his head gravely. "These wounds are too severe and are located in areas of the body that could not have been self-inflicted."

"Thank you, Healer Steppe, you are dismissed," said Lord Komph.

"Lady Marilana. Master Earek." Lord Komph addressed them with considerable gravity. "You have sustained unjustified and unforgivable injuries while in the custody of Lord Frishka—"

"I am being set up!" Frishka shouted. "I did not torture anyone."

"Lord Frishka, if you interrupt the Court one more time, I will have you gagged," the Head Magistrate said.

"Your Honors, may I speak?" Marilana said, calmly stepping forward.

"You may."

"Lord Frishka does not consider what he did to us torture. He made it very clear that he was punishing us for disobeying him."

A wave of uncertain murmurs swept through the courtroom. Frishka and Prinka took up a haughty stance when they heard this. Lord Komph and King Rylan studied Marilana suspiciously while Lord Quinre and Lord Hunmis looked at her with surprise.

"What disobedience did you commit that would require such punishment?" asked Lord Komph cautiously.

"We told the truth before the Court. I refused to repeat the lies Frishka insisted I tell you. As did Master Earek."

"That is a fact," Earek intoned.

The room filled with surprised whispers as Lord Komph leaned back in his chair, his expression thoughtful.

"You will pay for your disrespect, Marilana," growled Frishka. "You both will."

Marilana turned and met his angry eyes with a look of pride and honor. She said, "I do not respect or obey traitors. I serve only the legitimate royal line."

"My son would have been crowned king had you not gotten in the way," Prinka shrieked at the young lioness.

"Prince Marquiese is the rightful heir to the Crown," Marilana retorted. "And you are nothing more than an annoyance to him."

"I will be king!" growled Frishka taking a menacing step toward Marilana, while she moved not a muscle. "Marquiese will die, and I will take the Crown. Then you will pay for your interference." He looked up at the magistrates and snarled, "You will all pay!"

"Restrain him," Lord Komph said coldly.

Three guardsmen closed in on Frishka and forcibly restrained him. He snarled at them and struggled to throw off their paws, while his mother glared at Marilana with pure hatred.

"Order," the Head Magistrate called to the courtroom. "You will all come to order at once."

When the murmurs, whispers, and gasps sweeping through the courtroom died to a low hum, Lord Komph continued without commenting on Marilana's actions. "We have been called today to pass Judgment, and so we declare by law our verdict. We, the Magistrates of the Royal Court of Law, Lords Komph, Quinre, and Hunmis, declare that you, Prince Marquiese, are innocent of all charges of treason against King Rylan. We release you from custody." The eyes of all three magistrates fell upon Frishka, and Lord Komph continued. "As you have condemned yourselves with your actions and words here today, we now pass Judgment upon you. We, the Magistrates of the Royal Court of Law, Lords Komph, Quinre, and Hunmis, declare that you, Lord Frishka, and you, Lady Prinka, are guilty of Treason to the Crown as evidenced in this trial. By consent of His Majesty, King Rylan of Redsands, and His Highness, Prince Marquiese, you are hereby stripped of all titles and property, and henceforth banished from the Allied Nations and all lands there in."

He shifted his gaze upon Marilana and Earek and said, "Lady Marilana and Master Earek, we have decided to take a short recess before starting the trial to decide your guilt. We will open said trial the first day after the next Restday. You are to remain under guard in your rooms in the custody of His Highness Prince Marquiese. Court adjourned."

Marilana curtseyed as the magistrates and King Rylan left the courtroom. As she prepared to follow Marquiese out, she caught sight of Frishka sneering at her. She lifted her head and continued as if he were below her notice.

*

Marilana and four guards stood unmoving in the hallway as Marquiese and Master Castant escorted Earek into his rooms and supervised the removal of his wrist manacles.

They came back and walked the young lioness into her rooms. The leopard entered first, and the Crown Prince followed. He scanned the room and checked the bathing room.

"Remove her wrist manacles please," the royal lion told one of the guards. When the guard was done, Marquiese said, "Leave us."

When the door clicked shut behind them, Marquiese said, "First, I thank you for your actions in court. You caused Frishka and Prinka to condemn themselves in open court. That was the best thing that could have happened. The magistrates knew they had made the right choice when they heard that, and the public also knew the truth."

Marilana said nothing. She waited while Marquiese took a deep breath, his hesitation palpable. "Second, I do not like to ask this, but I must." Still Marilana waited. "I need to see for myself the extent of the damage that Frishka has dealt to you."

He stopped talking and met her eyes. She detected a shadow of pain and anger. She sighed. A small part of her had hoped he would not ask this. Another part of her knew it was just wishful thinking. She feared his anger upon seeing her wounds, and wished he had asked to hear the accounting of the events before seeing the result. At least then he would have understood the battle she had fought with Frishka not just the brutality of it.

"As you wish, My Lord Highness." She released the cloak and blinked back tears as it fell to the floor. She bent and gathered the hated skirt. She straightened and gazed into his eyes, raising the skirt as high as she could while preserving what little shred of modesty remained. The Crown Prince's face darkened and contorted with rage and disgust. Marilana could no longer hold back the tears welling in her eyes, as the full horror of the past few fifnights overwhelmed her. It was as if Marquiese's knowledge of her wounds made it all the more real to her; as if hiding it from him had been her last protection. Now that was gone.

While he scanned her legs for what felt like eternity, she looked into his eyes and tears flowed from hers. Abruptly he looked away and stormed out the door. Master Castant followed, his face showing a mix of pity and anger. When the door locked behind them, Marilana sank to the floor and wept.

*

Hours later, she sat exactly as she had, motionless, staring at her paws. The lock clicked behind her, the door opened, and three creatures entered. Marilana did not even twitch as the door closed and locked again.

"Marilana?" King Rylan's gentle voice filled the room. "Are you alright?"

When she did not respond, he knelt beside her and cupped her chin in his paw, gently lifting her face to his. Tears welled up again as she looked back at him. Eyes so like his son's. He sighed and released her. She buried her face in her paws again and the tears streamed forth again.

"My Lady, why are you weeping?" asked Altia, taking the King's place. Father Iscoot joined her as well.

"Father Iscoot and our young maid are concerned about you," said the King of Redsands, his voice even more gentle. "As am I."

Marilana looked up them, meeting their concerned faces and tried to smile.

"Thank you," she whispered through the tears. "I am sorry. This should be a happy meeting. We have achieved a great victory. I could not have done it without your help. From the depths of my heart you all have my thanks."

"I don't understand, Marilana," Altia asked softly. "If it is as you say, a great victory, why do you cry? You were so strong against Frishka. Why now do you weep?"

Marilana smiled at Altia. "I weep because my heart is broken, my dear friend."

"What do you mean, your heart is broken?"

"I always knew that in the end, no matter how the trial ended, that when I faced him, I would see my heart break. I will go on. I must go on. But my heart will always remain here. And for now, it is in pieces."

"But—"

"Not now, gentle one," interrupted Father Iscoot. "I think Marilana needs some time with her thoughts and some good rest."

The old leopard put a warm paw on Marilana's shoulder and squeezed gently. He said, "We have brought food and one dress that Altia managed to save for you. My child, everything will turn out right in the end. I feel it in my old bones."

Father Iscoot gathered his cloak, stood, and moved toward the door. Altia threw her arms around Marilana and hugged her tightly. She rose reluctantly, and King Rylan followed them toward the door.

"Sire," Marilana whispered. "A favor. May I have wood for a fire tonight?"

"A fire in summer?" he asked, surprised. But he relented without question, even if his tone was full of curiosity. "Of course you can. I will have wood brought." The trio left the room, and Marilana's tears tinseled her beautiful face, her golden fur becoming sodden.

26

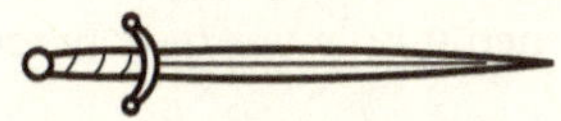

The Crown Prince and his chief advisor entered the room once again, their eyes seeking the unexpected source of heat and finding it safely in the fireplace. Marilana sat on the floor with her arms wrapped around her knees; her gaze intent on the flames.

"A fire in the middle of summer?" asked Castant in surprise.

"Yes," Marquiese replied, softly so as to not disturb the heavy silence pervading the room. "This is how Marilana does her deepest thinking. She told me once that it allows her to exclude everything around her and focus her thoughts completely."

He stopped a few paces away and took in her appearance. The medium blue dress was unadorned, but styled for a noble of the court. The gentle curves of the neck and slightly loose sleeves gave it a comfortable look. Her slumped shoulders and red eyes belied the nobility the dress gave her. The chain connecting her ankles poked out from under her skirt. He shook his head and knelt at the corner of the fireplace, facing her across the fire-lit stone before the hearth. Castant leaned against the mantel.

"Marilana," Marquiese spoke gently "You have not slept. You have not eaten. How are your wounds going to heal?"

Marilana said nothing in reply, but Marquiese noticed the slight tightening around her eyes. After a few seconds, Master Castant pushed away from the mantel.

"Should I get the healer, Highness?" he asked quietly.

"No healer," Marilana replied harshly. Her eyes traveled from the lion to the leopard and back again. "I do not need a healer, and I would not choose Healer Strunt if I did," she said. "He is not trustworthy."

"Be at peace, Lady Marilana," the Crown Prince said quietly. "We mentioned it only out of concern."

She dipped her head, closed her eyes for a moment, and sank back again, the flicker of spirit fading. Her voice was a mere whisper when she said, "Forgive me, Master Castant. I did not mean to be rude." And then to Marquiese. "You are correct, My Lord Highness; I have not slept and do need to sleep to recover my strength. My wounds are healing well enough with the aid of Maid Altia's remedies. I ate my dinner, but have not yet eaten my breakfast. And the additional reason for the fire was the burning of a hated garment."

Marquiese was not surprised to learn the fate of yesterday's dress, but listened more to the tone of her voice. She sounded tired, but not tired from lack of sleep; a tired that comes from resignation. She had resigned herself, he had heard it before, and never liked the dark thoughts that accompanied her logic in such a state. The only question now was what situation did she feel left her with no alternatives.

When she offered nothing more, he said, "Marilana, what you did yesterday in the courtroom was brave, foolish, and amazing all at the same time. I am grateful to you. However, I have not yet decided how to proceed with the charges against you."

She remained still her eyes seeking the flames.

"I have come this morning to ask you a few questions. I left here last night in a state of rage, but King Rylan and Master Castant convinced me to come back and ask my questions of you directly. I have already spoken with Earek this morning; he has shed a lot of light on the situation, but I need to know your story as well."

"Of course, My Lord Highness." Her voice was hollow and cold.

He stared at her, but her eyes did not wander. He said, "Before you illuminate Frishka's treatment of you, I have one question I need you to answer first."

He waited for her to acknowledge his words, but she only drew her shoulders back and straightened slightly. "I would like you to tell me why you have consistently addressed me as Your Lord and King Rylan as Sire since my release."

He watched her swallow before opening her mouth to speak. "I . . . I give you my fealty, now and always. I want you to know that." She looked up at him—he found the mix of fear, hate, and pleading unsettling—and began to whisper. "He demanded that I address him as my lord. I refused. I spoke to him always as an equal, and it made him furious. Out of control." He saw the fury building in her. He knew she was talking about Frishka, and his own rage began to build. "So I address you with what I denied him, with what was always yours. My fealty is yours."

Marquiese had to concentrate on his own breathing, controlling his own fury. He had expected the answer, but it did not make it easier to hear. Worse, he had more to know from her that would light his anger to ever-higher flames. He glanced at the fire for a moment, and then forced himself to look back into her eyes. "I must ask now that you repeat for me all that you have told my father and the magistrates."

Marilana straightened her shoulders. Her voice was strong again, and she spoke without hesitation. Instead of fury, sadness filled her eyes, as if she had known that he would ask, and had hoped against hope that he never would.

She spoke flatly of the secret door in her room and the events that led up to her arrest on The Beach. When she began to speak of Frishka's first visit, Marquiese could sit no longer and tore his gaze from her eyes. He stood and paced. Marilana continued on, recounting her tortures in detail.

When she finished, Master Castant fetched her a cup of water. "Drink," he said softly.

"Thank you," she murmured. After a few sips, she set the cup on the floor next to her and hugged her knees.

Marquiese finally stopped pacing, though he could not face her.

"Thank you. I know how difficult that was," he said. "I have a lot to think about. I will return to make sure your needs are being met." He hesitated, anger seeping into his posture and edging his voice. "I thank you for your fealty, Lady Marilana." He took a few steps toward the door, but Marilana's voice drew him up short.

"My Lord, might I speak with you about some new clothes?"

He stopped and glanced back at her. She had not moved. She stared into the fire without blinking. He wanted to rush back to her, to wrap his arms around her and protect her, but he coldly felt his duty and held his feet facing the door. When he did not respond, she continued more softly. "I ask only for a single dress of low merchant cut, hunter green, and divided for riding. Also a light traveling cloak, dark gray."

When she said no more, he stormed to the door and left without a second glance, fury burning at his insides.

*

"How dare she! How can she?" Marquiese roared, pacing King Rylan's study his fury fueling his motion. King Rylan and Master Castant watched with obvious surprise as he ranted and paced. "How can she betray me this way? Betray all of us? She hates Frishka. She fights him every way possible and yet she betrays me."

"What are you talking about, Marquiese? I have not seen any of this new betrayal. What in the world has Marilana done?

Have we missed something?" the King said, struggling to remain calm. "If so, please enlighten us, my son."

"It is not new. She has been doing it the whole time; I have just been picking up on pieces of it myself. What is worse, I know not what she is doing exactly. I just get hints, suggestions that prick my awareness." The Crown Prince spat the words.

"Was it something then that she said while describing Frishka's treatment of her?" asked Master Castant. "I am confused, Marquiese, because I do not think she betrayed you with a contest of wills."

"No. She did what she had to do. And, although I deeply regret her position, I am also very aware that she probably saved my life by doing so." He stopped pacing and stared at the carpet. "No, it was when she asked for the hunter garb. I recognized that she had a plan for the future, that by doing so she is planning to betray me, is still betraying me."

"Hunter garb?" Castant's voice could hardly mask his exasperation. "She asked for a dress and a cloak. I did not think it meant anything."

"She was very specific," replied Marquiese. "The dress is hunter green, divided for riding and low merchant cut, and a light traveling cloak in dark gray."

"But Marquiese, that could be mean anything. Hunters do not usually wear dresses," King Rylan interjected.

"No," Marquiese replied darkly. "But as you said, I know her better than you. I know why she wants those clothes. Her hunter garb has always been divided riding dresses. I just do not know what she intends to do. Wearing those clothes, she can disappear in a heartbeat."

He studied both of their faces before answering their confused looks. "Think it through. A low merchant dressed for traveling can go un-remarked and virtually unhindered anywhere in any city, town, or countryside. She knows that her appearance will attract attention, but she has lived with that her whole life. She knows that a cold sneering attitude and a quick knife can deter most unwanted advances."

"But a higher merchant or a lord could still force the issue," interrupted King Rylan.

"You are forgetting the color of the dress," Marquiese replied. "Hunter green. No merchant or lord would interfere with a hunter on the hunt. She is a bandit hunter on the move. Yes, it is a dress, but one made for fast movement and long travel. No one will bother her. After a fifnight, no one will remember her coming or going. She will be able to move through the forest as silently as ever, and the color of the dress and cloak will make her nearly impossible to see no matter the time of day or night. The forest is her preferred hunting ground." He passed a paw over his elegant mane.

"She has chosen a hunting ground and has decided she will hunt in summer; the colors are wrong for the other seasons. She will begin hunting soon," Marquiese said as he met their gazes.

"The next question is—who is she planning to hunt?" asked Castant.

King Rylan shook his head with downcast eyes. "That is a question I do not need to ask."

Master Castant and Marquiese glanced at him with slight surprise. He sighed heavily. "Is it not obvious? Frishka has destroyed her life. He has been banished instead of beheaded, and she still sees him as a threat. If she is also banished, how long does she have to find and kill him before he returns? She has sworn to kill him no matter how long it takes. She will do everything she can to prevent his return."

Marquiese looked at his father. "It would seem that you know parts of her character better than I do. I could not have seen her target so easily, although I can see now that it makes sense for her to seek revenge. I do not usually think of her as the revengeful type."

"I do not think it is revenge," said King Rylan, intently focused on Marquiese. "She has her motives, but she is the only one who knows what they are."

Marquiese frowned thoughtfully at his father. He sensed that Rylan knew her motives, but the fact that he was letting her keep her own council on who should know was warning enough for Marquiese not to pry. He would let the matter rest. He had duties to perform now that he was free, and he would think about Marilana when he had time. The deep feeling of betrayal lingered as he discussed the state of his reports.

Marilana had wept again after Marquiese and Castant left, but it was shorter this time. She feared she would never be able to hold back tears after being in his presence. Wearily she got to her feet and staggered to her breakfast tray. She ate the bowl of porridge and raspberries mechanically, not because she was hungry, but because she knew he would be displeased if she did not. With her belly full, she headed to the bed and collapsed on the covers. But sleep wouldn't come. She considered entering the healing trance, but she knew that would not clear her mind. She stared at the canopy lace for a long time before surrendering to a deep slumber.

She awoke several hours later as a guard escorted a servant with her lunch tray. Once again, she finished her meal of cold cucumber soup, pears, cheese, and flat bread without being able to appreciate the fresh summer flavors. For the rest of the afternoon, she reclined on the couch, basking in the sun's warmth; this time using the healing trance. Speeding her recovery would be beneficial for the trials, even if getting real sleep would help her think.

Marquiese returned to check on her, accompanying the servant who carted her dinner tray. He was a magnificent sight dressed in a bright blue silk coat and pants over a red shirt, his dinner attire. Marilana sighed inaudibly. She felt heat rise in her cheeks as the dazzling Prince gazed at her; she imagined she looked like a beggar in a crumpled dress. *Why am I blushing? How silly to worry about my appearance while under arrest. I need to focus on the next steps of my plan. I know he won't like what I have to do.*

"The servants reported that both the breakfast and lunch trays were completely empty. Are you getting enough food? We could serve you more, if you'd like.

"Thank you. I do not need anything more," she said.

"You appear to have at least rested. Did you sleep well, or do you need something to help you sleep?" Marquiese studied her with deep concern in his eyes.

"I slept well. Thank you," Marilana said.

Marquiese opened his mouth as if we had more to say, but Marilana cut him off. "I am fine, My Lord Highness. Truly. Thank you."

He nodded, satisfied with Marilana words. Master Castant smirked behind him. Marquiese shifted and then spun around and motioned to the servant and Master Castant to follow him out. Castant frowned, but turned and left.

As soon as she heard the door close, Marilana's eyes filled with tears. Wiping away the tears, she made herself eat every last bite of her dinner.

27

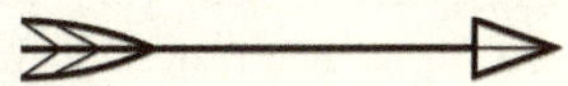

Marilana awoke late the next morning still wearing the blue dress, the only piece of clothing she had. As the grogginess of sleep wore off, the door opened. Marquiese and Master Castant entered just as Marilana was stepping away from the bed. She froze while smoothing her wrinkled skirt, surprised by the stream of servants that poured in behind the pair. Serving men carried steaming buckets; women carried towels and garments and items for the bath. One woman toted the breakfast tray. When she set the tray down, she set the table for four. *Who will join us?*

Marquiese studied Marilana for a moment; then grinned with amusement. He and Master Castant settled on the couch out of the servants' way and gazed out the window. When the serving men left and the door was locked, the serving women descended on Marilana, hustling her into the bathing room. After they undressed her and helped her into the bath, they scrubbed her, fussing over her fur and claws. When they finished bathing her, they helped her out, patted her down, and gave her a clean dressing robe. But they were not done yet; they worked her over with fragrant oils and silky powders; soon Marilana thought she might scream. It wasn't only that she objected to being pampered by servants; it was the fact that, aside from occasional tuts or sighs, they fussed over her in complete silence. Sensing their unspoken words and interpreting the glances of the women tending her, Marilana felt as though she might explode. The women dressed her in clean undergarments and a beautiful dark blue dress and escorted her out to join Marquiese and Castant.

Marquiese and Castant rose when the head maid curtseyed and gestured to Marilana. Marquiese looked her over with a critical eye before addressing the head maid. "You and your women have done well, Mistress Refrona. I thank you for your efforts."

The Head Maid grinned and curtseyed. The other maids bobbed quick curtsies before scurrying to the door at the urging of Mistress Refrona. Marquiese watched them go and then turned to Marilana.

Marilana spread her skirts wide and curtseyed deeply as she spoke. "I hope silence is not required for the rest of the morning. I was about to go mad. I have never had such a disconcerting bath. Maids usually chide and chatter until you think you cannot bear anymore, but by comparison, the silence is much worse."

Marquiese laughed and gestured for her to join him at the breakfast table. "Silence is definitely not required or even requested for breakfast."

Castant chuckled as he approached the door and knocked. The lock clicked and the door opened. Castant spoke softly with the guards outside and then retreated as the door opened. Marilana clasped her paws over her mouth and gasped with delight as Earek was escorted in by Captain Lorne. He appeared weary, but she could tell by his dark green linen suit, he too had been pampered. He smiled at her and looked deeply into her eyes to read her emotional state. She returned his smile; and lowered her paws.

Earek approached Marquiese and bowed respectfully. "Your Highness."

"Come, both of you, sit. Let us eat breakfast," Marquiese said gesturing to the table again.

He suited action to words and took the seat at the head of the table. Castant held the chair to Marquiese's right for Marilana, and gestured to Earek to take the seat across the table from her. Castant sat at the foot of the table. Captain Lorne leaned against the wall behind Earek, standing casually at the ready. Marilana narrowed her eyes as Marquiese and Castant conversed about trivial matters. As they spoke they questioned Marilana or Earek, asking their opinions, or inquiring if they had met someone or heard of an event. Marilana could see that the seating arrangement was intentional. It forced the one questioned to turn to look at the questioner while the others could observe unseen. When Marilana glanced at Earek, she could tell he was thinking the same thing. The seemingly innocuous conversation was heading somewhere, but Marilana could not predict where. Earek and Marilana recounted brief stories from their childhoods, but still the topics seemed frivolous. Marilana felt uneasy, almost hunted, by the time they sat back in their chairs and sipped tea.

Marquiese sighed contentedly. "That was a good breakfast; I definitely got plenty to eat. How about you, Earek?"

"Yes, Your Highness, thank you. I have had plenty, and feel a good deal better than I have for quite a while. The bath was very soothing and pleasant company is a nice change," Earek replied. He seemed relaxed, if a bit wary.

"Castant, you ate well and are content?" Marquiese asked.

Castant laughed, "Oh, yes, Highness, thank you for letting me join you."

"And you, Marilana, you have had enough?" he asked turning to her, his eyes scanning her face.

"Yes, thank you, My Lord Highness. I am quite well fed and feeling better," she replied quietly, studying his eyes in return.

"Very good. Well I have other duties to perform today, so I must go. I will return later perhaps." He set his cup down and stood. Everyone followed his lead and moved away from the table. "Earek, I assume you would like to say farewell to

Marilana. I am afraid I cannot let you two speak to each other for a while after today. This breakfast was all I could manage."

"Yes, thank you, Highness," Earek said with a bow to Marquiese.

He turned to Marilana and took one of her paws in his. With a bow he kissed her paw and gazed into her eyes. Squeezing her paw gently, he spoke softly, "Be strong, Sister."

"Be steadfast, Brother," she replied warmly, gently squeezing his paw in return.

Then he followed Captain Lorne out the door. After the door closed, Marquiese turned to face her.

"That is it? That is all you have to say to each other?" Marquiese said eyes wide with anger.

"Forgive us, My Lord, if you wanted more. What more can we say at this point? Our heads are barely above water as it is. What can we say to each other that is neither significant nor more heartfelt?"

"More heartfelt? Would you rather embrace like lovers and kiss? Or perhaps you want to remind him that your plan is not yet complete and to hold his tongue so you do not have to cut it out? Honestly, what should I think after that?" he said harshly, waving a paw toward the door.

"Please, My Lord Highness, I meant nothing like that," she said startled. "I did not mean . . . I just . . . ," she paused to swallow, her breathing quickened. "He is my brother. We are sworn to defend and support each other as family. We only meant to reassure one another. What else could have been construed by observation; it was a simple farewell between brother and sister bidden by law not to speak to each other." Her mouth slammed shut upon seeing the fury on Marquiese's face. Her breathing was quick and shallow. She wanted to step away from him, from his rage-filled eyes. Worry and fear blossomed in her. Not fear of Marquiese, but fear that she had done something to hurt him further—that she was somehow causing him even more emotional turmoil.

Marquiese inhaled sharply before speaking; his voice was constricted. "At least breakfast was pleasant enough." He turned away from her.

"Why?" she whispered and then she did step away from him. Seeing the renewed fury in his face made her wish she had not asked, but she could not help it. She had to ask; she could not see why he had gone through the trouble. She could not see what he had gained from the futile conversation, the pampering, any of it. She could not believe he was just making sure she was eating and getting her fill. She knew him too well for that to be the reason, or at least she thought she did. Facing his fury, she thought she might not know him at all.

"How dare you ask why I went through the trouble to make you comfortable, to see to it that you were cleaned, clothed, and fed. Do you presume to demand to know why I do anything? I could have left you the way you were, treating you as though you were not worth notice. I am the Crown Prince. I can do anything I want with you. Frishka ate meals with you. Why can I not? I am not he; I did not come here to torture you or to make demands of you. Can you not see? No, never mind. I have work I must do." With that he turned and stormed into the hall without a second glance.

Marilana collapsed on the floor and wept into her paws. She hardly noticed that Castant had not yet followed Marquiese out. He paused for only a second before leaving her to her confinement. She sobbed and shook uncontrollably. *How had he forced himself to be pleasant throughout breakfast if he hates me so much? Perhaps he brought Earek to breakfast because he does not hate Earek as much as he hates me. Perhaps Castant served as a distraction so Marquiese would not have to look at me the whole time.* She wept for hours with dark thoughts consuming her mind.

"If I may say so, that last bit did not go well," Master Castant said as he caught up to Marquiese and matched his forceful stride. Marquiese growled at him as he stormed toward his apartments. "I did not think you had intended to hurt her with a pleasant bath and breakfast," Castant continued.

Marquiese fumed in silence until they entered his study and were alone.

"Hurt her? I never intended to hurt her! You know I was giving them a chance to see each other, so they would know they were not permanently harmed; to forget the trial for a time and just be content. I never considered that we would have to force the conversation, or that she would further her scheming right in front of me. Earek at least is just following her lead. He is loyal to her. Of that I can be sure."

Marquiese paced the study, his rants tapering into angry mutters. Castant caught some of the more forceful mutterings of "hurt her" and "betray me" and sighed to himself. He thought he knew the root of the trouble, but, if he was right, Marquiese would have to figure it out for himself. Nothing anyone said could make him admit to the heartfelt truth. He might be able to pry at it, though, encouraging Marquiese to think about it indirectly.

"She collapsed on the floor weeping when you left."

Marquiese froze facing the wall; his eyes were open but his sight was directed inward. He spoke softly after a moment. "She was so afraid of me. I have never before seen her so overcome by fear. I know she fears when there is cause, but she is careful to control her emotions. For her to have completely lost her composure, Frishka must have come close to breaking her. I must be careful. She may not be of sound mind when he is near."

Castant remained silent. He suspected Marilana's state didn't have much to do with Frishka breaking her. She had said that he had come close to killing her, but did not have the ability to break her. Marquiese, however, would need to be watched carefully. Castant might have to intervene if Marilana was nearing the brink. He suspected that Marquiese could break her and not realize it until it was too late, given his and Marilana's emotional turmoil.

"Perhaps I should check on her later with Captain Lorne and let you check on Earek. She may need more time to settle down before seeing you again," Castant said gingerly.

Marquiese glanced over his shoulder, held his gaze, and then sighed and looked at the floor. "You may be right. Very well, I will not look in on her until it is time to gather her for court in two days."

Castant sighed, relieved that he had not had to convince Marquiese. He had to be wary of his friend's temper. Banishment was too good for all the upheaval and raw emotions Frishka had stirred up.

Marilana raced through the halls of the Royal Palace in the hated dress. Frishka's laugh pursued her and echoed down every corridor. She could not escape him, but still she ran. Somewhere Marquiese was being forced to mount a gallows. She had to get there to prevent him from dying, but the corridors continued unabated. Occasionally she could see the gallows and Marquiese out a window, but she was too far away to intervene, and the loathing on his face when she shouted out to him was enough to stop her in her tracks. Although she had seen his hatred of her, she still needed to reach him and stop Frishka from killing him.

She paused at another window looking down at Marquiese. He had reached the steps and men with spears were forcing him to climb the wooden scaffold. He twisted and dodged as best he could with his paws tied behind his back, fighting every step of the way.

Quickly she scanned what she could see of the courtyard searching for a door or even a window on the ground level. Searching frantically for a way down from where she was. Behind her she heard footsteps in a nearby corridor and Frishka's voice growing louder with each step.

"You will never escape me!"

The lock clicked. Marilana's eyes popped open. She threw herself off the couch, kneeling with her face to the door, her eyes on the floor. She fought intense panic and concentrated on slowing her breathing. *A dream. It had been a dream.* Her thoughts whirled in her mind as she came fully aware of her surroundings she remembered that Frishka was under guard in the tower dungeon. Fearing who had seen her submissive reaction, she looked up.

Master Castant and Captain Lorne stood staring at her in surprise; a maid nearly dropped the dinner tray before hurriedly setting it on the table and turning her back. Marilana buried her face in her paws and wept, sagging with relief.

"Leave us," Castant said quietly to the maid. He studied Marilana as she wept on her knees.

She murmured, "It was a dream," over and over again into her paws. Finally she collected herself enough to wipe away the tears. Castant approached her and knelt on one knee facing her.

"This is how he made you greet him." It was not a question, just a statement of fact.

"Yes," she answered, "When he came in with his men, I was to supplicate myself, and appeal to his mercy for shelter and protection." She emitted a wry laugh and further collected herself, not meeting his eyes. "Oh, how I fought the urge to kill him each time. Instead of submission, he received insults, and now I fly into position because my wits are scrambled from a dream."

"Your tears are not because you were afraid or ashamed. The relief was plain on your face when you saw who was here."

"Yes, tears of relief," she sighed peering down at her paws, "because he did not see my shame."

Castant did not respond. He did not have to. He knew that the "he" she spoke of was not Frishka but Marquiese. He knew now that his suspicions were correct, and King Rylan knew as well. How would he get Marquiese to see the truth? Marquiese had for some reason blinded himself to the possibility. He would reflect on it later.

"You need to pull yourself together, Marilana," he said firmly. "Marquiese will be back in the morning to collect you for court. You may be able to claim bad dreams, but he will not think well of it. The magistrates will definitely not like hearing any aspersions on your character or state of mind. They have already trusted your word more than they should have and it would reflect badly on their decisions, past and future."

"Yes, thank you, Master Castant, for the admonishment. I am alright now," she said calmly.

He nodded satisfied; then stood and left. Captain Lorne didn't say a word until they were in the hall, and then he spoke softly. "She is strong."

Castant nodded in agreement and knew the Captain would say nothing to Marquiese about what had happened.

28

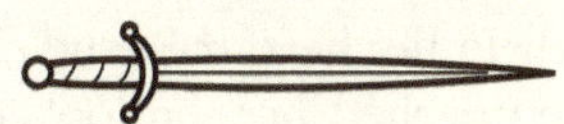

Marquiese was worried about Marilana because she was crying so much. He had assumed she would cry only upon losing a friend or a beloved pet. While he had been hiding in the Southern Tip he had seen her cry when Snow, the working mare that had foaled her most beloved stallion, had died. While helping her recover from her despair, he had watched her weep. He knew she had a tender heart and strong emotions. But she was adept at managing them so she would not lose control at the wrong time. She had stressed to him the importance of a bandit hunter being fully in control and able to focus completely on the job at present. She only showed emotion when she was somewhere that felt safe.

Part of him felt joy that she was able to relax in his home and feel safe in his presence, but he was also worried. The Royal Palace was not a safe place at the moment, not for him, and not for her. Yet she wept. The only conclusion he could reach was that she was closer to her breaking point than she was letting on. Her nerves were frayed and her control was slipping away. Frishka was responsible for pushing her so far, and she did not seem capable of regaining her composure. Perhaps she felt the stress and strain of the trial as keenly as he did.

Marquiese stared at the door to Marilana's room, nervous about what he might find on the other side. He had not seen her in two days, leaving her alone so she could relax without his anger flaring up when they met. He could not understand why she was betraying him. Standing beside him, Master Castant cleared his throat. Marquiese blinked to clear his thoughts, squared his shoulders, and nodded to the guard to open the door. He reminded himself to focus on the present job; he could not afford to slip up either. He wondered what he would do if she started to cry in the courtroom.

He had not realized that he had been holding his breath until he entered the room. When he saw Marilana standing calmly, he breathed a sigh of relief. He hadn't needed to worry quite so much. She held her head high and clasped her paws at her waist. As he approached her, he looked her over with a critical eye. Her fitted dress was clean and unwrinkled. She looked beautiful, in fact. She tilted her head slightly, giving her a humble air appropriate for her position and yet she stood with confidence. She offered him a precise curtsey with the look of focused determination in her eyes that he knew well; she was as ready as she could be to face whatever the day brought.

Marquiese motioned to the guard that had entered behind him and the guard moved forward with the chains to bind her wrists and to connect her wrist and ankle chains. Marilana held her paws out to the guard and let the manacles be locked around them. Then she lifted her skirt slightly to allow the guard to see her ankle chain. Once he was finished, he stepped aside ready to be part of her escort through the palace. Marilana calmly looped the chain over her arm so that the ankle chain no longer lay on the floor and looked at him expectantly.

Marquiese could only stare. Surprise supplanted all other thoughts. He had seen her in manacles many times before, but she had never done this; she had always let the chains drag on the floor.

"Why," Marilana asked ruefully, "should I let my chains drag and remind everyone that I am in chains? For Frishka it was a constant reminder that I was his prisoner. I wanted him focused on me. Now, I walk with the absence of the sound; I am prisoner by my own choice."

Marquiese smiled slightly and shook his head. It was a good reminder that she was very skilled at the arts of warfare—physical and mental. She hardly ever left any detail unexplored, using every object and action as a tool. Frishka had been a fool to even try to use her; she had pulled his strings in ways he had not even imagined. She had been the true master of the mental battles and had only let him control the physical because her other option had been to kill him. Marquiese wondered if Frishka had even now considered the possibility that she had manipulated him every step of the way.

Marquiese turned and led the way out of her rooms. He was not surprised to find Earek quickly gathering his chains as well in the hallway. He led the group toward the courtroom. He frowned slightly as he wondered in what way she manipulated him. She had seemed open and honest with him, but she was, after all, a great schemer.

Marilana followed Marquiese into the courtroom, Earek following a half step behind to her right, following her lead. She entered with all the grace and self-possession she could muster. She swept down to stand before the magistrates as if the guards were her own and present solely for her honor. Everyone in the courtroom caught the mood; discussions ceased abruptly, the magistrates stiffened, and King Rylan's small smile grew stony. Marilana remained serious and Earek too strode with an air of marked determination. Marquiese strode to the front and when he turned to check their positions, his slight grimace deepened and a touch of anger flared in his eyes. He turned away to coldly stare at the magistrates. Inwardly, Marilana cringed. She did not know how she could ever repair his opinion of her, but now she had to focus on what she had to say.

The magistrates stood. She curtseyed deeply, showing them the respect they deserved from a peasant, yet still with the air of a noble; the respect was her choice and all who saw knew it. Earek and Marquiese bowed enough to show respect for equals. Earek then crossed his chest with paw to heart, a proper gesture for a noble in the company of royalty.

Lord Komph watched her rise with a frown, and then spoke. "We now open the case of Prince Marquiese versus Lady Marilana and Master Earek with the charge of accessory to treason of the latter, against His Majesty, King Rylan of Redsands and His Highness the Crown Prince, Marquiese. All participants are present for this first session in order to hear the formal charges and the explanation of the trial procession. Lady Marilana Ranat, heir of the Southern Tip, and Master Earek Ranat, second heir of the Southern Tip, are charged with assisting the traitor Frishka in his attempt to undermine His Majesty, the King, Rylan Mercurer, son of Coryan Mercurer of Redsands, by taking action to apprehend Prince Marquiese Mercurer to face trial on a false charge of treason and to present evidence against His Highness in said trial." Lord Komph paused to look at all those standing before him; he let his gaze rest on Marilana. "Do you, Lady Marilana, deny these accusations?"

Marilana had not shifted her eyes from him and responded in a firm voice. "No."

Whispers swept the room. Lords Hunmis and Quinre exchanged surprised looks. King Rylan looked aghast. Lord Komph nodded slightly. Beside her Earek sighed. Only Marquiese did not seem to react at all.

"And do you, Master Earek, deny these accusations?" Lord Komph continued.

"No," Earek said firmly.

It was Marilana's turn to frown slightly. Marquiese still did not move.

"Very well. This trial will proceed to determine the degree of guilt of Lady Marilana and Master Earek as charged. The subsequent sessions of this court will be held with only one of the accused in attendance to obtain testimony for cross-referencing and verification of evidence presented. The Royal Court of Law, consisting of His Majesty King Rylan, myself Lord Komph, and Lords Hunmis and Quinre will determine the legality and authenticity of all evidence presented. I declare this court session adjourned."

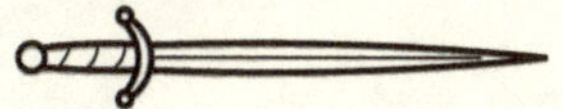

Marquiese paced in his study again, thinking about Marilana. Master Castant and King Rylan sat watching him. He had escorted Marilana and Earek back to their rooms without saying a word, and, in fact, had been unable to look at Marilana at all. He had realized what she was going to say when he saw how she held herself in the courtroom. He had also known that Earek would follow her lead whether she wanted him to or not. Earek would not let her go on alone. Strangely Earek's loyalty calmed Marquiese.

"Why?" Marquiese asked. "Why plead guilty to the whole charge when only part of it is true? Why plead guilty at all when you had been forced to cooperate? What does she think she will gain? I know she wants to hunt Frishka, but pleading guilty will not speed that end."

"Did you ask her?" asked King Rylan.

"Ask her? I could not even look at her after that performance," growled Marquiese.

"Do you think it is part of her betrayal?" asked Master Castant with a knitted brow.

"Yes, it is all part of her plan. I only wish I knew why."

"I say you should ask her," replied King Rylan.

"I will think about it," Marquiese said coolly.

29

Earek stood straight and firm before the magistrates. When Marquiese had gathered him for court that afternoon, he had said nothing. Earek was confident about what to say; he knew he must stay with Marilana. He knew what she had planned but hoped he could help protect her if he stayed by her side. He feared he would slow her down, but he had sworn to protect her, and he was just as guilty in this farce.

Lord Komph studied him closely. "Master Earek, you have pled guilty of accessory to treason. You have also provided testimony against the traitor you are claiming to have helped. You maintained you were forced into cooperation. Please enlighten us as to why you feel you are guilty."

"Gladly, Your Honor. I have told you the truth about what happened so the traitor could be condemned for his treasonous plotting. It is true that I was captured and taken to The Beach against my will. In that I had no choice. I was then compelled by threat of violence toward my friends to throw a net over Prince Marquiese," stated Earek calmly.

"Nothing you've stated reveals your guilt. You were forced into your actions," interrupted Lord Quinre.

"Yes, Your Honor. But I did have a choice in throwing the net that captured Prince Marquiese. However much I did not want to do so, I still made that choice," Earek said.

"Many would argue that as the alternative would have been worse, you made the only remaining choice," insisted Lord Quinre.

"That may be, Your Honor, but I had many options. I could have shouted when the gag was pulled from my mouth. I could have fought the men guarding me when they untied me. I could have thrown the net but intentionally missed capturing His Highness, Prince Marquiese. I could have done many things rather than the one the traitor requested. I made my choice. But in the end, I helped the traitor further his plans," Earek said firmly.

"If you had acted differently, what in your opinion would have happened?" asked Lord Komph quietly.

Earek winced. He had intentionally avoided this topic. Instead, he had been trying to demonstrate that he could have made a different choice. Lord Komph had perceived his avoidance and was angling for him to admit to having made the choice that saved Marquiese's life. He hoped Marilana would be forced to do the same.

Earek inhaled deeply before speaking. "The traitor made it clear that if I had made a different choice, I would most certainly be dead."

"And would that have saved your friends' lives?" Lord Komph persisted.

"No, my death would have accomplished nothing. I would have died, Prince Marquiese would have been captured, and Marilana would have placed the treason charges," admitted Earek.

"So by making the choice to throw the net, you helped to defend Prince Marquiese's life," concluded Lord Komph.

"Yes, Your Honor."

"Now tell me," continued Lord Komph, "why did you defend Prince Marquiese?"

Earek straightened and glared at Lord Komph. "As a loyal subject of Redsands, I have sworn to protect His Majesty, King Rylan, and His Highness, Prince Marquiese, with my life.

Furthermore, I regard Prince Marquiese as my friend and I would gladly give my life to protect him."

"Thank you, Master Earek." Lord Komph smiled slightly. "Court is adjourned."

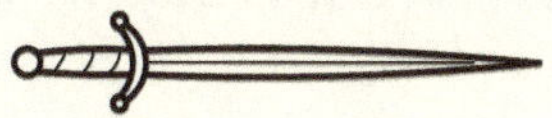

Marquiese could tell by Earek's slumped shoulders, that he considered the court session a lost battle. He smiled as he led the way into Earek's quarters. He turned to face him. "So, Earek, tell me, why did you fight so hard to plead your guilt?"

Earek sighed and shook his head. "This is not my day," he said sadly.

Marquiese laughed. "Really? I thought you did a great job."

"What do you mean?" asked Earek cautiously.

"You set the stage for Marilana's testimony tomorrow. We know that she is going to make the same argument. She and you both know that making the Court see that you made the choice willingly was the only way to prove your guilt. If she had voiced it first and swayed the Court, you would have followed nicely. Instead your plea is weaker; it was easier to show that you made the choice to save my life and therefore it was not treasonous. Tomorrow, when Marilana presents the same argument, it will be obvious."

Master Castant shifted slightly, "Do not underestimate Marilana. She has already thwarted one set of carefully laid plans. I do not believe that this will make much difference to whatever she intends. She is too familiar with the laws to rely solely on her testimony, and she knows Earek well enough to make sure his testimony won't affect her."

"Of course," said Earek levelly. "She was trained in law by Lady Annabella herself. The Lady has been training her to be her heir even if Marilana refused to see it."

Marquiese nodded. "I should have realized it. Lady Annabella knows the Magistrates' Creed as well as my father; they have to. That is how Marilana knew how to push the magistrates."

Earek smiled, "Well, I might not have helped her plans, but I did not hurt my plans."

"What do you know of her plans?" Marquiese asked frowning.

Earek studied him warily, "I only know that she wants to prevent Frishka from doing any more damage or harming anyone."

"That much I knew. Why, though, why does she care so much about Frishka?" Marquiese asked flatly.

"In part, it is in her nature to protect. She is, after all, a bandit hunter. She has seen him torture me, and she has been subjected to his torture. She does not want anyone else to fall prey to his scheming or torturing," Earek said coolly.

"Yes, I know. It is the other part that I do not understand. She is not revengeful."

"It is not revenge, Your Highness. You must discuss it with *her*," Earek said firmly.

Marquiese studied him, and then asked a different question. "What are your plans?"

Earek sighed then spoke calmly, "I intend to stay with Marilana wherever she goes, no matter her plans. I adopted her as my Sister, and I have no reason to stop being her Brother if we are exiled. I have sworn to protect her."

Marquiese nodded. "You love her."

Earek looked up and spoke carefully, but firmly, "I love her as my *sister*, Marquiese. I would do anything to see her happy and healthy. She has done so much for me without ever asking for anything in return. We are as close as any two friends can be, but I do not have romantic inclinations toward her. If she cannot wed the man she wants, then I will comfort her. I would only wed her if she insisted it would save her life to do so, and even then I would not bed her. She *is* my sister."

Marquiese smiled, sadness blooming in his eyes. "If you were to wed her, and you and she lived together as husband and wife, then you would bed her. It is only natural. I appreciate your words, though. I feel better knowing your feelings in this matter. If she is exiled, I would be relieved to know you were with her."

"Do you plan to exile her, Highness?" Earek studied Marquiese's face.

"I do not know. It is not up to me to pronounce sentence in this case. The magistrates and my father will have to decide your fate and hers," Marquiese said levelly.

"After the way I was questioned, it seems the magistrates intend to prove my innocence. If they do that, Marilana will be free to do as she wishes. I wonder what you will do then. Of course, your testimony comes after hers, so maybe you can influence the outcome as you wish." Earek persisted.

Marquiese was silent for a long time, studying Earek's face. Finally he turned without a word and left. Master Castant followed him to his study, where they were alone.

Castant said, "He is right, you know. Because you will have the last testimony, you can greatly influence the outcome of this trial. Lady Annabella will of course try to secure their innocence, but you are charging them with treason against Rylan and yourself."

"I understand that, Enton. I do not yet know how I want to proceed. If it were Earek's fate alone, I would pardon him and embrace his friendship. Marilana though…I just do not know what I want to see happen."

Castant held his gaze. Marquiese had not used Castant's first name since King Rylan had asked him to be an advisor. The informality signaled Marquiese's deep emotional turmoil. Marquiese felt as if he were caught in a river's eddies without anything to help keep his head above water. Sometimes he wanted to be rescued, and other times he wanted to let the current pull him under. All he could really do was keep swimming.

30

Marilana stood calmly in front of the magistrates. She wondered how Earek's testimony had been received. Marquiese had said nothing to her since the trial opened. She had refrained from opening the balcony doors. She could not break the conditions of her arrest while under Marquiese's care. She had hoped Marquiese or Master Castant would at least say how Earek was holding up. She was sure that, no matter how the Court had reacted, Earek felt his testimony did not go well.

"Lady Marilana, you have pled guilty of accessory to treason. You have also provided testimony against the traitor you claimed to have helped. You maintained to have been forced into cooperation. Please enlighten us as to why you feel you are guilty," Lord Komph said studying her closely.

"I pled guilty, Your Honor, because I am guilty. I chose to help the traitor further his plans. I enticed His Highness, Prince Marquiese down to The Beach, resulting in his capture and subsequent arrest," Marilana said levelly. She could tell by their reactions that she had said exactly what they expected her to say. She knew now that Earek had followed this course, too. She smiled to herself.

"So you made a choice. If memory serves, you stated in your testimony against the traitor that you felt you had no other choice; that he threatened to kill you and your friends if you did not cooperate. Is that correct?" Lord Quinre asked.

"It is, Your Honor. I chose the course that would save the lives of Master Earek and His Highness, Prince Marquiese," she replied in the same level tone.

"It would seem to me that you made the right choice," Lord Komph stated.

"Yes, Your Honor, but that does not remove my guilt. Even a correct choice can be treasonous. I freely admit to being guilty of making that choice."

The magistrates frowned at her for a few moments before Lord Komph spoke sadly.

"Very well, Lady Marilana. Court adjourned."

*

Marilana stood as calmly as she could while watching Marquiese pace in her rooms. Master Castant watched her thoughtfully with his arms crossed.

"How is it that Earek tried that plea yesterday and lost the debate, whereas you won?" Marquiese growled as he paced past her.

She swallowed hard then said, "It is a matter of perspective, My Lord Highness. Earek probably acted as though the choice he made was wrong and that he accepted it was wrong even if he had no other reasonable options. In contrast, I acknowledged my guilt in making a right choice. There was very little the magistrates could do; my logic was sound."

"Why?" he growled.

"Now it will seem as though Lady Annabella's praise of my character is just confirming my right in my guilt," she said dropping her eyes.

Marquiese stopped pacing and stared at her. "Why did you tell me that? Why expose your plan?"

"I will tell you anything," she said quietly.

"Why?" he asked surprised.

She looked up at him and studied his eyes; tears blurred her vision. "Do you not know?" she whispered.

He held her gaze, opened his mouth as if to say something, then clicked his teeth together, turned on his heel, and left. Master Castant shot her a commiserating glance before following Marquiese.

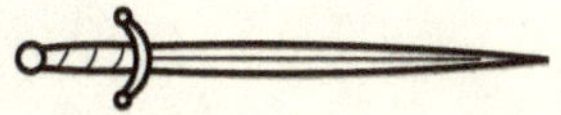

Marquiese stood alone in the royal sitting room peering out the high tower window at the distant shimmers of the afternoon sun on the water gardens. He had asked everyone to leave him to his thoughts.

I had once hoped to share this view with Marilana, so intelligent and beautiful; I had believed she would make an exceptionally strong ruler. I thought I could love her and hoped to earn her love in time. It was foolish to ignore her schemes; I will not make that mistake again. She schemes and betrays me, yet I do not see why. Now I must search my wits for an answer that everyone believes to be obvious. My father, Castant, and Earek know, or at least they think they know. Even Marilana thinks I should know. She is the answer to this riddle. I know she would have told me if I had insisted, but I feel I must figure it out on my own, somehow.

He was lost in thought until a timid knock at the door interrupted his reverie. It was time to dress for dinner. He still had no answer.

31

Lady Annabella's frustration with Marilana didn't show as she stood calmly in front of the magistrates. She knew the girl was scheming, and she was sure that whatever she said today would only further the girl's plan. Marilana knew her well enough to know what she wanted to say here. She also thought that whatever the girl was planning, there was a different way to approach it without being convicted of treason. Annabella focused on remaining calm. This was not the place to vent her frustrations.

"Lady Annabella," said Lord Komph with a bow of his head, "thank you for coming before us today. I know it must distress you to have your heirs on trial for accessory to treason. Please enlighten us about their characters, so we can better understand their motivations."

"Thank you, Your Honors, for allowing me to appear before you," she replied, bowing her head in return. "I have known Earek and Marilana for years. Earek's merchant father came to my estates frequently when Earek was just a boy. I have seen him grow into a man. He befriended Marilana and she has tutored him in skills she learned from me. He is well mannered, gentle-hearted, and strong when faced with challenges. He will make a fine soldier and a great leader."

"Marilana first became my Ward of State when just three years of age. Her parents entrusted me with her care when they left for a very important secret mission. Sadly, she has not seen them since. She has been a member of my household for thirteen and a half years and has been through many trying events that have shaped the kind-hearted, generous person she is today. Her love of life compels her to fight those who would take life from others. She became a bandit hunter to stop the predations of bandits on the innocent. She is fierce in her defense of her people. She has a vision of the future that would make the world a better place; as a noble, she can make that vision a reality. They both act as they see right."

"Thank you, Lady Annabella," said Lord Hunmis, "please answer this next question as honestly as you can. If they were faced with a difficult choice, say to save one life over another, what would they do?"

"A difficult choice indeed, Your Honor. I can honestly say they would try to save both lives. They would place a value on each life with respect to the other, a priority rating for each situation. They would then use the resources available to save the lives in peril according to the priorities assigned to those lives. If they saw an option that allowed them to save both lives, they would choose that one, even if it placed them at greater risk. If the option placed the highest priority life at greater risk, they would reject it and resort to the one that offered greater success toward the highest priority life," Lady Annabella explained.

"Lady, you seem to be saying that they would make the same choices or rate the lives involved in the same way. Why do you speak of them this way?" Lord Quinre asked.

"I speak of them as I know them, Your Honor. I trained Marilana in politics and law and my Captain-General trained her in warfare. Marilana, in turn, has passed on much of her training to Earek. In the past six months, Earek has begun formal training with me. They may value certain individuals differently, but, for the most part, they concur on the basic value of life. In this case, I can say they concurred in the lives they valued the most."

"And who was valued the most in this case?" asked Lord Komph.

"Prince Marquiese and King Rylan. Marilana and Earek's efforts were devoted to securing their lives," Annabella replied levelly.

"Neither Marilana nor Earek have mentioned King Rylan, so why do you suggest they were protecting him?" asked Lord Hunmis surprised.

"The traitor Frishka was aiming for the throne. Yes, he had to take out Prince Marquiese first, but his treason is against the Crown, and King Rylan was an intended future target. Marilana and Earek would have seen this from the start," Annabella said.

"So they did," replied Lord Komph. "However, they also tried to save each other, and that swayed some of their decisions."

"That's understandable. They have adopted each other as family, which means they've sworn to protect one another. They would have tried to save everyone involved, placing a fairly high value on each other's life, perhaps even as high as Prince Marquiese and King Rylan. And they would have safeguarded their lives so they could provide evidence against the traitor. Two identical stories that contradict the traitor's story would have been stronger than one story alone, and three stronger yet."

"What do you mean? Are you saying that they saved each other in order to condemn the traitor?" asked Lord Hunmis.

"By saving each other they were adding defenses around Prince Marquiese and King Rylan. Even now, by pleading guilty they are defending Prince Marquiese and King Rylan. They are telling the truth of events—that the traitor Frishka blackmailed them and that they gave way in order to prove his treachery."

"Yes," Lord Komph said slowly, "I see what you are saying. They have been open and honest. By claiming guilt, they are letting us know they have no other connections to the traitor. There is nothing more to learn from them. They were not innocent bystanders, but they were also not in league with the architects of the plot."

King Rylan and Lord Quinre nodded slowly with understanding. Lord Hunmis looked thoughtful. Lady Annabella nodded her head once in agreement.

Marilana peered out the windows of her room. Although the afternoon sunlight warmed her, she still felt cold. Captain Lorne, who had escorted the servant with her noonday meal, had given her a reassuring smile, but had remained silent. Annabella's testimony was long since finished. She could see her mother below, standing next to King Rylan and Marquiese and many others clustered on the stable road.

Twenty guardsmen stood by their mounts along the hedges, half on each side of the road. Four packhorses were being loaded with supplies to take the guardsmen and their prisoners past the border of Lentier, Redsands' ally to the west. It would take the group six nights to reach their destination. The third night would be their last camp inside Redsands. The morning after the sixth camp the prisoners would be released on foot with only the clothes they wore and one waterskin each. They would have to fend for themselves after that.

Commotion rippled through the two lines of guardsmen. Marilana glanced down and to the left to see the prisoners being escorted out. Frishka and Prinka, wearing only wrist manacles, had guards on each arm. She knew they would not try to escape, not now anyway. She did not know if they would allow the guards to escort them all the way out of the allied lands, or if they would be liberated sooner. She was sure, however, that they would head back to Maefair before too long. Frishka had been too confident not to have a backup plan in place. He had hinted at his second in command lying in wait outside Maefair, gathering an army to take the throne by force if needed. She wondered how soon that army would be ready to move against Maefair. She hoped she had enough time to hunt down Frishka and kill him before he could mobilize his army.

The guards stopped the prisoners in front of King Rylan and she could see him gesticulating. She considered opening the balcony doors to eavesdrop, but she could not risk doing anything that might further displease Marquiese. She also did not want to remind Frishka of her presence. She hoped in exile he would dismiss her from his mind, but she knew it was far more likely that he was just as focused on getting revenge against her as against Marquiese. She had stoked his anger too intensely for him to forget her. She would have to be very careful when hunting him; he would expect subterfuge from her.

Frishka spat on the ground at King Rylan's feet. The guards moved toward him, their paws reaching for their weapons. King Rylan held up a paw to stop them. The guards holding Frishka turned him toward a waiting wagon and helped him inside. Prinka was helped in after him and then the four guardsmen climbed in. The wagon was covered so the populace could not see the prisoners and potential assassins could not get a clear bowshot. Bandit hunters would wait for the prisoners to be released before hunting, but Frishka had made many enemies that would not wait to be given a lawful excuse to try to kill him. She herself would have sat waiting for him to leave the city with bow in paw if she could have. Never mind that he was protected by law until he left the allied lands or broke free of the guardsmen. He was too dangerous to let live.

When the wagon driver flicked his reins, the twenty guardsmen mounted and filed in alongside the wagon. Marilana fretted as she watched Frishka go; if only he had been sentenced to death. She turned her attention to Marquiese and watched as Annabella approached him. Together they approached the garden entrance and strolled along the path with just three men in tow. It was odd to see him without a group of guards surrounding him. The palace was, once again, a safer place for him. She intended to make it safer yet. For him and everyone else.

She watched them wander around the garden without an apparent purpose. She thought she knew what they were discussing. Annabella would know that her judgment on Marilana's and Earek's characters would help Marilana's position. But Marquiese was the only one who could truly sway the magistrates' decision. Marilana was sure that even with her guilty plea, the verdict would permit her and Earek to return to their places as Lady Annabella's heirs and would acquit their names of guilt. She needed to be sent out after Frishka, though. She had to at least appear to have been exiled so she could get close to Frishka without arousing too much suspicion. Hopefully Frishka would accept her into his camp if he believed she wanted revenge for being exiled. It was a difficult proposition for her to face, but it would let her get close to him inside his army. She hoped to find an easier way, but Frishka was cunning about his personal safety.

The question remained: how could she get Marquiese to exile her? By pleading guilty, she had hoped to force the magistrates to choose between exiling her and sentencing her to death. From King Rylan's expression during her testimony, and Marquiese's reaction afterward, it seemed they would dismiss the charge rather than face executing her. She could not understand why Marquiese behaved as if he did not want her to be guilty and yet still treated her as if she had betrayed him. He had to know how she felt, but he had asked her why all the same. She knew he had come to hate her for her actions against him. Had he forgotten the time they had spent together before their arrests? Surely he knew her friendship was strong and true. She needed him to do his duty, though, and allow the law to exile her. She had to find a way to get through to him— past his feelings of hatred and betrayal—and convince him to let her carry out her duty. She was the only one who could do what needed to be done; she was the only one Frishka would let his guard down for. Below, Marquiese and Annabella left the garden and entered the palace.

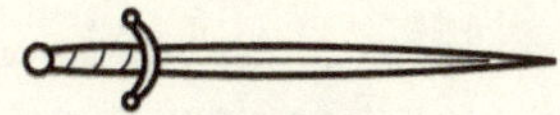

Marquiese entered the palace with Lady Annabella, walked to the first crossing hall, and then stopped. "I thank you for speaking your mind to me," he said to her quietly, "I need time to think about what you have said. Will you be joining us for dinner, My Lady?"

"I cannot, Your Highness," she replied shaking her head, "this is all too emotional for me. I do not feel right staying in the palace freely while my heirs are held captive here. I will be in camp with my men if you have need of me. Please think on what I have said."

"I understand. Thank you for all your assistance."

She curtseyed to him, then turned and walked toward the entrance hall, Captain-General Zariff following. Marquiese turned to a different hallway and started walking down the corridor, not paying attention to where he was going; he just felt the need to walk. His guard and Master Castant trailed behind him silently. As he walked, he thought about Lady Annabella's words. She had reminded him of his time in the Southern Tip. She had spoken of Marilana's loyalty to him. She had asked him to think about why he had befriended Marilana and Earek, and why he had asked them to come to the Royal Palace for their month of study before she named them her heirs. Finally she had asked him to put himself in Marilana's place and think through her position, reminding him that he, in fact, knew Marilana very well.

As he reflected on their conversation, he turned corners and wandered down hallways with no destination in mind. He climbed stairs only to pace more hallways. He passed servants and guests without taking notice of his surroundings. He did not just think about why Lady Annabella had said what she said; he knew that she wanted Marilana and Earek to be set free. She cared for them both as she would have her own children. They were her family and Frishka had torn them apart almost as soon as she had made the adoptions official.

Marquiese's thoughts followed her questions through to his answers—he forced himself to draw honest conclusions. He had befriended Marilana and Earek because they were intelligent and valued life, friendship, and trust. As he got to know them he found that their honesty and loyalty were as deep as their honor. They did not make promises lightly, and they would not break their word. Frishka had done this to them; he had driven wedges of doubt and confusion into their friendships. Frishka had used them as pawns to wage mental war on him. Now he struggled to determine what to do next. His emotions told him that they were his friends, as close to his heart as Master Castant. His sense of duty told him that they had been used to get to him, they were a liability now. Another part of him still felt betrayed.

Marquiese realized he had stopped pacing and was standing motionless, staring at a guarded door. The guards watched him, waiting to unlock the door if he wished to enter. He frowned at the door, thinking that Marilana was still betraying him; then he nodded to the guards to open it. Master Castant followed him into the room, but stopped just inside and leaned against the wall. Marilana turned away from the window and patiently watched him. Marquiese could see she was well recovered from her ordeal at Frishka's paws. She reported that her wounds were healing well, and she was much more in control of her emotions, at least in public. She appeared a little weary, but no more than could be attributed to the stress of the trial. She was stunningly beautiful. His heart ached to go to her, to hold her in his arms, to walk with her in the gardens, as he had done before. She was so strong, so brave, and she had, once again, saved his life.

In that moment he realized he could not condemn her as a traitor. Even though she had betrayed him and continued to do so, he could not sully her name. She had not betrayed the Crown; she had saved him and his father, yet he could not stop the sting of betrayal.

What is my reason for bringing her here? That is simple; she was my trusted friend. She did not choose to be Frishka's pawn, but she did choose to lead me down to The Beach. That is what she claims to be guilty of; she let Frishka use her. She knew it would cause me to distrust her, maybe even hate her. He had definitely been overflowing with anger since being charged with treason.

Then a memory surfaced. Marilana had rescued Brittia from bandits, and Brittia's family had told the whole town that Marquiese had been the hero because he had helped with the rescue. Marquiese had asked Marilana if she was angry because she had not received the respect or honor that she deserved. He could still hear their conversation. *I do not need them to tell me I have done well. I have saved her from a terrible fate, and that is all the reward I need.'*

'Despite how you two feel about each other?'

'I dislike Brittia for the way she treats other creatures in general, but I will not leave anyone to be a plaything for bandits. I know what they do to young girls; I know what they do to children. I will stand in their way as long as I can. Her hate is reward enough for me because it means she is alive to hate whomever she wants.'

He thought about what she had said as he studied her in silence, her face drooping into a puzzled frown. *She thinks I hate her. She is coping with my anger because it means I am alive to be mad at her. Yet how much does my anger really hurt her? We were once close friends. Most of my anger is toward Frishka. Have I been taking out my anger on others because I cannot strike out at Frishka?* He was suddenly ashamed, some of his anger leaked away.

Tension was still high in the palace, and he had been storming around lashing out at innocent bystanders. *I will have to make it up to my friends and the servants. They do not deserve my wrath. But some of my anger is directed at Marilana because she is somehow still betraying me. But do I truly hate her? When I look at her my feelings are far from hate. Does her betrayal against me make her guilty of treason? No!* His abrupt response gave him pause. Just four fifnights earlier he had charged her with treason, fully believing that she had allied with his enemy. Now he knew what she had done for him and the Crown. Unreasonably, he had allowed doubts to control his thoughts. *Why did I believed such lies? Why does any creature believe something they fear even when they know it is improbable?* He did not have an answer, so turned to the problem facing him. What was he to do with her? She had pled guilty but was certainly not a traitor.

He noticed that she had begun to grip her skirt tighter. His very prolonged silence was making her nervous. Looking deeply into her eyes, he saw concern. He approached her purposefully. She did not retreat, but he could see her worry tipping toward fear. He felt a growing need to comfort her, to chase away her fear, but he could not forgive her, not until he understood the nature of her true betrayal. When he stopped in front of her, she opened her mouth to speak. He raised his paw and placed a claw on her lips, signaling that she need not say a word.

"I do not hate you," he said simply. "I do not know how I feel toward you, and I have yet to decide what to do with you. I do know that you are not a traitor to the Crown."

He studied her a second longer. It was clear her fear and worry had been swept away by relief. He nodded gravely, then turned away and walked out of her rooms.

Marilana swayed on the spot where Marquiese had left her until his footsteps faded to silence. Then she stumbled to the couch and collapsed. *He does not hate me.* Her immense relief had left her light-headed. *He does not hate me.* The thought played in her mind until it took hold. He had stared at her, his face drawn with thought and anger, and she had feared that he would strike out. He had seemed furious. When he stalked toward her, his aura of power and judgment had been so potent that she had felt inclined to step away from him. She had been so tense, straining not to step back, an urgent need to say something growing stronger by the second—although she had no idea what she would have said. Her legs had nearly collapsed from relief when he said he did not hate her. She felt the shadow of his claw on her lips, the gentle pressure, the warmth of his touch, and she heard his words again. *'I do not hate you. I do not know how I feel toward you yet, and I have yet to decide what to do with you. I do know that you are not a traitor to the Crown.'* He did not hate her. She shook her head trying to clear her thoughts.

She faced an important decision. In order to continue to pursue Frishka she would need to sway Marquiese into exiling her, or she could stay close to Marquiese in an attempt to prevent Frishka from striking. Her heart burned to stay close, but she had to think rationally. If she stayed, Marquiese could order her back to the Southern Tip. He had not sorted out his feelings toward her, and he might just decide he needed time away from her. If she refused, he could misjudge her intentions. She also had to consider that Frishka still had spies in the palace. Frishka would know where she was and attack when she was not in a position to stop him. She wanted to make sure that didn't happen.

She could go on the hunt without being exiled, but Frishka would know her intentions and not let her get close to him. If she was exiled, however, she could try to trick Frishka and stop him before he returned to Maefair. Either way she might not find him in time, but she would have more freedom to try, and a better chance to succeed. She had to admit that all the options had slim chance of succeeding. However, she would feel more confident if she were out hunting, it is what she did best. Nodding to herself, she stood up and strode to the writing desk. She had a letter to write.

32

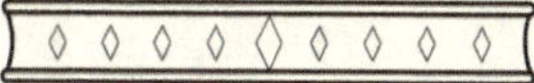

King Rylan entered the top tower room to find Marquiese still dressed in his dinner finery peering out at the darkness. Marquiese and he had spent less time in this room since Marquiese's mother died eleven years earlier. It had the best view of the grounds, and on nights like this provided a dazzling view of the stars. Expansive arched windows lined the walls in all three of the royal family's tower rooms, but this one was the highest, and the only wall section without windows faced south over the palace roof. This room had been Sahry's favorite for spending time with her family. King Rylan had never brought Prinka here, nor had Frishka been allowed to play here. He had reserved the Royal Family Apartments for his and Marquiese's personal time.

He had come here tonight to think, and apparently, so had Marquiese. He had noticed that Marquiese had been spending more time here since his return from the Southern Tip. He wondered if Marquiese had chosen this spot to think about Marilana. Peering out at the view, he understood why he might. Marilana had invited Marquiese to visit some of her most special places in the Southern Tip, and this room was one of Marquiese's; he would have wanted to share it with her just as she had shared with him.

Rylan approached Marquiese. Marquiese shifted slightly. He clutched a piece of paper in one paw. He sighed and decided to test his theory. He said, "She would love the view. The dark shadows of the trees hiding the wall. The winking lights of the garden lamps—stars below and above—the fresh air and the soft sounds of night enhanced by the feeling of distance and emptiness. I would like her to see it sometime if you choose to share it with her."

"She would have," Marquiese replied softly. "I doubt she will ever get the chance. I had hoped I would share it with her someday. Now I must remove any lingering hopes."

Rylan sighed again. He had been right, but something had made Marquiese finally choose his course. "At dinner you said you did not know what you were going to do; now you sound as if you wish you did not know your path. What has changed?"

Marquiese shifted uneasily; then gave Rylan the paper. Rylan retreated from the window to the shuttered stand lamp and opened the shutter. Marquiese followed and sat heavily in his favorite chair, leaning forward with his elbows on his knees and his paws clasped together.

"This was delivered to my apartments by Captain Lorne just as I returned from dinner. He said that it was given to him as he escorted the maid with the dinner tray. He promised to deliver it to me personally after dinner," Marquiese said levelly.

Rylan unfolded the paper and held it in the light to read:

Oh, woe is my laden heart,
Young lion of this land.
True that we've been torn apart,
Still with thee I make my stand.

From that autumn long before,
An equal I seemed to be.
Never an evil lore,
My heart I gave to thee.

Yet this court I will not bend,
And justice must be done.
My life the law will end,
While thine is safely won.

My love for thee is great,
My sacrifice cannot wait.

"A poem?" asked King Rylan surprised.

"She has many talents. She is intelligent," Marquiese sighed, "and she is wise."

"What is this about?"

"She is telling me to do my duty."

"Your duty, but I still do not understand. Your duty to do what?"

"My duty as the Crown Prince of Redsands. My duty to uphold the laws and procedures of the kingdom. I spoke with Lady Annabella this afternoon. She asked me to consider my choices carefully. I have thought long and hard on what I want for the future, what I want in regards to Marilana's future, and about our situation. I spent a good bit of time staring at Marilana in her room. While I was thinking, I realized that I do not hate her, that I do not consider her a traitor to the Crown of Redsands, and I also realized that I need to apologize to many people for my recent behavior. When I told her that I did not hate her or consider her a traitor—and I did tell her that I was unsure what to do with her—I could see her relief. I left before she could respond. She sent this after me."

"But what does she ask of you?" Rylan asked still perplexed.

"She is asking me to send her after Frishka, to send her into exile so she can protect me again. At the same time she is reminding me that my duty is to uphold the law, and the law states that if someone admits to being guilty of treason, they must be sentenced as guilty even if the Court decides they are not."

Rylan read the letter several more times, and sat in a chair facing Marquiese. "Marquiese, I hear your words, but I do not see how this tells you anything about your duty. Something more heartfelt perhaps, but not duty."

"No, not heartfelt. That is what someone who does not know her would think, that it is a letter of the heart, but I know better and can see the true meaning," Marquiese sighed, and then looked up at his father. "Father, you have said that I understand Marilana better than you and it is true. You must take each part of the poem separately, and then take the poem as a whole. She wrote it this way because she knows that very few people would be able to understand it. For me it is plain. In the first part, she tells me that she is saddened by what has happened, and that she regrets deeply that we stand in conflict with each other. She also says that she still gives me her fealty.

"In the next part, she says that she honestly did not know who I was when I was in the Southern Tip until I revealed myself to her here in the Royal Palace, and that her friendship was true and deep. The third part is the hardest for me. She is telling me that she set the Court in motion, and that she will only accept being sentenced as if she were guilty. She will insist that she is punished as set down in law, even if she is declared innocent. The law is specific—persons guilty of treason or accessory to treason are to be sentenced to death or exiled on pain of death. Either way her life as she knew it is at an end, and by doing so she has saved my life.

"Now take the whole poem together and the meaning of the last lines is clear. She still sees me as a friend and intends to save my life again. She fears that Frishka is not finished and that he will return, so she urges me to let her go into exile without delay. The sooner she can start on Frishka's trail, the sooner she can end his threat to me."

"So what will you do?" Rylan asked softly.

"The only thing I can do. She is right. I have a duty to uphold the law. As do you. By law she must be sentenced to death or exile. I will not see her die. She will go into exile. She and Earek both, The Goddess take me for it."

"So you have forgiven her betrayal?"

"No, I still feel her betrayal. She continues to betray me somehow, even in this. She is saving my life, but for her own purposes. I have determined that it is not part of Frishka's treason, though. Her betrayal is personal. It hurts only me. I must be strong and do my duty. She will continue her betrayal in exile, and I may never know what it is."

*

Marquiese had avoided Marilana after receiving her letter. At first he had wanted to go to her to try to change her mind. Later he had wanted to revoke the accessory to treason charge to negate the guilty plea. In the end, though, he knew that he was doing what must be done. Like any of his subjects, she deserved his honest duty. As much as he hated sending her out to hunt, he agreed that she had the greatest chance of anyone to succeed. He stood in front of the magistrates, knowing that they would ask him if Marilana and Earek were guilty. He had spent the entire Restday reasoning out what he would say.

Lord Komph looked down at him with pity. "Prince Marquiese, thank you for appearing before us in this matter. I am sure you have mixed feelings concerning the individuals involved. You have charged Lady Marilana and Master Earek with accessory to treason, and as you know, they have pled guilty to that charge. Please illuminate the Court as to what you wish of it."

Marquiese paused for a moment. Lord Komph was judicious. He did not ask Marquiese to condemn or acquit Marilana and Earek; rather he asked what Marquiese would like the Court to do. A very wise man.

"Your Honors," Marquiese spoke levelly, making eye contact with each in turn. "I do not ask that you condemn or acquit Lady Marilana or Master Earek. Their innocence of treason is evident in their testimonies. They chose to save my life and to protect King Rylan." The magistrates nodded. Marquiese continued, "In doing so, they assisted the traitor and for that they have pled guilty. They are honest and true. Their loyalty is to Redsands and their family and friends."

Marquiese paused again. The magistrates watched him and waited; they had agreed with everything he had said so far. But they would not like what he would say next. King Rylan sat stony faced behind the magistrates, braced for what Marquiese was about to say. His father had explored numerous alternatives before reluctantly agreeing with Marquiese's course of action, but found it profoundly appalling. Marquiese could not blame him, he felt the same way.

"Your Honors, after hearing their testimonies, I feel that they are innocent of treason against the Crown. My assessment of their actions means very little, however, because they have pled guilty." The magistrates frowned. "The law is clear. It is my duty and yours to uphold the law as it is written. The law states that persons who have pled guilty to treason or accessory to treason must be sentenced to death or exiled on pain of death. I ask that the Court see fit to sentence Lady Marilana and Master Earek to exile."

The courtroom sat in stunned silence. Time and again Marilana had demonstrated her knowledge of the law, yet no one had considered that she would wield it like this when she had pled guilty on the first day. She had set them up so that no matter what anyone said, she would have to be exiled or killed if the law was obeyed. Marquiese refused to let her be killed.

Lord Komph stood, "Thank you, Your Highness. We will deliberate and announce our verdict tomorrow. Court adjourned."

*

"I am sorry, Lady Annabella," Marquiese said standing in Lady Annabella's tent. "Marilana convinced me that I must uphold the law. I do not like it, nor do I like what she has done, but I agree that I must do my duty."

Lady Annabella sat in her simple camp chair. It was a sturdy lightweight chair that could be disassembled and reassembled quickly for storage in wagons on the march. There was a second chair, but Marquiese chose to stand. He felt like moving, but forced himself to remain still.

"I did not come here to hurt you, My Lady. I wanted you to know my reasons."

"I know your reasons, and I know hers. That does not mean that I like or approve of those reasons. Fool girl, I am sure she could have chosen a different path. She could have gone on the hunt after being acquitted. I am sure she could have done just as well that way," Lady Annabella said, angry but resigned.

"I think Marilana had sound reason for choosing this path. While I see other paths she could have chosen, she undoubtedly examined all of the options, and this was the one she felt she must take. She is smarter than I am most of the time."

"She is going to go hunt Frishka so he can no longer threaten you. Even if she succeeds, she can never come back home. How can you let her do this?"

"I said I did not like it. I do not want her to leave. Like you, I want her to be home and safe. She set this in motion when she chose to plead guilty," he replied hotly.

"I am sorry, Highness," she said looking down at her paws in her lap. "I love her as my daughter. I have guided her and raised her so that she could one day take my place. Now I am losing her. I took Earek as my second heir willingly, knowing that Marilana would be highly sought for courtship. And now she will not even be able to visit. I will not get to see the great leader she could have become. My life is crashing down around me, and I see no way out."

Marquiese knelt in front of Lady Annabella and rested his paw on hers, "I believe Marilana and Earek will keep their titles. They will be your heirs in exile from Redsands, but not from the allied nations. They can keep in touch with you, and you can go to visit them when they find a place to settle. I know it is not what you had wanted for them, but at least they will have the gifts you have given them. The magistrates and my father do not like what Marilana has forced them to do either. I believe this will be their choice."

Lady Annabella nodded, "Yes, it is something to send them with at least. And perhaps Marilana has a long-term plan that includes returning to Redsands."

Marquiese gaped at Lady Annabella. *Why have I not thought of that? Of course there are ways for an exile to be lifted, even for an accessory to treason charge.* Hope flickered in his heart. He would trust in Marilana. "Lady Annabella, you are welcome at the Royal Palace anytime, and you and your men are welcome to camp on the tournament grounds as long as you need. I hope you can trust Marilana's decision as I do. If you need anything from me, please ask."

She nodded sadly as he turned and ducked out of her tent. Marquiese was surprised to discover that he truly trusted Marilana's choice. He remained angry that she was betraying him and that she had manipulated the Court to this end, but he still trusted her reasons. He strolled to the edge of the camp where Master Castant waited with his horse and escort. He must have faith that Marilana would do what needed to be done and then hope she could find a way back.

33

Marilana stood nervously in her room facing the door, willing something to happen. No one had come to see her; no one had given her any sign as to what had happened. Captain Lorne had delivered her letter to Marquiese, and then nothing. She had grown increasingly uneasy over the past two days. The servants brought her meals and wash water escorted by the guard at her door. First Marquiese had stopped checking on her, then Master Castant, and even Captain Lorne was no longer escorting the servants. Were they all angry at her now? Were they trying to make her suffer by letting her wonder in silence? Were they hoping she would change her mind? Thoughts and questions ceaselessly spun though her mind. She wanted to pace, but she forced her feet to stay still. She closed her eyes and focused on slowing her breathing. *Calm,* she could do nothing more than she already had, she had to remain calm.

She heard approaching footsteps in the hallway. Her breath caught. She waited, but no one knocked. She released her breath in frustration. *Calm,* she reminded herself. The lock clicked, and she jumped in surprise. *So much for calm,* she thought ruefully. She watched the door open with apprehension, then sighed when Marquiese entered followed by several guards. Behind him stood Earek, chained and waiting beside Master Castant. She chided herself for a fool; they had collected Earek from his rooms first. She forced her face to appear calm and extended her paws for the manacles.

Once she was chained, she followed Marquiese out and fell in step beside Earek. They held their chains off the floor as they walked—prisoners by choice. She strode along the hallway, down the stairs and through the guard post to the courtroom, reminding herself to stay composed with every step. She swept into the courtroom with stately grace and curtseyed low to the magistrates. They responded with frowns, obviously troubled by what they had to say. She forced her trembling paws to stillness as she waited for their verdict. After a long moment of silence, Lord Komph stood.

"Lady Marilana and Master Earek, you have pled guilty to the charge of accessory to treason against Prince Marquiese. You have related the events that took place and your reasons for your actions. We are bound by law to pronounce Judgment upon you."

"We, the Magistrates of the Royal Court of Law, Lords Komph, Quinre, and Hunmis, have declared that you, Lady Marilana, and you, Master Earek, are found innocent of Accessory to Treason to the Crown as evidenced in this trial. However, as you have pled guilty to the charge, the law requires a sentence of guilt. By consent of His Majesty King Rylan of Redsands, and His Highness Prince Marquiese, you are hereby banished from Redsands. As we have declared you innocent, you shall retain your titles and rights as heirs to the Southern Tip in Exile and may remain in allied lands. Court adjourned."

Marilana sighed as she curtseyed deeply. She was exiled, but everyone in the courtroom knew it was because of the guilty plea. The façade of revenge may not work to gain access to Frishka's camp. She would have to consider how best to work around the difficulties. She followed Marquiese out and was surprised they did not stop at her rooms or Earek's. Marquiese led them up stairs and Marilana realized with surprise, that they were headed to the tower dungeon. Perhaps Marquiese was angrier with her than she had thought.

Marquiese and Master Castant escorted them into the dungeon. The guards remained outside. Marquiese sighed as he turned to face them.

"You will have to remain chained, I am afraid. You are still under arrest until you are outside Redsands, but I thought you would at least like to have each other's company. This dungeon is much better than the lower dungeons, and as you retain your titles, you have sufficient rank to be kept here. I will tell the guards that you are permitted to talk to one another."

"Thank you," Marilana said softly.

Marquiese shrugged. "It was the least I could do. You will have supplies from Lady Annabella when you go. She asked me to tell you that she has hope for the future, but she cannot come to see you go; she is far too emotional at the prospect of losing you forever."

Marilana could only nod as she fought back tears. She had known it would be hardest on Annabella. She had hoped to go alone so that Earek could stay with their mother. She would address that problem after she dealt with Frishka.

"Please, My Lord Highness," she spoke quickly as he turned to leave, "will you pass a request to her from me?"

When he turned back to her, he appeared pensive."Yes," he replied.

"Will you ask her from me to remain in camp with her men for at least a couple of fifnights? I would like to know that she is close to Maefair for a while. It will be good for her to be close to friends rather than alone in the Southern Tip. Will you also take Storm back to her? I do not wish to take him with me." She lowered her eyes; she knew Annabella would understand.

"I will share your words with her. I have already told her that her men can camp on the tournament grounds as long as she needs. And I will have her collect Storm from the stables. Good day to you."

He turned and climbed the steps to leave the dungeon. Master Castant followed and then they were alone. Marilana walked to a straw pallet and sat down with her back to the wall. Tears streamed down her cheeks. Earek moved over and sat next to her. In silence, he took her paw in his and squeezed gently. She turned her head and cried on his shoulder. It was good to have someone she could rely on again. She had missed the company of a friend during her long fifnights of arrest.

When she had cried herself out and regained some measure of composure, Earek regarded her closely. "So," he said studying her eyes, "what is the plan?"

She smiled at him.

"Always to the point, Brother," she replied lightly. "I have missed your strength these last few fifnights."

"My strength is nothing compared to yours, Sister," he said shaking his head. "I could not have done what you did. Taking the beatings and still fighting. I do not think I could have watched beatings without trying to stop them. Bearing occasional violence and missing a meal once or twice a day was easy compared to what you endured. No one has told me the details; I just have some idea of what you were going through. Are you healed?"

"Yes," she said leaning against him, "I have healed enough to travel hard and sleep in the open. I still have some bruises resolving, but nothing more serious. Are you fully recovered? We will both need strength these next few fifnights or months."

"Yes, I am fully healed. Now back to the point, what is your plan?"

She chuckled at his persistence. "Now we rest. Once we are escorted out of Redsands, we track the traitor and figure out how to get close enough to kill him. It is a simple plan that will have to be adapted as we go. I am glad of your company, Brother, but it will be hard going. I intend to push hard. I will leave you someplace safe if I must; you may not be able to keep the pace I intend to set. I wish that you had not chosen to follow me. I wish you were taking your place with Lady Annabella."

He nodded. "I will do my best to keep up. I am determined to not be left behind. I swore to Mother that I would protect you, and so I will follow you as best as I can. I wish you had not chosen to get us exiled. I also wish you were not putting Annabella through this emotional trauma. If wishes were gold, I would be rich just by being your friend. Because of you, I make lots of wishes."

"Some of those wishes are your own doing," she said ruefully.

He smiled. "Tell me this. Has everything gone according to your plan, other than me coming with you?"

"No," she sighed lowering her voice to a whisper, "not everything. I would rather have had Frishka beheaded, so I would not have had to plead guilty. Also, I would rather have had the magistrates condemn me as guilty of treason so that I could try to claim revenge as a motive to seek out Frishka. If I had done my job correctly, he would have welcomed my story as a way to get me to stay close to him. Then I could have worked my way close enough to kill him and all of his officers. Now I will have to try something else. It will be very dangerous, and you may have to follow at a distance to give me a way out. At least by being exiled, we will have the freedom we need to move about and not have to worry about spies."

"I will do what must be done to keep you alive," he whispered back.

They sat in silence for a while.

"Nothing in your explanation explains your tears, though," he said softly.

She shook her head and looked down at her paws.

"Marquiese has accepted that I must go forth with my plan, but he does not understand. He refuses to let himself see my reasons. I know that he could see if he let himself. At first I thought I had hurt him badly enough that he hated me, but he told me he does not. I do not think he trusts me anymore. My plan is hard for me to follow when I look at him. I would give much to give it up and stay with him. I will do what I must to keep him safe, so I will follow my plan."

Earek squeezed her paw again. "You love him. Deep down he knows that, but you are correct, he will not let himself believe it. He thinks you are betraying him; even now he feels fresh betrayal by your actions. Master Castant told me he decided your betrayal is personal and not against the Crown, so he is letting you be banished, but he could not let you be tainted by being condemned of treason. He seemed relieved by my insistence to go with you. I think he really cares what happens to you."

"Thank you, Brother. I hope your words are true. Only time will tell."

34

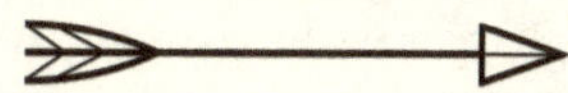

They spent the afternoon and the next day discussing plans for tracking Frishka. Late in the second afternoon, Marilana thoroughly examined the dungeon and discovered a way to scale the dungeon wall so she could sit in the upper barred window. It was not difficult even with her chains. The guards brought King Rylan to witness her accomplishment.

"Marilana, what are you doing?" King Rylan asked as he entered the dungeon.

The upper barred window was positioned where a second story window would have been and on the same level as the dungeon door and the guard's observation room. The floor of the dungeon was down a flight of steps from the door so the occupants could not try to overpower the guards opening or closing the door. The landing and stairs were narrow and the door opened inward. If someone tried to bar the door from inside the dungeon, one good shove of the door would send the prisoner tumbling to the floor below. The guard's observation room was opposite the door so that the guards could see any prisoners trying to hide by the door. Marilana was impressed by the functional layout. A lazy guard, though, may not take the time to check the observation room before attempting the door. It was a flaw easily remedied by having multiple guards. One stood watch in the observation room while others were stationed by the door. From the number of guards Marilana had been able to identify, there had to be a second guardroom on the second level down that housed a small garrison. That was also a good precaution. In all it seemed a very secure dungeon. Not all dungeons for high ranking prisoners were.

"Forgive me, Sire, if I have done something to disturb you or your guards. The view from this window is amazing," she said in awe.

The upper window looked out over the gardens and to the outer wall. It was higher than the window below and offered a better angle to see the garden paths. From here she could see almost anyone moving in her field of view, only a few garden trees blocked small areas. The lower window had several larger blind spots due to hedges. She had no intention of telling King Rylan that this upper window also had a good view into the guard's observation room. She had been counting guards as they changed shifts. Many of the guards had come to see her sitting in the window out of curiosity, giving her a chance to get a fairly accurate count in a short time.

King Rylan laughed and shook his head. "Marilana, you always do something unexpected. You may sit there if you wish, but be careful; I do not want you to break your neck climbing the walls of my dungeon."

She smiled at him as he turned to leave. She remained there until the dinner trays were served; then she hung from the lip of the window before dropping to the floor with an echoing clatter of chains. The space between the windows was great enough that her toes barely touched the top of the lower window as she hung from her paws. She joined Earek sitting on the floor and heartily ate her stew.

He studied her thoughtfully. "Do you always analyze the places you stay in?" he asked softly.

She smiled. "I am glad you understand what I was doing. Yes, I like to know everything I can about where I'm staying. Yesterday's brief examination was enough to show me the strengths of this room; it enabled me to sleep soundly. Today, I learned enough to assault it from the outside or the inside."

He lowered his bowl and spoon, concern on his face. "You could escape?"

She looked him in the eyes and said, "Not with King Rylan's precautions, but if someone less cautious put us here, yes, with your help. Perhaps even without your help."

He resumed eating his stew. "How easy would it have been to have escaped Frishka from your room?"

She smiled slightly. "I would not have left you to him. My room would have been exceedingly easy because it has a secret door that Frishka did not know about. I discovered it my first day, although I could not figure out how to open it. The more difficult part was how to get you to climb from your window to my balcony. It was a short space, but with very difficult paw holds. I am not sure you could have done it without ropes. I would have used the bed sheets to help you, but it would have been very risky. Of course, if it had come to that, I probably would not have risked losing the secrecy and gone out on the hunt before Frishka knew I had left my rooms."

Earek nodded. "I know you would have killed Frishka if it looked like that step was necessary. I knew you had outside help too. I could pick out some of the remedies in my food. I was grateful for them."

"I am sure Altia would like to know her risks were appreciated. I relied heavily on her to keep my sanity. It was not easy for her to see me tortured, or to know that you were being tortured too. She is very tender-hearted. And I am glad to know that you did listen to my lessons on herbs," she smiled mischievously.

"Just do not expect me to heal anyone any time soon. I might be able to tell you some of the names and detect them in food, but I still have no idea what each one is for or when to use them."

She laughed. "Herbs were never your talent; that is true."

"Why do you study your location so carefully?" he asked more seriously.

"Life is unpredictable," she sighed. "What would you do if you were attacked in your home?"

"Defend it. I have plans in place to defend my home," he replied.

"What would you do if you were attacked while camped in the woods?"

"I would have put plans in place to defend my camp."

"Correct. So why would you not put plans in place to defend yourself here or in someone else's home? Would you rely solely on their plans for defense? How do you know their plans will protect you?"

She watched as he absorbed her words. Many of her lessons to him were done this way. She preferred to make him think through the logic.

"I see," he said finally. "If you place your trust in someone else's plan, you are placing your life in their control. If you do not have a backup plan of your own, you could easily die if their plan fails to consider your safety. It is what you taught me about being a soldier. You must follow your orders, but your life is ultimately your concern and not that of your superiors. Good leaders try to preserve as many of their men as possible, but your own paws wield your sword."

"Correct," she nodded gravely.

"Do you ever trust anyone completely?"

"Yes, when you sleep you must trust those around you, so you need to know your closest companions well," she said without hesitation. It was a question she had been forced to consider at a much earlier age. She had been terrified of other creatures when she had finally awaken after her captivity by bandits, and had been unable to sleep soundly for fifnights until she had relearned how to trust. She paused then added in a softer tone, "And when you love, you find that you trust that person completely. It is still a dangerous thing to do, but it is impossible to not trust the one you love. Without trust, your relationship is meaningless and so is your love. I trust you completely; you are my brother. I can sleep soundly with you beside me because I know you will defend me. I trust Annabella completely, because I know she will not harm me. I may not trust her plans or defenses, but I trust her. It is a different way of trusting, but just as important.

"Trust your men to do their jobs, but have backup plans ready in case something goes wrong. That is the trust you must have when you sleep. That is the trust that went wrong the morning Frishka implemented his plan. I was not prepared well enough against someone sneaking into my rooms in the middle of the night. When you trust someone you love, you trust your emotions to them, not just your physical being. When that trust is broken, it cuts more deeply than any blade. If you die in battle, you can die knowing that you did the best you could, and your enemy cannot take your pride from you. When you have been betrayed, that is a death of a part of your soul that can take the rest of your life to heal. Or it may never heal," she said, her voice trailing off.

Earek reached across the trays of food and touched her knee with his paw. "You did not really betray him, though. You saved his life and mine. He understands that. This betrayal he claims is something else."

"He trusted me not to keep secrets from him, he trusted me to stop Frishka from getting so close. I failed him. I was not well enough prepared. Now I am leaving him and may never return. He may never have the chance to sort out his feelings, or to know my reasons."

"He will come to understand. This will not lead to a life of sorrow for you," he said quietly.

"When you are the betrayer, it is different," she said shaking her head. "I know I did the right thing, but while I placed the wound to my own heart, healing must come from the one I betrayed. He must first come to understand his own heart and decide if he can forgive. If he cannot, we will both be wounded for life."

They took their last bites in silence. Marilana climbed back up to the upper window and remained there awake for most of the night.

35

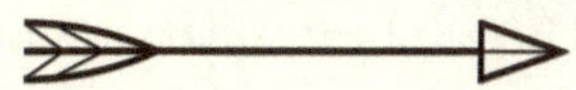

The next morning after breakfast Captain Lorne came to Marilana and Earek and had them brought out to the guardroom. Their chains were removed and they were given wash water and fresh clothes. A folding screen was set up in a corner of the room for Marilana. She was grateful. While she was happy spending time with Earek again, she still wanted her privacy. She set to washing with vigor; she had not been able to wash properly the previous day, and the luxury of clean wash water was wonderful.

When she was done washing she turned to the new clothes and had to stifle a sob. Her new hunter green dress of low merchant cut, divided for riding was folded neatly on top of a new traveling cloak in dark grey. Reverently she lifted the dress off the cloak and slipped it on. It fit perfectly, even considering the weight she had lost due to Frishka's care. She turned back to pick up the cloak and discovered a note that had been slipped in between the dress and cloak. She unfolded it slowly.

Good Hunting

She recognized Marquiese's writing. Her eyes welled up with tears. He had known when she had asked for the clothes what she intended to do. She dried her tears on the wash towel and then, draping the cloak over one arm, stepped around the screen to the waiting guards. Captain Lorne had set their lunch on a small table. Earek sat at the table dressed in a blue suit, also of low merchant cut, with a cloak of the same dark grey folded over his chair back. As she approached, Captain Lorne held the chair for her. She sat and they ate their lunch in silence. When they were finished, they waited together. Shortly a tall, young leopard entered the room and spoke quietly to Captain Lorne. He nodded and turned to Marilana.

"Lady Marilana," he said with a slight bow, "this is Lieutenant Guardsman Ranold. He will be in charge of your escort to the border. He is a good man. I must insist that your wrists be manacled before I escort you out of the palace."

"Of course, Captain," she replied with a gracious nod of her head, "thank you."

She and Earek calmly extended their wrists for the guards to lock on the manacles. When the guards stepped back, Captain Lorne led the way out of the guardroom and down through the palace. When they reached the stable lane doors, Marilana took a deep breath. She had not been outside since her last disastrous walk in the gardens with Frishka. She delighted in feeling the fresh air on her face and inhaled the sweet perfume of the flowers.

The scene she entered was like the one she had witnessed from her window. Twenty guardsmen stood holding their reins along the side hedges of the stable lane. King Rylan and Marquiese stood to one side. Several other lords and ladies stood witness. Master Castant frowned behind Marquiese. Only two pack horses were loaded, and, instead of a covered wagon, three horses were saddled. The tower guards escorted Marilana and Earek to stand in front of the King, but without holding their arms. Marilana spread her skirts in a deep curtsey. Earek bowed low beside her with fist to heart. King Rylan audibly sighed deeply.

"It is with great regret that I must send you Lady Marilana and Master Earek into exile. You have been acquitted of treason, but you have chosen to be exiled on pain of death. These men will escort you out of Redsands to the west along the same route as the traitor Frishka. Once they release you in Lentier, you will have to find your own way, your own futures as Heirs to the Southern Tip in Exile. If you return across the borders of Redsands without written summons from the Crown, you will stand in contempt of exile and can be killed on sight," he spoke out in a bellowing voice so that all could hear his words.

His face was hard, but his eyes were sad. She knew he did not want to do this, but Marquiese had convinced him. She deeply curtseyed again and met King Rylan's eyes as she rose. He responded with a slight nod. He, too, knew her intentions. She glanced at Marquiese and found him staring back at her. She could see anger in his eyes, but he also offered a small nod. She forced herself to turn away and walk calmly toward the waiting horses. Captain Lorne followed her to her mount.

"Good luck, Lady," he whispered.

"Thank you, Captain. Please keep a sharp watch," she replied as she let him assist her mounting. She had not needed his assistance, even with her wrists chained, but it had afforded a moment to pass the warning. He nodded as he offered her the reins. Marilana took a moment to settle her emotions. She sought the icy determination of the bandit hunter. She found the determination, but it was not the cold resolve she was use to. It was a blazing inferno, fueled by the strong emotions that had been kindled here in the Royal Palace of Maefair. Knowing she might never return to this place that had changed her so much, she turned the horse and followed Lieutenant Ranold down the road without looking back.

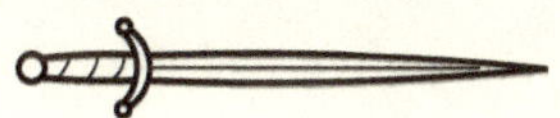

Marquiese watched the guards form up around Marilana and Earek as they rode toward the stables and the gate beyond. He glanced sideways and found his father watching too. When they had sent Frishka and Prinka off, it had taken restraint to not draw his sword and stab Frishka on the spot. It had been a relief to turn away from the traitor and know he was finally out of the Royal Palace. This time his emotions were a confusing lump in his throat. He felt betrayed by Marilana, angry at her for forcing this exile, relief that the ordeal was over, and yet he wanted to run after her to stop her. He had wanted to talk to her before she left, but had not known what to say, so he had slipped her a simple note. Would he ever see her again? He did not doubt she would succeed in her hunt, she had never failed. But what then? Did she have a plan for lifting her exile and Earek's? He hoped so, yet there was a yawning abyss being ripped in his heart. He felt only cold emptiness surrounding a tiny flickering flame of hope. His eyes followed them as they rode out of the open gate.

Turning he ambled toward the palace with King Rylan and Master Castant in tow. The others who had gathered also dispersed. Lady Annabella had refused to come watch her heirs leave on their exile. She doubted she could have watched them leave with the composure expected of a great-noble. At the back of the crowd, Maid Altia wept on Father Iscoot's shoulder. He met the leopard's gaze for a moment and saw great sadness and regret in his old eyes. Marilana and Earek would be greatly missed.

Appendix

Note on Time

The world in which Redsands is located varies slightly from our own planet of Earth. In Redsands, they have 24 hours in a day, but as most people cannot afford to own a clock, the daily schedule is based on the position of the sun in the sky. This system works fairly well as the difference in amount of daylight between summer and winter is only two hours. The clocks are therefore calibrated at High Noon when the sun reaches its highest point in the sky, also called its zenith. So the difference between High Noon and the common noon, is only a difference in language. However, how a person uses language can give clues about the individual. Most of the population uses dawn, dusk, and noon as references for the time of day. Those who are accustomed to clocks will measure in hours before or after these references.

When compared to a clock, the exact time of dawn and dusk changes throughout the year, but the daily schedule still uses these points as references since many activities require light. Candles, lanterns, and oil lamps can provide light for some activities, but candles and lamp oil are considered luxuries due to their expense, and are used sparingly by most. Other time-of-day references used to indicate passage of time include mid-morning, mid-afternoon, and midnight. Trackers, scouts, bandits, peasants, and others who spend much of their time in the outdoors can learn to measure the passage of time by watching the change of the length and direction of shadows or the movement of the stars and moon.

Note on Calendar

Redsands has a year consisting of 390 days. The year is broken into 13 months of 30 days each. Each month has 6 fifnights of 5 days, making 78 fifnights per year. The first day of the fifnight is called Restday, and every month starts on a Restday. The rest of the days of the fifnight are indicated by counting from Restday. School is held for the local children four days a fifnight for ten months, excluding three months of summer break and two fifnights for the New Year. Children attending school may also indicate the day of fifnight by indicating the day of the school fifnight. So the third day of the fifnight could also be indicated as the second day after Restday, or the second day of the school fifnight. Calendars, like clocks are a luxury not found in most homes. Months are indicated in reference to important annual events and the changing of the seasons. Each season is three months plus seven days with an equinox day at the beginning of spring and fall. Specific events are indicated by telling what day of the fifnight and how many fifnights or months before or after a reference day.

List of Important Days

*All days referenced by month from New Year for consistency of this list.

New Year—1st day of 1st month (start of 2nd month of winter)

School resumes after New Year break—2nd day of 3rd fifnight after New Year

Spring Equinox—8th day of 3rd month

First day of Spring—day after Spring Equinox

Last day of school year (Exhibition Dance)—last day of 5th month

First day of Summer—Restday of 4th fifnight of 6th month

National Day of Worship—Restday of 2nd fifnight of 7th month

First day of school year—2nd day of 1st fifnight of 9th month

Fall Equinox—3rd day of 5th fifnight of 9th month

First day of Fall—day after Fall Equinox

Annual Tournament in Maefair—4th day of 6th fifnight of 12th month

Tournament Ball—day after tournament, last day of 12th month

First day of Winter—1st day of 13th month

Winter Council in Maefair—last day of year, last day of 13th month

Last day of school for New Year break—last day of year

Note on Rank

Rank in Redsands is determined by birth and by merit. Birth determines caste: peasant, low-class merchant, mid-class merchant, high-class merchant, landed-gentry, noble, high-noble, great-noble, royal. Adoption and marriage are the primary ways to gain a higher caste. Disowning from family and abdication of duty will result in a drop in caste. When a non-heir child comes of age, they drop in caste unless they marry an heir to a caste title. Marriage grants the rights of the higher caste heir; these rights remain if widowed, but are lost in cases of divorce.

Rank within caste is determined by merit. Respect and common consensus are the currency of rank. In the peasant caste there is very little change in rank from orphans at the lowest to upper servants at the highest. Peasant rank is determined by wealth and hired position; these can be very fluid, causing drastic shifts in very short time. Successful farmers who own lots of land and upper servants who oversee other servants garnering the highest wages are granted the highest rank. With the merchant caste, the rank is a reflection of wealth and position on the Merchant Council. Possession of a Family name is a token of respect from the royal family and grants higher rank. The ability to maintain financial wealth influences the respect of the community and can grant higher rank as well. With the noble castes, from landed-gentry to great-noble, rank is granted by size of land governed and by respect from other nobles and the royal family.

The soldier class works within and outside the caste system. Soldiers are treated with respect according to rank, but are not granted the rights of the castes. For example, an officer (Lieutenant, Major, Captain, etc.) may speak up in public and attend gatherings as an equal to the merchant caste. However, an officer is only granted the rights of land ownership equal to a peasant and are not able to speak to the Merchant Council regarding laws or leadership. All of the children of soldiers of any rank are considered peasants.

Rank among soldiers is granted by merit alone. All soldier recruits start out as simple guardsmen. As they prove themselves worthy, they can be promoted. Officers are treated with the respect granted to the merchant castes. Knights of the Realm are treated with the respect granted to the noble castes. Soldiers must have a liege to whom they owe allegiance and from whom they take orders. Knights of the Realm can be soldiers or can be individuals of any caste, but they must accept the leadership and regulations of the Brotherhood of Knights to claim the title of Knight. Those who have proven themselves through competition of arms are granted the highest ranks. For example, Zariff is a Knight of the Realm who won many competitions and who has proven himself a very capable officer by gaining the position of Captain-General, he is therefore treated with respect equal to a great-noble, but is only granted the rights of property ownership equal to a peasant.

Characters Around Maefair

Around Mystillion:

Marilana—mair-ih-lain-ah—[lioness] bandit hunter known as The Ghost and ward of Lady Annabella Ranat. Rank: noble ward, equal to landed-gentry noble, but this is ignored, treated as orphan, lowest of peasant caste. Becomes great-noble heiress to Lady Annabella Ranat.

Annabella Ranat—ann-ah-bell-ah ra-nat—[lioness] The province of the Southern Tip is ruled by the Great-Noble Family Ranat. Lady Annabella Ranat is the only member of the family until she adopts her heirs. Rank: great-noble, highest of noble caste.

Zariff—zär-əf—[lion] commander of all Southern Tip troops in service to Lady Annabella, and a Knight of the Realm. Also Marilana's trainer and mentor. Rank: Captain-General in soldier class, equal to great-noble.

Brittia—brit-tē-ah—[lynx] daughter of Sleater. Rank: highest ranking high-class merchant heir in Mystillion.

Sleater—slē-tər—[lynx] established textile merchant, leader of Mystillion Merchant Council. Rank: highest ranking high-class merchant in Mystillion.

Corlda—còrl-dah—[lynx] wife of Sleater, mother of Brittia. Rank: high ranking high-class merchant.

Ceta—sē-tah—[lynx] sister of Sleater, Mystillion school headmistress. Rank: mid ranking high-class merchant.

Demdrake—dem-drāke—[lynx] first son of high-class Merchant Branish, also Corlda's nephew. Rank: high ranking high-class merchant heir of Bram's Fen.

Earek—air-ik—[rare black leopard] disowned second son of Yulan. Rank: orphan, lowest of peasant caste. Becomes great-noble second heir of Lady Annabella Ranat.

Yulan—ū-lan—[leopard] established tailor. Rank: second highest high-class merchant in Mystillion.

Xyta—zī-tah—[leopard] wife of Yulan, mother to Adrek, Earek, and Jarek. Rank: high ranking high-class merchant.

Adrek—ā-drik—[leopard] first son of Yulan. Rank: high ranking high-class merchant heir.

Vavinta—va-vēn-tah—[leopard] wife of Adrek. Rank: high ranking high-class merchant.

Jarek—jər-ik—[leopard] disowned third son of Yulan. Soldier in service to Lady Annabella. Rank: Lieutenant Guardsman in solider class, equal to low-class merchant.

Rose—rōz—[horse] teacher at Mystillion school, tutor to Marilana. Rank: peasant.

Caton—ka-tän—[silver fox] first son of a high ranking mid-class glass blower. Rank: high ranking mid-class merchant heir.

Klay—klā—[black bear] first son of a low ranking high-class blacksmith. Rank: low ranking high-class merchant heir.

Zara—zar-ah—[deer] also called Child and The Phantom, orphan trained to become a bandit hunter by Marilana. Rank: orphan peasant.

Hosten—hōs-ten—[cheetah] Lady Annabella's Head Horse Trainer. Rank: mid-class merchant.

Diof—dē-ôf—[zebra] low ranking high-class merchant son member of Mistress Rose's class.

Working Animals: Storm—Lady Annabella's white stallion war horse trained by Marilana, only accepts Annabella and Marilana as riders.

Arndt Family: [jaguars all] The province of Grudent (grü-dent) is ruled by the Great-Noble Family Arndt (ärnt). The Arndt Family includes Lord Armen (är-men), Lady Frena (frē-nah), family heir Frederick (fre-drik), non-heir son Warhaim (wȯr-hām), and non-heir daughter Graita (gra-ētah). Master Arndt and Master Warhaim ride with the Knights of the Realm.

Around Maefair:

Marquiese Mercurer—mär-kwēs mər-kyər-ər —[lion] Crown Prince of Redsands. Son of King Rylan and Queen Sahry. Posed as first son to Merchant Colbran, with his wife Adealy and daughter Lida in Mystillion for nearly three years. Friend of Marilana and Earek. Rank: royal heir to the throne of Redsands, second only to King Rylan.

Rylan Mercurer—rī-lan mər-kyər-ər—[lion] King of Redsands. Son of Coryan, father of Marquiese, married to Prinka Ebnic-Mercurer, adopted father of Frishka Ebnic-Mercurer. Rank: royal leader of Redsands, none stand higher within the kingdom.

Sahry Mercurer—sah-rē mər-kyər-ər—[lioness] deceased Queen of Redsands. Wife of King Rylan until death, mother of Marquiese. Rank: second to King, equal to Crown heir.

Prinka Ebnic-Mercurer—priŋk-ah eb-nik mər-kyər-ər—[tigress] Lady of Redsands, Lady-wife of King Rylan. Mother of Frishka Ebnic-Mercurer. Former non-heir princess of Ankenhun (ahn-kin-hoon). Rank: member of royal family, equal to great-noble.

Frishka Ebnic-Mercurer—frish-kah eb-nik mər-kyər-ər—[tiger] Lord of Redsands, second heir to throne of Redsands. Son of Lady Prinka Ebnic-Mercurer, adopted son of King Rylan, stepbrother of Marquiese. Disowned by royal family of Ankenhun. Rank: member of royal family, equal to great-noble.

Confidant—con-fi-dahnt—[lion] mysterious companion to Frishka. Banished from Redsands for violence against royalty and nobility.

Castant Family: [leopards all] The province of Draukshar (drak-shär) is ruled by the Great-Noble Family Castant (cas-tənt). The Family Castant includes Lord Withers (wi-thərs) and family heir Enton (en-tən). Lady Cheylotta (shī-lah-tah), deceased, mother of Enton, adopted sister of Queen Sahry. Both Withers and Enton rode with the Knights of the Realm. Enton replaced Withers as Noble-Commander of the Palace Garrison and King's advisor.

Ruberic Family: [mostly leopards] twelve in number. The province of Herinsford (hair-ins-ford) is ruled by the Great-Noble Family Ruberic (rūb-ər-ik). The Family Ruberic includes Lord Masod (mæs-ad) [leopard], heiress Ophelia (ō-feel-ē-ah) [leopard], daughter Heledia (hah-lē-dē-ah) [leopard], among others. Masod is cousin to Withers Castant and rode with the Knights of the Realm.

Kenhol Family: [leopards all] The province of Reine's Crossing (rens cross-ing) is ruled by the Great-Noble Family Kenhol (keen-hōl). The Family Kenhol includes Lord Ianto (yan-tō), Lady Valencia (vuh-len-see-ah), heir Banol (bān-al), Banol's wife Naseema (nay-see-mah), and daughter Ailse (ālz). Both Ianto and Banol rode with the Knights of the Realm.

Lord and Lady Bostwik—bas-twik—[zebras] high-nobles of county Pracbar (præk-bar) in the province of Abdshar.

Royal Magistrates: high-nobles from various regions around Redsands who have sworn to uphold the laws of Redsands and serve the highest court in the kingdom, the Royal Court of Law. Head Royal Magistrate: Lord Komph (kamph) [red fox]. Supporting Magistrates: Lord Quinre (kwin-ər) [eland] and Lord Hunmis (hun-mæs) [boar]. Healers consulted by the magistrates: Nacobi (nah-kō-bē) [beaver], Steppe (step) [goat], Jellon (jel-uhn) [wolf].

Gwina—gwin-ah—[caracal] Herb Mother, lives and deals herbs in northwestern part of city of Maefair. Great Aunt to Palace Maid Altia. Rank: peasant.

Soldiers of Maefair:

Lorne—lórn—[cheetah] captain in the Royal Palace Guards. Rank solider class equal to noble

Ranold—ran-ald—[leopard] lieutenant in the Royal Palace Guards. Rank: solider class equal to high-class merchant.

Hektor—hehk-tȯr—[gazelle] Errand Rider for the Crown of Redsands. Rank: solider class equal to landed-gentry.

Urdan—ər-dan—[caribou] guardsman of the King's Guard assigned to Marquiese. Rank: solider class equal to high-class merchant.

Karndel—kärn-del—[cheetah] guardsman of the King's Guard assigned to protect Marilana. Rank: solider class equal to high-class merchant.

Saffon—saf-ohn—[goat] guardsman of the Royal Palace Guards assigned to protect Earek. Rank: solider class equal to mid-class merchant.

Royal Palace staff:

Refrona—ree-fr-ō-nah—[grey wolf] Head Maid of the Royal Palace, in charge of all the servants in the palace. Rank: high-class merchant.

Altia—al-tē-ah—[caracal] Royal Palace Maid assigned to help Marilana. Rank: peasant.

Father Iscoot—iz-koot—[leopard] Royal Priest of The Goddess, Head Priest of the Royal Chapel in the Royal Palace of Maefair. Rank: high-class merchant.

Sir Libor—li-bȯr—[snow leopard] Royal Librarian, King's advisor, royal family tutor, rode with the Knights of the Realm. Rank: knight, equal to high-noble.

Strunt—struhnt—[giant anteater] Royal Head Healer, oversees all healers, assistant healers, and novice healers at the Royal Palace Infirmary. Rank: high-class merchant.

From Outside Redsands:

Carloth—kär-lawth—[lion] King of Precinlia (pre-sin-lē-ah), close ally of Redsands, border north of Maefair. Considered friend to King Rylan and Lady Annabella. Father of Clara. Rank: royal, equal to King Rylan, none stand higher in Precinlia.

Clara—klair-ah—[lioness] Crown Princess of Precinlia. Daughter of Carloth. Grew up in friendship with Marquiese and Dansho. Rank: royal heiress to throne of Precinlia, equal to Marquiese, second only to Carloth in Precinlia.

Dansho—dan-shō—[lion] Prince of Lentier (len-tē-ər), close ally of Redsands, border farthest west of Redsands. Grew up in friendly rivalry with Marquiese. Rank: second prince, royal standing below heir but above great-noble.

Zandor—zan-dȯr—[lion] Crown Prince of Coandor (cō-an-dȯr), member of allied kingdoms with Redsands, but has strained relations with Precinlia. Grew up in strong rivalry with Marquiese and Dansho. Rank: royal heir to throne of Coandor, equal to Marquiese, second only to Queen in Coandor.

Akadine—ah-kā-dē-in—[oryx] Prince of Rucdign (rūc-dyn), member of allied kingdoms with Redsands, situated north of Precinlia. Fierce personal rivalry with Dansho. Rank: fourth prince, royal standing below heir but above great-noble, slightly lower than Dansho.

Acknowledgments

This book would not have been possible without the help and support of so many people. First I must mention my wonderful husband who has supported and encouraged me and has been my most solid sounding board. Next I must mention my sons for always reminding me that there is more life to live. And my family for loving me no matter what comes of my endeavors. I must also thank all the friends and family who have read my first book, *Mystillion*, and are demanding I keep writing so that they can read the rest of Marilana and Marquiese's journey. Without that support and encouragement it would be much harder to be the author I am striving to be.

I am thankful for my editors, Mark and Ann, for finding all the places in my story that need changes to make it better, and for supporting my choices in regards to those changes. Thanks to Deanna for all her encouragement and exacting attention to detail, and Kathy for giving my world color and shape.

As always, I cannot leave out the most important helpers, David, and Kim, my wonderful beta readers. Without whose help I could not have seen this book from a readers perspective. Thank you all for all you have done to help bring this piece of the journey into existence.

About IA Mullin

IA Mullin grew up on a farm in rural Colorado. She helped raise crops and cattle. She learned the value of hard work and fostered a love of animals. She went to Colorado State University to further her interests in animals and science. She graduated with a Bachelor's degree in Zoology. Next, she attended Front Range Community College and attained the status of Certified Veterinary Technician with an Associate's degree in Veterinary Technology. She has worked as a kennel cleaner, vet assistant, and vet tech with various veterinary offices, the Larimer Humane Society, and volunteered with the Rocky Mountain Raptor Program, a rehabilitation center. She has raised cattle and pygmy goats. She loves all kinds of pets as well as nature and the outdoors.

In 2010, she chose to leave the veterinary field in order to raise her family. She began to write in earnest at that time. She had started her first manuscript in 1997 as a freshman in high school, but had only written in her spare time as a hobby. Now as a mother of two active boys, she has founded Avio Publishing, LLC and is very excited about the future as an independent publisher and author.

"It's been a long journey to this point, but I don't regret any step of it. It has lead me to understand that imagination is the substance of creation. If I can imagine it, I can create it, at least on paper." ~IA Mullin

Forthcoming Title

Redsands

The Kingdom of Redsands stands on the precipice of disaster. Outside forces are aiming to eliminate the royal family and throw the kingdom into chaos. Marilana, intelligent and deadly, has chosen the path to defend her homeland, her family, and her friends. Unfortunately her enemies are aware of her intentions and plan to render her skills useless. In order to survive, Marilana will need Marquiese and Earek more than ever before. Marquiese, however, is entangled in his own feelings of betrayal and loss. If the friends are to save the kingdom and themselves, they will have to push the bounds of skill, compassion, patience, and trust.

Can Marquiese sort out his feelings before all is lost?

Can the friends overcome the greatest threats they have yet faced?

Will they face the future together or fail in the last steps?

Find out how the story ends in *Redsands, Redsands Book 3.*

Learn More

The world of Redsands and other worlds yet to be explored are waiting to interact with visitors at Magewood.com the internet home of IA Mullin. Come learn more about IA Mullin, her worlds, and upcoming projects. See color maps, read short stories, and join other fans on the Mages of Magewood forum. Sign up for the Mages of Magewood email notifications for future releases, events, and special deals.

If you enjoyed this story, please leave a review or comments on Goodreads.com or wherever you purchased your book. And please encourage other readers to join your experience.

You, the readers, make these worlds come to life and sustain them.

Thank You.

www.ingramcontent.com/pod-product-compliance
Lightning Source LLC
Chambersburg PA
CBHW050600170726
48283CB00001B/51